As a therapist, I have seen how kids need a village of helpers. The entertaining cast of characters keeps the reader engaged, feeling the love they have for Emily and learning the lessons alongside her. Emily's House offers hope and insight on how to create a better life for yourself, regardless of the hand you've been dealt.

~Tami Olesen, Licensed Clinical Social Worker

This book is a must read for those that have lost hope, question God, or believe that life can't be different. Sharon's words and interwoven life teachings cause you to be excited about the idea that things never have to stay the way they began, and how the power of your choice can give you the feeling of belonging you need, and the future you choose.

~ Tara Rudolph, Life Coach and Founder of She Shifts Culture

There is a balance of sorrow, tragedy and hope, but Sharon Armstrong's story lends hope to our chaotic world. The blessings and curses of Emily's family give way to the big hearts of the people of Mountain Grove, and Emily is well on her way to having the house she hopes for, someday. I am looking forward to the sequel, or better yet, the series!

~ Kathy Anderson, Superintendent/Principal (retired)

There must be a sequel! The reader must know who and what Emily allowed in her future house as an adult, and to see how she will keep her promise to Ike, the owner of Good Eats, and be part of the Pass It Along Club. Emily's House, a Christian fiction, is perfect for female teens and adults.

Paula Finlay High School English Teacher (retired) Faith Christian High School

Mrs. Apple teaches Emily that she can survive her unhealthy family and make decisions that will ensure that her future home is nothing like her current one. She empowers Emily to decide what she wants in her life – to dream of Emily's House.

~ Zachary Louis, College Ministry Leader

As her alcoholic parents do the unthinkable, Emily is forced to take matters into her own hands. The townspeople of Mountain Grove walk alongside her in this new journey. This book navigates a dysfunctional family life, young love, anxiety, strained friendships, hard work and reimagines what a "normal" family can look like.

~ Hannah Maddalena, Youth Pastor & She Matters Director

Emily's House

~ a novel by Sharon Armstrong

Paperback ISBN: 978-1-953686-05-3
eBook ISBN: 978-1-953686-06-0

Library of Congress Control Number: TBD

WWW.LivingSpringsPublishers.com

Author's photograph by:
Vanessa Helder, The Helders Photography, Marysville, CA

To my wonderful husband, Chuck Armstrong, who loves and encourages me always.

To my mother, Violet Ann Cooper, who taught me to love the written word.

Acknowledgements

Special thanks to these wonderful family members for their advice, encouragement, and support:

Jim Armstrong and Jolyn Armstrong

Todd Armstrong

David Armstrong and Melissa Armstrong

For her many hours of research and editing, my heartfelt thanks to Kathy Anderson.

Thank you to Sister Makrina Finlay, Order of Saint Benedict, for her advice on proper conduct for my fictional character, Sister Mary Kathryn.

CHAPTER - 1

Emily stood at her front window as twilight settled over the village, waiting for the headlights of her dad's pick-up to come into view.

"Why do I do this?" she murmured, angry with herself for standing there like a crazy person.

She always worried when her dad was drinking, and today, he was not only drinking, but he had gotten into a huge fight with her mom, stormed off in his pick-up, and so here she stood, keeping watch. She decided to take a break and was just turning away from the window when she noticed headlights coming slowly down her street. She froze. The squad car slowed, then pulled directly in front of her house.

"Please, no!" she whispered, as the sheriff swung open his car door.

She kept her gaze on the sheriff's black boots as they swung out of the vehicle. The sheriff walked to the rear of the car and opened the door, where another pair of legs emerged, and her dad stumbled from the patrol car.

A couple walking by stopped and stared. Emily put her hands over her face and groaned.

"What's wrong?" snapped her grandmother, Pearl, from a chair that sat directly in front of the TV.

"The sheriff just brought Dad home," she said slowly. "He's drunk."

Pearl swore softly under her breath. "Darcy!" she yelled to Emily's mother, "The sheriff just brought Luke home! He's drunk!"

Her mother came out of the kitchen and stood near the front door, pale and wringing her hands.

Emily watched as her dad stumbled toward the house, his denim shirt tail flapping in the wind. The sheriff gripped his arm to steady him, and Emily gasped as her dad tripped over a pine tree root in the front yard. He would've crashed into the tree if the sheriff's strong grip hadn't held him firmly.

Mortified, Emily watched the scene play out like a bad movie, as more people stopped and stared as her dad stumbled toward the front door.

The sheriff pounded on the door, and Emily's mother quickly answered it.

"Ma'am," the sheriff greeted her mother stiffly.

Her dad didn't wait for her mother to respond, but pushed past her into the house, stumbling over the threshold, as the sheriff tightened the grip on his arm.

The sheriff steered him toward a ladderback chair, steadying him again as he tripped over a small, braided rug. Her dad clutched the chair with both hands, swaying back and forth.

"I didn't give him a sobriety test," the sheriff began, turning toward her mother, "but I'm pretty sure he would've failed it." His eyes softened as he continued, "I know he's got a family to support, so I'm going to let him sleep it off at home, just this once."

"Thank you," her mother murmured, lowering her eyes.

The sheriff turned to her dad, putting a meaty hand on his shoulder. "If it happens again," he hissed, bringing his face within inches of her dad's, "I *will* arrest you."

Her dad looked down and said nothing.

"He can pick his keys up at my office tomorrow morning, providing he's sober," the sheriff said to her mother, turning and walking toward the front door.

Her mother nodded silently as the sheriff walked past her, then quietly closed the door behind him.

Her dad staggered into the living room.

"Stupid sheriff needs to mine' his own bus'ness," her dad slurred, grabbing another chair to keep from falling over. "He's jus' been waitin' to pull me over...."

"Waiting to pull you over?" her mother sneered, as she walked up behind him. "You're lucky he didn't throw you into jail, Luke!"

Her dad turned around slowly, glaring at her mother, his eyes dark with loathing. "It's yer fault, Darcy!" he screamed. "Driven' me nuts with yer naggin'!"

Her mother backed away from him, and Emily became frightened.

Her dad swore at her mom, using words that made Emily cringe.

Out of the corner of her eye, Emily saw Pearl pull a worn slipper off her foot, raise it high in the air, and send it hurtling across the room, hitting her dad square in the back of the head.

Her dad's eyes bulged with fury as he spun around angrily, but Pearl had already turned back to watching her TV show.

No one said a word as her dad stumbled out of the room toward his bedroom, where he banged the door shut so hard the house shook. Emily and her mom just stared at each other as the windows rattled.

* * * *

"Emily Parks," her first period teacher called the next morning, taking roll at Whispering Pines Middle School.

"Here," she replied, keeping her eyes straight ahead.

She had awakened that morning with thoughts of staying home from school, knowing that news of her dad's drunk driving would spread like a dark shadow through the small village. The problem was, she had reasoned, if she stayed home every time her family embarrassed her, she would miss a lot of school. She listened as the teacher called the rest of the names of the students, her stomach churning one minute and twisting into knots the next, waiting for the first few knowing glances that would tell her that gossip about her dad had made its rounds.

When lunch time came, Emily stood in line in the school cafeteria and noticed the Bouchard brothers watching her as they ladled chicken noodle soup into two small bowls and set it on their trays. Emily kept an eye on them as she placed a tuna fish sandwich, an orange, and a bag of chips on her tray. As she looked for a place to sit, she realized the brothers were following her.

The brothers waited until she found a seat at a long table, then brought their lunch trays over and planted themselves directly across from her. They kept looking at her, whispering loudly, and snickering as they crumbled saltine crackers into their soup.

Emily didn't really know the two all that well, just that they were loud, over-sized mountain boys named Logger and Mack who lived in the sawmill region at the edge of town. She also knew they were troublemakers and decided to move to a different spot.

She stood up to leave, reaching for her tray.

"Hey Em'ly, wait a sec," Mack said, grinning at her with large, broken teeth. "I want to ask you somethin'."

She paused.

"Have you heard there's gonna to be a town election this year?"

She shook her head no.

Both boys began to howl with laughter.

"Yeah," Logger said, laughing so hard he could barely speak, "you better let yer dad know so he can run for Town Drunk!"

The boys screamed with laughter as the other kids turned to see what was going on.

Stung to the core, Emily grabbed her orange and hurled it at Logger. It bounced off his chest and landed in his bowl, causing soup to splash all over his white t-shirt.

Enraged, Logger jumped up swearing, calling Emily unspeakable names.

Before she could react, she saw a blur from the corner of her eye as a figure hurled himself into Logger, knocking him to the floor. Horrified, she watched as Jonathan Charles and Logger rolled on the floor, fists flying.

A crowd of students soon gathered round, yelling and screaming, and urging the fight on.

Jonathan straddled Logger, grabbed his shirt, and jerked his head up off the floor. "Don't you *ever* talk to her that way again," Jonathan hissed, his face just inches from Logger's.

"Get off me, you stupid pig," Logger bellowed, then swore and called Emily another name.

Jonathan's punch went straight to Logger's nose, and blood spurted everywhere. A girl screamed as teachers came running over.

Mr. Morton, the burly shop teacher, reached the boys first and dragged Jonathan off Logger. "What's going on?" he demanded angrily.

Logger got up; he and Jonathan straining toward each other, chests heaving and fists clenched, ready to fight again.

"Both of you calm down," Mr. Morton thundered, pushing them apart with big beefy hands.

"I saw everything," trilled Miss Graham, the Spanish teacher, as she came running over. "Emily started it all. I saw her throw an orange at Logger."

Logger glanced at Miss Graham and stepped back. "Yeah," he said, wiping blood off his nose with the back of his hand, "they're both crazy. Em'ly threw an orange at me and splashed soup all over my new shirt, and then this idiot jumps me."

Mr. Morton looked at Logger suspiciously. "Why would Emily throw an orange at you?"

"I dunno," he shrugged innocently.

"Let me handle this," Miss Graham snapped, turning to Emily. "I *demand* to know why you threw the orange at Logger." She crossed her arms and glared at Emily.

Emily stared back, trying to think of how to answer. If she told why she had thrown the orange, then everyone would know about her dad.

Miss Graham waited for an answer, her nose tilted smugly in the air. "*Well,*" she finally hissed, "I guess we know who the little instigator is then, don't we?"

Emily bit her lip and blinked her eyes quickly. "I'd like to talk about it in private, Miss Graham," she said evenly.

"You threw the orange in public," her teacher replied coolly, "so you will tell us why in public."

Emily stood silent as everyone stared at her. Jonathan stepped over to her side and glared at Miss Graham.

Miss Graham glared back. "And you, Jonathan...tell me why you attacked Logger."

Jonathan looked at Emily. "If she wants this talked about privately, then so do I."

Miss Graham's lip curled. "Very well then," she said coolly, "if you both wish to be stubborn, then you'll both have detention all week—and I'll be calling your father, Jonathan."

"Excuse me, Miss Graham," Mr. Morton said, stepping in, "there's a lot more to this situation..."

"I'll thank you to let me handle it," Miss Graham snapped, glaring at him. "I saw what happened, you didn't."

Logger and Mack stood behind her back smirking.

* * * *

After school Emily grabbed her backpack and hurried out of the classroom, wanting nothing more than to escape the stares and whispers of the other students. She knew by now that everyone had heard about the fight in the cafeteria, and about her dad.

She flew down the hallway toward a crowd of noisy students who nudged each other, staring as she walked by. She slowed down and stared back at them, determined not to let them think she was running away—even though she was. Emily held her head up and forced herself to walk calmly the rest of the way down the long hall, not stopping at her locker for books—even though she needed them for the weekend. She walked straight toward the double doors and down the stairs, her feet barely touching the steps as she hurried away.

"Stupid boys, stupid teacher, stupid *life,"* she said between clenched teeth, rounding the bend on the way to town. *Who, in this whole world, has a life as stupid as mine?* she seethed, giving a swift kick to a pinecone, watching as it somersaulted down the road.

A blast of cold wind came suddenly out of the north, causing her to hunker down into her jacket. The icy wind whipped her hair and stung her cheeks. She thrust her hands deep into her worn jacket pockets trying to keep warm.

Emily's family had moved from out west last summer, and her thin, California jacket was no match for this freezing wind.

As she turned onto First Street, a whirlwind of maple leaves twirled up around her, skipping and bobbing at her feet. The whirlwind danced nearby as she walked; first floating out a few feet in front of her, then quickly back to her side. Emily laughed, wondering if the north wind had sent her an escort into town. *Quit pretending,* she scolded herself as she huffed along, but the thought made her happy anyway.

In the distance, she could hear the Mountain Express blowing its whistle as it shuttled shoppers and commuters down the mountain to larger cities. Emily loved the wistful sound of the train whistle and felt her spirits rise. She stopped for a moment to inhale the crisp mountain air, enjoying the smell of smoke coming from villagers' woodburning stoves.

Who cares what people think? she thought, leaning into the wind. She had begun to shiver in the icy air.

As she walked by the green awning of *Montoya's Organic Produce,* she waved at Mr. Montoya, who was standing in an arched brick doorway sheltered from the wind, polishing fat red apples, and stacking them on a nearby pushcart.

"Buenas tardes, Senorita Emily," he called to her, with a smile that was almost as wide as the brim on his hat.

"Buenas tardes, Senor Montoya," Emily smiled back, trying to keep her teeth from chattering as she walked over to him.

Bowing slightly, he held out a polished apple. "May I offer da' lovely senorita one of my beautiful apples, picked jus' dees' morning from my orchard?"

"Thank you," she smiled, returning the bow. When she bit into the crisp apple, juice squirted out and ran down her chin. "Yikes!" she said, quickly wiping it away. She chewed hungrily; she had left the house without breakfast that morning, and her lunch had been left uneaten on the cafeteria table after the fight.

"Your apples are the yummiest," Emily said, taking another large bite.

She continued to shiver and hoped Mr. Montoya didn't notice. But he did.

"Senorita, you need warmer clothes," he said, eyeing her thin jacket.

"I know," she sighed.

"What ees warm enough for California, ees not warm enough for Virginia," he insisted, peering at her over his black rimmed glasses.

Emily could only shrug as she took another bite of apple, but Mr. Montoya wasn't finished. "When you move here in summer, that jacket ees fine. But now, *no bueno,* you need warm weenter jacket." Emily watched as he emphasized each word with his hands and tried not to smile. She didn't know why it felt good that he cared, but it did.

"I'll be buying one real soon," she promised, reaching over and giving him a quick hug. He started to say more, but she had already turned and was hurrying away. "Thank you for the apple!" she called over her shoulder.

As she passed Violet's House of Beauty, Emily glanced through the picture window. In the reflection of the salon's huge mirrors, she saw hairstylists gossiping with their customers—white teeth flashing as red lips rapidly mouthed the words.

I wonder if they're gossiping about my dad today, Emily wondered as she hurried by. She decided that she didn't really care.

There was a lull in the wind, and she could suddenly smell the wonderful aroma of baking bread that drifted out of Cooke's Bakery—*Home of World-Class Baked Goods*—as the sign on the door read. Emily hurried on as the bakery's warm scent wrapped itself around her, drawing her inside.

The bell jingled over the door as she entered. "Hey, Miss Mattie," she called out.

Mattie Cooke, owner of the bakery, was busy wiping down the top of a tall, pastry case. "Well, look who the wind blew in," she said, with a smile as big and bright as the moon.

Emily returned her smile and stuffed the half-eaten apple into her backpack as she walked over for a hug.

"Mr. Montoya must be givin' out apples again," Miss Mattie said in her plesant drawl, as she wrapped soft brown arms around Emily, hugging her warmly.

"Yes, ma'am," Emily laughed, returning the hug.

"That good man's gonna go broke handin' out free fruit to every soul that passes by," Miss Mattie chuckled. "Anyway, how're you doin' today, Sugar?"

"I'm *freezing*," Emily said, her body giving one last shudder as heat from the bakery began to work its magic. She realized what she had just said and regretted it, knowing another lecture was on its way.

"Sugar, you need to get you some *real* winter clothes," Miss Mattie scolded, right on cue. "Your little Califo'nia jacket can't keep out this Virginia cold."

"I know," Emily replied, wishing for the second time that she had kept her mouth shut. "I'll have my dad pick one up for me when he goes into Clayton this weekend for food and stuff."

"Have him buy you a good hat too, Em'ly—you've got to keep your head warm. And some gloves with a good linin'—and boots, you need some warm boots, Sugar."

"I'll tell him," she said, walking over and peering through the glass case at the wonderful array of sweets.

"How was school today?" Miss Mattie asked, following her over.

"Ummm...not good," Emily replied, lowering her eyes and letting them rove over each pastry. She blinked quickly, surprised that tears came to her eyes, and hoped Miss Mattie didn't notice.

She couldn't decide what she wanted; it was a toss-up between the light-as-air maple bars or Miss Mattie's enormous apple fritters.

Gus Cooper over at the filling station told her that he ate an apple fritter almost every morning.

"Them things is big as hubcaps and keep you filled 'til lunch," he had said.

Decisions...decisions... "I'll take a maple bar," she finally said.

Miss Mattie tilted her head slightly and gave her a funny look.

"Please," Emily quickly added. Miss Mattie was a real stickler for manners.

"I'll get us both one," Miss Mattie said. "I was jus' ready to take my break when you came in."

Emily grinned—Miss Mattie was always *just ready* to take her break when she came in.

"Let's sit by the window and you can tell me all about your not-so-good day at school," Miss Mattie said, giving her hands a quick wash in the little sink behind the counter. "Do you want your maple bar with or without chopped nuts?"

"With...please," she said, wishing she hadn't mentioned the school thing to Miss Mattie. She felt her stomach tighten into a knot.

She stood for another minute watching Miss Mattie put small paper doilies on two china plates. Food had to be served just so, according to Miss Mattie, and it wouldn't do to serve her world-class baked goods on anything less than doily-lined plates.

Emily dragged her backpack over to the small parlor table by the front window; there were no other customers in the bakery. She plopped down on a red striped chair and stared through lace curtains at Emerson Park directly across the street. Fallen leaves had blanketed the park, which was empty today except for a couple sitting near the statue of General John Emerson.

Emily had spent many afternoons reading library books in the lap of the General. He was sculpted in a sitting position holding a quill pen in one hand and an important looking document in the other—as though he were getting ready to sign it.

The problem was, no one in Mountain Grove knew a thing about General Emerson or the unsigned document. She had once heard a woman at the Village Grocer complain, "Who in their right mind would make a statue of someone signin' somethin' and not leave an account of what he was signin'?"

Emily had wondered the exact same thing.

Gathering her thoughts, she turned around just in time to see Miss Mattie round the glass case carrying the pastries; she had to turn sideways to squeeze through the narrow opening. Miss Mattie was a plump, bosomy woman. As she came toward her—regal as a queen carrying her maple bars—Emily was startled to see that she had put on a bright purple apron, with red and yellow chrysanthemums. Emily pressed her fingers against her lips to hide her smile, and turned toward the window, praying one of her belly laughs wouldn't erupt. The sight of Miss Mattie's aprons always shocked and delighted her.

Miss Mattie gracefully settled herself across the table. "What're you smilin' about, Sugar?"

"Oh, just something funny," she said, quickly taking a bite of her maple bar.

Miss Mattie took two delicate bites of her bar, then peered over at Emily and asked, "So what happened at school today?"

Emily swallowed before answering, her stomach knotting into a pretzel. She pushed the partially eaten maple bar toward the edge of the table, her appetite gone.

"Well..." she began, not wanting to tell the whole story. She picked at a crumb on the table, wishing again that she had kept her mouth shut about the whole thing.

"Jus' start at the beginnin', Sugar," Miss Mattie urged, laying a soft brown hand over hers. They sat in silence for another minute, the words stuck somewhere in Emily's throat.

"Before I tell you what happened at school today," she finally blurted out, "I have to tell you something else that happened yesterday—to my dad." The knot in her stomach cinched tighter.

Miss Mattie nodded for her to go on.

She took a deep breath and rattled it off without stopping. "Yesterday my dad was drinking and he and my mom got into a fight; my dad got really mad and jumped into his pick-up and took off. When he got to town, the sheriff stopped him for speeding and when he walked up to my dad's truck, he smelled alcohol."

"Did the sheriff arrest your daddy?"

"No," she said, fiddling with her napkin, "but he took the truck keys away from him and brought him home; the sheriff said my dad could pick his keys up this morning so he could make his wood deliveries."

Miss Mattie tilted her head. "Your daddy's lucky he didn't spend the night in jail."

"That's what my mom told him," she said, looking at her evenly, "but that just made him madder. He said the sheriff should mind his own business."

"What happened at school today that upset you?"

Emily sighed, forcing herself to tell the rest. "Two boys, Logger and Mack–they're brothers–must've seen the sheriff stop my dad. Today at lunch they made sure they sat across from me in the cafeteria. They kept laughing and looking at me; finally Mack said, 'Emily, have you heard there's going to be a town election this year?' When I shook my head no, they started laughing and Logger said, 'Be sure to tell your dad so he can run for Town Drunk.'"

Miss Mattie's eyes got big as dinner plates. "They said *that*?"

She nodded her head slowly.

Miss Mattie murmured something that she couldn't exactly hear and finally asked, "What'd you say to them?"

"I didn't say anything," she said, her bottom lip beginning to tremble. "I threw my orange at Logger, and it bounced into his soup, and splashed all over his shirt and he called me awful names. But this is the really terrible part...," she swallowed, trying to keep her voice from shaking, "...Jonathan Charles heard what Logger said and jumped on him and knocked him down to the floor." She buried her face in her hands.

"Go on, Sugar," Miss Mattie urged, "jus' tell it all and get it over with."

"Jonathan told him not to ever talk to me that way again," she said, remembering the awful scene, "but Logger swore at him and called me another name–so Jonathan punched him in the nose."

"Oh..." said Miss Mattie, looking somewhat pleased. "Well, what happened then?"

"The shop teacher ran over and pulled Jonathan off Logger, then my Spanish teacher, Miss Graham, ran over and told everyone that she'd seen me throw the orange and everything was *my* fault."

"*Your* fault!" Miss Mattie said, her eyes bugging out. "Didn't she even ask what'd happened?"

"Yes," replied Emily, "but I wouldn't tell her because I didn't want to talk about my dad in front of all the other kids. When I wouldn't tell, Jonathan wouldn't tell either...so now we both have detention all week, and Miss Graham's going to call his dad. Nothing happened to Logger and Mack; they just laughed at us behind Miss Graham's back."

"Hmmmmph," snorted Miss Mattie, her brown eyes blazing. "Someone needs to yank those boys' chains real good."

Neither said a word for a moment. When Miss Mattie finally spoke, her voice had softened. "Sugar, why didn't you jus' tell Miss Graham you wanted to talk to her in private?"

"I did, Miss Mattie, but she said no."

"Well, why in the world would she say that?"

"I don't know," Emily said quietly. "I don't think she really likes me..." Her bottom lip trembled. "I don't care about me though—I'm worried because Jonathan is in trouble."

She used her napkin to blot the tears that flowed freely down her wind-burned cheeks. "And what's Mr. Charles going to think," Emily cried softly, "he's always so nice to me."

"Now Sugar," Miss Mattie said, patting her hand, "I don't want you to worry another minute 'bout any of this; there's ways to take care of everything. I know Jonathan's daddy real well, and this can be taken care of quick as lightnin'."

"You'll explain everything to Mr. Charles?" she asked hopefully.

"I'll call him today. But you listen to me about somethin,' Em'ly," Miss Mattie said, her brown eyes blazing again. "I think this school situation needs a little *adult* attention."

Emily's heart sank. "But, I don't think my mom..."

"Now, now, you jus' listen to me," Miss Mattie soothed. "There's other adults in your life that can help if your mama's jus' a little too busy right now."

Emily closed her eyes and shook her head. This was a nightmare.

"Em'ly, don't you know that's why we're all down here together—to help one another?" Miss Mattie tilted her head to one side. "Wouldn't you help me if I needed it?"

Emily nodded.

"Of course you would, Sugar—and that's what I'm sayin'. This problem has grown way too big for anyone but an adult to handle. You tried. Jonathan tried. Now you need some help."

She looked at Miss Mattie, not really believing it could be that simple: things in her life were never that simple.

Miss Mattie looked directly into her eyes. "We'll get it all worked out, you'll see."

"I don't know..." her voice trailed off.

"Well, *I do*," Miss Mattie said, thumping the parlor table as she stood up. "Now, we had enough talk 'bout trouble. I'm goin' to get you a nice glass of milk to go with that delicious maple bar, and we'll have us a good visit. There's more pleasant things to talk about than those two rascally boys." She thumped the table again for good measure and walked back to the kitchen.

Emily sat picking at her maple bar, slowly swinging her feet back and forth. "What a mess," she sighed.

As she sat there, she thought of Miss Mattie's blazing eyes and the corners of her mouth tugged up into a little smile. She just loved it that Miss Mattie wanted to yank those boys' chains for her.

Maybe—just maybe—things could work out.

She couldn't help but tap her feet a little as she polished off the rest of her light-as-air maple bar.

CHAPTER - 2

The heavy bakery door slammed behind Emily as she left and headed toward home. She hurried past Good Eats Café, then crossed the street at the corner and continued up Elderberry Way. As she walked up the hill toward her house, she thought back to last summer of her first glimpse of Mountain Grove. She was sitting in the back seat of her dad's old pick-up as they drove through tall pines up the winding mountain road. She glanced out the side window as they came to a clearing and there she saw a towering sign that read: Welcome to Mountain Grove! *We Aren't Just a Town, We're a Family.*

She had fallen in love with the village right then. Someday she was going to buy a camera and take a picture of that sign, frame it, and hang it up in her room like a *Home Sweet Home* picture she had seen somewhere.

"Afternoon Em'ly!" someone shouted, breaking into her thoughts.

She looked across the street toward Cooper's Automotive and saw Gus Cooper, a grin on his weathered face, waving his grease-stained ball cap at her.

"Hi Gus," she shouted, waving back.

"I got some Orange Crush with yer name on it," he yelled through cupped hands.

"I'll come in soon," she yelled back, with another wave.

That was the really good part about living in a small town—everyone knew you and your family. But in her case, that was the really bad part, too.

As she walked on up the hill, pulling the thin jacket around her, a car honked. Glancing over, she saw Iris Head, owner of *God Bless America Real Estate,* waving. Iris pulled up to the curb and lowered the passenger window. "Just got my hair colored at Violet's, Em'ly," she said, touching her hair and looking very happy about it. "Need a ride? You look cold."

Emily smelled the acrid mixture of dye and hair spray wafting out the car window. "Not today, but thanks," she smiled, putting a finger under her nose to block the odor.

"Toodle-loo, then," Iris said, with a grin, and gunned her big white Buick up the hill, her bright, plum colored hair barely visible above the steering wheel.

Emily counted three American flags on her car as Iris zoomed off: one fluttering from the antenna, a small sticker on the back window, and an *America, Love it or Leave it* bumper sticker. Townspeople said that Iris Head was so patriotic that she "put the *P* in patriotism!"

Last spring Iris Head was the real estate agent who had handled the sale when her dad bought the woodcutting business. They had moved to Virginia from California because her dad had lost his job at an electronics store.

"That wasn't a good time," she muttered under her breath, as she hurried on, shivering in the cold. In fact, it had been a horrible time. If her grandmother hadn't given them money out of her savings to move, and make a down payment on the business, she didn't know what they would've done.

The townspeople often asked Emily what brought her family to Mountain Grove, and when she responded she always left out the part about her dad losing his job. She had the script memorized: "My dad was looking through some kind of an outdoor magazine and found an ad about a woodcutter in Mountain Grove who wanted to sell his business–so he called Iris Head at *God Bless America Real Estate* and she sent him all the information. He decided to buy it and we moved here."

She said it so many times that she could rattle it off in one breath. Then she would quickly change the subject, knowing the people in the village were so friendly, that in the next breath they'd invite her and her family over to a bar-b-que or Sunday dinner.

Her family consisted of three people: Luke, her dad; Darcy, her mom, and her grandmother, who everyone–including herself–called Pearl. And they never, ever went to bar-b-ques or Sunday dinners.

* * * *

As Emily walked up Elderberry Way, she saw her dad in the corner wood lot throwing oak logs in the back of his pick-up truck for a delivery. She was too far away to tell his mood, which stressed her out, since she hadn't talked to him since the sheriff incident.

Well, I either talk to him now about a new jacket, or freeze another week, she thought, as she hurried toward him.

"Hi, Dad," she said.

Her dad looked up and nodded as he heaved a huge log into the bed of his pick-up. He had a sour look on his face. Bolstering up her courage, she got right to the point. "Dad, I'm freezing in this jacket. Could you buy me a thicker one when you go into Clayton?"

He stared down at her thin jacket. "Yep," he said, so low she could barely hear him.

"Can you afford some gloves, and a hat, and boots, too?"

"I ain't made a' money, ya' know," he said, and turned back to his work.

"I'll write down my size and stick it on the bulletin board," she said over her shoulder, as she walked toward the house. She was pretty sure he would buy her whatever she needed. Nothing was ever easy with her dad, though.

* * * *

Emily could hear the TV blaring a daytime talk show before she even opened the front door. She wandered into the living room and saw Pearl sitting in her blue, overstuffed chair directly in front of the TV, a tall glass of amber liquid sitting on a half-table near the arm.

Pearl was like no other grandmother she had ever heard about. Other kids at school had grandmas who made dinner for them, played board games, and took them to Disneyland—unlike Pearl, who swore worse than any boy at school, drank until she passed out, and frequently hurled her slipper when she lost her temper.

Mostly, Emily just stayed out of her grandmother's way and didn't go near her unless she heard her snoring.

"Hi, Pearl," she said, not stopping.

Pearl just sniffed and kept watching TV. Emily glanced into the kitchen looking for her mother. Not seeing her, she hurried down the hall and tried the knob to her mother's bedroom. It was locked.

"Mom?" she called out softly, gently tapping on the door. No answer. *It's either a migraine or she's having one of her bad days,* Emily thought. Either way, she knew to just leave her mother alone.

Emily continued down the hall to her own bedroom, went in and threw her backpack on the bed. Looking around for a piece of paper, she found an old envelope and wrote her jacket and shoe size on the back. She could've gone shopping with her dad, but he would just buy her what he wanted to anyway. No one had much say about the purchases he made–from food to clothing–he controlled everything. Plus, the last time she'd gone, her parents had fought all the way to Clayton and all the way back. She vowed never to go with them again.

She couldn't decide what color jacket she wanted. *Maybe red,* she thought and jotted it down. *No, forget red.* She crossed it out. *Red jacket, red hair–not a pretty sight.*

She decided on black and forest green as her first and second color choices for the jacket–and black boots, of course, gloves and a hat. When her list was finished, she grabbed a book off her desk and headed out to the dated kitchen, where she pinned the envelope to the large cork bulletin board. The bulletin board was her family's main communication line. Sometimes she didn't see one parent or the other for a day or two–but she kind of knew what was going on by the messages they left. It was strange how those little notes could be so oddly comforting.

Emily checked her list over one more time, feeling a sudden rush of tenderness for her dad. He always made sure she had whatever things she needed–clothes, lunch money, food. *I wonder what he'd do if I ran outside and hugged his neck,* she wondered. The thought was so strange it made her laugh out loud.

* * * *

Emily headed out the glass slider toward her garden in the corner of the large backyard. It was well hidden behind a semi-circle of tall oleander bushes. The bushes arched out in a fan shape from the neighbor's fence on the left around to the back fence. There was a small arbor near the back fence, which was the only entry way. Emily planted sweet peas on each side of the arbor and as they grew, she intertwined them in the lattice until they covered the wood, making a beautiful archway.

Her anxiety floated away as she walked under the arbor; it was warmer here in her garden, sheltered from the wind. Emily stood for a moment and looked around the small sanctuary: Her metal rocking chair sat in the middle of the garden. She had found it all rusted in the wood lot when they first moved here, and carefully sanded the bowed arms and legs–and one bad spot on the seat–then spray painted it all a dazzling red. The chair was surrounded by neatly tended flower beds and clay pots filled with all kinds of wonderful flowers from Bloomin' Happy, the nursery owned by Mr. Charles, Jonathan's dad. Bamboo plants, ferns and mondo grass were poked into every bare spot imaginable, making her garden all but burst with greenery. Mr. Charles had also given her laminated sunflower posters from the seed company, which she had nailed to the fence like so many pieces of art in a museum.

What does Mr. Charles think of you now?

The question swooped out of nowhere, slamming into her thoughts like a wrecking ball. She slipped into her red chair and began rocking back and forth, her head tilted back as she stared up at the clouds. "Please don't let him hate me," she said to no one in particular, feeling absolutely miserable.

She opened the book on her lap, determined to corral her thoughts. She had to read the first paragraph over and over again until the words took hold—but took hold they did, and she was soon caught up in the plot of a grand adventure. She sighed contentedly. Sometimes it worked to read books and go live in another world for a while, sometimes it didn't. This book definitely worked.

Emily read for a long time until the sun went behind some clouds and it began to grow dark. She put her book down and just gazed at all the prettiness around her. When she first started her garden, she saved her lunch money and bought some purple pansies. Purple pansies were just about her all-time favorite; they looked like they had smiling faces with little squinty eyes.

She saved a little money to buy larkspur, her next favorite flower, and stopped by Bloomin' Happy to see if there were any in stock. That's when Mr. Charles had found out that she used her lunch money to buy the flowers. She hadn't ever meant to tell him, but it kind of tumbled out when he showed her his new shipment of blue pansies.

"Emily, have you ever seen a pansy this color?" Mr. C had said, pointing to a flat of them sitting on the ground.

She squatted down and cupped the pansies in her hand. "They're so beautiful; I didn't even know they came in blue," she murmured, stroking the velvety petals. "I'm saving *every bit* of my lunch money for these..."

And there it was, plopped out like a whale on the beach.

Mr. Charles looked shocked. "You aren't eating lunch so that you can buy flowers?"

"Just sometimes," she assured him, "but I eat a huge breakfast."

Mr. Charles was silent for a moment, then nodded his head toward the bright blue awning at the side of the nursery. "Come over here for a minute, I want to show you something."

He led her back to a corner where there was a rack of flowers that looked kind of droopy and had brown tinged leaves.

"Emily, these flowers aren't healthy enough to sell to my customers," he said, his eyes twinkling, "but with a little care, I believe you could rev them right up." Mr. Charles had eyes the color of blueberries, and they twinkled whenever he was happy—which was just about always.

"Would you like to give it a try?" he asked, already pulling flowers off the top rack.

"I'd love to..." Emily started to say, but her voice was all clogged up. She was so happy she could've done back flips through the zinnia beds.

After they loaded the droopy flowers onto a double-decker wagon, she noticed there were a couple of blue pansies on the wagon that didn't look droopy. She looked up at Mr. Charles and his eyes were twinkling again.

"Thank you, Mr. C," she said, reaching out and solemnly shaking his hand—she couldn't think of what else to do. She noticed that the twinkling in his eyes ramped up into Fourth of July sparklers.

She'd pulled the wagon home, unloaded it, and brought it right back to Mr. Charles. He had told her that she could keep it overnight, but she wouldn't think of it.

The next day, with the money she'd already saved, she went to Cooke's Bakery and bought a half dozen snickerdoodle cookies. Miss Mattie put them in a nice white box and tied them with a blue ribbon and gave her a tiny card to write *thank you* on.

Mr. Charles looked surprised when she handed the box to him. "Why Emily, thank you," he said, opening the box right on the spot. "Snickerdoodles! My all-time best-in-the-world-favorite," he beamed. "Well, you just come right over here, my good friend, and let's dig in."

They sat for over an hour, with Mr. Charles giving her tons of advice about flowers, as they hammered down on Miss Mattie's incredible cookies.

"Now listen, Emily," Mr. Charles said between bites of cookie, "if you want more flowers or greenery, I have plenty of work around here that you can help with. There are always plants to be watered or bags of fertilizer to stack; just let me know. Do you promise...no more skipping lunches?"

She had promised and taken him up on it the very next week, helping him move huge, smelly bags of potting soil and fertilizer.

* * * *

Emily pulled her thoughts back to the present and gazed around at all her flowers and plants. Mr. C had been right about the droopy and wilted plants—under her care the flowers and plants had flourished and bloomed, giving her a wonderful, peaceful garden.

Thriving. That's the word Mr. Charles used. She loved that word.

She stood up and stretched, then meandered over to the side fence that separated the neighbor's yard from hers. The house next door had stood empty since Emily had moved here, with a *For Sale* sign in the front yard. But just last week Emily had seen a SOLD banner across it. She peered through a knothole to see if there were any signs of the new neighbors, but the yard stood empty and unattended.

Someone really needs to take a mower to that yard, she thought, her eye roving over the knee-high grass and weeds.

Emily ambled down the fence a few feet to a gate leading into the neighbor's backyard. There was not only a gate, but also another arbor that matched the one at the entryway to her garden. It seemed so peculiar to her that neighbors had gone to all that trouble building a gate just to visit back and forth.

Peculiar, but nice, she decided.

She tried to open the gate, but something was holding it tight. She gave it a vigorous shake but it didn't budge. *Must be a latch of some kind holding it closed,* she thought as she turned back to her garden and went on a weed hunt.

The colder weather was causing some of her flowers to fade, she noticed, as she pulled weeds out of the pink begonia beds and some that had sprouted overnight in the marigolds. She also transplanted some Jupiter's Beard that looked like it was going to crowd out her Shasta daisies.

Her stomach was rumbling by the time she finished; she heard the church bells at St. Daniel's ring five times, so she dusted off her hands and headed for the house in search of some dinner.

The freezer held a big stash of frozen dinners, and she rifled through them, finally deciding on the Texas stuffed burrito. She tossed it in the microwave and punched 5 minutes HIGH. As it churned around, she dug a pack of salad mix out of the crisper drawer and snagged the bottled dressing from the refrigerator door before it closed. As she assembled her dinner, she heard loud snores coming from the living room and went to investigate.

Pearl slept upright in the overstuffed chair; her head lolled to one side. When she exhaled her snore sounded like a factory whistle. Just past her, the TV showed the evening news, and the tumbler of liquor stood nearly empty on the half-table.

Glancing at the clock, Emily sighed: six-twenty and her grandmother had passed out for the night. She would have to help her into bed.

She went over and gently shook her. "Pearl...Pearl...I'm going to help you into bed," she shouted, bending down and shouting again into her ear.

Pearl didn't budge.

She put both hands on her grandmother's skinny shoulders and pushed her up out of the chair. Pearl tried to stand up but toppled forward toward the TV. Emily grabbed her sweater and pulled her back to a standing position, thinking it was a good thing Pearl was so small. She managed to get an arm around her and shouted to be heard through her grandmother's stupor, "Walk Pearl! I'll lead you—just walk."

She led Pearl down the hall and into her little bedroom, then sat her on a chair so that she could turn back the bed covers. It always amazed her that Pearl kept her room—actually the whole house—so clean. Absolutely nothing was out of place.

She helped Pearl ease into bed and pulled off her slippers. She looked at the small shoes she held in her hands—they were so little, but Pearl could hurl them like missiles. She set them down by the bed so Pearl could find them in the morning.

Emily went out, softly closing the bedroom door behind her. Before she reached the end of the hall, she could hear the factory whistle going full force again.

In the kitchen, she picked up her plate, grabbed a fork and napkin and headed for her room. The sight of her backpack on the bed reminded her of what she had to face on Monday so she threw her jacket over it. She didn't want to even *think* about that mess.

She sat down at her small desk and dug a big hole in the steaming burrito, then turned on her small TV and clicked through the channels. Her favorite show, *The TV Doctor* wasn't on yet, so tonight she would have dinner with Judge Judy.

CHAPTER – 3

On Saturday morning, Emily flew down Main Street, bounded up the red brick steps to the library, and charged through the huge double doors, looking left and right for Mrs. Green, the librarian. From behind the check-out counter, Emily heard an astonishing blast of laughter. People stopped reading, and boys and girls listening to story-time looked up startled.

Mrs. Green's red hair popped up over the counter. "Sorry," she mouthed, clapping a hand over her mouth.

Everyone went quietly back to what they were doing with smiles on their faces; Mrs. Green's explosive laugh was wonderfully contagious.

"Good morning!" Mrs. Green sang out, when she saw Emily, a huge grin causing her ears to rise slightly.

"Good morning–I broke my reading record," Emily said breathlessly, thumping three books down on the return counter, and all but dancing with excitement.

"You read three books in one week! Wonderful!" said Mrs. Green, coming from around the counter to hug her. Mrs. Green was a great hugger. She hugged everyone–even grumpy old Miss Beasley, who tried skirting around the huge, oak library tables to avoid her.

"I wish I had a Blue Ribbon or reading medal to give you!" Mrs. Green laughed, giving her an extra squeeze. "What books are you going to check out this week?"

"More adventure stories, I *love* adventure."

"Oh, I love them, too," Mrs. Green fairly crowed. "Have you ever read *Julie of the Wolves*?

"Never," Emily crowed back.

"Well, my sweet devourer-of-books, *Julie of the Wolves* is a story of *high* adventure," Mrs. Green said, looping her arm through Emily's and steering her toward the fiction section.

When Emily first moved to the village, Miss Mattie had told her all about Mrs. Green's life, and her marriage to Mr. Green. Emily loved hearing the story more than anything, and pestered Miss Mattie to tell it to her again and again.

"I've known Miz' Green for years, Sugar," Miss Mattie would always begin. *When I met her she was Miss Redding, the librarian, and that woman loved three things: bein' single, travelin', and books.*

She earned her livin' by being a librarian—which was just the perfect job for her. But every spare minute that woman had, she traveled—and I'm talkin' all over the world! China, Rome, Istanbul! That woman had wings on her feet!

Well, Sugar—Miss Mattie would always continue—*the library and travelin' was her absolute life, until Mr. Green came along. What that nice woman thought could never happen DID happen, and she fell—not only head-over-heels— but back-flips and whirly-gigs in love with that man, and before you could even say, 'Happily ever after', those two were married and livin' in Mr. Green's house on White Pine Road—you know, just east of town, out past Grover's Fruit Stand.*

From the very beginnin' of her marriage, Miz' Green was as happy as peach pie. My goodness, how that woman loved bein' married! Why, she told everyone—friends, relatives, pastor, and postman, "Jus' call me 'Miz' Green'." She loved hearin' her married name over and over and over again. So all these years later—that's what everyone still calls her.

Miss Mattie told her that some people couldn't even remember Mrs. Green's first name anymore.

Last week, Emily had asked Miss Mattie to tell her the story one too many times and in exasperation, Miss Mattie said, "Sugar, I'm tired of tellin' that story five times a week. Please wait a month before you ever in this world ask me to tell it again."

Emily had been waiting forever to meet Mr. Green, thinking he must surely be the most handsome man in Virginia—maybe even in the whole world!

"I can't even read these crazy titles without my reading glasses," Mrs. Green was saying, pulling Emily out of her daydream. Mrs. Green was almost upside down trying to read book titles on the bottom shelf. She straightened up with a groan, putting her hands in the small of her back to get the kinks out. As she stretched, she caught sight of a line of people waiting at the check-out counter.

"Look at that line!" she wailed, hurrying off. "Emily," she called back over her shoulder, "would you mind fetching my reading glasses off the desk in my office? I'll be back in ten minutes."

"I wouldn't mind at all," Emily called out after her. In fact, she was quite excited to see Mrs. Green's private office.

Emily headed off toward what she was sure was the office part of the library. She passed through a small alcove; on the right was a door marked *Janitor's Closet,* and on the left she saw a massive oak door that stood slightly open. She peered inside.

The room was decorated with colorful maps and posters of places all over the world. She pushed the heavy door open further and went in, staring first at one wall, and then another, where a collage of photos caught her attention. She walked over for a better look, immediately recognizing pictures of a younger Mrs. Green, taken in every corner of the globe: Japan, Indonesia, China, and other places Emily wasn't sure of.

In one picture, Mrs. Green was standing with a group of Asian ladies in front of a pagoda; they all looked like they were saying "cheese" and giving the peace sign. In another she was surrounded by llamas and talking to a man in a weird pom pom hat; one of the llamas was trying to nibble her ear and another was licking her skinny leg. Emily stood there laughing, until she remembered she was supposed to be looking for reading glasses.

She went over to an oversized desk cluttered with unopened mail, papers, and books—but no reading glasses. She began sifting through the clutter to see if the glasses might be underneath. As she lifted some papers, an 8 x 10 framed picture caught her attention. She let the papers flutter back down on the desk as she picked up the picture, peering intently at a man with a huge grin.

"It can't be..." she murmured.

She stared for a full minute at the face that made Mrs. Green do back-flips and whirly-gigs. Mr. Green had a nice smile that made crinkles around his eyes, he was slightly bald with a small mole on his left cheek and had a large-ish kind of nose.

"No way!" Emily whispered, noticing a smudge on the glass of the picture. She held it at a different angle so the light hit it just right.

"Please tell me that's not lipstick," she groaned. But that's exactly what it was. In fact, there were two lipstick smudges where Mrs. Green had kissed each of her husband's cheeks.

Emily sighed and shook her head, carefully setting the picture back down on the desk--at the same time spotting Mrs. Green's reading glasses sticking up out of the pencil holder. She grabbed them and headed back to the fiction section. When she handed the glasses to Mrs. Green, she took a good look at her, too.

Mrs. Green had short red hair with cowlicks that sometimes looked like she had sprouted horns, an oversized mouth, with a smile that Gus Cooper said was, "bright as a Kodak flash", and green, mischievous eyes that danced at the mention of any book. Her laugh was way too loud, and sometimes she snorted when she laughed.

"These people definitely don't seem like what great love stories are written about," Emily said under her breath.

She checked out her books and left the library that day thinking Miss Mattie must be terribly mistaken. "Back-flips and whirly-gigs in love?" she sighed aloud. "I don't think so, Miss Mattie."

Emily walked to the park and headed toward the statue of General John Emerson. She clambered up the high pedestal and slipped into the statue's granite lap. The stone felt cold through her jacket, but the sun was bright and warming. She draped her legs over the General's arm and leaned her head up against his granite chest, where she hunkered in with her volume of *Julie of the Wolves.*

* * * *

Emily sat perched at the counter of Good Eats Café Sunday morning, feasting on a lumberjack breakfast of eggs, bacon, hash browns, and homemade biscuits. Glen Kingery, owner of the Village Grocer, sat two stools down, dressed in his usual black and red checked mackinaw, eating his standard eggs-over-easy. Iris Head was sharing a corner booth with Miss Violet and Miss Rose, sisters who owned Violet's House of Beauty. The three women had a standing engagement for breakfast each Sunday after church. Someone had told Emily that they always went to the early church service so there would be plenty of time to eat and visit afterward.

The rest of the people in the café were strangers: a drably dressed man and woman eating waffles with their little boy in the back booth, and a businessman who sat at a small table reading The New York Times, nibbling a sweet roll.

Emily kept glancing at the corner booth, entranced by Miss Violet who was known for her outrageous attire. This morning she was garbed in a lavender sarong and matching turban.

"Been cold enough for ya?" Mr. Kingery asked, breaking into her thoughts.

"Freezing!" she replied, watching him dip toast in his egg yolk. "Think it will snow soon?"

"Naw, not for a coupla months," he said, plunging a fork into a bite of ham.

Miss Violet's voice rose in the background, and they both turned and watched as she reenacted a scene from *Gone With the Wind,* which she'd watched the night before on the Turner Movie Channel. Her turban bobbed up and down as she waved her arms dramatically, and at one point, it slipped down over her left eye—but she hardly noticed, she was so enraptured with her own story telling.

Mr. Kingery looked at Emily, and nodded toward Miss Violet, "I didn't think they'd let a person inside a church in a get-up like that," he said in a low voice, turning back to his breakfast.

"Me either," Emily laughed, scooping up the last of her scrambled eggs.

Mr. Kingery blew on his coffee and took a sip. "You goin' to their charm school?" he asked, referring to the classes run by Miss Violet and Miss Rose in the back room of Violet's House of Beauty.

"You mean the Young Ladies Academy?" she asked, popping the last piece of bacon into her mouth.

"Whatever," he said, shaking his head. "I keep forgettin' they changed the name."

It didn't matter to Emily what they called it, she wasn't going and that's what she told Mr. Kingery, who laughed and added more sugar to his coffee.

Ike Peavler, owner of the café, came out of the kitchen wearing his signature chef's hat and green apron, carrying platters of French toast and sausages for the three ladies.

Emily watched as he served the food, trying to remember if she had ever seen Ike without his chef's attire. He sported a white chef's hat that towered like a stove pipe, and an apron embroidered with *Good Eats Café* across the bib; his name and title were written just beneath: *Ike Peavler, Owner & Chef.*

Ike took his work at the diner real seriously.

"Is there anythin' else I kin git you ladies?" he asked the women, setting the platters down in front of them.

"A pot of tea, if you please," Miss Violet trilled, adjusting her turban.

"I would enjoy some, too," Miss Rose said quietly. Miss Rose was as shy and demure as her sister was outrageous and flamboyant.

Ike went behind the counter and rigged up a tea service just the way he'd seen Millie, his waitress of eighteen years do it: a yellow flowered teapot with matching tea cups and saucers, served on a tray with lemon wedges, honey, and various sweeteners.

"Thank you," the sisters chorused, as he set it down in front of them.

Ike came over to where Emily and Mr. Kingery were sitting and began wiping off the counter with a white dish towel. "Millie's gotta quit takin' so many derned days off," he complained to them under his breath, wiping around their plates, "I'm a chef, not some dern parlor maid givin' tea parties."

"You oughta put some frills on that apron of yers, Ike," Mr. Kingery chuckled.

"Ha, ha, very funny," Ike retorted, glancing at Emily's plate. "How'd ya like yer scrambled eggs?" he asked her, changing the subject.

"They were yummy," she replied, putting a little grape jelly on her biscuit. "I tried to make scrambled eggs once, but they were stinky and tasted like burned rubber bands."

"Ya need to get you some cookin' lessons," Ike said, and went into his kitchen, returning with a skillet of hash browns.

"You want s'more of these?" he asked Emily.

She shook her head and looked up at him. "Do you give cooking lessons, Ike?"

He started to laugh but stopped when he saw the look on her face. "Well... I guess I could give a lesson or two."

"When?"

"When? hmmm..." He scratched his head. "Let's see, when's your next school break?"

She thought for a second. "Columbus Day."

"Well then, Columbus Day it is for cookin' school," he said, scooping a tall heap of hash browns onto Mr. Kingery's plate. "Come in early and you kin' help make eggs for my breakfast crowd."

"Where's Millie today, Ike?" Iris called from the booth. She stabbed her last bite of sausage, chewing it as she got up to help herself to coffee.

"Don't ask," Ike sighed.

"Let me guess...one of her daughter's is having a baby," Iris said, as she got her personalized mug from the rack on the wall. Each of Ike's regular customers had a mug with *Good Eats Café* stenciled on the front and their name written on the back. Ike had used a gold-colored Sharpie pen to write their name, thinking it gave just the right homey effect.

"You guessed right," Ike said. "Millie's got four daughters and each of 'em is havin' babies ta' beat the band." He shook his head. "She's over in Roarin' Springs helpin' with babies more 'n she's here."

Everyone in the café nodded in sympathy.

Iris poured herself some coffee then sauntered over with the coffee pot and poured Mr. Kingery a refill; she looked around the café to see if anyone else was holding up their mug for more.

"What's this I hear 'bout your granddaughter comin' to live with you, Ike?" asked Mr. Kingery, checking his watch. He didn't open his grocery store until ten o'clock on Sundays.

"Ya' heard it right, buddy boy," Ike replied, putting two tablespoons of finely ground coffee into his new latte machine. He set a cup under the spout and flipped the switch.

As the machine frothed and spewed, Mr. Kingery shouted above the noise, "How old is she?"

"How old is *who*?" Ike shouted back. He turned off the switch and took a sip of the latte, smacking his lips.

"Your granddaughter...how old's your granddaughter?" Mr. Kingery barked.

"Kelly Ann's fifteen, and smart as whip," Ike replied proudly, wiping his hands off on a white dish towel. "But whatever in this world I'm gonna do with a fifteen-year-old girl, I'll never know. I sure wisht my wife was still livin'."

Ike tapped the latte machine. "You want one of these?" he asked the grocer.

"Naw," Mr. Kingery shuddered. "I never touch that sissy stuff."

"How long is she staying with you, Ike?" Miss Rose asked, putting a dainty bit of butter on her French toast.

Ike shook his head. "That's the hard part–I don't know. What I *do* know is that ever since my daughter run off and married that Johnny Parrish bum, it's been downhill all the way fer her."

"Oh my, whatever happened?" Miss Rose asked, her cheeks pinking up.

"Why, Johnny drank likker ever' night of this world, and got my daughter to drinkin' it too," Ike said, shaking his head. "He run off after Kelly Ann was born, and it's been a real sorry state ever since. My daughter's gotta go into one of them rehab places to dry out."

"If you want my vote, Ike, I think you'll do just fine with Kelly Ann," said Mr. Kingery, downing the rest of his coffee, "and remember you gotta whole town full a' people to help you."

The ladies nodded their heads in agreement.

"Send her over to our charm... to our Young Ladies Academy," trilled Miss Violet, spooning sugar into her tea with great flourish.

"We'll introduce your granddaughter to other young ladies and direct her socially," Miss Rose added, then blushed, hoping she hadn't sounded too forward.

"I do thank ya, Miss Violet, Miss Rose," Ike said, his brow furrowed with worry. "That might be a plan if I kin talk her into it."

"When's she coming?" Iris asked, digging at her teeth with a toothpick. Miss Rose drew back in horror as Iris popped a piece of sausage out of a back tooth.

"I don't have th' exact time yet, Iris," Ike said. "I b'lieve in th' next coupla weeks or so. I pay for my daughter an' gran'daughter to fly out fer a visit 'bout ever' six months, and Kelly Ann and I git along jus' fine. It's jus' that I never had responsibility for th' girl all on my own."

"I bet it'll be fun, Ike," Emily said, thinking he looked really worried.

"Emily dear, you simply *must* come to our academy, too," Miss Violet trilled, keeping her eyes averted from Iris's tooth probing. "You could get acquainted with other girls your age, along with Kelly Ann.

That's not going to happen, thought Emily. She opened her mouth to give a polite refusal, but before she could say anything, she saw Ike's head jerk up.

"Well, wouldja look at that," he said, pointing toward the front window with his spatula.

Emily swiveled around just in time to see Miss Mattie stroll by in the biggest, most elaborate church hat she had ever seen in her life.

"Wow!" she said, hopping off the stool and running to the window.

Miss Mattie crossed the street and promenaded up Elderberry Way, in full view of everyone in the café. She looked majestic in an elegant, wide-brimmed, red, felt hat. The brim on one side was bent up in a sassy curve with a huge black feather arching out the top; the hat crown was circled with gold links that winked in the sunlight.

It was silent in the café as everyone stared, entranced as Miss Mattie—regal as a queen—sashayed up the sidewalk, then mounted the steps of the Mountain Grove Community Church, for their late morning service. Everyone in the café watched in silence until she disappeared through the giant double doors.

"Wow!" everyone whooped in unison.

"That was the' best hat show I ever saw," Ike laughed. "I thought her aprons was bright, but that hat beat 'em all."

"I loved it!" Emily grinned. "If I ever go to church, I'm going to wear a hat just like it."

"And a fine sight you'd be, Miss Em'ly," Ike said, with a sweeping bow.

Emily laughed as she walked over to the register and laid down her money for the breakfast. "Thanks for the good food, Ike."

"Yer more 'n welcome, darlin'," he said. "Now don't forgit our cookin' lesson."

"I won't," she said, pulling open the door. "Bye everyone!"

A chorus of good-bye's followed her outside.

As she trudged up Elderberry Way, Emily could hear singing coming from the church and a rush of loneliness hit her. She wished she could peek in through the church doors for one more look at Miss Mattie's hat. She went as far as to put a foot on the church step but changed her mind and decided to cross the street to the gas station and visit Gus instead.

She strode up to the gas island. "Good morning!" she called to Gus, who was busy checking the oil on grumpy old Miss Beasley's Cadillac. Emily wondered how she could skirt around the car so she didn't have to talk to her.

"Mornin' Em'ly," Gus said, grinning beneath his oil-stained ball cap. "He'p yer'thef to an Orange Cruth, I'll be finished in a 'thec."

"Sounds good," she said, wondering why Gus was lisping so much. She cut across the gas island in front of Miss Beasley's faded gold Cadillac. The vintage car stretched the length of the gas island, with chromed fenders that looked like silver wings.

Emily glanced toward the car and saw Miss Beasley glaring at her out the side window, which had been rolled down halfway. Emily wanted to dash straight to the soda machine but thought she should at least say hello.

"Morning, Miss Beasley," she sang out. "Would you like an Orange Crush?"

"Never touch the stuff, thank you," sniffed Miss Beasley, sticking her nose in the air.

Gus struggled to lower the hood on Miss Beasley's car. "This thing's big ath' a ski lift," he puffed, putting all of his body weight on the hood to get it closed.

Emily watched as Miss Beasley paid Gus for the gas, and with a final sniff, gunned her Cadillac out of the station. She watched in astonishment as Miss Beasley missed the driveway entirely, ricocheted over the curb, and bounced out into the street, her small head bobbing back and forth like a jack-in-the-box.

"That woman 'ith gonna git whip-lath' if the' don't slow down," Gus lisped, shaking his head, as he walked toward Emily, who stared, startled at the way his cheeks puffed out funny when he talked.

As they walked through the office door toward the soda machine, Emily glanced over at Gus' desk and let out a small scream.

"Whath's wrong," asked a startled Gus.

Emily pointed to the desk where a set of teeth sat, grinning at her.

"Whoopth..." Gus said, hurrying over to his desk. "'Scuse' me a sec..." He turned away briefly and popped the teeth in. "My ol' choppers git to agrivatin' my gums sometimes an' I take 'em out," he explained, pushing the teeth into place with a greasy thumb.

Emily stared in astonished silence.

"There we go...snug as a bug," he grinned, displaying a full set of even, white teeth. He motioned toward the soda box. "He'p yerself to a Crush," he said, acting like nothing unusual had happened.

Emily shook her head as she walked over to the soda machine, a blue square metal box with *Pepsi* written in faded red lettering. It stood on thin metal legs and the sodas inside were kept cold with chilled water. Gus had owned the gas station well over forty years and townspeople said his soda machine must be the original.

There was no coin dispenser, she just lifted the lid and grabbed a soda, shook the water off the bottle, and twisted off the cap. When Emily reached into her pocket to pay Gus the seventy-five cents he charged for sodas, he held up his hand and said, "No deal. Yer money's no good in here t'day."

She started to protest, but Gus kept his hand up. "I'm the one that did the invitin,' Miss Em'ly, it's on me."

"Well, thanks," she smiled, taking a large chug from the bottle.

"Let's get a load off our feet," he said, heading back outside to the row of slatted wood chairs that lined the front wall of his station. "Have a seat," he said, pointing in the direction of the chairs.

Gus' station was a regular meeting place for friends who loved to chew on various morsels of gossip. *Chin wags* were what Gus called them. Sometimes he and his old cronies would get to talking so much they would be irritated when they were interrupted by a paying customer.

Emily thumped down on a chair and Gus went back inside and came out wheeling his favorite old oak desk chair; the chair creaked and groaned as he sat down.

She took another drink from her Crush and asked, "Where's YipYap?" referring to Gus' old schnauzer that wandered around the service station.

"Las' time I saw 'im he was takin' a nap out back on a pile of oil rags," he answered, unconcerned.

"Has he said anything interesting lately?" she asked, trying to keep a straight face. Gus swore that when YipYap barked, he was actually saying words.

"Naw, he's been pretty quiet lately," Gus grinned. "Guess he's got nothin' to complain about."

About then, YipYap strolled around the corner of the station and went over to Emily, laying his head on her leg.

"Musta' heard us talkin' about him," Gus mused.

She patted the dog's head. "Want to know something funny about Miss Beasley?"

"Let's hear it."

"Did you know that Mrs. Green gives her hugs when she comes into the library?"

"You gotta be kiddin' me," Gus snorted.

"It's true," Emily cackled. "I've seen her do it—except she has to chase Miss Beasley all around the library to do it.

"Who'd want to try an' hug that ol'sour bird?" Gus shuddered.

"You should see them, Gus," she laughed. "Miss Beasley tries to keep a table between them, but Mrs. Green always catches her. Sometimes they go at a dead run!"

Gus snorted with laughter, giving a full view of his choppers. They were grinning at her the same way they had back on the desk.

"That beats all I ever heard," Gus said, wiping his eyes with a handkerchief. "I swear Miz' Beasley must eat crab apples fer' breakfast ever mornin'."

They both laughed.

"You know what I think, Gus?" Emily said, tossing her empty bottle into the recycling bin. "I think Miss Beasley likes the hugs."

Gus just shook his head. "Now *that* is hard to b'lieve," he said, leaning back in the chair and putting his feet up on a stack of oil cans.

"You better not lean back too far, Gus," she laughed. "We almost lost you last time."

Smiling, Gus put his hands behind his head and leaned the chair back at an alarming angle. "I know Em'ly, but my friends find it highly entertainin' to see me pitched over on my back with my feet stickin' straight up in the air."

She laughed and said, "Guess what?"

"What?" he asked, taking off his ball cap and setting it on his knee.

"Miss Violet invited me to the Young Ladies Academy today!"

"You goin'?"

"No way!" Emily snorted.

"That things been goin' on forever," he said, shaking his head. "It usta' be called *Miss Violet's Charm School,* but no girl t'day wants ta' go to a danged charm school."

"I know I don't," she replied, meaning it.

"Well, prob'ly wouldn't hurt t' give it a try," he shrugged. "Lotsa' girls go."

Emily was surprised, and a little disappointed, that Gus hadn't joined her in laughing off the whole idea, and decided she'd better change the subject quick. "You have any Ritz crackers with peanut butter?"

"I sure do, little lady. You know where I keep 'em."

Emily went into the office and fished out a couple of packs from under the counter and threw one to Gus when she came out. They crunched away watching village people stroll by; Gus had a story for just about every one of them.

They passed the rest of the morning having their own chin wag, feasting on crackers washed down with bottles of deliciously chilled Orange Crush—until she noticed people pouring out the church doors.

"Yikes, Gus!" she said, jumping up. "I've been sitting here all morning and I've got tons of homework to do."

As Gus stood up and stretched himself, she could hear bones popping. "Well Em'ly, I sure enjoyed our visit. You have a standin' invitation to join me anytime."

"Thanks," she said, and with a wave took off up the street.

Turning up Elderberry Way, Emily glanced over at the church hoping to catch sight of Miss Mattie in her hat one more time. She didn't see her and was tempted to hang around a few minutes, but knew she had a test to study for.

She was almost home before she remembered her books were in her locker, forgotten when she'd hurried away from school on Friday. She had no way to study for a test or anything else.

CHAPTER – 4

Emily could hear her ancient alarm clock buzzing in the distance. Her eyes shot open, dread filled her, and her heart took off at a gallop. *What was it?* She tried thinking through the fog. The problems came rushing in like a tsunami: drunk dad, Miss Graham, Logger, Mack, Jonathan, Mr. Charles.

She groaned, hitting the snooze button, and pulled the blankets up over head. "How am I going to get through this?" she moaned. When her alarm blared for the third time, she made herself get up and head for the bathroom.

Looking at her image in the bathroom mirror Emily thought, *this is the worst day of your life, and it's a terrible hair day too,* and quickly brushed her auburn hair up into a ponytail. As she brushed her teeth she leaned forward into the mirror for a closer look at her nose.

"It can't be!" she whispered, checking her nose at another angle.

"My freckles are fading!" she gasped, not quite believing it. She looked again, gingerly touching her nose with her fingertips. It was true! Her freckles had gone from reddish brown to sand color. She danced a little jig. *Yes...yes...yes*! She wasn't doomed to looking at spots in the mirror for the rest of her life.

Okay, so maybe this won't be such a bad day after all, she thought, quickly pulling on her black jeans, and red pull-over sweater. A person could face about anything if their freckles were fading.

Feeling ravenous, she strolled into the kitchen and was surprised to see her mother standing by the sink in a faded pink robe. Straggles of uncombed hair hid her mother's profile as she stared out the window.

"Morning, Mom," Emily said hesitantly.

Her mother turned and glared at her. "What're you doing up this early?"

"I go to school this early," she replied, tilting her chin up bravely.

Her mother shrugged and went back to staring out the window.

"You okay?" Emily asked, her anxiety rising.

Her mother shook her head no.

"Can I do something?"

"There's nothing you or anyone else can do," her mother replied coldly, refusing to look at her.

Emily just stared at her, not quite able to breathe right anymore. She opened her mouth to say something, but there was nothing to say.

Look at me, she pleaded silently, feeling invisible and unwanted. She hated these feelings.

A sudden burst of rage washed over her. *Everything isn't about YOU,* she wanted to scream. *When I go to school today all the kids will know that Dad was driving his truck drunk; my teacher hates me; a boy tried to help me, and he's in terrible trouble now. And his dad...I can't even imagine what his dad must be thinking of me...*

But she just stood there paralyzed, staring at her mother's back, her heart racing so fast it caused her to feel weak.

Okay Emily, breathe. An inner voice took over. *Walk out of the room, get your backpack, go to school.*

She turned, willing her legs to move toward her room. She had to get out of this house.

Jerking her backpack off the bed, Emily rushed back down the hall, heading for the front door. Her mother was still staring out the kitchen window when she hurried by.

"Bye, Mom," she whispered, not waiting for an answer. Once outside, Emily stood on the other side of the door, trying to get her breathing under control. She found herself trembling.

Her stomach started to rumble when she was halfway down Elderberry Way, and she realized she had forgotten to eat breakfast. "Who cares," she murmured, as waves of nausea washed over her.

Walking by the park she looked up at the statue of General Emerson and wished she could spend the rest of the day nestled in his lap, but trudged on. As she walked, she tried to cheer up by switching her thoughts to "Little Women," the book she read out in her garden yesterday, imagining that she had the same wonderful home life as the March sisters in the story. But it didn't work. Her home life was pathetic, and there was no use pretending it was anything else.

As she rounded the bend to the school grounds, she groaned. Mr. Charles' Dodge Ram was parked in the school parking lot next to

Miss Mattie's blue Mazda. With the awfulness of the situation firmly upon her shoulders, Emily walked onto the school grounds.

* * * *

In the principal's office of Whispering Pine Middle School, Mattie Cooke glared at Miss Graham, her voice fairly crackling with anger, "I'd say that one very *big* problem is that you look down on Em'ly."

Mr. Godfrey, the principal shifted uncomfortably, wondering if he should intervene on the conversation.

Miss Graham, the picture of poise, appeared unruffled. "Really, Mrs. Cooke, I don't see *what* you are so perturbed about. I merely mentioned to Mr. Charles that his son might want to find more suitable company than Emily Parks. Look at the trouble she's gotten him into already."

Mr. Charles stepped in. "Jonathan chose to get involved, Miss Graham—and that isn't the issue here. Two boys were cruel to Emily—that *is* the issue."

"How was I to know the issue if Emily and Jonathan wouldn't tell me what was going on," Miss Graham shot back at him. "And quite frankly, Mr. Charles, she might as well get used to it; I doubt that her family is going to change anytime soon."

Miss Mattie rose to her feet, a brooding tornado. "Now you jus' listen to me for one minute, Miss Graham," she hissed, "you have one *snooty* attitude. Of course Em'ly isn't going to tell you anything; you'd make it worse by blaming her—just like you're trying to do now."

"Ahem," Mr. Godfrey interrupted. "Maybe I could insert a little something here, if you'd kindly take your seat, Mrs. Cooke."

He waited for her to sit down before he turned to Miss Graham. "Perhaps, Miss Graham, one thing you *could* do is get to know Emily a little better and not just see her as an extension of her family." He paused, then continued, "I'm concerned about your attitude toward Emily, and that it will be detected by the other children. That's unacceptable."

Miss Graham glared at him, opened her mouth to say something, then clamped it shut.

"I plan to talk to her about the food throwing incident," Mr. Godfrey continued, "but I'm also going to let her know that if she isn't comfortable talking to her teachers, that I'm always here. She needs all the support she can get."

"You mean you *aren't* going to punish her?" Miss Graham trilled. "Why, you're letting the whole school know that you're on *her* side."

"Good!" replied Mr. Godfrey, looking her straight in the eye. "You need to let them know that, too."

Miss Mattie resisted the urge to jump up and plant a big kiss on Mr. Godfrey's bald forehead.

"Miss Graham," he continued, "you know that Emily has never caused a problem at school. She's on the Honor Roll and tries her best; let this go and get behind her more. She's bright and well spoken, but she's got a tough road ahead of her."

He turned to Mr. Charles. "And about Jonathan's behavior, I think his actions could've been a bit more tempered, and I'm going to call him in and talk to him about that. But to be perfectly honest, at his age I probably would've done the same thing—at least I hope I would have."

Miss Graham glared at him.

"What are you going to do about the Bouchard brothers?" Mr. Charles asked.

"They need their rear ends kicked from here to Richmond," Miss Mattie snorted, not one to mince words.

Mr. Godfrey looked at her and nodded. "They are a problem," he agreed. "As anyone can tell you, they go from one episode of troublemaking to the next. I think the next step is to bring the superintendent in on it."

"Can you get them some counseling?" Mr. Charles asked.

"Yes, if they would agree and their parents would agree to it," he said, gathering up papers, "and *that's* the problem." He stood to his feet. "You good people will have to excuse me now," he said, "I have another meeting in five minutes."

They all stood up.

"I know we'll all do everything in our power to help Emily," Mr. Godfrey said, looking directly at Miss Graham. He walked them to the door and shook everyone's hand as they left. He saw the anger written all over Miss Graham's face, but he didn't care.

Mr. Godfrey followed them out into the main office. "Send for Logger and Mack Bouchard in about forty-five minutes," he said to the school secretary. "I want to see them in my office."

* * * *

Out in the parking lot, Miss Mattie was still worried. "Do you think we should try an' get Em'ly transferred out of that woman's class, Joe? Miss Graham doesn't like her one bit, you know."

"I know, Mattie, but Emily is going to encounter a lot of *Miss Grahams* in her lifetime," he replied, "and besides, she's the only Spanish teacher here. Just keep an eye on things; you'll know if she needs help."

"I hope you're right," Miss Mattie said, looking worried as she gave Joe Charles a quick hug good-bye. "That woman is one nasty ole' hen and she's peckin' on Em'ly."

He smiled. "I think your smoldering eyes will cut down on any pecking, Mattie."

"Hmmmph," Miss Mattie snorted as she opened her car door and got in. She paused for a moment then poked her head up over the top of the car. "...And Joe, I hope you give that fine son of yours a Medal of Honor for jumpin' that rascally boy."

He chuckled as he unlocked his truck. "We'll see, Mattie. We'll see."

* * * *

Spanish was the only class Emily had with Jonathan, and it was just before lunch. Miss Graham hadn't said anything to either one of them when they came into the classroom, so when the bell rang dismissing them for lunch, Emily got up from her desk and started for the door.

"Emily," Miss Graham trilled, "I would like to speak with you a moment.

Emily saw Jonathan hesitate at the door and motioned for him to go on, but he walked back into the classroom.

"Jonathan," Miss Graham hissed, "*you* are dismissed. I wish to speak with Emily."

He stood his ground, looking at Emily.

"It's okay, Jonathan, I'll talk to you later," she said, keeping her voice lighter than she felt. If he wasn't in trouble anymore, she wanted to keep it that way.

He hesitated, but finally headed out the door. She wished she'd remembered to thank him for helping her.

She wasn't exactly sure what to do, so sat back down at her desk. Miss Graham tidied up the room, waiting for the class to clear of the other students.

As Miss Graham erased the blackboard, Emily happened to glance down at her feet. She'd never noticed before, but Miss Graham had *huge* feet. Her ankles were normal, but from her heel to her toes her feet shot out like boat oars. To make matters worse, she wore big white flats with no hint of a heel, which just emphasized the enormous length of her foot.

As Emily sat staring, she wondered if Miss Graham had ever done any broad jumping in high school. With feet that big, she could probably leap like a kangaroo. Emily was lost in thought trying to imagine Miss Graham as a teenager, when she happened to glance up— Miss Graham was glaring at her. Emily kept her eyes raised and away from Miss Graham's feet, but she knew it was too late, Miss Graham had already seen her gawking. Miss Graham walked back to where Emily was sitting, her big shoes clattering on the tile floor. "They're size 12, in case you were wondering," she said in a cold voice.

Emily just sat there. What could she say?

"I want to speak to you about the cafeteria incident," Miss Graham said, scowling at her. "I don't know why you refused to talk to me, and then brought the whole village in on it. You made me look incompetent."

Emily was dumfounded. "I didn't bring in the whole village..." The words died on her lips; she knew it was useless.

"And if I had my say," Miss Graham continued, "there would be severe consequences for your little food-throwing incident." She sniffed. "Your actions were simply inexcusable."

"What about Logger and Mack?" Emily asked, growing angry.

"They're being dealt with," Miss Graham retorted, walking back to her desk, her big shoes echoing. She took her lunch out of a desk drawer. "You may go now," she said, glaring at Emily. "I just wanted you to know that you don't fool me."

Emily was furious and unafraid. "I'd like to stay in, if you don't mind," she hissed, barely getting the words out through clenched teeth.

"I have lunch duty and you can do as you please, but let me tell you something, Emily," Miss Graham said, shaking a finger at her, "I *won't* be made a fool of."

Too late for that, Emily thought as she heard Miss Graham clatter out the door.

Emily didn't know why, but her anger suddenly melted away, and she felt sorry for Miss Graham and her enormous feet. *No one really likes her,* she thought, *and she doesn't seem to have any friends.* The thought of being Miss Graham's friend was quite alarming.

"I know one thing," she murmured, pulling a piece of paper out of her binder, "if I ever *were* her friend, I'd tell her to not wear white flats with those big feet of hers."

Emily spent the next ten minutes writing. Looking up at the clock, she saw that she'd just have time to buy a sandwich before the afternoon bell rang. On her way to the lunchroom, she went by Jonathan's locker and stuffed the note of thanks through the small air vent in his locker door.

* * * *

Emily knew she had to get it over with.

After school she headed straight for Bloomin' Happy nursery to talk to Mr. Charles about the whole school mess. Dread increased with each step, and she wished a flying saucer would land in downtown Mountain Grove, or an earthquake would split the streets open and block the way—*anything* so that she didn't have to do this. *Quite pretending, and just get it over with,* Emily scolded herself, even though she didn't have a clue as to what she was going to say. She walked slowly through the wrought iron gate at Bloomin' Happy Nursery, shutting it quietly behind her. Mr. Charles was unloading flats of red peonies from a hand cart.

"Hi, Mr. C."

He swung around looking surprised. "Why hello, Emily!" he said, a grin spreading across his face. He set the flowers down on a wood-slatted potting table and dusted off his hands. "How did things go at school for you today?"

"Well, things were pretty awful for me at school," she replied, glad he'd gotten right to the point. "How was it for you?"

He laughed. "Oh, kind of awful, but life gets that way sometimes. Come on over and sit down where it's a little warmer." He led the way to the patio area and pulled out a canvas folding chair and sat it under the portable heater. "Would you like some hot cocoa or anything?"

"No, thanks," she said, surprised that he was being so nice to her.

He sat down on top of a short step ladder. "We had a pretty good talk with Miss Graham and I think everything is worked out on our end. How about on yours?"

"Ummm...Miss Graham hates me," Emily said, deciding not to sugar-coat anything.

Mr. Charles looked startled. "*Hate* is a pretty strong word, Emily..." He started to reassure her that Miss Graham didn't really *hate* her, but then he wasn't so sure himself. "Do you need any help?" he finally asked.

"I probably would if you and Miss Mattie hadn't shown up," she said. "So thank you for that. I'm just sorry Jonathan got into trouble."

He held up his hand, interrupting her. "Jonathan chose to get involved; you didn't ask him to—so don't worry about that. His choice."

"You know what I mean, Mr. C. It started with my family and all."

"I know, but that's not your fault either," he said, smiling at her. "But getting back to Miss Graham..."

"Well, I know I shouldn't have thrown the orange," Emily sighed, "but Miss Graham would still feel the same way about me whether I threw it or didn't throw it. So, at first, I decided to hate her the same way she hates me, but then I felt sorry for her because of her big feet and all..."

"Her *what?*" Mr. Charles interrupted, his eyes wide.

"Her big feet...Miss Graham has huge feet and no friends and I kind of feel sorry for her. She needs a friend to tell her not to wear big white shoes..." Emily stopped rambling and just stared at him. "Do you know what I'm trying to say, Mr. C, because I'm not even sure."

"Actually, Emily, I think I do."

She nodded and stood up. "Well, I need to go. I was just afraid you were mad at me and I wanted to talk to you about it..." Her voice trailed off, and she turned to leave.

"Emily..."

She turned and faced him, afraid of what would come next.

"I just wanted you to know that I think you're a really great person," he said, meaning it.

"You do?"

"I do," he smiled. "Come on over Saturday if you need work. I have a few bags of fertilizer we can toss around."

Emily grinned at him. "Are you sure you aren't tossing me some now?"

He appeared puzzled, then burst out laughing.

She smiled and walked out the gate with the sound of his booming laughter ringing in her ears. She couldn't remember when she'd ever felt happier.

* * * *

Walking up First Street, toward home, Emily heard the roar of a truck behind her. She turned and watched as the biggest U-Haul she had ever seen in her life zoomed by. The truck turned left onto Elderberry Lane, and she quickened her step to see where it was going.

When she finally turned onto Sycamore Street, there was the barge-sized truck, backed up into the driveway of the house next door to hers.

New neighbors! Nearly bursting with excitement, she hurried up to the house. Two men with arms the size of tree trunks were unloading the U-Haul, but there was no one else in sight. Emily stood a moment more peering down the street, hoping her new neighbors would drive up, but no one followed the U-Haul. Disappointed, she turned and walked into her own house.

* * * *

Emily was hurrying down the steps of the library, eager to dive into the books she had just checked out, when she caught sight of Miss Violet walking toward her. She slowed down.

Miss Violet was picking her way along the sidewalk on five-inch heels, being very careful to avoid the wet, slippery leaves that had fallen from trees in Emerson Park. Perched on her head was a tall, white furry hat—much like one worn by a conductor in a marching band. She seemed to be doing a dual balancing act of teetering on her high heels, while trying to keep her hat from toppling off.

Strolling beside Miss Violet on a glittery leash was the ugliest bulldog that Emily had ever seen in her life. The dog's face was squashed in, and its wild-looking eyes bulged as it strained against a sequined harness; the teeth on its lower jaw came straight up over its top teeth, making Emily wonder how the dog could chew without biting its own nose.

Emily picked up her speed a little as she and Miss Violet drew near; it was Emily's plan to whiz right by Miss Violet before she could bring up the Young Ladies Academy.

"Good morning, Emily," Miss Violet said, as she carefully navigated the sidewalk, a small, flowered scarf fluttering in her hand.

"Good morning, Miss Violet," Emily replied, seeing her smile reflected in Miss Violet's enormous rhinestone sunglasses. She attempted to zip by but was stopped by the perfumed scarf waggled in her face.

"Emily," Miss Violet trilled, blocking her way like a Dallas Cowboy lineman, "we would be ab-so-LUTE-ly delighted if you would join us at our next session of the Young Ladies' Academy."

"Thank you," Emily replied, attempting to scoot around her, "but I'm pretty busy.

Miss Violet stepped sideways, blocking her with a maneuver the Cowboys would have been proud of. "One should always make time to better oneself, don't you think?" she asked, standing her ground.

"Well, I hadn't thought about it—but I sure will," Emily said, jumping as Miss Violet's dog growled and nipped at her legs.

"Now, naugh-ty, naugh-ty," scolded Miss Violet, shaking her ringed finger at the dog.

Emily hesitated, then took off at a trot, making her escape while Miss Violet scolded the dog.

Laughter caught Emily's attention as she walked up Elderberry Lane. She glanced across the street and saw Gus and his cronies sitting out front of Gus's station, a chin-wag going full force. The men noticed her and lifted their hands and waved. She considered going over and joining them—she loved listening to their stories—but decided to just head for home and her books instead.

When she arrived home, her house seemed unusually quiet as she closed the front door. Even Pearl's chair in front of the TV sat empty. Wondering where everyone was, Emily went down the hall. She heard snores coming from Pearl's room, and knew she was taking a nap, then she went looking for her mother.

"Mom," she whispered tapping on her door. Her mother didn't answer. She had been depressed for days, rarely emerging from her room. Sighing, Emily went out into the kitchen and checked the bulletin board, where there were three notes pinned to the cork. The first one was a reminder her dad had written to himself, *Johnson's needs wood on Monday.* That meant her dad was out on a delivery. The second note was a list of the deliveries he had the rest of the week. She studied it, noting that there wasn't anything scheduled for Wednesday, so her dad would be home all day. She made a mental note to go somewhere after school that day, maybe a movie or the library, knowing that if her dad wasn't working, he would begin drinking in the morning and her mom would join him when she got up. By afternoon World War III would start.

The third note was in her mother's handwriting with a list of things she wanted on the next shopping trip into Clayton. One item listed was St. John's Wort, which Emily knew her mother took for depression.

"Why doesn't she just go to the doctor," Emily murmured, shaking her head. She had seen an episode on *The TV Doctor* where they had talked about all kinds of medicines available for depression. Emily made a mental note to try and talk to her mother about it.

She heard her dad's truck pull up in front, so she moved away from the bulletin board. It irritated him when he saw her reading it. "Why are you so nosey?" he asked suspiciously, the last time he saw her looking at the notes. She made sure that he didn't see her doing it again, knowing his next step would be to just take the whole bulletin board down. He was weird that way. Before she went out to the backyard, she opened the kitchen window slightly so she could keep tabs on what was going on inside the house. When both parents were home, things could get very volatile, very quick.

As she sat in her red chair reading in the warmth of the garden, loud thuds could suddenly be heard coming from the backyard next door. Emily jumped up, excited to see the new neighbor. Peering through a knot hole in the fence into the overgrown yard, Emily spied an older woman, round as an apple, who stood whacking away at tall weeds. The woman was wearing a floppy straw hat, with daisies in the crown; about all Emily could see of her face were two rosy red cheeks.

The woman was soon joined by an equally round man who looked as though he had also dipped into the rouge pot. "Helena, why don't we rent a rototiller and take care of this entire back yard at one time," he said, watching the woman thump away with a hoe.

"Oh, I don't know, dear," the woman replied, as she assaulted another weed. "Let me hoe for now." *Thwack!* "I find it so soothing being out here." *Thwack!*

Emily watched as the man, clearly distressed by the energy his wife was giving to the weeds, tried again. "You know, Helena, I believe I saw an equipment rental place on Second Street. Why don't you come in for some lemonade while I run over there?"

He didn't wait for an answer, but gently took the hoe out of his wife's hands and leaned it up against a tree.

"You may be right, Herbert," the woman said, allowing herself to be led toward the house, "that ground is a little harder than I thought." She pulled out a hanky and patted away sweat on her upper lip, as the man propelled her toward the back door.

"A nice glass of lemonade will cool you right down, Helena," he said, glancing back at the hoe.

I bet he hides that thing, Emily laughed to herself.

"Maybe I could work on those weeds just fifteen minutes more, Herbert, and then go in," the woman said, pulling back a little. But the man held her arm firmly as he clucked and coaxed her all the way into the house. Emily chuckled as the couple went inside, liking these rosy, round people already.

Emily sat back down in her red chair and tried to finish reading, but could no longer concentrate. From inside the house, she could hear bottles clinking as her dad got liquor out of the cabinet, and poured himself a drink.

She re-read the paragraph three times and then put the book down; her stomach started to churn as she heard her mother join her dad. She closed the book, deciding to leave by the side gate, and go to Emerson Park to read.

As she unlocked the gate, she remembered the open window in the kitchen, and hoped with all her might that the new neighbors stayed inside their house. She didn't want them to hear her parents when they started fighting. "Why didn't I just leave that stupid window closed," she muttered, quietly shutting the gate behind her.

CHAPTER – 5

"Good morning, Ike," Emily sang out, as she blew through the door of Good Eats Café.

"Good mornin,' darlin'," Ike said, looking up from the newspaper he was reading. "What're you doin' out this early?"

"Don't you remember," she asked as she hung up her jacket on the coat rack near the door, "you told me to come on Columbus Day for my cooking lesson?"

"Oh!" he said, appearing somewhat surprised. "Well, I remembered the cookin' lesson, I just didn't remember t'day was Columbus Day." He folded his newspaper and stuck it under the counter. "Come on back to my kitchen, an' I'll git you outfitted in a hat an' apron."

Millie, Ike's full-time waitress of thirty years, walked by with a coffee pot. "I 'spose you also forgot I was takin' the afternoon off," she said, cocking her head.

"Takin' the afternoon off!" Ike bellowed. "You take off more days than Santy Clause. What about my lunch crowd?"

"I told you last week I was takin' Monday afternoon off for my gran' baby's hernia operation and you just forgot—so don't be *Santy Clausin'* me!" She stomped over and poured Bill and Iris Head a refill, then stomped back to the rear booth to refill a truck driver's mug.

"Heav'n help me," Ike grumped, as they headed back to his kitchen. "I gotta git me some of that Jingo Balooga stuff. My memory's gone."

"It's called *Ginkgo Baloba,* and I hope you get yourself the jumbo, extra-strength bottle," Millie shouted into the kitchen.

"That Millie's sure a spitfire," Ike said, shaking his head, as he brought out a freshly laundered chef's hat from a cabinet near the stove. He carefully placed the hat on Emily's head. "This thing's a little big for you, Em'ly," he said, adjusting the hat this way and that, squinting as he tried to get it at just the right angle.

Emily was glad she'd worn a ponytail. It helped wedge the hat on, so it didn't fall down over her eyes.

When Ike was satisfied with the tilt of the hat, he pulled out a green apron. "Now jus' put this part over your head..." he helped her get the neck piece over the chef's hat. "Dad gum, we shoulda' put the apron on first," he said, fussing with the hat again.

"Put a little fold in that apron, Em'ly, so it don't drag on the floor." Ike watched carefully to make sure she got it right. "Okay, now pull the strings up and tie 'em around your waist."

He had her turn in a circle to make sure she was properly dressed for kitchen duty.

"Perfect!" he announced, beaming at her. "You look jus' like a chef straight out of one of them la-ti-da restaurants in New York City!"

I don't think so, Ike, she thought, feeling ridiculous. The chef's hat soared above over her head, while the apron drooped around her ankles.

"I got three orders for a full breakfast with scrambles," Millie called back to them, through the opening from the dining area. She stuck the order ticket up on the chrome spinner.

Ike grabbed the ticket off the spinner, and turned to Emily, "Ok, now for the fine art of makin' scrambled eggs."

He went over to a huge stainless-steel refrigerator, swung open the door and stuck his head in. "Let's see," Ike's voice echoed inside the refrigerator, "we got our eggs, we got our cream." He closed the refrigerator door and turned to a spice rack, "and we got our salt and pepper." He snagged a whisk off the utility rack and a large bowl off the utility shelf.

"Em'ly, do ya know the mos' important ingredient in scrambled eggs?" he asked, breaking six eggs into the bowl and pouring in a little cream.

She shook her head.

"Well, darlin,' it's *air*."

"Air?"

"Yes, sireee, it's what makes yer scrambled eggs's fluffy," he said, positioning his whisk like a weapon above the eggs. "Eggs don't come with air ya know, so you gotta beat it into 'em—like this..."

Ike began beating the eggs slowly at first, then faster and faster, spinning the whisk around like a propeller. He cranked the spinning up a notch and his arm became a blur. Emily looked on wide-eyed as Ike ramped it up even more and went into a regular whipping frenzy. She clamped a hand over her mouth to keep from laughing. Ike looked like a mad man thrashing eggs.

When the eggs were beaten to his satisfaction, Ike leaned against the counter huffing and puffing. "There ya go, Em'ly," he gasped, wiping sweat off his forehead with a corner of his apron. "Jus' beat th' crud outta them eggs and they'll be fluffy as cotton balls."

Emily stood there staring at Ike, wondering if she should get him a chair. He looked like he was going to collapse.

"Okay, Em'ly, you have a go at it," Ike said, after he'd caught his breath. "I'm gonna cook these up while you crack more eggs in that large bowl for the next order–and remember, you gotta beat th' crud outta them."

Food orders started flying in as the breakfast crowd streamed into the café, keeping Ike glued to his grill.

"You 'bout got those eggs ready for me, Em'ly?" he shouted.

"I've got the eggs all cracked open, but there's so many I can't whip them right," she shouted back.

Ike looked over at the prep table and saw that Emily had cracked all five dozen of his eggs into a gigantic salad bowl and mixed them together–every last egg he had. About then, Millie barked in an order for two eggs over-easy and three eggs sunny side up for Glen Kingery and Sheriff Mobley, who headed up law enforcement in Mountain Grove.

"Tell 'em that scrambled eggs and omelets is on the menu t'day, Millie," Ike whispered, nodding his head toward the huge bowl of eggs.

Millie peered into the kitchen, scowled, and shook her head. "I'll tell 'em, but they ain't gonna like it."

Millie hurried back to the booth Glen Kingery and Sheriff Mobley were sharing. "We've only got scrambled eggs and omelets on the menu t'day, gentlemen."

"What?" howled Mr. Kingery. "If there's anything I can't stand, it's havin' my eggs all swished together. Ike knows that!"

"Shhhh," Millie hissed. "He's teachin' Em'ly to cook an' she went an' cracked open all his eggs. Your gettin' 'em scrambled, so hush."

* * * *

"Well, Em'ly, you did yerself proud today," Ike said, grinning at her after the breakfast crowd had left. "You sure know yer way aroun' with a spatula."

"Sorry I cracked open all your eggs and burned a couple of batches," she said, taking off the chef's hat and apron, and tossing them in the laundry bin.

"Why, that was nothin'," Ike replied with a wink. "I've burned 'em m'self a time or two."

Millie came out from the storage room with her jacket on. "Why don't you hire Em'ly here to help you with your lunch crowd, Ike, she's a real worker."

He scowled at her. "Well, I 'spect Em'ly's got better things to do than hang 'round here all day."

Millie pulled the café door open. "See ya' later, alligators," she sang out, letting the door slam behind her.

"See ya," Ike said, looking depressed.

"I don't mind helping you, Ike," Emily offered. "Just show me what to do."

He looked relieved. "You sure?"

"Positive. What do I do?"

He set up a quick system for customers ordering food. Since she didn't know all of the menu prices, he told her to just write down the orders and he would figure out everyone's bill.

"Do ya' know how to make change?"

Emily nodded that she did.

"Well, we're in business then," he said, briskly rubbing his hands together.

The first of the lunch crowd to come through the door were Mr. and Mrs. Green.

"Emily, how good to see you," said Mrs. Green, giving her a hug. She beamed up at the man standing beside her. "This is my husband, Mr. Green."

Mr. Green gave her a huge smile as she shook hands with him. Emily peered closely to see if she'd missed something from the picture she'd seen of him in the library office, but he looked exactly the same, except for his smile, which was much better in person.

"Nice to meet you Emily, do you work here?" Mr. Green asked.

"No, this is my first time," she explained, walking them to a back booth. "Millie had to go to her grandbaby's hernia operation, so I'm helping Ike with the lunch crowd."

Mr. and Mrs. Green grabbed their personalized coffee mugs off the rack on the way back to the booth. It was easy to find their mugs, because they were the only two green ones. Ike had thought it was a real nice touch, matching their mug color with their last name.

"I'll have an egg salad sandwich on whole wheat toast," Mrs. Green said, not even looking at a menu. Mr. Green ordered a steak sandwich. Emily wrote it all down carefully on the order pad, making sure to put *well-done* for Mr. Green's steak. She gave their order to Ike and went to get the coffee pot to fill their mugs.

Mr. and Mrs. Green were holding hands across the table, laughing like school children when Emily returned with the coffee. Mrs. Green's face glowed as she stared at her husband, and the crinkles around Mr. Green's eyes shot out like sun rays as he looked at his wife. Emily glanced at them as she poured their coffee, expecting to see little hearts float out the top of their heads like in the cartoons.

I just don't get it, she thought, as she went to wait on another customer. *Shouldn't they look more like movie stars to be that much in love?*

Jonathan came in for lunch, looking like he'd had a rough morning at Bloomin' Happy, followed by Gus, who tossed his grease-stained baseball cap on the hat rack next to Emily's jacket. They both sat down at the counter.

"I'll be with you in a second," Emily smiled at them.

"Well, it looks like you finally got some good help around here," Gus shouted back to the kitchen.

Ike came out with Mr. and Mrs. Green's order. "Here you go Em'ly," he said, handing her the platters. "You better hush Gus, or Millie won't be servin' you anymore."

"Promises, promises," Gus said, as everyone around him chuckled.

About then the café door opened and eight people walked in. "Heav'n help me," Ike said, and bolted back to his kitchen.

Emily took Gus and Jonathan's order, put them up on the chrome spinner, and hurried to wait on the other customers. When she looked up she saw Mr. and Mrs. Green at the register waiting to pay their bill. She managed to make change for them, and said to Mr. Green, "I'm glad I finally got to meet you!"

"And I can't tell you how glad I am to meet you," he grinned.

Emily ran to clear their table. As she swept their two empty platters and coffee mugs into a rubber tub, she saw a five dollar bill lying beside Mr. Green's plate. She carried the dirty dishes back to the kitchen and held the money out to Ike. "Mr. Green left this by his plate."

"Well, that's for you, darlin'." "Jus' put any money you find on the tables straight into those pockets of yours."

"Thanks!" she said, suddenly feeling very happy.

As Emily brought out Jonathan's burger and fries, she glanced over to see two customers at the register waiting to pay their bills, another customer was signaling for a coffee refill, and a booth in the back needed clearing.

Jonathan noticed too and stood up. "Let me take care of the cash register, Emily, and you go ahead and help those other people."

"But your cheeseburger will get cold," she protested.

"It'll be fine," he said, heading for the register.

Relieved, Emily ran with the coffee pot and gave everyone refills and quickly cleared the empty booth, stuffing the three-dollar tip into her pocket. She heard Ike ding the bell, signaling more orders were ready, and flew back to the kitchen.

As she carried the food out, Gus was clearing tables as Jonathan handled the steady stream of paying customers.

She set Gus's tuna melt on the counter and served two chili dogs to the couple sitting at the back table, then hurried back into the kitchen. "I don't see how Millie does this all by herself," she told Ike, as he handed her a hot pastrami on rye for a trucker sitting at the counter.

"She's a whiz alright," he grinned. "Sometimes she looks like a reg'lar octypus out there waitin' on everyone."

Emily gave the hot pastrami to the trucker as Gus thumped a tub of dirty dishes onto the counter. "Well, I done enough maids' work for t'day," he said, handing Emily the wad of money he'd picked up from the tables. "I'm gonna' eat and git' back to my fillin' station."

She grinned and gave him a quick hug. "Thank you, Gus!"

The café slowed down and Jonathan went back to the counter and dug into his cheeseburger.

"Thanks for your help, Jonathan," Emily smiled, setting a large Pepsi on the counter in front of him. "Your burger must be cold by now; let me get you another one."

"It's okay, I don't have time," he said, squirting catsup on his cold fries.

Emily cleared the last table, her pockets stuffed full of bills. Jonathan gulped down his burger and hurried over to the register to pay.

"Hey, buddy," Ike called out to Jonathan from the kitchen, "yer money's no good in here t'day."

Jonathan started to protest.

"No, I mean it," Ike said, peering at him over the swinging doors. "Yer burger probably got cold while you was helpin' out, an' I don't want you payin' for it."

"Well thanks, Ike," he smiled, and turned to Emily. "Need help with anything else?"

"No, I'm leaving, too," she said, pulling the apron off over her head. The neckpiece of the apron caught on the elastic band holding her ponytail. "Ow," she gave it a hard yank.

Jonathan laughed and reached around her to work the material free from her hair. Emily moved in closer to him, inhaling the clean smell of his shirt as he freed the apron. She liked the woodsy, masculine smell of him.

He handed her the apron.

"You smell good," she said, leaning in and sniffing again.

"And you're goofy," he laughed, giving her pony tail a tug.

After Jonathan left, Emily walked back to the kitchen to say good-bye to Ike.

"Looks like you took in quite a haul, young lady," Ike said, looking at her bulging pockets. "What're you gonna do with all that money?"

She didn't even have to think about it. "I've been wanting a digital camera," she said, feeling excitement surge through her.

Ike shook his head. "Them cam'ras are too complicated fer me, but I sure think it's a jim-dandy plan for you." He flipped over a hamburger, and said, "Don't ferget', there'll be a paycheck here for you on Friday, too."

"No way, Ike," she said, shaking her head, "you gave me cooking lessons."

"Cookin' lessons is one thing," he said, punctuating each word with his spatula, "but keepin' you workin' all them hours is another."

"You don't need to pay me. Like Miss Mattie says...that's why we're all down here—to help one another.'"

"An' she's right as rain, Em'ly, but for this kind of help, I'm *payin'* you," he said, meaning it. "I might need me a good waitress next time Millie goes traipsin' off."

"Thanks for showing me how to cook eggs," she said, putting her jacket on.

"Yer sure welcome, darlin'," he grinned. "Now remember, with them eggs you gotta...."

"I know, I know," she grinned, as she headed toward the door, "you gotta' beat the crud outta them."

* * * *

As she walked home, Emily was deep in thought, with visions of the new camera she would soon have enough money to buy. Turning onto Sycamore Street, she was surprised to see a car parked in the driveway at the house next door. The car's trunk was open, and the round woman she had seen through the knothole in the backyard fence was unloading groceries. Embarrassed that her new neighbor might have heard her parents fighting the other day, Emily slowed down a bit, not sure if she wanted to meet her right now. It was too late though. The woman had spotted her and was giving a friendly wave, smiling at her behind large owlish glasses. Emily had no choice but to walk over.

As she approached, Emily saw that the woman had a sweet round face to match her round figure. Her cheeks were rosy, and her soft gray hair was pulled back in a bun; she wore a bright red flowery dress, and her eyes lit up as Emily walked toward her.

Emily instantly felt tender toward her. "Hello," she said, shyly.

"Hello, dear," the woman smiled, her cheeks blooming to a deeper red.

"I'm Emily," she said, extending her hand. "Welcome to the neighborhood!"

"Thank you, dear," the woman replied, giving a gentle two-handed shake. "I'm Mrs. Apple."

Apple? Emily was startled! *A rosy, round woman named Apple?* It was so funny that Emily actually snorted. Mortified, she cleared her throat and tried desperately to think of something to say.

"Where'd you move from?" she finally managed, but she was already jiggling with laughter.

Stop!! She scolded herself.

"We moved up the mountain from Whitefield, a little town south of Clayton," Mrs. Apple replied, looking at her oddly. "Do you know where that is?"

"Uh-huh..." she managed to croak, as she slipped her arms over her stomach, trying to control her belly laugh.

"My goodness, dear," Mrs. Apple said, peering over her glasses, "it looks like you're in quite a happy mood today."

With a squiggly voice, Emily asked, "Would you like me to help carry your groceries in?" Which she really didn't want to do, but she needed a chance to bring her embarrassing cackles under control.

"Why, yes... thank you," her new neighbor replied rather hesitantly. "Just carry them through the living room, and straight back to the kitchen. I'll be there in a minute or two."

As Emily carried the grocery bag up the front steps, she couldn't control herself, and snorted with laughter. She clamped a hand over her mouth and looked back at Mrs. Apple, who was staring at her like a bug in a Mason jar.

She tried to get her mind to think about other things, but every time she pictured the round woman offering her hand and saying, "I'm Mrs. Apple," her laughter erupted like a bubbling volcano.

"Stupid laugh, stop it!" she ordered herself sternly, trying to gain control. But that seemed to have just the opposite effect, and she began to heave with uncontrollable laughter. She was laughing so hard, she barely managed to set the groceries up on the Formica counter in the kitchen.

"I get those giggling fits myself sometimes," said a man's voice, behind her.

Emily spun around, and there stood the round man she had seen in the back yard the other day.

"Oh good," she managed to say, snorting twice.

She clamped one hand over her mouth and held the other out to shake his hand. "I'm Emily," she said, with a muffled croak.

"How do you do, Emily, I'm Mr. Apple."

His name sent laughter racking through her. Mr. Apple stood there blinking his eyes as she howled, snorted, and cackled.

But a wonderful thing happened Mr. Apple started laughing, too. In fact, once he got started, he heaved and chortled right along with her. They held their sides laughing, and when Mr. Apple snorted, they both screamed with laughter. At one point, Mr. Apple made a brave attempt at conversation, but only brayed like a donkey. Emily brayed back.

When Mrs. Apple came in, she said, "What on earth..."

But neither one could answer because they were both holding onto kitchen chairs and counter tops, laughing uncontrollably as tears ran down their cheeks.

Mrs. Apple just shook her head. "I'll make us all some hot chocolate," she said, skirting around them. "You two are a real case."

Later, as they sat drinking hot chocolate in the Apple's warm kitchen, Mrs. Apple said, "Now, does anyone want to let me in on the joke?"

Mr. Apple held up his hand. "Don't ask, Helena, because we don't know—and you'll only set us off again. Right, Emily?"

Emily shook her head, trying not to even *think* about it. Mr. Apple knew about belly laughs—you just had to leave them alone, or they erupted again.

* * * *

The next day Emily burst into Miss Mattie's bakery. "I have new neighbors now," she sang out happily.

"Well now, that's jus' fine, Sugar," Miss Mattie said, with a smile that rivaled a harvest moon. "Tell me all about them."

"Well," she said, warming up to the subject, "it's two older people, and they are both round with red cheeks, and just *guess* what their name is?

"Apple?" quipped Miss Mattie.

Emily's jaw dropped. "How'd you know?" she cried, more than a little disappointed. She had wanted to shock Miss Mattie and make her laugh.

"I know because they came in for a half dozen of my fine cranberry croissants and we introduced ourselves."

"Did you burst out laughing when you heard their name?"

"I certainly did *not,"* Miss Mattie replied, looking shocked, "please tell me that's not what you did."

"Yes, I sure did," Emily laughed, "but they didn't know what I was laughing about. When I met Mr. Apple, he laughed with me—

and that made it even funnier. You should've been there, Miss Mattie! We had to hold onto things to keep from falling on the floor we were laughing so hard."

"Hmmm...I don't know 'bout you, Em'ly," Miss Mattie said, trying to look stern. But Emily could see the corners of her mouth tugging up.

* * * *

Later, as they sat at a table and shared an apple fritter, Emily remembered. "Miss Mattie, I saw you in your big hat on Sunday!"

"You did?" she smiled. "How'd you like my church hat, Sugar?"

"It was beautiful," Emily said, licking icing off her fingers. "I'm going to have a hat like that someday if I ever go to church."

"Is that so?" Miss Mattie said, as she stood up to wait on a customer. "I'll bring you back some milk to go with that fritter."

Miss Mattie soon returned with a glass of milk and a stack of unopened doilies and picked up the conversation right where they had left off.

"Now, I was jus' thinkin' Sugar, since you liked my church hat an' all'," Miss Mattie said, ripping open the package of doilies, and stacking them in a holder, "I jus' got me a new catalog of fine hats and there's a section for young ladies. T'morrow after school, you come on by 'bout closin' time and we'll go up to my place and have us a look in that catalog."

Miss Mattie lived in a large apartment over the bakery and Emily couldn't have been more excited if she had been invited to Paris! She had never seen an apartment over a bakery, or looked through a catalog of fine hats.

It was all she could do to keep from clapping her hands like a child.

CHAPTER - 6

Emily kept squirming as she watched the big round face of the school clock during her last period class. Each circle of the minute hand seemed to take forever; she couldn't wait to take off for the bakery and see Miss Mattie's catalog of fine hats. She looked at the clock so many times, the girl sitting next to her asked, "You got ants in your pants?"

Emily glared at her and tried to sit still, but as soon as the bell rang, she grabbed her backpack, and dashed out the classroom door. She ran all the way to the bakery and burst breathlessly through the door.

"My goodness, Em'ly," Miss Mattie said, as the bell over the door nearly fell to the floor jangling. "Somebody chasen' you?"

"I couldn't wait to look at the hat catalog!" she said, laughing.

Miss Mattie grinned and got her a cinnamon twist. "You jus' sit tight 'til closin' time, Miss Em'ly!"

Promptly at four o'clock Miss Mattie shut off all of the front lights and put the *Closed* sign in the front window. Emily helped her clear out the pastry case and they went back to the kitchen, where Miss Mattie took off her jungle green apron with orange pineapples and purple monkeys and put it in the wash bin.

"There's my collection of aprons, Sugar," Miss Mattie said, pointing to a pegged wall at the back of the kitchen.

Emily walked over and beheld a dazzling array of aprons—all in eye-popping colors of reds, greens, blues, purples, and yellows.

"I collect them," Miss Mattie said proudly. "There's one for each day of the month."

"Wow," Emily chuckled, rummaging through them. She especially liked the plum- colored apron dotted with elephants and toucans in primary colors.

Miss Mattie began shutting off the kitchen lights, then went into the bakery area, pulled down shades, and snapped off more lights. Finally, after giving the bakery one final glance, they went to the front door and Emily followed her out.

"This way, Sugar," Miss Mattie said, after she had locked the bakery door. They turned and walked twelve steps to the wooden staircase, then up the steps leading to Miss Mattie's apartment.

Miss Mattie unlocked the door and motioned for her young friend to go in.

Emily stared around the cozy apartment; the interior was warm, homey, and cheerful with its over-stuffed couch and colorful knick-knacks. It brought to mind a picture of a pleasant cottage Emily had seen in a Beatrix Potter book. Wonderful aromas still wafted up from the bakery through the vents in the floor, perfuming the air with cinnamon, vanilla, and freshly baked bread.

While Miss Mattie hurried off to get the hat catalog, Emily walked over to the huge bay window overlooking First Street. Across the street she could see Emerson Park and the statue of the General; the library was to the right of the park; Elderberry Street and the church grounds were to the left. She saw a man in a suit, with a neatly trimmed beard emerge from the church basement, and wondered who the church was housing this time. The pastor often let people who were passing through stay overnight in the church's furnished basement.

"Now, here we are, Sugar," Miss Mattie said, interrupting her thoughts, as she plumped down on the sofa while holding a thick catalog.

Emily went over and scrunched up next to her, resting her head on Miss Mattie's soft shoulder. Miss Mattie hummed softly, licking her thumb to turn pages. When she came to the section titled *Young Ladies' Fine Hats,* Emily gasped. Feathers, rhinestones, beads and gold braids adorned the stylish hats. She had never seen such beautiful headwear.

"Show me which one you like best." Miss Mattie handed over the catalog.

Emily looked and looked, flipping the pages back and forth as she compared the hats; she finally narrowed her choice down to two. The first was green and peaked at the top; it was shaped sort of like a picture she had seen of Robin Hood, except this hat flared up on one side, with a gorgeous brown feather that swept up and back. The second hat was wide-brimmed and flared out stylishly. It was light blue with the same sassy curve that Miss Mattie had worn on Sunday. It had a bright blue plume that arched back gracefully.

"That's my favorite," she said, pointing to the blue hat. "I love it. It looks like the one you wore."

"It is beautiful," Miss Mattie agreed, reaching for a pen to mark the page. "Is that the one you want then?"

"No! I didn't mean for you to buy it for me," Emily gasped. "It's way too expensive. Look!" She pointed at the price: *$74.95.*

"Now, Sugar," Miss Mattie began, "I've been wantin' to have someone come to church with me for a long, long time. It gets lonely sittin' in that pew all by myself." She folded the edge of the page to mark it. "We need to make a trade here. I'll trade you this fine hat for your fine company—and I think I'm gettin' the better end of the deal."

"I don't know, Miss Mattie..."

"Well, I *do,*" she said, looking at her evenly. "Do you have a blue dress?"

Emily nodded her head.

"Then wear it to my house Sunday morning at 9:30. I'll order this hat by express mail and we'll have us a good time at church."

* * * *

Emily's mind was all awhirl as she left the library on Wednesday. She decided to head over to Bloomin' Happy for the next thing on her "to-do" list. Her dad wasn't working today, so she had made a list of things to do to avoid going home after school.

When she arrived, Mr. Charles was helping Juan Montoya look for plants to put in front of his produce market, so she went and sat down under a green umbrella in the patio area. As she sat enjoying the pungent smell of evergreen and potting soil, she tried to figure it all out. She had spent an entire hour on the internet at the library looking at different cameras to buy, once she had enough money. All she had gotten for her trouble was a headache, and she still didn't have a clue what she really wanted.

What the heck is a mega-pixel anyway? she wondered.

She tried to listen as Mr. Montoya explained how he was fixing up the outside of his produce market. Ordinarily, she loved listening to him speak with his wonderful Spanish accent, but today she was restless and the small talk made her itchy.

At last Mr. Montoya headed toward the gate. "Adios, senorita," he said, waving to her.

"Adios," she replied, heaving a sigh of relief.

"I'll have one of my boys put everything in a wagon this afternoon and pull it to your store," said Mr. Charles. "Do you need help putting the shrubs into the soil?"

"No, gracias," Mr. Montoya said with a grin, "my wife, Debora, has been after me to get more exercise." He patted his slightly protruding belly to prove his point. "I eat too many of her delicioso apple pies."

Mr. Charles laughed and waved good-bye, then turned to Emily. "Out flower shopping?"

"No, I'm actually tree shopping," Emily said, reining her thoughts in. "I get too hot in the summer when I'm out in my garden reading—there's no shade. I thought if I planted a tree now, it would be big enough by the time it starts getting hot."

"Well, a tree would shade you eventually," he agreed, pulling up a stool and sitting down, "but you might not want to shade some of those flowers you've planted. I'd advise buying an umbrella instead of a tree; that way you can take it down when you don't need it." He grinned. "Your flowers will love you for it."

"Ummm...I didn't think of that," she said, staring off at nothing in particular.

Mr. Charles studied her. "What's on your mind today, Emily? You look like you've sailed off to the land of whimsy."

She grinned. "Well, I want to buy a camera, and I can't figure it out—what kind of camera, what features. I made $52.00 in tips on Monday when I helped Ike, and I'm saving up."

"Terrific!" he said.

"Do you know anything about digital cameras?"

"A little. What do you want to take pictures of?"

"Oh, my garden, people...stuff like that." Emily skirted around the question. She didn't want to tell him *exactly* what she wanted to take pictures of.

"Well," he said, scooting his stool a little closer, "I'll tell you what I know, but I'd advise you to talk to an expert. Drop in at Taylor's Camera Shop on Second Street and talk to the owner; his name is Miles. He also gives photography lessons; my wife is thinking about taking some."

She couldn't think of where the shop was.

"It's two doors down from Good Neighbor Pharmacy," he said, standing up to go wait on another customer.

She watched as he helped a woman in a business suit, who was shopping for a Boston fern for her office. It didn't take long to find. Mr. Charles rang it up, handed her a receipt, then came back over and sat down.

"From what you've told me, Emily," he said, getting back to their conversation, "I think a ten or twelve mega-pixel camera would work for you. Have Miles recommend a lens and he can help you decide whether to get a *point and shoot*, or one you set manually—but of course they cost more."

"How much?"

"I'd guess they start at around $450.00 to $500.00 for a good one."

Emily sighed.

He tapped his pen on a receipt pad. "You want to work after school the next few days?"

"Sure," she said, growing excited.

"Okay, here's what I need help with," Mr. Charles led her to a pretty area with a fountain in the center. "My plants and flowers look pretty sitting around in kind of a hodge-podge order, but I want my customers to have an easier time finding things."

He pulled out a folded sheet of notebook paper and laid it on a potting table. "I've mapped out how I'm going to reorganize my inventory."

"I want to start right here," he said, pointing to an area near the back gate that led out to the parking lot. "If I put large items by this gate, it will be easier for the customers to get things out to their car. I've ordered two small flat-bed hand carts that should be in this week. I'll have those sitting by the gate, also."

He handed her a pair of gardening gloves. "Let's start with the potting soil. I'll carry the fifty pounders and you should be able to handle the twenty-pound bags."

They each hefted bags and carried them over by the gate, starting two separate piles. After a dozen trips back and forth, he asked, "Do you think you'll become a professional photographer?"

"Is that a good job?"

"Anything can be a good job," he said, stepping over a garden hose, "but I would say the main thing is to try and earn your money doing what you love."

"Is that what you did?"

"It's what I *finally* did," he said, heaving the last bag of soil onto the pile. He looked at her. "Emily, your face is as red as those holly berries you're standing next to. I have some bottled water over under the awning. Let's take a break."

She took a long swallow of the water Mr. Charles handed her. He pulled up two patio chairs and said, "Have a seat, Emily, I'll be right back."

He bolted into the Village Grocer and came out a few minutes later with two large chocolate chip cookies and two bananas. "I bet you haven't eaten since lunch," he said, handing her one of each.

"No, I haven't," she said, eagerly taking the food he offered, "and the mac and cheese they served in the cafeteria today wasn't all that great."

She hammered down on a cookie as Mr. Charles sat down and peeled a banana.

"Tell me about your work," she said.

"Well, Emily," he said, flicking his banana peel into a metal waste barrel, "I used to work in a big city, for a big company; and I made big money..." He took a bite of the banana. "...but the problem was, I didn't see my family very much, and the other problem was—I didn't even *like* the work. I got involved with it because friends told me how much money I could make."

"So how come you moved here?" she asked, popping the last bite of cookie into her mouth, as she hunkered into her chair for a good story.

"Well, when I realized I was only seeing my kids about two hours a day, I made a goal to change that," he said, finishing the banana. "That's something you should always do, Emily, set a goal and write it down. It gives you a target to shoot at. Otherwise, you're aiming at nothing, and that's what you'll get."

"Hadn't thought of that," she said, peeling her banana and giving the peel the same flick into the waste barrel.

"I decided that I wanted my kids to grow up around family," he continued, stretching out his legs and locking his fingers behind his head. "Mountain Grove is where my grandparents lived when I was a boy, and I have lots of family here. But that was only half the battle; I also had to figure out how to earn a living here. So I started thinking about what I did that made me the happiest. That took some real brain storming. I knew I loved the outdoors and working with my hands. I asked my wife for input, too. That's something else that's important, Emily—get input from people you trust. They may have knowledge or insight that you don't have."

Emily hoped she could remember all this.

"My wife thought about it for a while," Mr. Charles continued, "and finally said, 'Well, it's simple: you love outdoors, you love working with your hands, you love gardening. Why don't you open a nursery in Mountain Grove?'"

"Bingo! She hit the nail on the head!" Mr. Charles grinned. "That very day I started planning how to open a nursery in Mountain Grove; and *Presto-Chango!*—just like magic—here I am."

She laughed. "Just like magic?"

"Actually, Emily, magic had nothing to do with it. Planning did."

She nodded. "Then what happened?"

"Well, I found this huge empty lot," he said, sweeping his hand around the nursery. "I liked it because it was already fenced, and it was next door to the Village Grocer. Foot traffic, Emily. All the people going to the market would walk right by my nursery and I'd have instant customers, and wouldn't have to do a lot of expensive advertising to get them."

"Did you put that side door in?" she asked, nodding her head toward the glass door that led directly inside the Village Grocer.

"No, it was already there; that also helped me make a decision about this site. I brought my wife and kids over to see what they thought. My wife thought it was perfect. So, I stood here in the middle of this empty lot with my family and said, 'I am so *bloomin' happy* here', and that clever wife of mine said, '*Bloomin' Happy*...hmmm, I think you just found a name for your nursery.'"

"It's a great name," Emily laughed. "What happened next?"

"Well, I learned everything I could about running a nursery business, leased the land, brought in all the fixtures and built my little patio space and awning, then *Abracadabra!*—just like magic—here I am in my new business."

"Only it wasn't magic, it was planning."

"Bingo," he said. "You're a fast learner, Emily."

She left Bloomin' Happy that day with another twenty dollars in her pocket and a head buzzing with new ideas. *Imagine doing something you love and getting paid for it!* She nearly hugged herself with the idea. The first thing she'd do is write down her goals so she'd have something to aim at, then she'd drop in at *Taylor's Camera Shop* and see if Miles Taylor could help.

* * * *

"Where you been, Sugar, I haven't seen you for days," Miss Mattie said, as Emily bounced through the door of the bakery.

Emily was so excited the words tumbled over each other. "I've been working for Ike and Mr. Charles—and guess what? I'm going to buy a digital camera with the money I've made. It'll be ten or twelve mega-pixels and I can blow the pictures up and put them on the wall if I want to."

"You don't say," smiled Miss Mattie, putting a chocolate éclair and a powdered donut into a bag for a customer. "Now that's a fine idea, Sugar."

Miss Mattie completed the sale and said good-bye to the man and his little boy. After she and Emily had decided on a piece of coconut cream pie to share, they took it over to the small parlor table near the front window and sat down. Words spilled out non-stop as Emily told Miss Mattie all her plans for buying a camera.

"I still have to earn a few hundred dollars more," Emily chatted on, as she nibbled the pie, "for the camera and memory stick—but I'll get it."

Miss Mattie grinned at her. "Your mama and daddy mus' be real proud knowin' you're workin' hard and savin' for that camera."

Emily stopped chewing and just stared at her. She finally said, "My parents don't know about it."

"They don't know?" Miss Mattie said, her eyes bugging slightly. "Sugar, why not?"

Emily sighed and looked away; she didn't want the conversation to go in this direction. She noticed customers at the other tables were craning their necks to hear.

Miss Mattie noticed too, and motioned Emily to follow her to the kitchen. "Blessy," she said to her part-time help, who was busy washing a large baking pan, "would you mind watchin' the bakery for a few minutes while I talk to Em'ly?"

"I'd be proud to, Miz' Mattie," Blessy smiled, drying her hands and hurrying out of the kitchen.

They sat down on a bench near the big mixer. "Now tell me all about it," Miss Mattie urged.

Emily sighed. "I don't think you understand my family, Miss Mattie," she said. "They sort of turn things around in their minds. My dad would say I don't need people's charity, and he can buy me a camera. And my mom—well, I can't really explain it, but it's like she gets upset when I do normal things. Sometimes I think she just wants my life to be like her life and Pearl's."

"Who's Pearl?" Miss Mattie asked.

"My grandmother."

"You call your grandmother *Pearl*?" Miss Mattie's eyes bugged out again.

"I call her Pearl and so does my mom," Emily replied, "and it's *her* mother. I don't know why. We don't talk much in my family and everybody gets mad if I ask questions. Pearl throws her slipper at me."

"Your grandmother throws her slipper at you?" Miss Mattie asked, punctuating every word.

"It's okay," Emily laughed. Only it wasn't okay, and she couldn't understand why she was laughing, when her heart was growing heavy as a stone. "I just wanted you to understand that things aren't that simple at my house and that's why I'm not going to tell my parents about working for a camera."

Emily could feel her throat starting to clog. *Oh no!* she thought, as the tears welled up. Miss Mattie wrapped soft brown arms around her, as big tears rolled down Emily's cheeks and plopped on her sweater.

"I'm s-s-s-sorry," Emily cried, burrowing her face into Miss Mattie's shoulder.

"It's all right, Sugar," Miss Mattie said, rocking and crooning, and holding her close.

Emily tried to gulp down the great heaving sobs, but it was useless.

* * * *

The next day Emily trotted down First Street and straight into Good Eats Café, her taste buds tuned for one of Ike's good root beer floats. Everyone in the café greeted her as she hopped onto a red stool.

"Hi, Ike. Hello, Miss Millie," she said, then noticed Gus who was sharing a booth with Montana Chan, editor of *The Mountain*

Grove Gazette, the village's weekly newspaper. She waved to them both.

"What's this *Miss* Millie stuff," Millie grumbled, as she came over to take her order.

Emily was taken back. "Well," she explained, "Miss Mattie says I need to say *Miss, Mr.* or *Mrs.* before an adults' name, unless they tell me to just call them by their first name—like Ike and Gus did."

"*Miss Millie* makes me sound like an' old maid or somethin'," Millie groused. "Just plain ole' Millie is fine." She took Emily's order for a root beer float and trounced off.

"Mattie Cooke is a real crusader when it comes to manners," Montana said, jumping into the conversation, as he carefully measured a half teaspoon of sugar and stirred it into his coffee.

Gus eyed Montana as he sweetened his coffee. "Why doncha' just skip that sugar, Montana, there ain't enough in there to choke a roach."

Montana shuddered, and continued talking to Emily. "I remember the time I ordered a pineapple strudel from Mattie and sat down at a table in the bakery to read my newspaper. Mattie brought my order over, but I was so engrossed in reading my paper, I didn't say anything. When I reached down for my strudel—it was gone," he laughed. "I looked up and she was taking it away because I hadn't acknowledged her or said, 'thank you'."

"An' you better look 'er in the eye and say it," added Gus, laughing along with everyone else.

"And by the way, Emily," Montana said, "please call me Montana and not Mr. Chan. Tell Mattie I said it was okay."

"Tell Em'ly how you got yer name, Montana," Gus said, hammering down on his cheeseburger.

Montana glanced at him and sighed. "Gus, my friend, you give me no rest over my name. Why do you find it so entertaining?"

"'Cause yer the first Asian I ever knew who dressed like a cowboy and was named Montana," Gus cackled, giving a full view of his choppers. "Just tell 'er. No one enjoys a good story 's much as Em'ly."

"Yes, tell me," Emily laughed, as Millie set a large root beer float down in front of her.

Montana shook his head. "I'm going to need more coffee for this one, Millie."

As Millie refilled his coffee mug, Montana pushed his cowboy hat to the back of his head, crossed his snakeskin cowboy boots, and got comfortable.

"It is a simple story, Emily," he began. "My parents emigrated from China and moved to Montana. They were not familiar with American names, so my brothers and I are named for the area where we were born. I was the first born and got the state name. My younger brother got the city name, Billings–and, of course, we call him Bill. My youngest brother is named after the county, and you don't *even* want to know what his name is."

"Sure we do," Gus howled.

"Then, my friend, you'll have to look it up yourself," Montana said, giving Emily a quick wink.

"I jus' say thank the Lord you weren't born in *Massachusetts*," Millie said, pouring more coffee.

"Or *Virginia*," Ike added, with a grin.

"You've got a point there," said Montana, continuing his story. "My parents dressed us the way a lot of people dress in Montana; they assumed that's how all Americans dressed. I've always worn cowboy boots and a cowboy hat, and I like buckskin and fringes," he said, lifting his arm and waggling the fringe on his jacket.

"Don't let Gus harass you, Montana," said Millie. "I think you look real dapper."

"Why thank ya, ma'am," Montana replied in his best Southern drawl, as everyone in the café chuckled.

"Now, if Gus has had enough fun with my name for today, I need to get back to work. Gotta keep those presses rolling."

He put money on the table for his coffee and thumped Gus on the back. "I'm honored to be such an unending source of humor to you, my friend."

"Bye, Montana," everyone yelled.

"Yippee Ki-yea," Montana replied, as he walked out the door.

"Say Em'ly," said Ike, as he rang up her root beer float on the cash register, "wouldja' be interested in helpin' me out with Saturday's lunch crowd? Our travelin' Granny here has another gran'baby to tend to in th' afternoon."

Millie gave him a dirty look.

"Sure," said Emily, "can I have a cooking lesson, too?"

"You sure can, darlin'. Come in early Saturday mornin' and we'll have a go at flapjacks and waffles. And why doncha' take this menu with you, an' study th' prices. That way you can handle th' customer's bill all on yer own."

Emily paid her bill and sailed out of the café with visions of a ten mega-pixel digital camera dancing in her head.

CHAPTER – 7

On a cold, windy Saturday morning Emily left her house early to get to Good Eats Café by seven-thirty. She was excited that Ike was going to teach her how to make pancakes and waffles, and even more excited that, in the afternoon, she would help in the café and earn more money for her camera.

At the end of the driveway she was surprised to see Mrs. Apple getting into her car.

"Good morning," she called.

"Well good morning, Emily," Mrs. Apple said, smiling at her. "You don't happen to know where Good Neighbor Pharmacy is, do you?"

"Sure," she replied, "would you like me to show you?"

"I'd appreciate it. Hop in," Mrs. Apple said, unlocking the door to her Oldsmobile. "Mr. Apple is out of one of his medications and needs it right after breakfast."

Mrs. Apple drove slowly. "I've been wanting to talk to you," she said, turning on her windshield wipers to clear off the morning mist. "Would you mind giving me your phone number? I'd like to hire you to help us put some of our extra belongings up in the attic."

Emily hesitated for a moment trying to think of how to answer. "My dad's cell phone is the only one we have," she began, "and he's always got it with him, plus he really doesn't like anyone else asking to use it.

"Oh," replied her neighbor, looking puzzled. "What would the rest of the family do in an emergency?"

"Beats me," she shrugged.

"Well," Mrs. Apple said, furrowing her brow, "why don't we plan a time right now then? Would Thursday after school work for you?"

"Sure, that'd be fine," Emily was delighted with the prospect of making more money for her camera.

"And maybe you'd like to stay for dinner," her neighbor smiled. "Homemade chicken pot pie is on the menu."

"Yum!" she said, her mouth actually beginning to water.

She gave Mrs. Apple directions to Second Street. As they turned the corner, Emily said, "The pharmacy is up there on the left, right across the street from St. Daniel's Catholic Church."

"What a lovely old church," Mrs. Apple murmured, as they pulled up in front of it. "You know, I've heard of this church. It has a monastery, I believe."

"A *what?*" Emily asked.

"A place where nuns or monks live," Mrs. Apple replied, craning her neck for a better look. "If you look up the hill there behind the church, you'll see their living quarters."

Emily looked, and could just make out the quaint buildings through the trees. The modest, one-story structures were made of the same stone as the church, surrounded by a massive wall that extended down each side of the church, ending on Second Street. "I never noticed those buildings before," Emily said, peering out the side window. "It looks peaceful back there."

"Mmmm...and it must be at least a hundred years old," Mrs. Apple murmured. "And would you just look at those blackberry bushes growing on the east wall there. I wish I had time to stop and pick some for Herbert. He loves a good berry cobbler."

The clock on the dashboard showed that it was almost seven thirty, so Emily said, "I'll jump out here and walk to the café. If you pull into the driveway over there," she said, pointing across the street to the pharmacy, "there's a parking lot in the back."

"Let me give you a ride to wherever you were going," her neighbor offered.

"You don't need to; the café is just around the corner."

Emily got out and walked in front of the car to cross the street. The traffic was light. She looked to the right before crossing, and then to the left just as a car came careening by. It veered so close that she had to jump up on the hood of Mrs. Apple's car to get out of its way.

She turned and looked through the windshield at Mrs. Apple, who stared back at her in jaw-dropping astonishment.

"It's just Miss Beasley," Emily shouted to her through the windshield, feeling a little shaken herself.

They both watched as Miss Beasley turned into a parking space in front of the post office, nearly running over the skinny postman who was busy scooping letters from a curbside mailbox. Miss Beasley's front tires bounced up the curb onto the sidewalk, then rolled back down into the street and came to a halt. Unperturbed,

Miss Beasley got out of her old Cadillac, and strolled into the post office.

Emily turned to wave goodbye to Mrs. Apple, surprised to see her frozen to her seat, with her mouth still hanging open.

* * * *

She arrived at Good Eats Café eight minutes late. "Good morning, Ike," she shouted back into the kitchen. "Sorry I'm late; I had to show my neighbor where the pharmacy was."

"Good mornin' darlin'," he called, coming out of the kitchen, "no problem. Come right on back an' we'll git you outfitted in yer chef's attire."

Emily groaned. She'd forgotten about the stove pipe hat and baggy apron.

The café was soon humming with the breakfast crowd.

"Two orders of blueberry pancakes, two eggs over easy, Ike," Millie shouted into the kitchen.

"That's yer cue, Em'ly. Pour th' batter."

She picked up the dispenser that held the pancake batter, then flicked a little water on the griddle.

"When th' water dances on yer griddle, the temp'ture is jus' right," Ike had told her.

She pulled the trigger on the dispenser, releasing a measured amount of pancake batter, then repositioned her dispenser and did it five more times. Ike told her that customers got three pancakes each with their order.

"Put you a handful of blueberries on each flapjack," Ike said, "and when bubbles form around th' edges, flip 'em over."

Emily was kept hopping between the waffle iron and pancake griddle. The morning flew by, and she was surprised when Ike told her it was time to get set up for the lunch crowd.

"Well, Em'ly, think ya kin' cook flapjacks an' waffles on yer own now?" Ike asked, as he cleaned up the grill.

"I sure do," she smiled. "That was fun!"

Millie came into the kitchen, pulled off her white apron, and threw it in the laundry bin under the sink. "I'm outta here."

They had about twenty minutes of slow time before the lunch crowd started coming in. "We might not have our usual Saturday crowd," Ike said. "They're havin' that lumberjack competition ov'r at Monett today, an' I know lots of people were talkin' 'bout goin'."

That was fine with Emily. She didn't know how she was going to juggle seating customers, taking orders, working the cash register, and clearing tables.

The café door opened and a truck driver, Iris Head, and Glen Kingery trotted in, and she ran to seat them.

The truck driver seated himself at the counter and Mr. Kingery made a b-line for the men's room. Iris Head grabbed her mug off the rack on the wall, poured herself some coffee, and sat at her usual booth, spreading real estate listings out in front of her. Today she sported a rhinestone American flag on her blue suit lapel that winked little red, white, and blue lights.

"Cute pin," Emily grinned, when she went over to take her order.

"Listen to this," Iris said, pushing a tiny button on the flag.

Strains of *America the Beautiful* filled the air and Emily burst out laughing.

"Want to hear the *Star Spangled Banner*?" Iris asked, grinning.

"Next time," Emily laughed, "I have to go wait on other people."

Gus came in and thumped down on a red stool, craning his neck around the café. "Montana been in yet t'day?"

"Not yet," said Ike, "but I see you rubber neckin'. What's up buddy boy?"

"I went over to th' li'bery an' Miz Green looked up the county name fer where Montana was born. You ain't gonna b'lieve what his brother's name is," he said, grinning like a crocodile. He looked toward the door again.

"Well, what is it?" Ike asked.

"You'll see," Gus said, hardly able to sit still. He ordered a Spanish omelet and kept his eye on the door.

When Ike brought the omelet to Gus, he watched him douse it with hot sauce. "You wanna glass o' milk or somethin' to neutralize that fire your puttin' on them eggs?"

"No way," said Gus, "I got my system tuned perfect; my gut wouldn't know what ta do if I was ta pamper it that way."

Gus' head swung around each time the bell over the door jangled. After a few minutes, everyone in the café turned their heads in anticipation when someone came in. The tension was palpable by the time Montana finally strutted in, decked out in snakeskin boots and a ten-gallon hat.

Gus hooted and swiveled around on his stool. “I found out your little brother’s name,” he sputtered, flecks of omelet flying out of his mouth.

“Tell me you didn’t,” Montana groaned, lowering his cowboy hat down over his eyes.

“Yessirr, I surely did,” Gus replied, leaning back on his stool like he was about to deliver the Gettysburg Address.

“Well, my friend,” Montana said, “why don’t you just get it over with and tell Ike and all the fine people in this café what my brother’s name is.”

“Custer!” Gus crowed. “Your brother’s name is Custer, as in *Battle of Little Bighorn* Custer. I cannot b’lieve my good fortune in findin’ this out. Does he dress like a cowboy too?”

Montana groaned and shook his head, as he sat down on a stool next to Gus. “I don’t suppose I could talk you into forgetting this whole name thing, could I?”

“No way, this is rich,” Gus crowed, diving back into his omelet, as Montana ordered a waffle from Ike.

“Is your brother in the Army like General Custer?” Emily asked, history being one of her favorite subjects.

“You mean th’ *cavalry*, doncha Em’ly,” Ike shouted from the kitchen.

Everyone in the café burst out laughing.

“I’m doomed,” Montana groaned.

“Let ‘er rip, Montana,” Gus said. “We wanna hear ever’thing.”

“Okay, okay,” Montana said, holding his hands up in surrender. He pushed his hat to the back of his head, swung around and sat facing everyone in the café. “My brother’s name is Custer County Chan...”

He got no further because Gus began to hoot with laughter.

Montana sat watching him as he snorted, and howled, and pounded the counter with his fist.

Ike came out from the kitchen and shook his head. “I need to be sellin’ tickets to this show.”

“Go on, tell the rest of it,” Gus gasped, tears streaming down his face. He dug for his handkerchief.

Emily could feel a belly laugh coming on and clamped a hand over her mouth.

Montana glanced over at her. "Not you, too," he moaned. He cleared his throat to finish the story. "Okay here's a little bio on my brother, then I'm finished...done...end of story. Custer was my parent's third son. Since I was the firstborn, I got the state name, and my brother Billings was named after the town we lived in. The only regional name left for son #3 was the county. Thus, *Custer County Chan.*

Montana looked from person to person, and it was silent. Thinking they were satisfied with the information he had given them, he turned around and buttered the waffle Ike had set on the counter for him.

"Well, tell us about yer baby brother, Montana," Gus said, nudging him with an elbow.

Montana groaned. "Throw a couple of pieces of bacon on this waffle, Ike, and I'll finish the story. I'm not going to get any peace from this guy until I do."

Ike brought a small plate from the kitchen with three pieces of bacon on it, and set it down near Montana, then leaned on the counter eyeing him.

Montana poured syrup on the waffle and tried to finish his breakfast, but the restaurant had grown silent as the customers waited expectantly for him to tell the rest of the story. He noticed and quit chewing.

He turned around. "You guys are something else," he laughed, shaking his head.

Everyone else burst out laughing too.

"Okay, I'll finish my family history, and then maybe I can eat my breakfast in peace."

Customers smiled and settled back in their seats for a good story.

"Custer is a free spirit sort of guy," he began. "He travels, and writes, and he's a great photographer. So he combines the three and that's how he makes his living. And of course, he's not married–all of this to my parents' dismay."

"He earns his money taking pictures?" Emily asked, suddenly very serious and very interested.

"He sure does, my young friend," Montana said, "but in my family, this is looked down upon. My parents wish that he would find a steady job, get married, and have children."

"What do you think?" she asked, peering at him intently.

"I think that as long as he doesn't have a family, he can earn his money any way that makes him happy." Montana took a bite of waffle, and continued, "When he meets the right girl, he'll settle down. For now he should see the world, do whatever he wants. He's only in his twenties."

"Do you see yer family very often, Montana?" Ike asked.

"I try to. My wife and I like to keep our kids in contact with family. My brother Bill still lives in Billings and my parents do too, so we try to make it up every six months or so. I see Custer more often; he blows into town about every three or four months. I'll bring him in next time he comes. I'm sure he'd *love* to meet you, Gus."

"So," said Emily, repeating herself," your brother takes pictures and earns money doing it?"

"You seem very interested in my brother's lifestyle, Emily," Montana said, with a grin.

"Oh, just thinking," she replied, and went back to clearing tables.

The three men at the counter looked at each other and smiled.

* * * *

On Sunday, Ike was serving Gus link sausages and a Denver omelet when he happened to glance out the front window of his café.

"Gus, turn around quick," Ike gasped.

Gus swiveled around and let out a whoop, as both men flew to the window.

They stood frozen to the spot as Miss Mattie and Emily sashayed by, crossing the street at the corner and going up Elderberry Lane. Miss Mattie was decked out in a wide, plum colored Sunday hat with an arched red feather, and Emily was equally decked out in a blue wide-brimmed hat, with a big white feather that swooped up and back. The two men stood transfixed in front of the window watching the two ladies. Ike draped an arm over Gus' shoulder and murmured, "We ain't never gonna see a sight like this again th' rest of our whole lives."

"That's fer sure," Gus said, pulling his ball cap off his head and putting it over his heart. "This has got ta be th' church's finest hour."

The men watched mesmerized as Miss Mattie and Emily marched up Elderberry Lane, regal as queens in their church hats. The men stood respectfully at attention until the two ladies had mounted the steps to Mountain Grove Community Church and disappeared through the big double doors.

"We ain't never gonna see a sight like that again th' rest of our whole lives," Ike repeated.

Gus nodded, keeping his hat over his heart.

* * * *

Everyone was seated when Miss Mattie and Emily entered the sanctuary. As they walked up the church aisle, heads began to turn and smiles appeared.

It was a high day at church.

As Pastor Britton looked out on his singing congregation that morning, his gaze fell upon two fine ladies—one brown and one white—singing with mouths wide open, the hallelujah chorus, in the most amazing set of Sunday hats he'd ever seen.

He later told his wife, "It was the most astounding sight of my life. If I'd had my Nikon, I would've taken pictures from the pulpit right then."

* * * *

On Monday morning, Emily stood in front of the bathroom mirror hurriedly getting ready for school. The noise level in the next room was deafening. Her parents' shrieking had been going on for hours. Their fighting had awakened her about three o'clock that morning, and she'd been awake since, a pillow over her head to drown out the noise. Her stomach hurt and she was nauseated. She studied her pale face in the mirror and quickly brushed her teeth. She had to get out of there.

"Em'ly!" her dad yelled.

Her stomach knotted, but she didn't see any way to avoid him.

Grabbing her jacket and hoisting her backpack onto her shoulder, she walked out into the living room. "What?" she asked. There were empty bottles strewn everywhere; both her parents looked drunk and angry.

"I jus' want you to help settle a 'lil argument here..." Her dad swayed and almost fell over.

"I don't want to be in the middle of your fight, Dad," she said, holding her stomach as the pain nearly doubled her over.

"Yeah, she's too good for us, Luke!" her mother mocked, with an expletive that made Emily cringe.

"Too good for us, huh?" her dad slurred.

Her stomach recoiled and she bolted for the door. She barely made it outside before she vomited all over the lawn.

She leaned against a fence post and wiped her mouth off with the bottom of her sweatshirt; she was reeling and needed to sit down somewhere. Her mind searched for possible places to go. She would rather die in the street than go back inside that house, and school didn't start for another two hours.

Her thoughts flew to her garden; she slipped around the side of the house and quietly unlatched the gate to the backyard. She crept to the oleanders, glancing toward the windows at the back of her house. She didn't see her parents, so she hurried through the archway into the garden, and collapsed in her red chair. She wrapped her jacket tightly around her; it was cold outside, but she didn't care.

She rocked herself, tilting her face back so it was warmed by the sun. Her stomach began to calm down, and she tried to rest and not think about anything. Her mind felt worn out with the constant maneuvering around her parents, and she was exhausted.

As a gentle breeze blew, she felt her throat begin to tickle. She sneezed, not just once, but one blast after another. "Stupid allergies," she moaned, then sneezed again.

"Is that you, Emily?" asked Mrs. Apple from the other side of the fence. At the same instant she heard her parents muffled shrieks; they were fighting in the kitchen now.

"Yes, it's me," she said, quickly going to the gate, bending over slightly to relieve the pain.

The fence rattled a bit. "Will this gate open, Emily?" Mrs. Apple asked. "I was just going into the house for some hot chocolate. Maybe you'd like to join me."

"I've never been able to open it from this side," Emily said, giving the gate a hard push. "Is there a latch on your side?"

"Why, I believe there is..."

Emily heard a click and the gate swung open. There stood a smiling Mrs. Apple in her purple flowered dress and wedged shoes.

"Oh, isn't this the most marvelous thing," Mrs. Apple said, peering at her behind large glasses. "We can visit back and forth anytime we want."

Emily crossed her arms over her stomach, as pain speared through her belly. From inside the house, the roar of her parents' profanity could be plainly heard.

"I don't think that would work, Mrs. Apple," she said, clutching her stomach to relieve the pain. "My parents don't like people coming over; I should just come to your house."

"I see," Mrs. Apple replied, frowning as she listened to the yelling that came from Emily's house.

Inside the house a dish crashed against the wall.

"Mrs. Apple, I have a really bad stomachache," Emily groaned, nearly doubling over. "I need to go lay down somewhere."

"Oh, my goodness," Mrs. Apple said, putting an arm around her. "Come on dear, I know just the thing for your tummy." She scooted Emily into her own yard, closing the gate firmly behind them.

Emily followed her across the yard to the back door, then through the kitchen, and into the cozy living room. Mrs. Apple had her lie down on the flowered sofa, tucked a fluffy pillow behind her head, and covered her with a soft afghan that smelled of lavender.

"I'll be right back," she said, hurrying off.

Mrs. Apple soon returned with a large spoonful of something thick and white. "Just swallow this, and you'll feel better right away," Mrs. Apple said, tipping the spoon so that Emily swallowed every drop.

Relief spread immediately through Emily's stomach. She felt so much better that she sat up. "I can't believe it stopped hurting already. "How'd you know what I needed?"

"Oh, I know all about a nervous stomach, dear," Mrs. Apple said, peering at her over her large glasses.

"A *what?*"

"A nervous stomach," she said, setting the spoon and bottle down on the end table. "My parents fought all of the time, too, Emily."

Emily pulled the afghan up around her neck. She really wanted to pull it over her head and hide from embarrassment. "I wondered if you could hear my parents fighting."

"Yes dear, I can," Mrs. Apple replied. "I've heard them many, many times. How long has your stomach been hurting you?"

"It started a few months ago, but it's getting worse. I threw up on my lawn."

Mrs. Apple sat down beside her and took her hand. "Promise me you'll come over when things get so bad your stomach hurts."

"I don't know...," she started to say, but Mrs. Apple interrupted her.

"No Emily, *really*. I want you to come over when your parents are fighting; it's not good for you to be over there. I *know*!"

"How do you know?" Emily asked.

"Because when I was a girl, my home life was *horrible*," her neighbor said, shaking her head sadly. "But there was physical abuse in my family."

Emily was shocked and didn't know what to say. "I'm sorry," she finally blurted out. "There's no hitting in my family, just drinking and screaming."

"I know that too, dear," Mrs. Apple replied evenly.

"You do?" Emily's jaw dropped. "How could you know that?"

"From the first time I heard your parents fighting, I listened, and I watched. I only heard yelling, not screams, like someone was being hurt. When I met you, I looked closely to see if you had any marks or bruises. If I'd thought you were being hurt, dear, I would've called the police."

Wow! Emily thought, staring at her. *She looks soft, but she's a tough lady!*

"I know it seems nosy," Mrs. Apple continued, "but we *all* have a responsibility. I wish a neighbor had called for help when I was a little girl. Do you understand what I'm saying, dear?"

Emily nodded her head. "What did you do about the abuse at your house?"

"*Do*? Why there was nothing I could do. I was only a child." Mrs. Apple's face eyes filled with tears, and she dabbed them with a flowered hanky. "I'm so silly. You'd think after all these years I wouldn't be such a crybaby."

Emily patted her shoulder and tried to think of something to say, but all she could think of was what her neighbor had just told her.

"There's a happy ending to my story that I'd like to tell you about," Mrs. Apple finally said, after a few minutes of sniffling and blowing her nose. She glanced up at the clock on the mantle. "My goodness Emily, don't you have to be in school?"

Emily looked at the clock and groaned; school started in twenty minutes. She would have to hurry to make it on time. She threw off the afghan and grabbed her backpack.

"Wait dear, you're not leaving without eating something."

"I'll be fine," she protested, but Mrs. Apple would have none of it.

"It'll only take me a minute to scramble an egg and put it on an English muffin," she said, hurrying off to the kitchen. "You can eat it on the way to school."

"But..." Emily started to say, but Mrs. Apple was already out of the room.

"Feel free to freshen up in the bathroom," Mrs. Apple called from the kitchen, where the sound of an egg cracking could be heard.

Emily sighed and headed to the bathroom, where she washed her face and rinsed out her mouth, desperately wishing she had a toothbrush. Mrs. Apple had her breakfast sandwich all ready when she came out.

"I put a little cheese on it," Mrs. Apple said, looking pleased, "and you need to eat every bite." She handed Emily the sandwich, folded in a napkin.

"Thank you," Emily said, loving the smell of the warm bread and egg.

"You'll feel better when you get something on your empty tummy," Mrs. Apple said, giving her an extra napkin to tidy up with. "Come back after school and we'll have hot chocolate, and I'll tell you all about my happy ending!"

Mrs. Apple hugged her good-bye and stood in the doorway until she was all the way down the walk. "Have a wonderful day!" she called out, waving a hankie.

Emily hurried down the street, biting into her warm breakfast sandwich as she walked. She almost felt like skipping. She couldn't remember anyone ever making her breakfast or hugging her when she left for school.

Just like TV! she thought, as she hurried happily down the street.

CHAPTER – 8

After school, Emily hurried back to the Apple's home, eager to hear Mrs. Apple's story, and extremely happy that she didn't have to go back to her own house just yet. In the warm kitchen, Emily sat at the chrome dinette table while Mrs. Apple filled two mugs with steaming hot chocolate, then heaped them high with whipped cream. Mrs. Apple set the mugs on the table and laid a spoon beside each. "I'll be right back," she said, and hurried out of the room. Emily spooned a couple of bites of the thick cream into her mouth. It was freshly whipped and tasted heavenly! She sipped deeply the delicious chocolate, smacking her lips it was so good. Mrs. Apple came back and sat down across the table from her, handing her a small gift wrapped in pink wrapping foil. "I bought this for you while you were at school," she smiled.

"What is it?" Emily asked, eagerly tearing away the wrapping.

It was a small book.

"Thank you," she said, looking the book over. The cover was parchment decorated with tiny violets; a matching pen was tucked into a little pocket on the front. Emily began thumbing through the pages and found that they were all blank. She looked up at Mrs. Apple, puzzled.

"It's a journal, dear," Mrs. Apple said, taking a sip of her chocolate. "It's a part of my story and how I had a happy ending to my life."

"Okay...." Emily replied hesitantly.

"My journal became my plan," Mrs. Apple explained. "A plan for a different life than the one I had as a child."

Emily glanced at her doubtfully. "How do you plan out a whole life?"

Mrs. Apple set her cup down and looked at her evenly. "By making decisions about what you want in your life later on—and what you *don't* want." She took Emily's hand. "I want you to remember this, Emily. You have no control over the family you live with now—the family you were born into. But one day, you *will* have control, and you need to start deciding right now what you want that family to be like."

"But I'm only fourteen."

"I know," Mrs. Apple said, "but if you don't start planning now, and gear your mind, you're in great danger of patterning the family life that you've been raised in." She peered at her over her glasses. "In fact, statistics show that you are at great risk for it."

Emily sighed. This had become an extremely depressing conversation. "So you're saying I might copy the family life I have now—even though I don't like it?"

"Yes dear, because it's all you know."

"But how can you fight something that big?" she asked, scooping out another bite of whipped cream.

"Well, the first thing to do is what we're already doing—talk about it," Mrs. Apple said. "The second thing is to make some sound plans about the qualities you want in a husband, and what kind of home the two of you will have." Mrs. Apple peered at her over her glasses. "I know it sounds rather unromantic, dear, but it's a sure way of having a 'happily ever after'."

"Is that what you did?" Emily asked.

"It's exactly what I did, and that's how I found my Herbert," Mrs. Apple said, her cheeks pinking up to a pretty glow.

Emily licked the whipped cream off the back of her spoon. "Actually, I've been thinking that I probably won't get married. It seems simpler to just take care of myself." She took another drink of chocolate. "This is extremely yummy, by the way!"

"Thank you, dear. It's my mother's recipe—made from scratch with real chocolate."

She waited, letting Emily enjoy her beverage, then said, "You know, Emily, I don't blame you for feeling that way about marriage right now, but you want to leave options open for yourself—in case you change your mind."

Emily clanked the spoon into her empty mug, got up and went to the kitchen sink where she rinsed it out. "Okay, so what's the journal for?" she asked, turning toward her.

"I want you to start looking at families that are happy and thriving. Write down in your journal the things you see that they do to make their lives and family life work," she replied. "Do they speak kindly to each other? Do they help one another? Do they have fun together? Be specific, *nothing* is too small to write down in your journal, Emily. Then let the things you've written about influence you, and *not* your home life."

"I sort of do that already."

"Wonderful," Mrs. Apple beamed. "Then you're on the right track!"

"What else did you put in your journal?" Emily asked, growing more interested.

"I wrote down the qualities I wanted in a husband," she said, her eyes softening, remembering.

"You mean if he's cute?" Emily asked.

"No, Emily, not his looks; those don't count a whit in the long run," she said, then thought a moment. "For example, I had a neighbor, Mr. Post, who was so kind and thoughtful to his wife. I'd sit on my porch and watch them garden together. It was what I wanted one day, so in my journal, under the category of *Future Husband*, I wrote *kind, gentle*. Then there was my math teacher, Mr. Davenport. He was the funniest man, and made his students laugh every day. There wasn't much laughter in my home—so I wrote *sense of humor* under my husband category." She looked at her evenly. "Do you see what I'm talking about, dear?"

"I get it," Emily said, not really wanting to talk about a *husband* category.

"And when you know what you're looking for," Mrs. Apple continued, "never settle for anything less, or overlook something in a man that you know might be a harmful thing."

"I don't think anyone's perfect, Mrs. Apple," she said, feeling tired all of a sudden.

"Of course not, dear. But there's a big difference between someone who forgets to hang up his trousers, or leaves coffee grounds in the sink, and someone who drinks every night of this world, or screams at you, or hits you. I think you know what I mean, don't you, dear?"

Emily nodded. The lack of sleep, the hot chocolate, the warm kitchen, had made her so sleepy she could hardly keep her eyes open. "I'm glad you found someone nice like Mr. Apple," she yawned.

"Me too," Mrs. Apple smiled, looking like a hoot owl blinking behind her large glasses. "But remember, I *knew* what I was looking for. Use your journal like a best friend too—tell it all your deep dark secrets!"

"Now there's a scary thought!" Emily smiled, stifling another yawn.

Mrs. Apple noticed and stood up. "Come with me, dear."

She led Emily down the hallway to a small bedroom. The warm, taupe room was cozy with the afternoon light filtering in. It held a set of twin beds with red comforters, and a beautiful, braided rug, that brought warmth to the wooden floors. Mrs. Apple drew the comforter back on one of the beds and plumped up the pillow, then went over to an antique dresser and took a small blue flannel nightgown from the top drawer.

"Change into this warm nightie, dear," Mrs. Apple said, holding it out to Emily, "then crawl between the sheets and rest just as long as you need to."

Emily started to protest, feeling like she had already taken up enough of her day, but Mrs. Apple shook her head. "No, dear, I insist. You look completely worn out."

She *was* completely worn out and took the gown from her without another word. Mrs. Apple left the room, shutting the door softly behind her. Emily set her new journal on the nightstand, and quickly changed into the old-fashioned nightgown, loving its sweet, clean smell. She crawled between the warm flannel sheets; the last thing she remembered was laying her head down on a pillow that smelled of the fresh outdoors.

When she awoke, the sun was slanting in through the blinds, and she knew it must be very late in the afternoon. She could hear Mrs. Apple humming in the kitchen and a delicious aroma wafting in through the heater vents. As she lay still in the peaceful room, she heard Mr. Apple go into the kitchen, his voice hushed as he spoke to his wife about something. Mrs. Apple responded and they both chuckled quietly. She glanced at the nightstand, then sat up and reached for her journal. She leaned back against her pillow, pulled the pen from the little pocket, opened the journal to the first page and wrote:

Emily's House:

1. Warm flannel sheets.

2. Good smells from the kitchen.

3. Lots of laughter.

She closed the journal and put it back on the nightstand, then turned over on her side and drew the comforter up under her chin. *I'll just lie here five more minutes,* she thought, closing her eyes.

When she opened them again, Mrs. Apple was gently shaking her; the room was dark except for a shaft of light coming in from the hallway. "Dinner's ready, dear," Mrs. Apple whispered. "Come and eat a little and then you can come straight back to bed."

Emily smiled in the dark. Later she would add one more thing to the list in her journal: *Someone calling you to dinner.*

* * * *

Emily walked down Jack Pine Road past the picnic grounds, on her way toward the river. The stand of trees in the picnic grounds looked positively aflame: fiery reds; brilliant yellows; deep oranges, all vividly alive and bursting with color. She enjoyed them all the more, knowing it was their last days. Miss Mattie had told her that the brilliant leaves only lasted awhile, then fell to the ground in brittle brown piles. She stopped for a moment to stare, wishing she had a camera to capture it all. She slowed down as she approached the river, not wanting to stumble onto the same group of kids that had been there last time. She adjusted her cap to shade her eyes and peeked out from behind some bushes, looking up and down the beach. No one was in sight.

On the previous trip to the river, she'd walked out of the woods practically on top of a group of boys sitting around a campfire smoking weed. They looked startled when they first saw her, but then laughed and asked if she wanted to join them. She stood there gawking at two boys who couldn't have been much older than twelve. They stared back at her with bleary eyes and lopsided grins. One of the older boys stood up and glared at her menacingly. He was so high that Emily knew she could outrun him, but it still frightened her. She decided from then on, that when she went to the river, she would make sure no one was around before coming out into the open.

She walked across the empty beach to the river's edge, then tip-toed like a tightrope walker over a small group of rocks to a huge boulder out in the river. She scrambled up its side, sat down on its flat granite surface and gazed around, awestruck by the incredible beauty of her surroundings.

Aspen trees lined the whole river. As the wind blew, golden leaves fluttered down onto the water, where they bobbed downstream like a tiny fleet of banana boats. Puffy clouds, the size of fairy-tale castles floated overhead, while a fly fisherman in a canvas hat silently fished upstream, adding to the tranquility of the setting.

The sound of the river roaring over stones and boulders calmed something deep inside of her. In the distance, she heard the Mountain Express, and caught a glimpse of it winding its way down the mountainside. Its whistle echoed off the mountain, sounding much like a circus calliope.

Emily watched the distant fly fisherman as he stood braced against the current, his fishing rod weaving back and forth, as he let the line out. He turned his head toward her, and she saw a huge grin appear underneath his hat. The fisherman waved at her.

Who is that? she wondered, feeling a bit alarmed.

He waved again.

Jonathan!

She didn't know what to say—and wouldn't be heard over the river's roar even if she said it—so just sat there waving.

Now what? If she turned the other way, he might think she was trying to ignore him; but she couldn't sit there waving all day.

She didn't have to think about it for long, because Jonathan reeled in his line, and was soon high stepping through the water toward her. He was coming so fast that water splashed up in his face.

She stood to her feet laughing. "Slow down, you're drowning yourself!"

He was laughing too, as he waded up to the rock and handed up his fly rod. "How'd you get up on there?" he grinned.

She laid the fishing rod down on the boulder and pointed to the stones she'd crossed over on. He went in toward the shore and stepped up on the first rock, then jumped from rock to rock until he reached the boulder. He stared at it. "Where'd you get a toe hold on this thing?"

"Can you make it up in those waders?" she asked, pointing to where she had climbed up.

"We'll find out," he said, digging a toe into a chip on the boulder. He scrambled, but his waders made the rock slippery.

Emily grabbed his arm and pulled, giving him just enough of a tug so he could heave himself up onto the rock. They were laughing like children by the time he made it to the top.

"I didn't know you fished!" she said, staring at the fishing flies pinned to his hat.

"I come here a lot," he grinned. "Do you fish?"

"I've never in my *whole life* even tried it!"

"Really?" he laughed. "Want to give it a try?"

"Sure!" she said, eagerly. "What do I do first?"

Jonathan picked up the rod and handed it to her. "Well, first you hold the handle with this hand," he said, placing her right hand on the fly rod. "And you hold the fishing line with your left hand," he said, pulling out a little of the thick line for her to grab. "You have to let the line out slowly. It's kind of tricky though because you've got to..." He appeared to be at a loss for words about what to tell her next.

"Here, let me show you," he said, moving around behind her. He pulled out some line with his left hand and had her grab hold. "Now with your right hand, weave the pole back and forth like this," he showed her the right motion to use to get the line to sail out. When he let go, she kept the whipping motion going, but forgot to let the line out.

"Like this," he laughed, reaching both arms around her. With his right hand over hers, he showed her the right weaving motion again; he took the fingertips of her left hand and cupped them in his, showing her how to hold the line so it could easily sail out. His chest felt warm against her back and she could feel his arm muscles flex as he showed her how to cast. When the line finally plopped down on the water surface, it didn't seem like more than a second before the tip of the rod began jerking up and down.

"You've got a fish!" Jonathan yelled.

"I've got a fish! Oh my gosh, what now?" She was so excited she almost fell off the rock.

Jonathan laughed as he grabbed her. "Hurry! Reel it in!"

"There it is," he yelled, as the fish flew up out of the water.

"I saw it! Oh my gosh!" she cried again, nervous with excitement, as she frantically reeled the fish in.

Jonathan's vest had a net attached to the back and he quickly undid the Velcro and got it ready. When she had reeled the fish in close enough, he reached down and scooped it up.

Emily stared wide-eyed as he held the net up at eye level for her to see. "Your fish, madam," he said, with a sweeping bow and a big grin. "It's a rainbow trout."

"I can't believe it," Emily laughed, looking up at him, noticing the intense blueberry color of his eyes. "What do we do now?"

"I'll clean it for you, and you can take it home," he said, smiling down at her.

"I don't know how to cook fish."

"Have your mom do it," he shrugged.

She tried to picture handing her mom a gutted fish and asking her to fry it for her. "I don't think that would work," she said, trying not to laugh. "You take it home."

He was silent for a moment. "Want to cook it right here on the beach?"

"How can we do that?"

"I'll show you," he said, gathering up his fishing gear.

They hopped back over the rocks to the shore, and he took off his waders. She watched as he dug a knife out of his pocket and laid the fish on a flat rock. She turned her head while he gutted it. When he was through, he went to the water's edge and washed it off.

"Gather up sticks and dried leaves, and paper if you can find it. I'll look for some rocks."

Emily came back a few minutes later with an armload of sticks, leaves, and a paper cup. Jonathan was squatting down, putting the rocks in a circle.

"Perfect!" he said, taking the leaves and cup from her. The leaves were put in first, then the paper cup was torn up and tucked in with the leaves. After pulling some matches out of his tackle box, he set fire to the whole thing. When the fire was high enough, the small sticks were thrown on top.

In no time a nice little blaze was going. "Now for the fish," he said, skewering a stick up through one of the fish's gills and out its mouth. Emily looked away again.

The skewered fish was set across two large rocks on either side of the fire; the rocks kept the fish about five inches above the flames.

"Does it take long to cook?" she asked, squatting down beside him.

"No, only a few minutes," he said, turning the fish over. Emily could see one side was already getting brown.

Jonathan turned the fish twice more, poked it with his finger, and announced that it was done. She noticed that the outside was a little black. He went over to his tackle box, got out a paper towel, and laid the fish on it. Emily walked over as he was pulling out the skewer.

He stood up. "Try this," he said, breaking off a piece of fish. "Watch out for bones though."

She took the fish from him and popped it into her mouth, surprised at how good it tasted. "Yum!" she said, smiling up at him.

"Here's more," he said, handing her an even bigger piece.

"No! You eat some too," she said, pushing his hand back.

"We'll share." He broke the piece in half and put it up to her lips. She looked up at him; his eyes were two blueberry pools looking at her in a weird way. She gulped the fish down and quickly looked away.

He finished off the last piece of fish and smiled at her. "I didn't think you'd do it."

"Do what?"

"Fish...then eat the fish," he grinned. "Most girls wouldn't, you know." He playfully tugged the bill of her cap down over her eyes.

"Really?" she laughed, pushing the cap back up. "I thought it was fun."

"Me too," he said, staring at her in that weird way again.

She stepped back. "I've got to get home, but thanks for showing me how to fish, and cook a fish..." She was rambling as she backed away, then turned to go.

"Wait," he said, gathering up his fishing gear. "It's getting dark, and you shouldn't walk through the woods alone. I'll go with you."

They hiked out through the shadowed trees and bushes, and Emily was glad she had waited for him. It was creepy in the semi-darkness.

As they passed the picnic grounds, they heard jeers from some of the kids who hung out there. Emily spotted the boys she had seen smoking pot on the beach, and they appeared to be in the same high condition again. She also saw two other familiar figures–Logger and Mac.

"Last time I went to the river, I accidently walked right into the pot party those guys are having," Emily laughed, nodding toward the picnic grounds. "They were all high!"

Jonathan looked alarmed. "Those guys are nothing to fool with, Emily."

"I could've easily outrun them all," she said, lightly.

Jonathan turned to her. "Why don't you let me know next time you're going to the river, and I'll go with you."

"I'll be careful," she replied, side-stepping his offer.

* * * *

Emily didn't know why she felt nervous going into the camera shop.

Just go in and get the price of a camera so you know how much money you'll need to save, she told herself.

She peeked into the shop to see if it was crowded and saw two men inside, then pushed the door open and walked in.

"May I help you," asked the tall man with a full beard.

"Are you Mr. Taylor?"

"I am, but call me Miles," he grinned.

She introduced herself and said, "I'm interested in buying a camera and taking photography lessons. Mr. Charles said I should come and see you."

"Great! Glad you came by," he replied, turning to the other man, who had a ponytail and a row of earrings in his left ear. "This is my friend, Custer Chan, world-renowned photographer."

She couldn't control the smile that tugged at her lips. "You're Montana's brother," she said, feeling delighted as she shook his hand.

"I am," he smiled at her. "But don't let this guy fool you," he said, nodding at Miles, "I'm not world renowned."

"But you do make your living taking pictures," she said.

Custer laughed. "I suppose my honorable brother told you all about me!"

"Just that you make your living traveling and taking pictures, and that your parents wish you'd get married and settle down," she told him.

Both men burst out laughing.

"Tell me what kind of photography you're interested in, Emily," Miles said, "and I'll try and help you figure out what you need."

"People and landscapes are my favorite things," she said.

"Okay, got it," Miles went to the back of the shop. He brought out three different cameras and spent the next forty minutes going over their different functions and prices.

"That was a big help, thanks for explaining everything," Emily said later, tucking the brochures Miles had given her into her backpack. "I'm saving my money, and I'm pretty close to having enough for the least expensive camera, but I sort of like the one that costs more. I'll have to think about it."

"That's a good idea," Miles said.

"When do your photography lessons start?" she asked.

"That's what Custer and I were just talking about when you came in," Miles said. "Custer is going to be in town for a while, and he'll be teaching a couple of classes in our next session–which starts Monday."

"How much are classes?"

"Let's see, $75.00 for the six-week course."

Emily was relieved that she could afford it. "Okay, I'd like to sign up then." She unzipped a pocket on her backpack and pulled out her tip money. As she counted the money out, it dawned on her that she didn't have a camera to use.

"Wait," she said, feeling very disappointed, "I can't take lessons if I don't have a camera."

Miles looked up from the receipt he was writing her. "I have one I'll loan you." "No problem."

Relieved, she smiled and handed him the money. "See you both on Monday then," she said, grabbing her backpack, and heading for the door. She found herself humming as she walked home.

* * * *

"Seventy-five dollars for six weeks of photography lessons?" Custer said, after Emily left. "I thought you told me *two hundred* and seventy-five!"

"Call it a life investment," Miles shrugged. "I liked her. She didn't whine or try to wheedle anything for free."

"I liked her too," Custer agreed. "Smart kid."

CHAPTER - 9

Emily walked up Second Street, bracing against the brisk, cold wind, on her way to Good Neighbor Pharmacy. She had promised Mrs. Apple she would stop by and pick up another prescription for Mr. Apple, who didn't seem to be weathering the cold very well.

"I may take him to Florida for the winter if he doesn't start improving," Mrs. Apple confided.

At the pharmacy counter, Mr. Carver, the pharmacist, went over a list of instructions on the pill bottle with Emily. "Mr. Apple needs to take this on an empty stomach to get the greatest benefit," he told her. She nodded as the pharmacist went on with more instructions, memorizing everything he said.

Leaving the pharmacy, Emily glanced across the street at the blackberry bushes growing up the thick wall that surrounded St. Daniels church. She thought about Mr. Apple loving blackberry cobbler and wondered if she should go pick some.

Of course I should, she thought, as she hurried across the street.

The north wall of the church ran along Jack Pine Road, and as Emily turned the corner, she was surprised to see a nun dressed head to toe in a flowing black habit, busy plucking berries, and putting them into a small bucket that hung from her arm.

"Oh...hello," Emily stammered.

The nun jumped a bit, looking startled. "Why, hello," she replied, her face breaking into a huge grin beneath her veil, revealing a row of berry-stained teeth.

"Is it okay if I pick some berries for a sick friend?" Emily asked, stifling a laugh.

"Help yourself," the nun replied, with another purple grin. "The berries are quite sweet this time of year. I've been sampling them myself."

"I can tell," Emily said, grinning up at her.

"Oh, are my teeth purple?" the nun asked, baring her teeth to give Emily a better look.

"Yes, extremely," she laughed.

The nun laughed too. "My name is Sister Mary Kathryn," she said, extending a berry-stained hand.

"I'm Emily," she replied, giving the nun's hand a hearty shake.

"Do you have anything to put the berries in?" the sister inquired.

"Ummm...no," Emily replied, looking around, "except for this plastic bag from the pharmacy."

"It's too small, and will leak berry juice," Sister Mary Kathryn said firmly. "I'll give you my bucket, and we'll fill it together. What's your sick friend's name?"

"Mr. Apple."

"Oh..." Sister Mary Kathryn said, looking surprised.

"I know it's an odd last name," Emily said, and they both burst out laughing.

Sister Mary Kathryn handed Emily her bucket. "Well then, we'll pick a bucket of berries for Mr. Apple," the sister said. "How does that sound?"

"Like something out of a bad fairy tale," Emily replied, and Sister Mary Kathryn laughed so hard, she snorted twice.

As they picked berries, Emily asked, "How will I return the bucket to you?"

"Hmmm," the sister said, pushing her veil back over her shoulders, as she tried to think it through. Her face brightened. "I know, we have teatime for guests on Tuesday afternoons at four o'clock. Why don't you come and be my guest, and bring the bucket then?"

Emily hesitated. "Is it okay if I do that? I'm not very religious."

The sister burst out laughing again. "Of course it is, and I love your honesty."

When the bucket was full, Sister Mary Kathryn handed it to Emily, but didn't release it. Instead, she said a quick prayer. "Father, I pray that you will restore Mr. Apple to good health, and that these berries will be a blessing to him."

"Thank you," Emily said, meaning it. She started to hug Sister Mary Kathryn, but hesitated, not knowing if she should, when all of a sudden she felt herself enfolded in swaths of soft black cloth.

"God be with you," the sister said, giving her a bear hug.

* * * *

It was Saturday afternoon, an exquisitely beautiful fall day, with the sun so bright you needed sunglasses in November. Emily breathed it all in as she headed for the library. When she heard the bells at St. Daniel's ring twice, she realized she was late, and started running. She had promised Mrs. Green she would be there at two o'clock to help reorganize books in the children's section.

She flew up the library steps and rocketed through the big double doors, not seeing Miss Rose, who was just exiting with a tall stack of books. They collided, and the books exploded in all different directions, tumbling to the ground.

"I'm so sorry, Miss Rose," Emily said, stooping to pick the books up. "Are you all right?"

"Well, yes, I believe I am, Emily," she said, looking somewhat shaken, as she smoothed down her dress. She looked down to see if her stockings had been damaged by the falling books.

Emily reached out and steadied her as she checked first one leg, and then the other.

"I'll have to run right home if my stockings are torn," Miss Rose said, peering intently at her right leg. "It isn't proper to go about town with runs in one's stockings."

"Are they okay?" Emily asked, checking the back of her legs for her.

"Yes, only a small snag that hardly shows," Miss Rose replied. She looked at Emily sternly. "One should always remember to enter doors graciously, dear," she admonished.

"Okay, I'll remember that," Emily replied, and tried to scoot by her.

"If I may have but a moment of your time," Miss Rose said, smiling sweetly, as she gripped Emily's arm with the strength of a Sumo wrestler. "I would like to extend an invitation to our Young Ladies Academy; a new course is starting in eight days." Her sweet smile broadened. "May we count on you being there, dear?"

Emily was stuck and her mind couldn't come up with an excuse quick enough. To her horror, she heard herself saying, "Okay, I'll come."

Miss Rose patted her arm, smiling demurely. "We'll see you on the 15th then!" she said, and hurried out the door.

Emily stood there frozen. *What have I done?* she thought. *Could someone just shoot me now!*

Sighing, she turned and went to the check-out desk where Mrs. Green was renewing Miss Beasley's library card. "There you go, all set for another year," she told Miss Beasley, giving her the new card and a big hug.

"Thank you," sniffed Miss Beasley, standing ramrod straight. She tucked the library card into her pocket, wheeled around, and marched out of the library, sniffing at Emily as she passed her.

* * * *

How come you hug Miss Beasley?" Emily asked Mrs. Green, as they were carrying books back to the children's reading room.

Mrs. Green tilted her head to one side. "Because everyone needs to be hugged or touched."

"It doesn't seem like she enjoys it much," Emily said, picturing Miss Beasley standing stiff as a flagpole, as Mrs. Green hugged her.

"She's a little uncomfortable with it," Mrs. Green agreed, "but that's because she's still getting used to it. If I thought she really didn't want me to hug her, I wouldn't do it." Mrs. Green grinned. "At least she doesn't make me chase her around the library tables as much as she used to."

They both laughed.

"We never hug at my house." Emily said, and immediately regretted it.

Mrs. Green looked at her sharply.

Why do I let words fly out of my mouth that way? she thought, turning quickly and putting *The Tale of Peter Rabbit* on a bookshelf. She was so annoyed with herself; she could've stuffed the complete works of Beatrix Potter down her throat.

"Who taught you to be such a great hugger then?" Mrs. Green asked, plowing right into the subject.

She had to think about it for a moment. "I went to preschool when I was four, and the preschool teacher hugged as much as you do."

"See?" said Mrs. Green. "Can you remember how it felt the first time she hugged you?"

Emily thought back. "I was embarrassed, but it felt good."

Mrs. Green smiled. "I'd probably be chasing you around library tables, too, if the preschool teacher hadn't made you comfortable with hugging." Mrs. Green looked her square in the eye. "Emily, do you know that you can do the same thing at your house?"

"Do what?"

"Hug your family."

"Hug my mom or Pearl?" she said, her eyes growing wide with alarm. "No way! I *know* they wouldn't like it." It made her itchy just thinking about it.

"Probably not at first," Mrs. Green agreed, "but try just a pat, let them get used to your touch."

Emily arched her eyebrows and looked at Mrs. Green doubtfully.

Mrs. Green arched her eyebrows right back, and said, "What have you got to lose?"

"Ummm, my head when Pearl throws her slipper at me."

They both burst out laughing, as heads turned in the library.

"Shhhh!" whispered Mrs. Green, still laughing. "Just try it and let me know what happens. If it works, fine. If it doesn't..." she shrugged, "oh, well...you tried."

* * * *

Emily sat staring at the journal Mrs. Apple had given her. She felt like a cat walking around cornered prey, not quite sure how to approach it.

She opened it to the first page, which she had titled, *Emily's House,* and looked at the entries she had written when Mrs. Apple first gave her the journal:

Emily's House:

1. Warm flannel sheets.

2. Good smells from the kitchen.

3. Lots of laughter.

4. Someone calling you to dinner.

After her talk with Mrs. Green today, she decided to add another thing to her list:

5. Hugging. Lots and lots of hugging.

Emily reread the list and grew excited at the thought of having a home where these things happened every day, not just occasionally at a neighbor's house, or at the library. *I'll be in control of what happens in my own house*, she thought happily. It made her want to dance around the room.

She focused once again on the journal, deciding the first ten pages would be used just to add to the list of what she wanted in her house one day; the remainder of the book would be used to journal. She carefully counted off the pages and put a small clip on them, then flipped over to where her journaling entries would begin. *This must be the hardest part,* she thought, tapping her bottom lip with the pen, *putting my thoughts out in the open, instead of keeping them stuffed inside my head.* She wrote the date, and that seemed to make it her own. She didn't quite know how to speak what was on her mind. Should she write, *Dear Journal* or write it like an essay for school?

What would she like it to be?

She decided to take Mrs. Apple's suggestion: the journal could be like a best friend. She had never had one, and it might be good practice.

She began her first entry:

October 26

Dear Journal,

I wonder about my life and how it can come out okay. Mrs. Apple thinks that writing to you and writing down the things I want in my life will help. I don't know if she's right, but her life came out okay.

Today I did something really stupid! I let Miss Rose pressure me into going to that dumb Young Ladies Academy! I almost knocked her over running into the library and felt so terrible, that when she asked me to come, I said YES!

COULD SOMEONE JUST KNOCK ME IN THE HEAD, PLEASE!! I am so S-t-u-p-i-d!!!! Plus, I can tell everyone WANTS me to go, especially Mrs. Apple, who has been after me to make friends my own age. I told her people my age would want to come over to my house—but they can't! Then they would want to call me on the phone—I don't have one! At least not one I can use. My life is too weird. Mrs. Apple said I could give them her number and bring them to her house—but that just makes things weirder. She's worried that if I don't make friends my own age right now, when I go off to college, I won't know how, and I'll be lonely or I'll pattern my life after my parents and NEVER have friends over.

Maybe she's right. I really don't care if I have friends my age, but that's probably not good. I guess since I'm stuck going to that goofy YLA, I could try making a friend there. E.

She closed her journal feeling an odd sense of relief after putting her thoughts on paper; it seemed to clarify things for her. Maybe—just maybe—Mrs. Apple was right about all of this.

****

Emily put on her black jacket and pulled on her old boots, deciding to head for town on her dad's day off. When she walked into the kitchen, she saw her mother, still in her ragged bathrobe, getting a cup of coffee.

"Good morning, Mom," she said, walking up to her. She decided it was now or never to try the touching stuff she and Mrs. Green had talked about.

Her mother said hello and grew uncomfortable as Emily drew closer to her.

How'd she know I was going to touch her? Emily wondered.

Her mother leaned into the counter like she was doing something.

"I'm going downtown, I'll see you later," Emily said, standing just two steps away from her.

"Okay," she murmured, fiddling nervously in a drawer and bringing out a spoon to stir her coffee. Her mother took her coffee black.

Emily stepped forward and patted her mother's shoulder. "Bye, mom."

Her mother flinched. "Bye," she said coldly, not turning her head.

Disappointed, Emily stood a moment longer, then turned and walked away. Mrs. Green's suggestion seemed a gigantic flop.

As she walked by the living room, the TV was blaring one of the morning talk shows. Pearl was hissing at a young man, whose very pregnant girlfriend sat beside him, yelling insults at an ex-girlfriend. Emily started to just walk out the door, but the thought came to her that nothing would ever change, unless she changed it.

She turned from the door and walked back over to her grandmother.

"Bye Pearl, I'm going downtown," she shouted over the TV.

"So?" Pearl said, glaring up at her. She had her slipper clutched in her right hand, ready to throw it at the TV.

"I just wanted to say good-bye," Emily said, reaching over and patting her awkwardly on the shoulder. She looked into Pearl's eyes as she did.

Pearl's eyes shifted back to the TV for a second, and then back to her. "All right," she said, her voice not quite as gruff. "Well, bye."

Emily turned and walked toward the front door, hesitated, and glanced back. Pearl was staring at her. Emily smiled, and Pearl raised a blue-veined hand, and gave her a little wave. Emily waved back.

* * * *

"That's a very cute hairdo you have today," Miss Mattie said, peering at Emily's French braid. She took a dainty bite of the Danish they were sharing. "Does your mama or daddy have red hair?"

Emily shook her head. "I don't know where my red hair comes from," she replied, biting into her pastry. "I just wish it'd go away. I'm going to dye it when I get older."

"You're going to *dye* it!" Miss Mattie cried. "*Why?* It's beautiful!"

"No, it's not," Emily insisted. "Plus, I have freckles to go with it—but at least they're fading."

"Now let me tell you somethin', Miss Em'ly," Miss Mattie said, leaning forward, her face only inches away from Emily's. "God gave you that red hair and He planned every freckle on your face. They're a blessin'!"

"Ummm...I don't think so," Emily said, biting off another piece of Danish.

"Well, I *know so*," Miss Mattie insisted, "and when you realize it's true, you jus' come on back into my bakery and say, 'Miss Mattie, I found out you were right; my hair and freckles are a real blessin' from God.'"

Emily rolled her eyes.

"I'll be waitin' for you to do it," Miss Mattie insisted, thumping the table.

"Well, don't wait too long," she laughed. "This," she said, pulling the braid straight up in the air, "is *not* a blessing."

"Oh, you'll see," said Miss Mattie, with a grin.

Emily grinned back at her and said, "Tell me the story of Mrs. Green again."

Miss Mattie moaned, "Is my month up already?"

"Yes ma'am, it sure is," she said, hunkering in for a good story.

"Well, if I have to tell it again, jus' remember—Miz' Green also has red hair. And you better believe that Mr. Green loves every strand on that woman's head." Miss Mattie squinted at her. "Are you *sure* my month is up?"

"I'm sure!"

Miss Mattie sighed and shook her head, but Emily could see a slight grin. "Well Sugar," she began, "I've known Miz Green for years. When I met her she was Miss Redding, the librarian and that woman loved three things..."

Emily leaned back and finished her Danish. How she loved a good story.

As Emily picked up her backpack and got ready to leave, the bell over the bakery door jingled, and a giant of a man entered, accompanied by a very petite teen-aged girl. The man, who had a lower jaw that jutted out like Miss Violet's bulldog, had an unlit cigar stub clenched firmly between his teeth.

"Afternoon, ma'am," he smiled around the cigar, displaying front teeth the size of piano keys.

"Good day, sir," Miss Mattie replied, graciously, as she walked over to wait on him.

"My name's Callahan, J.T. Callahan," he said, extending his hand, and giving her a smile that displayed a full keyboard. "Just bought the little car dealership east of town."

He rolled the cigar stub to the other side of his mouth. "And this here," he said, turning to the petite girl standing beside him, "is my daughter Bitsy." His homely face lit up as he introduced his pretty daughter.

"Pleased to meet you both," said Miss Mattie. "And this," she said, turning to Emily, "is my friend Em'ly. Em'ly meet Mr. Callahan and Bitsy."

Bitsy? Emily stepped forward and shook each of their hands. "What's your real name, Bitsy?" she asked.

"Oh, it's Bernadette Claire-Marie," she cooed, "but goodness knows that's waaaay too big a name for lil' ole'me. So Big Daddy just calls me Bitsy, doncha,' Big Daddy?"

"That's right, darlin'," he said, looking at Bitsy like she was topping on a dessert. "Yessir," he repeated, hooking his thumbs in his suspenders, "we bought old Pete Jenkin's car dealership out on the highway, didn't we, Bitsy?"

"We sure did, Big Daddy," she giggled, with a flutter of her eyelashes.

Emily and Miss Mattie exchanged quick glances.

"Where did you and Bitsy move from, Mr. Callahan?" Miss Mattie asked.

"Jus' call me J.T., ma'am," he said, shifting the cigar stub again. "Me 'n Bitsy and Bitsy's mama moved here from Louisiana." Only he pronounced it *Weezianna.*

"My Bitsy here is a first-class cheerleader," he grinned, turning to her. "Aren't you darlin'?"

Bitsy fanned her eyelashes. "Oh Big Daddy! You're embarrassin' me."

"Show Miss Mattie and Em'ly some of your cheers, honey."

"Oh, Big Daddy," she said, with a slight pout, "no one wants to see my ol' cheers."

"Why *sure* they do, darlin'!" he boomed. "Now go on..."

"Well, if you're gonna insist."

Miss Mattie and Emily stared in disbelief, as Bitsy took two steps back and began dancing in place, and raising her arms, began shaking invisible pom poms.

"GIVE ME A *B*!" she shrieked.

Every customer in the bakery turned and gasped in amazement.

"B!" Big Daddy bellowed, with a foolish grin on his face.

"GIVE ME AN *I*!"

"I!" Big Daddy hooted, waving hands the size of catcher's mitts.

"GIVE ME A *T*!" she screamed, this time throwing in a high kick.

"T!" Big Daddy spun around in a circle, as Miss Mattie reached out and clutched the counter for support.

"GIVE ME AN *S*!"

"S!" Big Daddy brayed, grabbing Miss Mattie's hand and giving her a twirl.

Emily looked around at the customers. Their jaws had dropped open, and some had chewed up pastry in their mouth, which wasn't a pretty sight!

"GIVE ME A *Y*!"

"Y!" hooted Big Daddy.

After shrieking the last letter, Bitsy jumped straight up in the air and did a cartwheel toward a table where an elderly man was seated. He gasped, and nearly fell over backwards trying to get out of the way of her flying feet. Another customer had to grab his saucer of apple pie as Bitsy flew toward him, her right foot brushing his table.

"Heaven help me," Miss Mattie gasped, holding onto the counter for support.

"Good, ain't she," Big Daddy laughed, nudging her. He removed the cigar stub from between his teeth and gave Bitsy a loud whoop, clopping his catcher's mitts together in a hardy round of applause.

Bitsy and Big Daddy left the bakery shortly afterward, with a dozen mixed donuts, and a promise to return *real soon*. Miss Mattie collapsed into a chair as soon as the bakery door shut, and Emily made her a cup of tea, waiting on customers until Miss Mattie had fully recovered.

* * * *

On Wednesday afternoon Emily sat beside Miss Mattie on her over-sized sofa thumbing through a family picture album. She was thrilled to her toes at being invited up to the apartment over the bakery to look at family pictures—and she was staying for supper too! The room was snug and warm with the smell of chicken roasting in Miss Mattie's oven.

"This is me in my younger days with my baby sister, Eula," Miss Mattie said, pointing to two young girls with beautiful brown skin, and enormous eyes staring shyly at the camera. Miss Mattie turned the page.

"And here's my Herman," she said softly, touching the picture. "The finest man God ever made."

"How long were you married?" Emily asked, staring at the nice-looking man with a pleasant smile and large kind eyes.

"Fourteen years and three months, Sugar," Miss Mattie sighed. "The finest man God ever made," she repeated softly.

"Did you have any children?"

"No, Sugar we didn't," she replied wistfully. "That's one of the low places of my life—that no child ever called me mama. Herman would've made a fine daddy, too."

Mama. Emily mouthed the word softly, liking the feel of it on her lips. She leaned her head against Miss Mattie's soft shoulder and continued looking at pictures. *Mama,* she thought, a sigh escaping her. *Mama.*

"I think our supper mus' be jus' about ready," said Miss Mattie, closing the picture album and putting it on a side table. "Next time it's your turn to bring your family album and show me pictures."

Emily sat straight up. "I don't have a family album."

"Well then, how 'bout jus' some of your baby pictures."

"I'll check with my mom," Emily said. "I've never seen any pictures of me."

"Well Sugar," Miss Mattie said softly, "I'm sure they're jus' put up safe somewhere. Everybody has pictures." Miss Mattie patted her leg. "Come on and you can help me serve up our supper. You crumble up the bacon for the green beans, and I'll slice us up some of that delicious chicken that's been slow roastin' all afternoon."

All right, Mama, she whispered softly, as she followed Miss Mattie to the kitchen.

CHAPTER – 10

"Mom, do you have any pictures of me when I was a baby?" Emily stood behind her mother as she worked on the computer.

"*Why?*" her mother asked, clearly not pleased about being interrupted.

"I don't know. I just wanted to see what I looked like when I was little."

Her mother considered it a moment, then said, "I think they took one of you in the hospital when you were born."

"How about when I got older?"

"That's the only one," her mother said, growing irritated. "We didn't have a camera."

Emily felt stung to the core. *That was it?* No record of her childhood: a first birthday, a first tooth, a picture of family members looking at her lovingly–which also would have been a first.

Nothing. Nada. Zippo.

She could barely speak. "Do you mind getting me the picture?"

"I think it's in that shoe box at the top of the coat closet," her mother replied, irritably. "You can find it. I'm right in the middle of this."

She waited a brief second, hoping her mother would caution her to take good care of the only baby picture they had of her, but her mother went back to surfing the web.

Emily's heart began to race when she found the shoe box high on the closet shelf under some vacuum cleaner attachments. She took it down carefully, cradling it as she hurried to her room. She sat down on her bed and carefully opened the lid. The box contained an old address book, various coins, bobby pins, the top to a lipstick case, and other odds and ends. It looked like the contents of a woman's purse had been dumped into it. At the bottom of the box she found a yellowed envelope with a small stack of photos in it. Her hand trembled slightly as she lifted them out.

The first picture was an old black and white of two people that she didn't recognize. The edges of the picture looked like they had been cut with small pinking shears. She studied the picture closely; the young woman looked familiar. The next picture jolted her. It was of a young couple that looked like her mom and dad, staring happily into each other's eyes. Then she realized that it *was* her mom and dad. They were hugging in front of a sign that read, *Wedding Bells Chapel, Reno, Nevada.* Her parents' wedding picture. How terribly odd. Her mother's hair was long and parted down the middle; she was smiling up at her dad, who looked deep into her mother's eyes and smiled back. *He had loved her!* Emily could scarcely breathe as she studied the picture, and the reality of it hit her. *Her dad had loved her mother.*

The next picture was of a newborn dressed in a white cotton gown, squinting up at the camera; the baby had lots of red hair. This must be her. She sat staring at the picture a long time, looking deep into the eyes of the baby that she had once been. Here was the complete record of her babyhood and childhood. The baby could have been one of many—except for the hair. She hadn't seen too many newborns sprouting red hair, and it oddly pleased her.

The next picture was of a beautiful little red-haired girl in a blue party dress. She looked about two. So there was another picture of her! Her mother must have forgotten. Excited, she hurried to show it to her mother.

"Isn't this a picture of me?" she asked, holding the picture out for her mother to see.

Her mother turned and actually twitched when she saw the picture, then reached out and snatched it from Emily's hand.

"It's someone you don't know," she hissed. "Just get your picture and don't nose through everything."

"Is it a cousin or some other family member?" Emily asked, wanting desperately to know. "That little girl has red hair, too."

Her mother stood up, glaring at her. "You know I don't like answering a lot of questions." She tried to walk by her.

"But *why*?" Emily asked, putting her hand on her mother's arm. "Why don't we ever talk or ask questions? I don't know anything about me, or you, or any of our family. Do I have cousins or aunts and uncles?"

Her mother shook Emily's hand away. "There's nothing to talk about," she hissed, and went to the shredder and stuck the corner of the picture in. The machine was old, and it slowly churned to life as her mother fled the room.

Emily dove for the shredder, grabbing the picture and pulling straight up. She felt it rip. Her hand shook as she checked it for damage, but only the baby's shoe had been damaged.

Emily heard the lock click on her mother's bedroom door and knew she wouldn't see her for the rest of the day. Guilt started to well up, but she pushed it away. "It's okay if I ask questions," she said out loud. "I haven't done anything wrong." She tucked the picture of the little girl into her pocket and went back to her room.

She carefully gathered the pictures up and put them in a small box. These few pictures made a pretty slim beginning for a family photo album, but it was a start. She knew she should keep the picture of the little red-haired girl hidden, so she stuck it in a manila envelope and hid it next to her journal.

* * * *

Emily walked up behind her sleeping grandmother and gently laid a hand on her shoulder. Pearl started slightly and glared up at her with muddled eyes. When she saw it was Emily, her face softened just a little, and she growled, "What'd you wake me for?"

"I wanted to know what color your hair was when you were my age," Emily said, sliding down to the floor beside her. As she slid down, she unconsciously grabbed her grandmother's hand.

"You woke me up outta' my nap to find out what color my hair was?" Pearl snarled.

"I need to know," Emily said, her eyes imploring her grandmother to answer without getting mad.

Pearl touched the flattened gray wires of her hair. "Why, it was th' same color as yers," her grandmother replied slowly, her watery green eyes looking somewhere in the past. "Exactly th' same. I had freckles too, but they all faded." She peered closely at Emily. "Yer's are fadin' too."

They sat staring at each other. She never knew her grandmother had such soft hands. They felt frail and papery.

"I have pictures somewhere," Pearl growled, the hard edge returning to her voice. "Maybe I'll show 'em to you sometime." She pulled her hand out of Emily's.

"I'd really like to see them," Emily said, standing up and turning to leave.

"Em'ly..."

She turned and looked at her grandmother.

"We looked just alike, if that's what you was wonderin'."

* * * *

"It's my mom and dad's wedding picture," Emily said, handing the picture to Mrs. Apple. They sat before a roaring fire in the Apple's living room.

"They were a sweet-looking couple," Mrs. Apple said, studying it for a moment.

"What happened to them?"

Mrs. Apple looked at her. "Happened?"

"Yes. What happened to the couple in the picture? How did they start out that way and end up in the mess they're in?"

Mrs. Apple stared out the window and didn't answer right away. "That's pretty difficult to know dear, but let me try..." She returned the picture to Emily. "The best I can do is guess. But what I would guess is that their habits got them into trouble."

"*Habits?"* Emily sighed. Maybe Mrs. Apple was too old to know about this stuff.

"What kind of home did your parents come from?" Mrs. Apple asked.

"They never talk about it," Emily said, starting to feel depressed. "The only other family member I know is my grandmother."

"Do she and your mother have a good relationship?"

She couldn't help it, she burst out laughing. "Oh, it's just swell! Mrs. Apple, nobody in my house even talks to each other; they scream or throw things. I don't know what kind of home they came from."

"Well, dear, then here is my guess on that, too. Whatever habits they lived with as children came right into their marriage. Maybe not right at first, but later. As problems came up, they probably had no skills to handle them—so they handled them just the same way their parents had."

Emily stared at Mrs. Apple. "That's really sad," she said, hugging the sofa pillow.

"It's very sad, dear," Mrs. Apple said, looking at her evenly. "What can you do about it?"

"What can *I* do about it?" Emily stared off into space. "Nothing. There's nothing I can do about it."

"But you keep trying."

"Yes," she whispered.

"Tell me again the advice you heard from your TV doctor," Mrs. Apple said.

"*'You can't control your parent's choices; you can only control your own',"* she recited. "But that doesn't make me any less sad for my parents."

"Of course not, dear," her neighbor said, peering at her over her large glasses. "But you don't have the power to make it any better for them; you only have the power to make it better for yourself, and your children."

"I know it in my head," she whispered sadly, "but my heart hurts for them—for us. I keep trying to think of stuff to make it better."

"I know, dear, I did exactly the same thing when I was a young girl. But your focus has to be on your own future, and your own habits. That's *all* you can control."

Mrs. Apple took Emily's hands in hers. "And never ever be afraid to ask for help."

"Help? What kind of help?"

"Therapy, if you need it."

"Is that what you did?"

"Yes, I went to a therapist for a while," Mrs. Apple said, releasing Emily's hands as she thought back. "I also had wise friends—older friends, of course. When you're young, your friends don't know much more than you do."

Emily put her head back on the sofa. "Life's not simple, is it?"

"No, not always, dear," Mrs. Apple said, taking her hand again. "But the wiser you handle it, the simpler it will be. I promise."

* * * *

Later, as they were having lunch together, Emily sniffed a wonderful aroma coming from Mrs. Apple's oven.

"Is that what I think it is?" she asked.

Mrs. Apple laughed. "Yes, it's berry cobbler made with those beautiful blackberries you brought us." She went over to the kitchen counter. "And here's the bucket for you to return to your nun friend—all washed out."

"Thanks," Emily said. "Want to come with me when I return it?"

"It sounds like fun," Mrs. Apple said, "but I won't be able to." She looked at Emily. "I need to talk to you about something."

Emily felt her stomach tighten with apprehension.

"I've decided to take Mr. Apple to Florida for the winter," Mrs. Apple said. "His doctor thinks it's a good idea, since he keeps having relapses in this cold Virginia air."

Emily couldn't speak at first. "When are you going?" she finally whispered.

"In a few days."

"How long will you be gone?" she asked, hoping she didn't cry.

"'Til March or April," Mrs. Apple said. "Whenever it starts to warm back up." She patted Emily's hand. "I'm sad to leave, too dear, but he just isn't doing well."

Emily could only nod her head.

Mrs. Apple noticed and said, "Let me give you my cell number while I'm thinking about it." She got up and found a small notepad and pen. "Call anytime you need to talk," she said, trying to sound upbeat. "Remember, I'll only be a phone call away."

Emily nodded, not trusting herself to speak, as she took the number, deciding not to remind her neighbor that she didn't have a phone.

"I'll miss you," she said, biting her lower lip.

"I know dear, I'll miss you too," she said, taking Emily's hand and patting it. "Just remember the things we've talked about and keep writing in your journal. I'll be back before you know it."

The timer went off on the stove and Mrs. Apple grinned. "How about some hot berry pie with a scoop of vanilla bean ice cream?"

"Ok," she said, her spirits rising. "But let's give some to Mr. Apple first." She was secretly hoping that the yumminess of it would perk him up.

"He's napping, dear."

"Oh," Emily replied, feeling her spirits sink again.

* * * *

Emily felt nervous as she carried the empty bucket onto the church grounds of St. Daniels. She wasn't sure where the library was exactly but figured it must be somewhere behind the church. She strode down a narrow walkway that went by the bell tower and saw three buildings. She stood wondering which one was the library.

"May I help you?" asked a friendly voice behind her.

She turned around to see a tall priest with a big grin.

"I'm looking for Sister Mary Kathryn," Emily said. "I'm supposed to have tea with her in the library and return this bucket." She held it out as proof of her mission.

"Oh yes, Sister Merrie Kate," the priest said. "She's quite fond of berries."

"Sister *who?*"

"Merrie Kate," the priest smiled. "Just a nickname, of course. You'll understand as you get to know her."

"Oh..." Emily replied, with a grin. "Actually, I think I already do understand."

"I'm Father Patrick," he said, extending a hand.

"I'm Emily," she replied, shaking the priest's hand.

"Well Emily, this way to the library," he said, gesturing for her to follow. The priest took off at a trot and Emily nearly had to run to keep up with him.

Father Patrick stopped in front of one of the buildings and pointed to the library sign. Emily thanked him and went in. She took a seat and Sister Mary Kathryn hurried in a few minutes later, grinning from ear to ear.

"I'm so glad you came," she said, and Emily found herself once again enfolded in the great swathes of Sister Mary Kathryn's dark habit. "Now let's get our tea," the sister said, holding her at arm's length.

An ornate table had been laid out with a beautiful tea service. Emily noticed another nun seated close by having tea with an elderly woman.

Sister Mary Kathryn poured their tea into delicate china cups. "Sugar?" she asked, using silver tongs to offer a sugar cube.

"No, thank you," Emily replied, taking the cup. She watched as the sister dropped four sugar cubes into her own cup, stirred and tasted it, then threw in another cube for good measure.

"Let's sit right over here," the sister said, looking as pleased as if the Queen of England had come for a visit.

They sat facing each other in tall ornate chairs that looked like wooden thrones; Emily's feet didn't even touch the ground. The nun seated nearby smiled at her, and Sister Mary Kathryn introduced them. "Sister Susan, meet Emily."

Sister Susan grinned and introduced her elderly friend, Mrs. Brooks. Each of them murmured their hellos, and Sister Susan and Mrs. Brooks went back to talking.

"So how did Mr. Apple like his berry cobbler?" Sister Mary Kathryn asked. She sat with her teacup in her lap, ankles crossed, swinging her feet like a schoolgirl.

"I heard that he loved it," Emily said, "but Mrs. Apple is taking him to Florida soon. He's not getting any better."

"Does their leaving make you sad?" the sister asked, peering at her over the teacup.

Emily nodded.

"It shows on your face," the sister said, leaning forward and patting her hand. "Now tell me all about your good friends."

To her amazement, Emily blurted out the whole story of her neighbors—from belly laughs with Mr. Apple, to Mrs. Apple giving her a journal.

"Ahhh," Sister Mary Kathryn said, taking a sip of her tea. "Just as I suspected. They're very special friends."

Emily nodded, biting her bottom lip. She felt like she might burst into tears.

"Well, then," Sister Mary Kathryn said, clasping her hands and looking pensive, "let's think of some things for you to do, so you can stay busy while your friends are gone."

"Invite her to our music Mass," blurted out Sister Susan.

Sister Mary Kathryn and Emily looked at her.

"Excuse me," Sister Susan said, her face reddening, "I couldn't help overhearing."

They all laughed and Sister Mary Kathryn asked, "Do you like music?"

Emily nodded.

"Wonderful!" she replied. "Would you like to come to our informal song service on Wednesday nights to hear us play?"

Emily was intrigued. "What instrument do you play?"

"The sax is my favorite."

"You play the saxophone!" Emily felt a belly laugh coming on.

"Oh yes—and the banjo too—but I really prefer the sax."

"And she's very good at it," spoke up Sister Susan, blinking behind her large glasses.

"Sister Susan plays the bass," Sister Mary Kathryn informed her. "And the third member of our trio is Sister Caroline, who plays the guitar.

"Are you jazz players?" asked Emily, knowing a bit about music herself.

"Well," confided Sister Mary Kathryn, with a twinkle in her eye, "we have been called *The Blues Sisters*."

* * * *

"How in the world did I get talked into this?" Emily muttered, as she slogged up the street toward Violet's House of Beauty.

As she pushed through the door of the hair salon, she was greeted by a platinum blonde hairstylist. "How ya doin,' honey?" the woman smiled, her small jaw working overtime on a wad of pink bubble gum.

"I'm doing okay," she replied, walking over to greet her. "My name's Emily."

They shook hands. "Pleased to meetcha' Em'ly, my name's Charmagne. Rhymes with *champagne*."

Charmagne's tongue darted out as she blew a small bubble. "You goin' to the Young Ladies' Academy?"

Emily couldn't help sighing. "Yes, I am."

The hair stylist nodded toward the back of the salon. "The Academy's that way, honey."

Emily turned and saw the sign over the doorway: *Young Ladies Academy, Miss Violet & Miss Rose, hostesses.*

She heard clattering and turned to see where it was coming from. Miss Violet came into view tottering on five-inch heels, fluttering a laced handkerchief. Emily gazed in amazement at her gold parachute pants, topped with a gold embroidered vest and matching open-toed shoes. Gold earrings, the size of ketchup bottles, dangled from her ears and swung wildly as she tottered in. Emily stifled a laugh. Miss Violet looked like a character straight out of *The Arabian Nights*. Her bulldog stood at her side glaring.

"Emily! Welcome!" trilled Miss Violet, fluttering the handkerchief at her.

Emily smiled weakly and her eyes began to water, as vapors of Miss Violet's *Evening in Paris* perfume fogged in around her.

Miss Violet reached down and picked up the dog. "Mitzi," she cooed, "you simply *must* say hello to Emily!"

Mitzi had on a gold jacket that matched Miss Violet's, and a collar that matched her earrings. Emily reached out and gently patted the dog's head. Mitzi bared her ugly teeth and snapped at Emily's fingers.

"Mitzi! You naugh-ty, naugh-ty thing!" Miss Violet scolded. "Say you are sorry right now!"

She held the dog up to Emily's face, as though she expected Mitzi to bark an immediate apology.

"It's okay," Emily assured, stepping back.

"Mitzi, Mitzi," Miss Violet cooed, as she rubbed noses with the dog. "Whatever would Miss Gaynor think of your naughtiness?"

"Who's Miss Gaynor?" Emily asked.

Miss Violet appeared taken back. "But surely you've heard of Miss Gaynor."

Emily shook her head.

"You know, dahling, Mitzi Gaynor, the actress. Come now, Emily, you simply *must* have heard of her!"

For a moment, Emily was tempted to pretend she had heard of her, but instead shook her head again.

"She is *simply* a classic!" Miss Violet said, rolling her eyes heavenward. "Mitzi Gaynor is my *dearest* and most favorite actress from the fifties. I simply *adore* her movies."

"Oh," Emily murmured, wishing she had never asked.

"Well, *do* come right on in and meet the other girls!" Miss Violet trilled, setting Mitzi down beside her. Emily followed at a safe distance to give her lungs a break from the perfume. As Miss Violet tottered ahead of her, she noticed the bulldog's rear end and Miss Violet's rear end waddled exactly the same way.

Miss Violet fluttered her lace handkerchief this way and that as she walked. Emily had never seen her when she wasn't fluttering something: a scarf, a handkerchief, or an empty cigarette holder. She had asked Gus about the empty cigarette holder.

"It's on account of th' fact that Miss Vi'let smoked like a chimney stack for thirty years," he had told her, "until all them reports come out on lung cancer and such. She give up smokin' pretty easy, it was that dang cigarette holder she missed. She went to carryin' it around *empty*—flappin' it in yer face like a dern baton."

"There is a seat right over there, *dear*," Miss Violet was saying—only she pronounced it *de-ah.*

Somewhere along the way—and nobody could remember when—Miss Violet had acquired a slight English accent.

Emily had asked Gus about that, also.

"She's highfalutin'," Gus had said, "watches too many old movies."

Emily sat down in a blue folding chair and turned to greet the petite girl sitting next to her. She was startled to see that the dark-haired girl had two tissues stuffed up her nose and tears streaming down her face.

"Hi," she said, trying not to stare at the tissues. "I'm Emily.

The girl waved at her miserably.

"Do you have a cold?" Emily asked.

"Naw, its Miss Vi'let's perfume," the girl said, her voice sounding like a clogged drain pipe. "I swear that perfume mus' kill ever' bug in th' county. My name's Kelly Ann, pleased to meetcha."

Kelly Ann...Kelly Ann... Where had she heard that name?

"Are you Ike's granddaughter?" Emily asked.

"Yep, that's me," she grinned. "Straight from Atwater, Mississippi."

CHAPTER - 11

Kelly Ann, who dressed for the occasion in blue jeans with stylish rips in the legs, and a rainbow-colored sweater, kept up a steady stream of blowing and honking all during the meeting of the Young Ladies Academy. Emily almost laughed out loud, as Kelly Ann gave her side glances each time she dramatically blew her nose and moaned. After class was over, Emily decided this was as good a time as ever to start making friends. It would certainly make Mrs. Apple happy anyway.

She turned to Kelly Ann and said, "I'm going to the bakery when I leave here. Want to come?"

Kelly Ann's eyes actually lit up. "Would ah' ever," she whooped. "Let's git outta here. Ah' love me some sweets."

Emily laughed, enjoying her new friend's drawl, which was as thick as chowder. Kelly Ann threw on her denim jacket and bolted toward the door. Emily felt a twinge of guilt, thinking she should go over and say good-bye to Miss Rose and Miss Violet. In the end, she just waved at them and bolted after Kelly Ann.

When they entered Cooke's Bakery, Kelly Ann ran straight for the glass case. "This stuff smells better 'n gooseberry pie fresh outta the ov'n," she said, peering intently through the glass case.

Emily smiled at Miss Mattie and turned to introduce Kelly Ann. As she gave the introduction, Kelly Ann mumbled "Hi" and kept her eyes glued to the pastries, not even looking at Miss Mattie.

Emily was shocked at her rudeness, and when she looked up at Miss Mattie, she saw fire in her eyes. Everything got quiet.

Kelly Ann noticed and looked up at a tight-lipped Miss Mattie. "Did I miss somethin'?"

"Yes, ma'am, you did," said Miss Mattie, evenly. "You missed greeting me properly. Emily, would you make the introductions again, please."

Cringing with embarrassment, Emily said, "Kelly Ann, this is my friend, Miss Mattie. Miss Mattie this is Kelly Ann, Ike's granddaughter from Mississippi."

Miss Mattie extended her hand with a smile and a nod, "Welcome to Mountain Grove, Kelly Ann. I'm pleased to meet you."

"Likewise," said Kelly Ann, ignoring Miss Mattie's hand and turning back to the glass case.

Miss Mattie's eyes smoldered.

Mortified, Emily said, "Kelly Ann, can I talk to you a minute...in private? Excuse us, Miss Mattie."

In the corner of the bakery, Emily whispered fiercely, "If you don't have better manners, Miss Mattie will boot you out of here."

"She'll what!" Kelly Ann yelped. "What is this, Russia or somethin'?"

"Shhh!" Emily hissed. "Miss Mattie is really strict about manners. When I introduce you, look at her and say, 'Pleased to meet you, too—not *likewise*'. That's rude! Then shake her hand—and do it like you mean it."

"Oh fer Pete's sake..."

"Shhh! Come on."

Emily made the introductions again.

"Pleased ta' meet you, Miss Mattie," Kelly Ann said, looking directly into her eyes. She gave her a hearty handshake, even added a curtsy. Emily couldn't tell if Kelly Ann was just being sassy.

"It's very nice to make your acquaintance also, Kelly Ann," Miss Mattie said, the fire gone out of her eyes. "Now, what can I get for you ladies today?"

"I cain't decide," Kelly Ann said with a shrug. "How 'bout we could buy two things an' split 'em?" she said, turning to Emily.

Emily nodded eagerly, and both girls chose the pastry they wanted, then went and sat down at one of the small round tables near the front window. It wasn't long before Miss Mattie came out from behind the glass case with the pastries, wearing a bright yellow apron, dotted with purple palm trees, and flying red parrots.

Kelly Ann's eyes bulged. "What in th' world is that woman wearin'?" she whispered, as Miss Mattie sashayed toward them.

"Shhhh," Emily laughed, nudging her arm.

Miss Mattie set two doily-lined China plates on the table. One plate held an enormous Napoleon; the other held a cream puff drizzled with chocolate. They were both sliced down the middle for sharing.

"Would you like to sit with us?" Emily asked Miss Mattie.

"Thank you, I'd love to," Miss Mattie said, pulling up a chair. She watched as the girls feasted on her world-class pastries. "So how was Miss Violet's class today, ladies?" she asked.

Both girls looked at each other and rolled their eyes.

"We learned about proper place settings, and which forks go where, and all that," said Emily, wasting no time in polishing off her half of the cream puff.

"Well, that's somethin' good to know," Miss Mattie said, pushing a couple of napkins toward them. "Especially if you ever go into a fancy restaurant!"

"I guess so," said Emily, wiping off the blob of whipped cream that had dropped on her shirt. "It's just that Miss Violet is so goofy, with her English accent and those big earrings."

"Yeah," Kelly Ann added, "I was skeered one of her earrings was gonna swing 'round an' knock 'er tooth out or somethin'."

They all laughed.

"She's pretty flamboyant, all right," Miss Mattie agreed. Then changing the subject, she asked, "How long have you been in town, Kelly Ann?"

"Oh, near a week or so," said Kelly Ann, bits of her Napoleon spraying out of her mouth. Emily cringed and handed her a napkin.

Miss Mattie waited for her to swallow her food, and asked, "How do you like livin' in Mountain Grove so far?"

"Well, I'm used to a town that goes a lil' bit faster, ma'am," she said. "There's not a whole lot ta do 'round here." She shrugged. "But I know how to dig up fun, so I'll be fine."

"Is that so?" said Miss Mattie, a worry line creasing her brow.

The girls finished their pastries and pulled money out of their pockets to pay. Miss Mattie held up her hand and said, "You girls go spend your money shoppin'; this is my welcome treat for Kelly Ann."

Emily hugged her. "Thank you, Miss Mattie. I'll see you later."

"You're welcome, Sugar," said Miss Mattie, hugging her back.

Kelly Ann was already at the door. "Thank you, ma'am. Nice meetin' you."

"You're welcome, Kelly Ann. It was good to have met you too."

Miss Mattie stood at the window, watching the girls cross the street. Their heads were together, and Kelly Ann was laughing.

"Hmmm, I wonder 'bout that girl, "Miss Mattie said out loud, as warning signs popped up in her mind, like so many jackrabbits in a field.

* * * *

Monday came too soon. Emily sighed as she sat down in her Spanish class, putting her backpack on the floor next to her.

"Attention, class!"

Emily looked up at Miss Graham, who stood with her arm around Bitsy Callahan.

"Attention, class," Miss Graham repeated. "We have a new student joining us."

Miss Graham waited until all the students were looking her way. "Class, this is Bernadette Claire-Marie Callahan," she said, and actually smiled down at Bitsy. "Her family has moved here recently from Louisiana, and I want you all to make her feel very welcome.

Bitsy flashed them all a smile and fanned her thick lashes. Emily noticed her dimples for the first time, as some of the boys shifted in their seats.

"Now remember, Miss Graham," she cooed, "you promised to call me Bitsy. Bernadette Clarie-Marie is jus' too long a name for lil' ole' me."

Gag me with a spoon, thought Emily. *A big spoon.*

"Of course, dear," Miss Graham cooed back. She turned to the class and said, "I need someone to show Bitsy around at lunch time. Who would like to volunteer?"

Most of the boys in the class immediately raised their hands. Miss Graham gazed around the room, trying to decide who to choose. Some of the boys began to flag their hands back and forth, make grunting sounds to get Miss Graham's attention.

Emily shook her head and looked away in disgust.

Miss Graham glanced at Emily, then over at Jonathan, who was thumbing through a book, appearing to be quite disinterested in the whole matter. "Jonathan," she trilled, "would you mind showing Bitsy where the cafeteria is?"

Jonathan looked up, shifting uncomfortably. "Actually, Miss Graham, I thought I'd go home for lunch today."

"Nonsense!" sniffed Miss Graham, giving Emily a side glance. "Here are two lunch tickets for the cafeteria. I think you're just the one to show Bitsy around."

Emily glared at her, thinking she would like nothing more than to knock Miss Graham in the head.

Without any more discussion, Miss Graham patted Bitsy on the back, and said, "You two have a nice lunch!"

"Thank you, Miss Graham," cooed Bitsy. She started for her seat, then stopped. "Oh, and by the way...I *really* love your shoes," she said, smiling up at her. "I'm gonna ask Big Daddy to buy me some cute flats like that."

"Why thank you, dear," Miss Graham said, looking foolishly pleased, as she clomped over and handed the two lunch tickets to Jonathan.

* * * *

Dear Journal,

I wonder if there is anyone in the whole world meaner than Miss Graham, or dopier than Bitsy Callahan? Miss Graham insisted that Jonathan take Bitsy to lunch today, and she kept glancing at me to see if I cared. I didn't, but it made me mad that she put Jonathan on the spot that way. Well, maybe I cared a little. I sincerely hope Bitsy gagged on her sandwich and it spewed out her nose.

E.

* * * *

Emily blew into Good Eats Café after school and saw Montana sitting at a booth. She went over and greeted him. "I met Custer the other day at the camera shop," she grinned.

"Really!" said Montana, wiping the table off with his napkin. "Did you two have a good talk?"

"He gave me advice on what camera to buy."

"So you really *are* interested in cameras."

"I'm interested in *photography,"* she said, correcting him, "and guess what? I'm taking lessons from Miles Taylor in a few days."

"Well, how about that," Montana smiled. "As the official news reporter of this fair village, I should have better tabs on what our young citizens are doing."

She grinned and headed for a stool at the counter.

"Whoa, Emily!" Montana said. "Custer will be here any minute. Sit down and join us."

She hesitated, wanting to sit with them, but feeling like she might be intruding. Before she could invent a getaway, Millie appeared with her order pad.

"Git a load off yer feet, Em'ly," she said, shooing her into the seat across from Montana. "You two 'bout ready t' order?"

"We'll give it another minute," Montana started to say, but the café door flew open and Custer strode in decked out in a leather vest, red plaid shirt, and jeans tucked into snakeskin cowboy boots. As he headed toward the back booth, he looked surprised to see Emily sitting across from his brother.

"Hey, everybody," Custer said, as he tossed his cowboy hat on the rack next to Montana's.

"Howdy, partner," Montana said, in his best southern drawl. "Nice boots!"

They all peered down at Custer's pointed boots; they were the exact style and made of the same snakeskin as Montana's, except Custer's boots were red.

"Good to see you all," Custer said, as he slid onto the seat next to his brother. "Are we having a party?"

"No, my honorable brother," Montana said, handing him a menu. "Emily was just telling me that she'd met you over at Taylor's, so I invited her to sit with us. I thought you could dispense some more of your photographic genius."

"Good! Glad you joined us," Custer smiled at Emily. Millie twiddled her pencil waiting for everyone to decide what they wanted.

Emily just wanted a root beer float. Montana picked up the little sign on their table that read, *Blue Plate Special*, and held it up for Custer to see.

Custer nodded.

"Two Blue Plate Specials, Millie," Montana said, "and give us the works—mashed potatoes and gravy, fried chicken, corn on the cob. We want all the trimmings."

"*And* all the fat," Millie groused, gathering up the menus.

"Party pooper," Montana growled, as Millie left with their orders.

"So, Emily," Custer said, "how did you become interested in photography?"

"I don't really know," she said, trying to think back. "Some of the kids at school have a photography club, and after I saw some of their pictures they'd hung in the hallway, I wanted to try it too. Now when I see clouds in the sky, I want to take a picture of it, or if I see people doing stuff, I think, *That would make a good picture.* But I don't have a camera, so I just think about it."

"So your mind converts things into a picture?"

"Sometimes. Like when we're sitting here," she said. "I'd like to get a ladder, set a camera above us at an angle, and title it, *Three Friends.*"

Both men grinned and Custer said, "Wow! You really *do* have the bug."

Emily smiled.

"And I am honored that you consider us friends," Montana added.

She blushed, wishing she would learn not to let her thoughts just pop out of her mouth.

"How much more money do you need to buy your camera?" Custer asked.

"Well, I had three hundred dollars, but I paid $75.00 to take the photography class," she said. "If the camera is five hundred, plus tax, then I think I need about three hundred more."

"You'll need a little more than that," Custer said, "because you'll need to buy a memory card; the one that comes with the camera usually holds about fifty pictures. A card that holds 1000 pictures is about forty-five dollars. Plus, you'll need a camera case to protect your investment. A good one costs around fifty dollars."

"And maybe I should get a tripod," she said, as Millie set a huge root beer float down in front of her.

"Knock yerself out, kiddo!" Millie grinned.

"Wow! Thanks Millie, I've never seen a root beer float this big!"

"Well, that's 'cause I only give extra scoops to hard workers," Millie said, handing her a long spoon. "Thanks honey, for fillin' in for me so I could be with my gran'babies." She reached over and gave Emily a quick hug. "Eat up before it melts."

"I love these things," Emily said, taking a long pull on her straw. "Yummy!"

"You must've scored big with her," Montana said, as Millie went to get their Blue Plate Specials. "She's never given me anything extra, except a lecture on my cholesterol."

They all laughed.

"So, do you have any way to come up with another four hundred dollars, Emily?" Custer asked, getting back to the subject.

"Sure!" she said, surprised he was interested. "Sometimes I work for Ike or Mr. Charles. Miss Mattie needs help on Wednesdays." She spooned a large bite of ice cream into her mouth, relishing its creamy texture. "Don't worry," she said, pointing her long spoon for emphasis. "I'll get it."

"I have no doubt of that," Custer said, glancing over at his brother. They winked at each other as Millie set their plates down in front of them.

"I hope you boys are goin' for a long walk after eatin' all this," Millie lectured. "Your cholesterol will be jumpin' over the moon." She hurried off to wait on another customer.

The men ignored Millie and dug into their meals, chewing happily.

"If I may quote you, Emily," Custer said, between bites, "This is *yummy*!"

"Great stuff!" Montana agreed, reaching for the saltshaker. As he did, the fringes on his suede jacket dipped down into his gravy.

"Shoot!" said Montana, lifting his elbow and carefully wiping off each fringe. "What kind of a cowboy has gravy on his fringes?"

"Absolutely shameful," Custer agreed, checking his own fringes.

Emily laughed, happy to be in their company. "Tell me about some of your photography jobs," she said to Custer.

He dug into his mashed potatoes. "Well, let's see, which one should I tell about?"

"Tell her about your assignment in Kenya," Montana said, slathering butter on his corn. He glanced over to make sure Millie wasn't watching.

"Ah yes, Kenya, where I nearly got harpooned in the rear by a rhino," Custer mused. "Don't ever climb a short tree if a rhino is chasing you, Emily."

"Thanks for the warning," she laughed. "What happened?"

"Well, I'd been hired by National Geographic to photograph animals of the African plain with their young," he began. "I wasn't that experienced..."

As Custer told his story, one by one, heads turned in the café and customers began to listen. In no time, Custer had them all howling over his photo shoot, as they pictured a pony-tailed Custer sprinting across the African plain and being treed by a female rhino.

"I'd still be in that acacia tree if my driver hadn't rescued me," he laughed.

When she had finished her float, Emily stood up and smiled at the two men. "Thanks for your help and advice," she said, laying three dollars on the table.

"Hey, your money's no good in here," Custer said, handing it back to her.

"Well...thank you," she said, feeling awkward. "And thanks for the advice and great stories." She could barely hold her stomach in, she was so stuffed.

"Bye everyone!" she called over her shoulder. The restaurant patrons all yelled their goodbyes as she left the café.

"Can't her parents give her a hand with some of the money?" Custer asked, after Emily was safely out of hearing range.

"I think most of their money goes for booze," his brother replied.

"You're kidding!"

"I wish I were, honorable brother, I wish I were. That girl has it pretty rough at home. She's a great kid, too."

Custer shook his head and stared down at his plate for a minute. "I think I may need to hire someone on a photo shoot I'm doing around here," he said finally. "Would you happen to have Emily's phone number?"

"And I was thinking I might need someone to help over at the newspaper office," Montana said. "And no, I don't have a phone number for her."

Custer reached for his black leather planner. "I wonder how I could get ahold of her then?"

"Her dad's cell phone is the only one they use, but I wouldn't recommend trying to reach her that way. I have a feeling it would cause trouble. You can find her here, or she's at Mattie's bakery a lot."

They put their cowboy hats on, paid the bill and left. Out on the sidewalk, Custer said, "If you see Emily, tell her I'm looking for her."

"Will do," Montana said, giving his brother a brief hug before heading across the street to the newspaper office.

* * * *

It stormed the next day, so after school Emily headed for the library. She curled up in an overstuffed reading chair in the fiction section and opened her latest adventure story. As she read, a shadow fell across her book. She looked up to see Jonathan smiling down at her, water dripping off his jacket.

"That must be a really good book," he grinned, "you didn't even hear me when I walked up to you."

"So how was lunch with Bitsy yesterday?" Emily blurted out, then bit her lip. She couldn't believe what had just come out of her mouth.

Jonathan looked surprised, then burst out laughing. He knelt down by her chair. "I know what you've been thinking about," he teased. "Were you jealous?"

"No!" she said, trying to appear indignant.

"Good," he said, pretending to believe her. "Bitsy is really goofy."

"She is?"

"She definitely is," he said. "An air-head, too."

"She is?"

"Absolutely," he grinned. "You want to hear more?"

She smiled back, suddenly feeling wonderful... expansive... ready to do something fun. "It's stuffy in here, want to walk to the river?" she asked, tossing her book aside.

"Did you forget that it's storming outside?"

"Oh...right," she said, feeling herself blush.

"I have to take care of some paperwork at home, anyway," he said, reaching over and squeezing her hand. "I just wanted to see you for a few minutes."

"You did?"

He nodded. "I wanted you to know that I wished I'd handed that lunch ticket to one of the other guys yesterday. I didn't realize, until later, what Miss Graham was doing."

"You do? I mean, you didn't?"

"No. I usually expect the best from people, but that was a set-up against you— and it was pretty rotten."

"I wanted to knock her in the head," she confessed.

Jonathan laughed. "I like a person who says what's on their mind."

That's a relief, she thought, liking the feeling of his hand on hers.

"Well, I need to get home," he said, squeezing her hand as he stood up. "I'm applying to a school in England for their foreign exchange program, and I need to have the application in the mail by tomorrow."

"That's exciting," she said, smiling up at him. "Thanks for coming by."

"See you later," he said, giving her pony tail a gentle tug, before he turned and left.

She found herself humming as she returned to her book.

* * * *

Emily trudged up First Street looking for Kelly Ann; they had become good friends in a short time. Emily had been a loner for so long that it surprised her how much she enjoyed hanging out with someone her own age. They had gone to the movies together, had lunch at Good Eats, and hung out at the park a number of times. It turned out that Kelly Ann was a lot of fun, and Emily liked being around someone who made her laugh.

As she turned the corner and headed toward Second Street, she spotted Kelly Ann walking toward her with a group of kids.

Kelly Ann gave her a big grin. "Hey, Em'ly!" she yelled from half a block away. "We're headin' for th' picnic grounds, wanna' come?"

The picnic grounds? she thought. *Didn't Kelly Ann know about the picnic grounds?*

"I already have plans," she said, as they drew closer. She started to just walk on by, but then she stopped. "Kelly Ann, could I talk to you for just a sec?"

She walked out of hearing range and waited for her.

"What's up?" Kelly Ann asked, as she hurried over.

"Kelly Ann, do you know what they do over at the picnic grounds?"

"No, what?" she shrugged.

"They smoke, and drink, and do drugs."

Kelly Ann burst out laughing. "You goofy. I've been 'round all that b'fore."

"But..."

"Don't worry, Emmy Lou," she laughed, reaching over to hug her. "I kin take care of myself. See ya later!"

She watched forlornly as Kelly Ann rejoined her friends. They walked up the street and turned right on River Road, toward the picnic grounds.

She sighed, wondering if she should have said more. She also wished she had never told Kelly Ann that her middle name was Louise. *Emmy Lou* wasn't exactly a name she wanted to be tagged with.

* * * *

"What're you thinkin' so hard about, Sugar?" Miss Mattie asked, as Emily plowed into a cream-filled donut. They were sitting in their usual spot after school, while Miss Mattie "took her break."

Emily looked up a little startled and blushed. "Next week is my birthday, and I want to ask my mom and dad for a memory card for the camera I'm buying, but then I'd have to answer a lot of questions."

"Your birthday! How wonderful!" Miss Mattie said, with a smile as big and bright as the moon. "You havin' a party?"

"No," she said, sounding shocked. "I never have a party. My parents don't like to be around people, remember? Especially a house full of people. They'd faint."

"So how do you celebrate?" Miss Mattie asked. "A family dinner with cake and ice cream? Or do they take you out for dinner?"

She just stared at Miss Mattie. "Do you know how uncomfortable that would be?"

She popped the last bite of donut into her mouth, but when she looked up, she saw that Miss Mattie was waiting for an explanation.

She sighed, then explained, "We never sit down to dinner, and I don't want to anyway." She looked evenly at Miss Mattie. "If my parents are together more than five minutes, they fight. For my birthday they'll buy me a gift and put it on the kitchen table. When I thank them for it, my dad will say, 'Well, Happy Birthday' and my mom will too if she's not too depressed."

"How 'bout a birthday cake?" Miss Mattie asked, her brow furrowed.

"Nope," she shrugged, "and I don't want them to get me one. It would be way too weird to pretend, for even five minutes, that we're a normal family while they sing *Happy Birthday.*" She allowed herself to picture such an extraordinary scene. "Way too weird."

Her mind scampered around for something else to talk about, but Miss Mattie had more questions.

"You mean that you've *never* in your life had a birthday cake?"

"I don't care about that, Miss Mattie," Emily said, desperately wanting to change the subject. "Really I don't."

Miss Mattie looked like she was ready to yank someone's chain, and Emily burst out laughing. She just loved Miss Mattie!

Emily stood up and went over to her, putting her arms around her in a bear hug. "Miss Mattie, on a scale of one to ten in my life, a birthday cake is a *one*–a minus one. *Normal* is important and *peace* is important. That's what you are to me, and I need that way more than cake."

She heard Miss Mattie gulp, and when she looked, she saw huge tears sliding down her beautiful brown cheeks. Emily scooted her chair over and put her head on Miss Mattie's shoulder as she continued to gulp.

CHAPTER – 12

Emily hurried down Elderberry Lane and glimpsed Kelly Ann waiting for her in front of Gus' station, looking very cute in dark pants and a beautiful blue sweater.

"Happy Birthday!" Kelly Ann yelled, running up and throwing her arms around her.

"Thank you," she laughed, returning the hug. "Are you announcing it to the whole village?"

"That's a great idea!" Kelly Ann said, cupping her hands around her mouth.

"Don't you dare," Emily laughed, pulling her hands down.

Kelly Ann ran a few steps ahead, stopped and shouted at the top of her lungs, "EVERYONE IN MOUNTAIN GROVE...IT'S EMILY'S BIRTHDAY TODAY !!!"

Emily ran up to her. "Stop!" she said, laughing.

Laughing and fussing, they continued walking toward First Street, as Kelly Ann yelled the birthday message to anyone she saw. She had invited Emily to the movies for her birthday–her treat.

"I have ta' stop in at Gran'pa's and git somethin'," Kelly Ann said, as they neared First Street.

"The movie starts in about twelve minutes," Emily reminded her, wishing she'd worn something nicer than her black sweater and blue jeans.

"It'll only take us a sec," Kelly Ann said, making a bee line for the café. She pushed the café door open and motioned for Emily to go in ahead of her.

The first thing Emily noticed were pink and white balloons bobbing all around. She glanced toward the middle of the room and saw a table pulled to the center of the café–on it was a three-tiered cake, also in pink and white. The café was packed with people she knew, and everyone was smiling at her.

"Surprise! Happy Birthday! Surprise!" they all sang out at once.

Emily stepped back toward the door, feeling like she was going to faint.

"Go on in, goofy," Kelly Ann laughed, gently pushing her forward.

Miss Mattie, dressed in a beautiful peacock colored dress and matching hat, walked over to Emily with her arms out. "Happy Birthday, Sugar!" she said, giving her a warm hug, and a smile as bright as the new moon.

Emily was speechless as she looked around the café at the streamers, balloons, and beautifully decorated tables. She finally found her voice. "You did this for me?" she whispered to Miss Mattie.

"I couldn't think of anyone I'd rather do it for!" Miss Mattie smiled, taking her by the hand and leading her over to the cake.

Emily read the inscription: *Happy 15th Birthday Emily!*

Touched beyond measure, she whispered, "Thank you!"

As Emily looked around the room, everyone had smiles that seemed to wrap around their heads; she'd never seen so many sets of teeth grinning at her. She smiled back, her eyes filling with tears.

Gus stood up on a chair and using one of Ike's big cooking spoons as a baton, he took the stance of a musical conductor. He tapped the spoon on the back of the chair to get their attention, raised the spoon high and began to bellow, *Happy Birthday to You!*

Everyone joined in. *Happy Birthday to You...*

Emily looked at the circle of people around her: There was Kelly Ann grinning foolishly as she sang; Mr. and Mrs. Green stood with arms around each other, happily belting out the song. Next to them were Mr. and Mrs. Charles, and Jonathan; Custer and Montana, who were busily taking notes, and snapping pictures for the newspaper; Miss Rose stood next to Miss Violet, who was holding Mitzy; the dog was dressed in a tiny, blue party dress with a red geranium behind her ear. There was Bill and Iris Head, Mr. Kingery, Mr. and Mrs. Montoya, Ike and Millie, and a couple of people she didn't even know...all singing with mouths wide open...

Happy Birth-day, deeeeeeeeear Em-i-ly! Happy Birthday to YOU!!!

After the song, everyone broke into a thundering round of applause. Emily laughed and did a slight curtsey. Custer stepped to the center and told everyone to find a seat. Every empty space held folding chairs, which were quickly filled; the rest of the guests crowded into the café's dining booths.

"We are here to celebrate Emily, and her journey through the teen-age years," Custer announced.

The whole crowd hooted.

"Now Emily," he said, turning toward her, "we've all been down the path you're on, and some of us, who've gone before you, would like to offer a bit of advice."

She grinned, clasping her hands in anticipation.

Custer paused and looked at his list. "The first to speak will be Gus."

Everyone applauded as a dapper looking Gus came forward, wearing a blue suit. He stood by the cake, adjusting his tie self-consciously. Emily took a seat, then Gus bowed slightly and said to her, "Well now, Em'ly, what I learnt' durin' my teen years was never to sass my pa."

Everyone in the crowd smiled.

"When I got to be 'bout fifteen, my pa started irritatin' the life outta me," Gus began, with a grin. "He insisted on givin' me drivin' lessons—as if any fool don't know how to drive. One day we got in that old Pontiac of ours for my practice drive, and it all went pretty well, 'cept my pa made me drive too durn slow.

" *'Slow 'er down Gus,'* he said to me over and over again, 'til he liked to git on my last nerve. Well, I knew he was old and slow—he was 'bout thirty-six at the time—and I figured I could show him how to live a little."

"About the tenth time he told me ta' slow down, I sez', '*Hang on, Pa. We're gonna have us a lil' fun.'* I punched th' accelerator on that ol' blue Pontiac, and we was off like a scalded hog."

The crowd roared.

"I careened aroun' them corners and, boy, did I ever make the gravel fly! My ol' pa was white as a ghost an' hangin' on fer dear life, hollerin' at me ta' beat th' band." Gus imitated his father clutching his seat, and Emily doubled over with laughter.

"Well, I started gettin' a little concerned over his re-action," Gus continued. "I tried making some smart aleck jokes, but that wasn't goin' over too big either."

The whole room was laughing, some wiping their eyes with tissues and napkins.

"Well sir," Gus continued, "I figgered I'd better stop that car in a public place, 'cause my pa had gotten a tad bit madder than I'd expected him to." Gus grinned, shaking his head. "I knew he'd wallop me good if I was ta' go home, so I pulled up in front of the Grand

Movie Theatre. I timed it jus' right, too, because all my friends was jus' comin' out, an' they would see what a big man I was to roar up in that ol' car." He chuckled and shook his head again. "Then I said, loud enough for my friends to hear, '*There ya are ol' man. That's how ya' drive.*'"

The crowd moaned.

"Well sir," Gus said, giving a full display of his choppers, "my pa was ord'narily a quiet kinda man, and I thought if I chatted a bit with my friends, he'd behave hisself. But I had guessed wrong–*real wrong*.

My pa got outta that car and come 'round to the driver's side, threw open that blamed door, and yanked me out by my shirt. Now, I was intent on retainin' my dignity in front of all my friends. But Pa...well, he saw it otherwise, and didn't give a dern about my dignity. In fact, he de-molished my dignity by liftin' me up outta that seat like a two-year-old and placin' me, not too gently, on my rump right on th' sidewalk. He never onc't raised his voice, but it was cold as steel. I can still hear it. He says, 'If you come near this car for six months, I'll *thrash* you.'

Well sir, there I was in front of God an' all my friends, sittin' on my rump as my ol' man zooms off, scatterin' gravel and dust all ov'r me. He liked ta' skeered me ta death. For an old man, he sure was strong." Gus looked at Emily and smiled. "So, jus' a word of advice, Em'ly. Be careful who you sass."

The crowd whistled and applauded, and Ike shouted, "I can testify to all that, Em'ly, since I was one of th' friends comin' outta the movies. That old man liked ta scared us all ta death." He and Gus both snorted with laughter.

The crowd applauded once more, then Custer got up and introduced the next speaker, Mr. Charles.

"Well, Emily," Mr. Charles began, the crowd quieting down immediately, "my tale is almost as sad as Gus'."

Everyone grinned, eager for the story.

"I got my first job at sixteen making deliveries on my bike for an auto parts dealer," he began. "When I got that first paycheck, I felt pretty good. I was a man of the world now and felt like I needed to prove it to a certain young lady." He glanced over at Mrs. Charles, who smiled.

"So," he continued, "my first purchase with that paycheck was a pack of Marlboro cigarettes!"

The crowd hissed and booed.

Mr. Charles laughed and held up his hand. "Now give me a chance to finish."

"I knew the young lady I was trying to impress walked home every day from school, and I knew the route–since I often followed her."

Emily heard Miss Mattie chuckling beside her.

"Well, I got my smoking equipment all together–a Bic lighter, which was the second thing I purchased with my paycheck–and my Marlboros, which I rolled up in the sleeve of my T-shirt, just like I'd seen in the movies. I took a couple of cigarettes out so no one could tell it was a brand new pack. I stood behind a huge walnut tree in the corner of Mrs. Sydney's front yard–well out of sight of Mrs. Sidney, since she was a family friend. I knew this certain girl walked right by that tree every day, and there I hid, ready to light up."

The crowd was absolutely quiet, eager with anticipation.

Mr. Charles grinned. "I kept glancing around the tree, and finally saw her walking down the sidewalk toward me. I lit my Marlboro up and quickly began to puff away; I wanted my timing to be just right. So I counted off thirty seconds, and stepped out from behind the tree with the cigarette dangling from my lips, like I'd seen in a James Dean movie."

The crowd hooted, and Glen Kingery shouted, "I wanted to look like Marlon Brando when I smoked my first one."

Mr. Charles laughed and continued, "But alas, this tale has a sad ending. The person walking toward me wasn't the girl I was trying to impress; it was my tall and terrifying Aunt Mary, who had just emerged from visiting her friend, Mrs. Sydney!"

The crowd roared. Emily watched Gus and Ike hang onto each other, cackling like old hens.

"I wanted to swallow that cigarette," Mr. Charles continued, "but it was too late. Aunt Mary had already seen me, and the smoke billowing around my head. She walked up to me, stuck her hand out, and barked like a drill sergeant, 'Okay kid, give me that awful thing!' I handed her the smoldering cigarette, she threw it on the sidewalk, and ground it out with the toe of her shoe. That's when my prayer life began!"

"'Raise your right hand,' Aunt Mary ordered, and she didn't mean maybe. I raised it quick.

"She looked me dead in the eye and said, 'You can either swear to me that you'll never again touch another cigarette—and I mean for the rest of your life, Buster—or we can go find your dad right now and tell him about it. Which one is it?'"

"Well, I couldn't take that oath fast enough, and before you could say *cancer free,* I'd promised never to smoke again."

The crowd cheered, and Iris Head shouted, "Tell us what happened to the girl."

"Well, I'd love to tell you," Mr. Charles said, "but I don't know where she disappeared to. I was just grateful that she hadn't been there to witness Aunt Mary making me take the oath."

Mrs. Charles popped her head up and said, "I saw you behind the tree, and ran the other way when your Aunt Mary came out of Mrs. Sydney's house."

After the laughter and applause had died down, Custer got up and said it was time to cut the cake. "After the cake is served," he announced, "there will be two more speakers to warn Emily of the perils of being a teenager."

Everyone grew silent as Miss Mattie began to light the candles. Emily hoped that Custer was getting plenty of pictures of her very first birthday party.

When all the candles were lit, Miss Mattie held out her arm and Emily went and stood in the soft curve of it. "Now everyone sing real loud," Miss Mattie said, holding Emily close to her. "We want people over in Monett to hear us celebratin' our Em'ly."

Everyone put their whole heart and vocal cords into the second singing of *Happy Birthday*. Emily laughed, and Ike wondered if the roof would hold.

At the end of the song, Emily just stood there smiling at all of them.

Blow the candles out!" everyone shouted in unison.

"Oh!" she said, then began puffing out the candles.

Impulsively, Miss Rose broke into a chorus of *For She's a Jolly Good Fellow*, not quite sure of how to sing the feminine version.

After another round of hooting and applause, Miss Mattie cut the cake. Mrs. Green and Mrs. Charles helped, handing out generous portions to each of Emily's guests.

Custer waited until they'd all been served, then called Ike to the front to tell about the blunders of his first date. Then it was Millie's turn to tell about the time she and her girlfriend had sneaked into the movies, and been caught by her uncle. Emily wore herself out laughing.

After the final two speakers, Custer stood up, smiled, and said, "Now Emily, if you'll come forward please, we have a gift for you."

Feeling slightly embarrassed, she walked to the front and Custer handed her an envelope.

"Should I open it now?" she asked.

"Please," Custer said.

She noticed that he couldn't quit grinning, as she tore the envelope open. Inside, there was a folded piece of paper, which she set aside, then opened her card and read it. There were so many messages that three sides of the card were filled, margin to margin. Everyone had written wonderful things about her and signed their names.

"Thank you so much," she said, clutching the card close to her heart, as she smiled out at the crowd.

"Open the other paper," everyone shouted.

"Oh!" she grinned, reaching for the paper. She unfolded it and saw that it was a gift certificate from Taylor's camera shop. She gawked at the amount: $350.00!

"Oh my gosh!" she murmured.

"Happy Birthday!" they all shouted.

"Oh my gosh," she repeated, looking out at the crowd. "Thank you all so much!"

She hugged every guest and thanked them for coming.

Even strangers who had dropped into the café for lunch gathered round, congratulating Emily and wishing her a happy birthday. On their way out the door, they could be overheard remarking about the wonderful people that made up the village of Mountain Grove.

* * * *

November 7

Dear Journal,

Today is my fifteenth birthday and it has been the best day of my whole life! I had a birthday party, with balloons, and candles, and a cake. It was the first time I've ever heard anyone sing Happy Birthday with my name in it!

"Happy Birthday, dear Em-i-ly. Happy Birthday to you!"

I keep hearing it over and over again in my head. Everybody was smiling, and Custer kept taking pictures. They told funny stories and we all laughed and laughed. They even gave me a gift!

I can still see their teeth smiling at me. It was the best day of my life. E.

* * * *

"Thanks for the movie," Emily said, as she and Kelly Ann left the Grand Theatre the next day, hanging a right at the corner.

"Yer welcome and happy birthday a'gin," Kelly Ann replied, giving her a quick hug. "You sure looked shocked yesterday. I thought you were goin' ta faint or somethin'!"

"Me too!" Emily laughed, zipping her thick, black jacket against the cold.

The sun disappeared behind the mountain peaks, as they passed the alley at the rear of the Grand Theatre.

"Pssst! Kelly Ann!" they heard from the shadows of the alley.

Emily and Kelly Ann looked at each other, then peered into the darkness of the alleyway, instinctively holding onto one another for safety. They both jumped as a dirty face appeared out of the shadows.

"Gilbert!" Kelly Ann yelled. "What th' hockey puck are you doin' hidin' in that alley? You near scared us ta death!"

A skinny, bare-foot boy dressed only in jeans and a light T-shirt emerged into the partial light. "Shhhh!" he said, waving his hands to quiet her down. "I run off, an' I'm afraid my ol' man's lookin' for me."

He motioned for them to follow him into the alley. Emily hesitated, but Kelly Ann whispered, "It's okay! I've known Gilbert forever."

When they were well off the street, Kelly Ann lit into him again. "Gilbert what in thunderation are you doin' out here in this cold, with no coat or shoes?"

"My ol' man got drunk and blew a gasket," he whispered, wrapping his skinny arms around his body, trying to stop shivering. "I had t' run, or he woulda beat the snot outta me. I didn't have time t' grab my shoes or coat."

The girls looked at each other, not quite knowing what to do.

"Do you have any place to go?" Emily asked.

He shook his head miserably. As he did, she caught sight of the right side of his face; his eye was bruised, and almost swollen shut, with a nasty cut above his eyebrow.

Emily was instantly enraged. "Gilbert, did your dad do that to you?"

He just looked down at the ground and wouldn't answer her.

"We need to get the sheriff," she said angrily.

"No!" Gilbert yelled and tried to run past her. Kelly Ann reached out and grabbed his arm.

"It's okay Gilbert, we won't tell," Kelly Ann said. "Don't run away."

"If ya'll tell anyone," he said frantically, "I'll run 'n hide in th' woods."

"Jus' calm down Gilbert," Kelly Ann said, hanging on to his arm, "nobody's gonna' tell nothin'."

"I won't tell, if you don't want me to," Emily said, alarmed at his reaction. She moved a couple of steps away from him; he smelled as if he hadn't bathed for a long, long time.

"I jus' need a blanket and some kinda food," he said. "I'll hide at the picnic grounds 'til he sobers up."

"Gilbert, your daddy stays drunk for days, sometimes weeks," Kelly Ann said. "You know you can't live outdoors in the winter!"

He leaned back against the wall of the theatre and sank down to the ground, wrapping his skinny arms around his legs, trying to stop shivering. "Ya'll jus' go on, I'll figure it out." He could barely speak he was shivering so hard.

"Why won't you let us get some adults to help you, Gilbert?" Emily asked.

"No!" he shouted again. "No sheriff, no adults, no anybody. I kin take care of m'self. I don't need them nosy county workers comin' 'round."

"Gilbert was in foster care once," Kelly Ann explained. "He hated it."

"Were they mean to you, Gilbert?" Emily asked.

"Naw, they weren't mean or nothin'," he mumbled. "I kin jus' take care of m'self without nobody nosin' in my business. Jus' forgit I asked ya'll for help."

He huddled on the ground, shivering miserably.

"You won't survive the night in this mountain cold, Gilbert," Emily said, squatting down beside him. "The temperature can go down to zero."

"Yeah," Kelly Ann said, "you'd be deader 'n a mackerel by mornin', Gilbert."

He shrugged. "I'd rather be dead then have them county workers breathin' down m' neck."

Kelly Ann looked at Emily. "Doesn't that church up the street give people a place to stay sometimes?" she asked.

"I think so," Emily replied. "I see people coming in and out of their basement."

"You think they'd let Gilbert stay there?"

"We'd have to go ask."

Kelly Ann looked alarmed and turned back to Gilbert. "Thunderation Gilbert, why are you so derned stubborn? I don't wanna go poundin' on some preacher's door in the middle of the night."

"I ain't sleepin' in no church basement either if I hafta see an adult. I'm tellin' you, they'll call the county on me, and then they'll lock up my ol' man."

Emily stared at him. "Why are you protecting your dad, when he hit you that way?" she asked in disbelief.

"It's complicated," he mumbled, not looking at her.

"I don't know a bowl 'a beans 'bout talkin' to a preacher," Kelly Ann moaned. "And we hafta ask him for a room for you *and* tell him he can't see you? He'll think we're crazier than a pet coon!"

Something rose up in Emily, she didn't know if it was determination or pity, but she stood up. "I'll go if you want."

"You'd go alone?" asked Kelly Ann, looking surprised.

"Sure," Emily said, taking off her jacket and wrapping it around Gilbert. She pulled off her beanie and stuck it on his head. "You keep Gilbert company. I'm going to run all the way, and I'll be back in a jiff." She was already starting to tremble from the cold.

"You swear you won't tell that ol' preacher 'bout me or nothin'?" Gilbert was upset again. "Ya gotta swear it!"

"I promise, Gilbert. Don't worry, everything will be fine," she said, sounding a lot more confident than she felt. All she knew was that she couldn't leave Gilbert out in this cold all night.

"I feel bad makin' you go alone," Kelly Ann said. "I'll come if you want."

"I'll be fine," she assured her, her teeth beginning to chatter. "Just make sure Gilbert is still here when I get back. I sure don't want to do all this for nothing."

"Oh he'll be here, if I hafta sit on him," Kelly Ann assured her.

* * * *

Emily had to knock three times before the porch light at the parsonage came on. She was shivering uncontrollably, and it wasn't all due to the cold.

Pastor Britton opened the door dressed in black sweatpants and sweatshirt. "Why, hello!" he said, looking surprised.

"Hello, your holiness..." she began.

The pastor laughed. "Please, just call me Pastor Alex. And come in, you're shivering like a Chihuahua out there."

Emily followed him into a cozy living room, lit by a fire that hissed and sizzled in the stone fireplace. Pastor Alex motioned toward it and said, "Stand over there and warm yourself."

The logs were so hot they popped and flicked sparks against the screen. "I don't know if you remember me," she began, turning to look at him as she warmed herself by the fire. "My name is Emily, and I come to church with Miss Mattie sometimes."

His eyes lit up. "Of course I remember you," he grinned. "You and Mattie wear those great Sunday hats."

Emily noticed his ears went way up when he smiled.

"What brings you to my door this evening?" he asked.

She didn't quite know where to begin, but about then Pastor Alex's wife, an attractive, dark-haired woman, came into the room carrying three steaming mugs on a tray.

She smiled at Emily. "I was making hot chocolate when I heard you come in," she said, setting the tray on a tufted ottoman. "You're just in time."

Pastor Alex made the introductions. "Emily, this is my wife, Penelope."

"Nice to meet you," Emily said, looking into Penelope's dark eyes. They were almond shaped and beautiful. "Should I call you Mrs. Britton?"

"No, Penelope is fine," she smiled. "And it's nice to meet you, too." She motioned toward a small sofa. "Please sit down, Emily."

She handed Emily a mug of hot chocolate, then joined her husband on the larger sofa. They both looked at Emily expectantly, waiting to hear what she had to say.

"I've come because I know someone who needs help," Emily began.

They both nodded for her to go on.

"The problem is," she continued, "I promised I wouldn't give out any details because he's afraid—but he needs a place to sleep for a few nights. He said he would sleep outside, but my friend told him he'd be deader than a mackerel in the morning if he did that. So what I'm asking is if he can sleep in the church basement." She had rattled it all off without stopping once.

Pastor Alex and his wife sat looking at her with their mouths open.

"And I thought your church hat was a surprise!" said Pastor Alex, standing up.

"Let me see if I have this straight, Emily," he said, rubbing the back of his neck. "You want me to open the church basement for someone, and not ask you any questions about it. Is that right?"

"Yes," she replied, "and he's not in trouble with the law, he's just having some personal problems. My friend and I will get him some food—I have money. I can also give you money for the electricity he uses, or a deposit if you're afraid he'll steal something. But I'd appreciate it if you'd lock up anything too valuable, because I don't have a lot of money."

Emily sat blinking at him, waiting for an answer.

"Well, Alex," Penelope said, standing up, "I think we've found a modern-day Good Samaritan." She smiled at Emily, and sat down next to her, putting an arm around her. "It's really nice of you to look out for this boy," she said, giving Emily a gentle squeeze. Penelope turned and looked at her husband. "Don't you think it's wonderful of her, Alex?" she asked, demurely.

Pastor Alex stared at both of them as they sat there blinking at him, waiting for an answer.

Dear Lord, he thought. *Two women on a mission.* He was a goner.

CHAPTER – 13

"You mean, the preacher said yes?" Kelly Ann was so excited she began jumping up and down, clapping her hands like a child.

Even Gilbert was smiling.

"He sure did," Emily laughed, "and not only that, but he said Gilbert could help himself to the food pantry in the basement."

Kelly Ann eyed her curiously. "Where in thunderation did you get that jacket?" she asked, taking in the stylish pink ski jacket that fit Emily perfectly at the waist.

"Penelope—Pastor Alex's wife—loaned it to me until tomorrow," she said, turning around so Kelly Ann could see the back. "Cute, huh?"

"A preacher's wife dresses like that?" Kelly Ann said, touching the material. "I thought they wore long ol' black coats that look like they jus' come from a funeral."

Emily laughed and showed her how the silver buckles on the front of the jacket hooked together.

That's just darlin'," Kelly Ann said, having her turn around again.

"Who *cares* 'bout a stupid jacket," Gilbert exploded. "What about that ol' preacher? Is he gonna be snoopin' aroun' or call the law?"

"No Gilbert," Emily said, turning to him. "He's not going to do anything except unlock his basement door and turn on the heat."

"That's what *he* says," Gilbert growled, "but how do ya know he's tellin' th' truth?"

"Because I trust him," Emily said. "Now come on, your feet and legs are all blue, and you're not shivering anymore. When you stop shivering, you're on your way to freezing to death. I saw it on a TV show." She wasn't a hundred percent sure about him being near death, but she thought it wouldn't hurt to scare him a little.

"I swear Em'ly," Kelly Ann whispered, as they hurried up Elderberry Way, "is there anything in this whole blamed world you haven't heard on that TV of yours?"

"Not much!" she laughed, noticing that Kelly Ann was also grinning.

They looked up the hill as they crossed First Street, and there, like a warm oasis, was the church basement all lit up. Gilbert stepped off the sidewalk into the shadow of a tree. "Kelly Ann, ya'll go check and see if anyone's waitin' inside that basement to turn me over to the county."

Kelly Ann started to argue with him, but finally said, "I'll go see Gilbert, but if you run off, I'll chase you down an' twist your ears 'til they're on backwards."

Kelly Ann came running back a few minutes later and said, "Come on Gilbert, you gotta see what's laid out for you." Laughing, she grabbed his arm and began dragging him up the hill to the church. She threw open the door of the basement and there, all warm and cozy as a nest, was a bed piled high with quilts. A fresh pair of clean pajamas lay folded on a chair, and a small table held a hot plate, a small pan, and three cans of soup.

"Look! This dern place even has a shower!" Kelly Ann said, peering inside a small bathroom.

Hallelujah! thought Emily. She had walked a few paces behind Gilbert, with the jacket collar up over her nose.

"Okay, Gilbert," Emily said, taking over. "You go warm yourself up in that shower and we'll heat up the soup for you."

Gilbert started to protest but saw the look on her face and didn't argue.

"Take these clean p.j.'s with you, Gilbert," Kelly Ann ordered, "and throw your mess of clothes out here." She handed him the pajamas. "And don't ferget to wash that mangy head of yours. I'm gonna bring some scissors tomorrow and take care of that hair."

"You ain't gonna touch my hair tomorrow or any other day," Gilbert roared, "and I'd like ta' know what yer gonna do with my clothes."

"They're goin' with me, straight into grandpa's washer. Yer clothes smell like you been sleepin' with the dogs!"

"What's wrong with 'at?" he mumbled, as he headed for the shower.

They heard the shower start. "I hope he doesn't try to run away in those striped pajamas," Kelly Ann laughed.

"I'll take my jacket with me," Emily said. "He won't go back out into that cold."

Emily opened two cans of vegetable beef soup, dumped them into the saucepan, then went to the pantry in search of a spoon. When she opened the pantry door, she saw that it was actually a small room with shelves, stocked with all kinds of food and supplies. Emily found a large spoon in a plastic bin, grabbed a few napkins, and went back out to the hotplate.

"Where're we going to find Gilbert a jacket and shoes?" she asked, stirring the pot.

"I'll ask gran'pa if I can borrow some of his," Kelly Ann replied.

"Won't he wonder why?"

"I'll tell him somethin', Emmy Lou," she shrugged. "If you can ask a preacher for his basement, I can ask gran'pa for a pair of shoes. Jus' be back here tomorrow around 8:00, so I don't havta' go onto the church grounds alone."

* * * *

As Emily approached the church the next morning, she saw Kelly Ann pacing at the side of the church grounds, trying to keep warm; her boots crunched on the frosted grass.

"Where in thunderation have you been," Kelly Ann exploded, as Emily walked up to her. "I been freezin' my 'tater off!"

"You didn't have to wait outside for me," Emily said, shocked at her outburst. "You could've gone inside with Gilbert, where it's warm."

"Oh sure, and have that preacher come 'round wantin' to talk to me."

"What's wrong with that?" Emily asked.

"'Cause Miss Smarty Pants, I was afraid he'd ask me 'bout the Bible—of which, I don't know a bowl a' beans about," she said, her breath making puffs of steam with every word.

"When you meet a preacher they don't give you a Bible quiz, you know," Emily said, glancing down at a bag near Kelly Ann's feet. "What's in that duffle bag?"

"Some warm clothes for Gilbert 'n a pair of grandpa's work boots." She eyed Emily's plastic Wal-Mart bag. "What's in yers?"

"Penelope's ski jacket."

"Shoot!" said Kelly Ann. "I think I'd fer'get to return that cute thing!"

"It was tempting!" Emily smiled. "Your grandpa didn't mind lending Gilbert his boots?" she asked, nodding toward Kelly Ann's bag.

"He didn't *lend* 'em, he give 'em to me for charity."

Emily gave her a side glance. "I don't even want to know the story behind that one."

"Ever' thing I told him was the absolute truth," Kelly Ann said, as they headed around the church to the basement. "I jus' hope Gilbert doesn't ever wear 'em into Grandpa's café!"

"That's what I thought," Emily said, laughing.

They knocked quietly on the door and heard scampering sounds. Pretty soon a pair of eyes—one of them bruised—peered out a small window.

"Gilbert, open the blamed door," Kelly Ann yelled. "No one out here is gonna drag you off to the county."

"That guy's nervous as a cat," she whispered to Emily, as he fumbled with the lock.

They heard a click and the door swung open. They walked in and Kelly Ann handed Gilbert the duffle bag. "Here's your clothes and a pair of Gran'pa's long underwear," she said. "And there's some thick socks in there too and these..." She handed him the work boots. "Hope you wear a size eleven!"

"I dunno what size I wear," Gilbert said, inspecting the boots. "All my shoes was give to me."

"Well, if they're too big, wear two pair of socks. It's for sure, they aren't too small," she said, looking down at his bare feet.

They stood there not knowing what to do next. "I need to take this jacket back to Penelope," Emily finally said. "You want to come Kelly Ann?"

"No," she replied abruptly. "I got other plans."

"What 'm I supposed ta' do all day?" Gilbert complained. "I can't go nowhere 'til my eye gets better."

"I'm going over to the library if you want me to pick up a book for you to read," Emily offered.

"Now that oughta set your pulse to beatin' real fast, Gilbert," Kelly Ann yawned.

He ignored her. "I dunno Em'ly, I ain't actually sat down and read a whole book b'fore."

"Can you even read?" Kelly Ann asked.

Emily was more than a little shocked at her rudeness.

"Well, 'course I kin read, stupid," he said, his eyes growing dark with anger.

"Don't git your feathers ruffled, Gilbert; lots of kids can't read," Kelly Ann said. "Anyway, I'm outta' here. I'll come by later."

"I'll be back in a while with a book, Gilbert," Emily said, "and I'll bring you some donuts. You like donuts?"

He nodded his head miserably and she left feeling sorry for him. Maybe she would bring a board game tomorrow and play games with him. She would have to go back home if she did it today, and she had no plans to go back to that war zone anytime soon.

"Where are you headed?" she asked Kelly Ann, when they were outside.

"Well, I can tell you one thing, it isn't to the library, or the bakery," she said sarcastically.

Emily watched her friend walk away, wondering what had put her in such a bad mood.

Penelope answered right away when Emily knocked on the parsonage door; she looked like she was on her way out. Emily stared at her, she wore Levis tucked into cute snow boots, and a red puffy jacket with matching earmuffs.

"I wanted to return your ski jacket," she said, handing Penelope the bag wondering if all pastor's wives dressed that way.

"Thanks!" Penelope smiled, tossing the bag on a bench in her entry hall. "I was just on my way to get a manicure touch-up. Would you like to come? My treat."

"Thanks, but I already have plans," Emily said, glancing down at Penelope's hands.

Penelope noticed and held her hands out. "This shade is called *Hot Chili Peppers*," she smiled. "Do you like it?"

Emily laughed and nodded. "It's really pretty, but my fingernails are too short to polish." She pulled her hand out of her glove. "Look!"

"No, they're not!" Penelope said, inspecting her fingers. "Nail polish looks pretty on long and short nails!"

It sounded like fun and Emily was tempted, but she said, "Maybe some other time. I promised Gilbert..." She clamped her hand over her mouth. "I mean, I promised *my friend*, that I'd get him a book from the library and some donuts."

Penelope laughed. "Your friend's name is safe with me."

"He's just afraid for certain people to know," Emily explained, wishing she could just blurt the whole problem out to

Penelope. She decided to change the subject instead. "Thanks for loaning me your jacket last night, I appreciate it."

"Well, I appreciate what you're doing for your friend," Penelope grinned, wrapping a red and white knit scarf around her neck. "I like your spunk."

Penelope locked her front door, and they went down the walk together.

"Could I have a rain check on the manicure?" Emily asked. "It sounds like fun."

"Absolutely," Penelope smiled. "Did the basement work out last night for your friend?"

"The basement was great—perfect for what we needed," Emily said, thinking of the shower for Gilbert.

* * * *

Emily returned to the church basement that afternoon with a book for Gilbert and a box of mixed donuts. Kelly Ann was already there keeping him company as she did her homework. Gilbert let out a whoop when he saw the pastries.

Emily took off her jacket and gloves and threw them on a chair, then walked over and offered Gilbert a donut out of the box. He snagged a chocolate donut and one that was jelly filled. When Emily took the box over and offered Kelly Ann a donut, she caught a whiff of cigarette smoke. She froze in her tracks and just stared, not knowing what to say.

"What?" Kelly Ann glared at her.

"I didn't say anything."

"No, but your eyes are sayin' it all."

"You smell like cigarette smoke."

"So?"

"Do you smoke?"

"You're not my mama, ya know," Kelly Ann snapped.

Emily felt like she had been slapped. She went over to Gilbert and handed him the book she had been so sure he would enjoy. It didn't seem so exciting to give it to him anymore.

"I read this, Gilbert, and I thought you'd like it, too," she said dully. "It's about a boy who survived a plane wreck." She handed it to him, then walked over to the chair and put her jacket back on and started to leave.

"Em'ly," Kelly Ann said.

She turned.

"You need to quit worrin' 'bout me so much. You don't know if I was smokin'—and even if I was, it isn't that big a deal."

Emily went over and sat down on the floor next to Kelly Ann, refusing to make eye contact with her. She leaned her head back against the bed, so tired she could barely speak.

"It *is* a big deal if you do what the other kids over at the picnic grounds are doing," Emily said, "and I know they go way beyond just smoking cigarettes. They smoke pot, they do drugs and alcohol. Just like my parents do, just like your parents do. *That* is a very big deal." She closed her eyes. "Anyway, you're right, I'm not your mama. But I care about you."

Emily couldn't remember when she'd felt so tired and depressed. She wanted nothing more than to go somewhere and sleep for a long, long time. It made her even more depressed that she had no place to go.

"You sleepy?" Kelly Ann asked, her voice softening.

Emily nodded, and tears sprang to her eyes.

"What'd you do, stay up all night watchin' movies?" Kelly Ann asked.

"No," Emily said, "my mom and dad stayed up all night drinking and fighting."

Neither one said anything for a moment, then Kelly Ann stood up and walked over to the food pantry. "I saw some cots in here when I was gettin' food for Gilbert."

She dragged out a cot and set it up, then went back into the pantry and came out with two blue plaid blankets and a fluffy pillow and made up a bed for her.

Emily watched silently.

Kelly Ann walked over and held out her hand. "C'mon," she said pulling her to her feet. "You sleep and I'll do my homework, then we'll go to Grandpa's an' get us a cheeseburger." She gave Emily a quick hug. "Sorry for bein' in such a bad mood, it's jus' some guy I like that's been irritatin' me."

Emily was too tired to care. She took off her jacket and boots, crept under the blankets and slept soundly for the next two hours.

* * * *

Emily and Kelly Ann took turns checking on Gilbert, making sure he didn't need anything.

One Wednesday they showed up at the basement door at the same time.

"Where've you been?" Emily asked, hugging her friend. "I haven't seen you for a couple of days."

"Oh, jus' hangin' out with that guy I told you about," Kelly Ann replied, knocking on the door. She turned to Emily. "Isn't there any boy yer interested in, Emmy Lou?"

"No," she replied. "And I don't want there to be either. Being single is less complicated."

"Don't trust men, huh?" Kelly Ann said, knocking on the door again.

"Something like that," Emily said.

They saw Gilbert peek out the window.

"Open up, it's just us," Kelly Ann yelled, rolling her eyes at Emily.

When he opened the door he looked different.

"Who in thunder lowered yer ears, Gilbert?" Kelly Ann asked.

"Who did *what*?" he asked.

"Who gave you the hair cut?" Emily asked, thinking he looked way better with short hair.

"Oh...that ol' preacher came snoopin' aroun'," he said, looking self-conscious. "Me 'n him been talkin' the last few days and he asked if I wanted a dern haircut, so I said 'sure why not.'"

"He give you those clothes, too?" Kelly Ann asked.

Gilbert nodded.

"Yer lookin' alright Gilbert," she said, giving him a thumb's up. "He give you a Bible too?"

"Naw, but I went to his ol' church on Sunday."

Kelly Ann looked shocked but didn't say anything.

"You goin' home anytime soon?" she finally asked.

"I sneaked back one time and had a look–but my ol' man's still drinkin'."

"Did you tell the preacher about your daddy?" Kelly Ann asked.

"I had to," Gilbert replied. "But he an' his wife have a foster care license and fixed ever'thing up with the county so's I could stay awhile. He said I could stay in his house, 'cept its only a one bedroom."

"Well, it's good that you have a place to stay," Kelly Ann said.

Emily noticed his eye was almost completely healed, and he didn't look so wild anymore with a haircut. And one sniff told her that he had been having a shower on a regular basis.

* * * *

Emily felt the weight of the season settle quietly on her shoulders as she walked beneath the bare trees that lined First Street. She glanced up as she passed the giant cornucopia painted on the front window of Montoya's Organic Produce and paused at the plate glass window of Violet's House of Beauty. It read: *Thanksgiving Perm and Haircut Special - $79.99.*

Emily hurried on, noticing that the holiday theme raced up and down First Street. The front window of Cooke's Bakery was covered with a Norman Rockwell painting of a family sitting down to their Thanksgiving meal. Taped to the bakery door was a small sign that read: *Order your Thanksgiving yeast rolls early!*

The huge corner windows of Good Eats Café had pilgrims sailing off on the Mayflower, and across the street, Bloomin' Happy had a display of cardboard pilgrims, with dried corn shocks as a background.

It all depressed her.

Why? she wondered. *Why Thanksgiving? Why didn't she get depressed on Fourth of July or Christmas?* Thanksgiving made her want to crawl under the covers and not come out until spring. She didn't want to go home but knew that with the season fairly bristling in the air, any villager she met would ask about her Thanksgiving plans. It was an extreme embarrassment to her that she didn't have any. *No, Mr. Charles, we don't sit down and have turkey together. No, Mrs. Green, friends and relatives don't come and join us—there's nothing to join. No, Ike, I don't know what my favorite part of the turkey is.*

She'd heard all the questions before and didn't want to tell them that she had never in her whole life sat down to a Thanksgiving meal. She didn't even know what cranberry sauce tasted like. *My life is so weird,* she thought as she crossed First Street and headed up Elderberry Way.

Gus! she thought as she walked by his station. Gus was a bachelor and lived alone; he would be a safe bet not to bring up Thanksgiving. She set off at a trot across the street and found that she was actually humming as she crossed the gas island.

"Hi Gus" she said, as she opened the door to the gas station office. Gus had his feet up on the desk with YipYap in his lap, giving him a thorough brushing with a small wire brush.

"Well, look who the wind blew in, YipYap!" Gus smiled, showing an even row of white choppers. "Sit yersef' down, Em'ly. I was just tellin' YipYap that we need to get our Thanksgivin' bird ordered. What're you doin' for Thanksgivin'?"

She stood there dumfounded. "I'm not sure," she finally mumbled, wondering if it was too late to bolt for the door.

"Yessir! Me and YipYap love Turkey Day better 'n 'bout any day there is, don't we, YipYap?"

She would've sworn the dog bobbed his head up and down.

"'Course YipYap's favorite part is the gizzard, and I'm a drumstick man myself," Gus continued, a soft glow in his eyes, as he sailed straight toward memory lane. "I 'member when I was a boy, our table was fit to bustin' with food. My mama was a wonderful cook. And people sittin' 'round to a fare-thee-well. Family come from all over and 'course anyone within shoutin' distance was invited over. I kin still smell that turkey roastin' and those giblets stewin'. And those pies my mama made! Why no one in the county could make pun'kin pies like mama. She even grew her own pun'kins!"

"That's nice," Emily mumbled, her spirits sinking through the floor. "How are you today, YipYap?" she asked, hoping to change the subject. She patted the dog's head.

"Oh he's got his mind set on turkey gravy. I put a ladle full over his turkey and mashed 'taters..." and Gus was off again.

She stood there nodding her head, a smile frozen to her face, as she tried to figure the quickest way out of there.

A horn honked, and she was relieved to see Mr. Charles' Dodge Ram pull into the station. "Well, I'll let you wait on Mr. Charles, Gus," she said, heading for the door.

"Just sit a spell, Em'ly," Gus said, getting up from his creaky chair. "I'll only be a sec."

"I have stuff to do, but thanks." She made a bee-line for the door while she had the chance.

"Hi, Mr. C!" she called out, walking swiftly across the gas island.

"Emily, just a minute," Mr. Charles said, "I've been wanting to talk to you." He put his credit card into the slot on the gas pump and made his gasoline selection.

Please don't ask what I'm doing for Thanksgiving, she thought, as she turned and walked over to him.

"What are you doing for Thanksgiving?" he asked.

Her heart froze. "I'm not sure yet," she replied, desperately wondering if there wasn't some sort of Thanksgiving-free zone in Mountain Grove.

"Well," he said, twisting off the gas cap, "my family has decided to skip the traditional dinner this year."

Thank goodness! Emily felt herself thaw out a little.

"What we've decided to do is serve other folks their Thanksgiving meal at Creekside Villa, the rest home east of town. I was wondering if you'd like to join us?" He set the gas nozzle to fill automatically.

"Sure!" she heard herself saying. She wasn't too keen about hanging around an old folk's home all day, but what the heck! Now she had Thanksgiving plans and wouldn't have to dodge everyone for the next week.

"Super!" he grinned. "We plan to meet in the parking lot of the facility Thanksgiving Day at two o'clock sharp."

"I'll be there!" she said, an enormous weight lifted off her shoulders. She turned and walked back toward town, happy that she had Thanksgiving plans and no longer needed to avoid people. The library would be her first stop.

* * * *

On Thanksgiving Day at two o'clock, a nice sized crowd assembled in the parking lot of Creekside Villa Convalescent Home. The land, which had a beautiful creek running through it, had been donated by Mr. Montoya, and it adjoined his apple orchards. Emily glanced around, relieved that there were other villagers in the crowd. She didn't want to be the only non-family member.

"If I could have everyone's attention," Mr. Charles yelled through cupped hands. "The staff here has given us a few pointers to remember." He glanced down at a yellow sheet of paper fastened to his clip board. "First, these folks have small appetites and will probably eat only half of what is served them. Second, more than the food, they are hungry for company. That's why we're doing this one-on-one, so you can give them individual attention. They'll probably want to reminisce about their lives and previous Thanksgivings, so just be good listeners."

"Okay, here's our strategy," Mr. Charles continued, loosening a small stack of papers from his clip board. "I have the names of all the patients–well I guess we're supposed to say *residents*–so I have the names of all the *residents* who don't have family members coming to visit them today." He hesitated as he flipped through the papers. "Actually, some of them don't have family members visiting *ever*.

A slight murmur ran through the crowd.

"I've matched you all up with a specific resident," he continued. "Step forward as I call your name, and I'll give you your assigned person with their room number. The staff's instructions are to just go to their room, introduce yourself, and wheel them into the dining hall."

Wheel them? Emily thought. *Are these people sick?*

Emily was the first to be called. Her sheet read, *Mrs. Tupper, room 210.*

Mr. Charles' Aunt Mary, who Emily had only met a couple of times, was next.

Aunt Mary read her paper out loud, "Mrs. Sanchez, in room 208." She looked toward the building with a puzzled expression. "Where in the world do you go, Joe?" she asked Mr. Charles. "Room 208 should be on the second floor, but there isn't a second floor."

"They're wings, Aunt Mary," he explained. "Room 208 would be in the second *wing*."

As Aunt Mary turned to go, Emily walked over. "My resident is in room 210, which must be near yours. I'll go with you."

"Let's do it," said Aunt Mary, smiling as they headed inside. "By the way kid, you look very cute with that French braid."

"Thank you," Emily smiled.

Jonathan hurried over to them, and said, "My resident is in room 206; I'll go with you two."

As they walked toward the gold-washed, Tuscany style buildings, Emily noticed that Aunt Mary kept glancing at her and Jonathan with that smile adults sometime get when they think something is cute.

Give it a rest, Aunt Mary, Emily thought, as she scooted closer to Jonathan to avoid a fallen tree branch.

"Those red dome awnings set the building off so nicely, don't you think?" Aunt Mary asked, breaking the silence.

"Looks like pictures of Italy," Emily agreed, glad that Jonathan was along. She didn't know why, but places and situations seemed safer when Jonathan was around.

Inside the building, Emily noticed they had kept up the villa theme, with an interior that was attractive and cheerful. A lone nurse sat at a desk, and to the right was a large room with a TV, but no older residents were in sight. The nurse noticed Emily craning her neck around and said, "The residents who are mobile are already in the dining room, the others are in their rooms waiting for you." She smiled and added, "This is a very big day for them."

As the three walked down the long hall of wing two, Jonathan said, "Here's my room," and disappeared into room 206, and Aunt Mary did the same at room 208. Emily hesitated at the doorway of room 210. *What was she supposed to say to the resident anyway?* She had forgotten to ask about that part.

She found Mrs. Tupper behind a drawn curtain waiting patiently in her wheelchair. She had a sweet face, dotted with age spots, and a cap of white hair.

Her eyes lit up when she saw Emily, and she offered a small hand. "Gladys Tupper," she said, barely able to speak above a whisper as she introduced herself. Emily guessed she was somewhere in her nineties.

"I'm Emily," she said, suddenly very glad to be there. "Happy Thanksgiving!"

"Thank you," Mrs. Tupper smiled. Her head shook with slight tremors.

"Is there anything you'd like to take with you to the dining hall?" Emily asked.

Mrs. Tupper pointed to a lavender shawl folded neatly across her bed and leaned forward as Emily draped it around her small, stooped, shoulders. "It sometimes gets chilly in the dining hall," she whispered.

She pushed Mrs. Tupper at a fast clip down the hallway. Ahead she could see Aunt Mary pushing Mrs. Sanchez's wheelchair; they were talking and laughing like schoolgirls. She thought about starting a gab session with her new friend, but Mrs. Tupper didn't seem like the talk and laugh out loud type.

As Emily flew down the long hall, she noticed Mrs. Tupper clutching the arms of her wheelchair, as if she were afraid of being pitched to the floor. Emily slowed down and from behind came the whoosh of another wheelchair. Jonathan pulled alongside, pushing a man who was hunkered down with a red plaid blanket tucked around him. All Emily could see of the elderly man was the back of his head, with its thick thatch of grey hair, and ears that stuck way out.

"Race you!" Jonathan smiled.

"Want to race, Mrs. Tupper?" she asked her elderly charge.

Mrs. Tupper glanced up at Jonathan, and smiled, "No, but I bet *you* do."

Emily felt her face grow red.

"What's your favorite part of the turkey, Mrs. Tupper?" she asked, quickly changing the subject.

As they entered the dining hall, she saw a vacant table and scooted Mrs. Tupper's wheelchair over, positioned it, and sat down to her left. Jonathan took the chair to her right, with his resident seated next to him. Emily introduced Jonathan to Mrs. Tupper, and he introduced her to Mr. Volpi. There was a sudden bustling, as servers came in with wheeled trollies loaded with Thanksgiving entrees. After she was served, Emily's mouth watered as she stared down at her Thanksgiving plate laden with turkey, dressing, mashed potatoes, green beans, and *cranberry sauce*. She couldn't wait to finally taste it.

Mr. Charles stood up to say the blessing, and she bowed her head, but she couldn't help peeking at the cranberry sauce as he prayed. At the end of the prayer, everyone chorused *Amen* and dug into their food. Emily made sure Mrs. Tupper had her eating utensils, then eagerly reached for her own—but couldn't find them. She looked everywhere, even under her plate and napkin.

Jonathan noticed and quickly stood up to get her some.

"It's okay," she said, and started to get up. "I'll get it."

"Just sit, I'll be right back," he said, and hurried off toward the kitchen.

She sat back down and looked across his empty seat at Mr. Volpi, who was staring at her. His ears stuck way out from his thin face, and his nose looked far too large for him. He turned and watched as Jonathan trotted off.

"He's taken' care of ya, huh?" he said to Emily, in a raspy voice.

She felt herself blush, as she nodded.

"He's an alright guy," Mr. Volpi said, with a wink.

Jonathan handed her a set of blue plastic utensils and she thanked him, digging right into her cranberry sauce. The tart, sweet flavor burst inside her mouth.

"Yummy," she said to no one in particular.

"You actually *like* cranberry sauce?" he asked.

"It's the best!" she replied, not wanting to tell him it was the first time she had ever tasted it. She quickly polished it off.

"Here, take mine," he said, picking up his plate. "I hate the stuff!"

"Well if you're sure you don't want it..." She was delighted as Jonathan scooped his cranberry sauce onto her plate, and she could feel his eyes on her as she eagerly ate it all.

When she popped the last spoonful into her mouth, he leaned over and whispered, "You're sort of *weird,* you know that?"

Stung to the core, she quickly looked up at him, but he was smiling down at her with that funny look in his eyes.

"Yes, I do," she whispered back.

He laughed, and then turned to talk to Mr. Volpi.

She turned her attention to Mrs. Tupper, who was smiling, and thoroughly enjoying her exchange with Jonathan. "What was Thanksgiving like when you were a girl, Mrs. Tupper?" she asked.

Mrs. Tupper stopped smiling. "Would you mind if we talked about something else, dear? It nearly plunges me into a depression to talk about it."

"Really!" Emily exclaimed. "Why?"

"Well, because we never had a Thanksgiving!" she warbled. Leaning in toward Emily, she confided, "My family was a real *mess*!"

"Mine too!" Emily said, delighted that Mrs. Tupper shared her sentiments about Thanksgiving. "So what else would you like to talk about?"

"I like talking about my husband, Oliver," she said, her eyes growing bright. She leaned in toward Emily. "I was a war bride, you know!"

"I want to hear all about it," Emily said, happily digging into her mashed potatoes.

* * * *

At the end of the day, she wheeled an exhausted Mrs. Tupper back to her room. A nurse came in to get her into bed, and Emily helped. She adjusted Mrs. Tupper's blankets, then leaned over and hugged her frail shoulders, holding her like a child. "I had fun today. Is it okay if I come and see you again?" Emily asked.

"You really *want* to?" Mrs. Tupper whispered, looking up at her.

"I really do," she said, taking Mrs. Tupper's small, boney hand into hers. "I'll come back in a few days."

Mrs. Tupper closed her eyes and nodded her head happily, too exhausted to speak another word. Impulsively, Emily leaned forward and kissed her forehead, then tiptoed out of the room.

CHAPTER – 14

What should I do with these last days of Thanksgiving vacation? Emily wondered, as she walked up First Street.

Kelly Ann wouldn't be back from visiting her mother until the day before school started. She had visited everyone on First Street, and even worked a shift at Ike's café.

She looked up and spied Bitsy, dressed in a short skirt, tights and boots, scampering down the street toward her. Her first inclination was to wheel around and go in the other direction, but she knew Bitsy had already seen her.

"Hey, Bitsy!" she said, as Bitsy scampered up to her.

"Br-r-r-r! Isn't this weather just the coldest?" Bitsy cooed, rubbing her mittened hands together. "I was just on my way to that silly old theatre to see a movie. Goodness knows, at least in Louisiana we had movies that weren't a hundred years old."

Emily forced a smile and hoped Bitsy wouldn't invite her to come along.

"I was jus' huntin' for that cute Jonathan Charles, to see if he wants to go with me," Bitsy said, fanning her lashed eyes. "Ya'll don't know where that boy hides himself, do ya?" she asked with a dimpled grin.

Emily's stomach did a somersault. "No, he's pretty good at hiding," she managed to say.

"Just give me one of your *wildest* guesses where he might be," Bitsy cooed, with another flutter of her eyelashes. "I know ya'll are friends."

Thoroughly annoyed, Emily tapped her chin. "Hmmmm,". "Let me think..."

"I know," she finally said, trying to keep a straight face, "why don't you check in the back room of Miss Violet's House of Beauty. Maybe he's hanging out there, having tea with Miss Rose."

"No kiddin'?" Bitsy's small mouth dropped open.

"You wanted my wildest guess," Emily shrugged.

"Why that boy!" Bitsy said all aflutter. "You know, I have the biggest *crush* on him! Can you imagine someone bein' that sensitive and havin' tea with a nice ol' lady!"

"Hard to imagine," Emily said, giving her best smile. "If he's not there, be sure to ask Miss Rose or Miss Violet where to find him.

Tell them you're *huntin'* for him so you can invite him to the movies."

"Why you are the most *helpful* little thing!" Bitsy giggled.

"Anytime!" Emily said, with an innocent bat of her own eye lashes.

Bitsy turned and made a beeline for Violet's House of Beauty. Emily waited until she had disappeared through the glass door, then trotted off in the opposite direction trying very hard to control her belly laugh.

Miss Rose and Miss Violet will faint when they find out Bitsy is chasing Jonathan, and doing the inviting, Emily thought happily. *No, they won't just faint–they'll go into a coma!*

* * * *

Dear Journal,

Okay, so why do I give a rip if that dopey Bitsy is chasing Jonathan? I don't want to care, but I do. In fact, I want to knock her in the head when she says his name. I hope Jonathan really was hiding from her. The boys at school trip over themselves and stutter when Bitsy bats her stupid eyes at them. Last week Christopher Douglas walked into the flagpole when Bitsy smiled at him. He got a bloody nose and chipped tooth for his trouble. Boys!!!! E.

* * * *

Emily sat in the photography class rapidly taking notes, not wanting to forget one word Miles Taylor said. This was her third session. Custer had taught the first two, and then left for an assignment in the New England states. Miles was teaching the rest of the classes.

"Next week, class, we are actually going to be taking pictures out in the field," Miles told his photography students, as the class wrapped up. "So, come dressed for an hour in the outdoors."

Emily exited the camera shop with an extra spring in her step. Outdoor photography was her favorite, and she couldn't wait for the next class. There were so many winter scenes she wanted to capture but couldn't because she only had the camera that Miles loaned her to use in class. She was within $183.00 of having enough money to buy her own camera though, thanks to the villagers' generous birthday gift.

She pulled up the collar of her jacket against the cold wind and headed up Second Street to visit Mrs. Tupper. Creekside Villa

Convalescent Home was just past the medical center, about a half mile walk.

Christmas was only two weeks away and a light snow had fallen, causing Mountain Grove to resemble a winter scene on a Currier & Ives Christmas card. There were festive lights outlining every building, and a pine-coned wreath on every door. A life-sized manger scene graced the lawn of St. Daniel's church across the street, and the loudspeaker outside Good Neighbor Pharmacy played, *Have Yourself a Merry Little Christmas.* She hummed along, thinking maybe she would go to church with Miss Mattie this Sunday.

Up ahead, she noticed two familiar figures crossing the street. She did a double take, then stopped in her tracks, feeling lightheaded as she stared at Jonathan and Bitsy walking up the street together, their backs to her. Her heart began to hammer as she stared at the two of them, watching in disbelief as Jonathan put his arm around Bitsy, who was doing some kind of silly hip-hop step.

Her stomach knotted, and she felt like she was going to throw up. Emily watched for a minute, then wheeled around and hurried down the street in the opposite direction, ducking under the marquee at the Grand Theatre, where she stood with her back against the wall, trembling.

She edged over and took a cautious glance around the corner of the building to make sure they hadn't turned around. They were still walking in the opposite direction, up Second Street, clinging to each other as Bitsy kept up her hip-hop. Emily couldn't take her eyes off them, as Bitsy tried to jump up into Jonathan's arms. He put her down but kept walking with his arm around her.

Stricken, she ran out from under the marquee, flew in the opposite direction to the corner as fast as she could, turned, and sped up Elderberry Way. All thoughts of visiting Mrs. Tupper vanished. She dashed across First Street, and ran toward the park, where she crawled up the pedestal, straight into the General's lap. She put her face against his chest. It was freezing cold, but she didn't care. Right now, the General was the only male in the world she trusted.

* * * *

Emily stayed in her garden most of the next day, not quite understanding the sadness that weighed on her heart like a stone. When she tried to read, she found she was reading the same paragraph over and over again, not remembering a word of what she'd just read.

Why would Jonathan say he thought Bitsy was goofy, and then hang out with her? No, more than just hang out, he had his arm around her. The thought looped tediously through her mind again and again, like a child's rope- skipping chant. Finally, she tossed the book aside, went out her side gate, and headed for town.

When she passed Gus' station, she saw him giving Iris Head's windshield a thorough going over with a squeegee. He called out to her, but she didn't feel like small talk so she waved and kept going. As she approached First Street, she saw Kelly Ann coming out of the Village Grocer struggling with two very large grocery bags and she hurried over to help her.

"Yer jus' the person I wanted to see," Kelly Ann grinned, handing her one of the bags.

"Wouldn't it have been simpler to use a grocery cart?" Emily asked.

"I'm only takin' 'em to grandpa's, and I didn't know they'd be so heavy," she said, tucking a stalk of celery down inside the bag. "Besides, I been lookin' for you anyway. Wanna go see a movie?"

"I don't know," Emily said, hesitating. Her mind galloped through a list of excuses for not going. In truth, she just didn't want to take the chance of running into Jonathan and Bitsy.

"What's up with you?" Kelly Ann asked suspiciously.

"Nothing."

"Well you better notify yer face. It's lookin' sad as a hound dog."

Well," Emily said, deciding she better put an end to the questioning, "I'm trying to decide if I want double butter on my popcorn when we go the movies."

"Now yer talkin'," her friend laughed, as they hurried up the street lugging the heavy bags.

* * *

They watched an old movie from the nineties, inhaling not only double buttered popcorn, but a box of Good & Plenty candy, two large root beers, and a Butterfinger candy bar split down the middle.

"Does this place ever git movies that aren't eighty years old?" Kelly Ann complained, as they walked up the aisle toward the movie exit.

"It sure doesn't," Emily replied, tossing her empty Good & Plenty box in a trash bin. "You have to go into Clayton for the new movies."

"That figures," Kelly Ann sighed, rolling her eyes. "So whaddya wanna do now?"

"Well...." Emily said, furrowing her brow as she thought about it. She finally shrugged. "I don't think there's much for us to do at eight o'clock at night." She just wanted to go home anyway. She had sat through the entire movie thinking about Jonathan and Bitsy, deciding she'd like to knock both their heads together, with a swift kick to follow.

"I know," Kelly Ann said, perking up, "let's go to the Grange Hall, they have a dance ever' Saturday night."

"First of all," Emily said, frowning, "I don't know where the Grange Hall is, and second, I don't want to go to a dance."

"Don't worry, Emmy Lou," she laughed, grabbing Emily's arm and pulling her up the street, "they won't let us in anyway, it's for adults. I jus' like to watch through th' window."

Emily pulled back. "Excuse me for saying so, but watching people dance through an open window doesn't seem like a whole lot of fun."

"Come on, goofy," Kelly Ann said, laughing as she propelled Emily up the street.

Oh, what the heck, Emily thought, suddenly caught up in the silliness of it. "How far is it?" she asked.

"It's right over there on River Road," Kelly Ann said, pointing to an area across the road from the picnic grounds.

Emily could barely see the log structure tucked back in a stand of trees. Funny she had never noticed it before. As they crunched across the gravel parking lot, Kelly Ann had to raise her voice to be heard above the music blaring through outside speakers. "Let's stand over here," she shouted, "it's ever'body's favorite spot."

"Who's everybody?"

"Oh," Kelly Ann replied, looking a little sheepish, "the kids come over from the picnic grounds and look in the window when they're bored."

Great endorsement, Emily wanted to say, but kept her mouth shut.

They peered in the low window and watched older couples bobbing up and down, dancing to an old Merle Haggard song. Emily didn't recognize anyone and soon grew bored. "Is this all there is to it?" she shouted above the music.

"Just watch," Kelly Ann shouted back.

About then Gus came dancing into view with a plump, attractive looking dark-haired woman.

Emily burst out laughing. "Who's Gus dancing with!" she hooted.

"That's Carlotta," Kelly Ann said, laughing along with her. "Mr. Montoya's sister."

They watched as the two went spinning around the room and collided with another couple. Then they careened in the opposite direction and nearly upset the punch bowl.

The girls howled with laughter.

"How long's he been seeing her?" Emily cackled, as she blotted away the tears of laughter with her sleeve.

"Oh, she's been after him for years," Kelly Ann said. "She brings Uncle Gus homemade tamales to the gas station, and I think he goes ta' her house too—but he won't tell me."

"*Uncle* Gus?" Emily asked. "Are you related to him?"

"Naw, but he and Grandpa have been friends forever, and that's what I grew up callin' him."

She watched until Gus and Carlotta had danced to the other side of the room and out of sight. "You sure know a lot about people in this town."

"Well," her friend drawled, "I get out and meet people." She gave Emily a quick glance. "And I don't just sit around Grandpa's café, or hang around the library or bakery, like some people I know."

Emily glared at her, feeling more than a little annoyed. "You know what?" she said, not bothering to hide her irritation. "I'm really tired of your comments about what I do, and don't do." She turned to walk away.

"Oh thunderation! Don't be mad," Kelly Ann cajoled, hanging onto her arm. "How come yer so touchy all of a sudden?"

Emily knew why but wasn't about to tell her about Jonathan and Bitsy, so she just shrugged, and said nothing.

"I'll quit givin' ya' such a hard time," Kelly Ann grinned. "Let's jus' watch a while longer, the booze starts flowin' and it gets really funny. Some of 'em get so drunk they fall down."

Emily couldn't believe what she was hearing. "I don't think drunk people are funny," she said, glaring at Kelly Ann. "Does Gus get drunk too?"

"Naw, Uncle Gus doesn't drink, but a lot of 'em do." She tilted her head to one side. "Why are you so fussy?"

"I can't believe you think it's funny when people get drunk!"

"Oh come on, Emmy Lou, it's jus' life."

"No, it isn't *just life!"* she said heatedly. "Why would you say that? Don't you want something better?"

"Sheesh! Lighten up, wouldja?" Kelly Ann said, turning away from her. "I never thought about it, okay?"

"Well, you'd better think about it," she said. "Do you want your kids to have a life like ours?"

"All right. All right!" Kelly Ann said, growing angry herself. "Let's leave. And would you kindly just calm down fer Pete's sake."

They walked down the street in an uncomfortable silence. Kelly Ann finally spoke up. "I didn't know you were so all-fired worried about life."

"Aren't you?" Emily asked, glaring straight ahead.

"I told you, I never think about it," she said. "I jus' do what comes next."

"Do you have any kind of plan," Emily asked, "besides just doing, *what comes next*?"

"Well yeah, sorta'."

"What?"

"Oh, I don't know," Kelly Ann said, "I figure if I git a good education, that'll help me out some–so I keep my grades up."

"That's good," Emily agreed, taking a deep breath, and feeling her anger subside. "What else?"

"I dunno," she shrugged. "I'm just tryin' to keep my head on straight, stayin' with Grandpa, hopin' my mama is gettin' help so she doesn't drink herself ta' death." Kelly Ann looked at her evenly. "But you know what Emmy Lou? So far it all kinda'stinks. Havin' fun helps me to keep my mind off it."

"What about when you get married and stuff?" Emily asked.

"I'm fifteen, not forty. Why would I worry about that now?"

"Kelly Ann, I'm not saying to *worry*, I'm saying to *plan* so that it doesn't happen."

"So *what* doesn't happen?" Kelly Ann said angrily, throwing her hands into the air.

"So that you don't marry a person who drinks, just because it's what you're used to. So that you have a good home to raise your kids in, not one that stinks." Emily stopped and turned toward her. "Look, it's really good that you're getting good grades and all that, but there are other things that can trip you up. Smart people can make stupid decisions, you know!"

"I know, I know," Kelly Ann sighed. "I know all about how drinkin' runs in families and all about *generational* problems." She sighed again. "Sometimes I think I'm just doomed."

"Well you're *not* doomed," Emily said, putting her arm around her. "And neither am I. We can think and plan different lives than our families have." She gave her an extra squeeze. "It's really good that you're getting good grades, too!"

"You're plum crazy," her friend laughed.

"Crazier than a pet coon," Emily agreed, laughing along with her. "And you just wait until we're in Wal-Mart again. I'm buying you something."

"Oh really," Kelly Ann laughed. "And jus' what are you buyin' me, may I ask?"

"A journal."

"*A journal!* What in thunderation for?"

"Oh, you'll see."

"You really *are* crazy!" Kelly Ann laughed, hugging her again.

* * * *

"What do you wanna' do now?" Kelly Ann asked, as she and Emily left the school grounds, the last day of school before Christmas break. A wind gusted and the girls hugged themselves against the cold.

"I'm not sure," said Emily, shivering.

"Want to go over to your house?" Kelly Ann asked.

Emily was at a loss for words. "I don't think that would work," she finally said, pulling up the collar on her jacket.

Kelly Ann stopped and stared at her. "Oh, I get it," she finally said. "I never brought friends to my mama's house, either. Never know what to expect, right?"

"Well, actually, I know exactly what to expect," Emily replied, with an impish grin. "My parents would take off for their room, and my grandmother would throw her slipper at you."

They were still laughing when they walked by Gus's station.

"Anyone gonna share the joke with me?" Gus called out. He was polishing his vintage pick-up, nicknamed the *Leapin' Lena.* The villagers had so nick-named the truck because Gus had never quite mastered the clutch and was often seen leaping down First Street.

Emily and Kelly Ann turned into the station.

"Look out! Here comes trouble," Gus said, with a grin that nearly wrapped around his head.

Kelly Ann stuck her tongue out at him.

"What're you two girls up to today?" he chuckled.

"Well, I don't know what *we're* up to," Kelly Ann replied playfully, "but we know what *you* were up to Saturday night."

"What're you talkin' about, Miss Sassy."

"How's Carlotta?" she asked, batting her eyelashes.

"Oh law, where you been snoopin' now?"

"Through the window of the Grange Hall. You're quite the dancers, you and Carlotta."

Gus took off his ball cap and scratched his head. "Ya know, I b'lieve I'll just talk to someone with a few manners," he said, turning to Emily.

"How're you doin' Em'ly?"

"Great!" she replied, trying not to laugh. "How about you, Gus?"

"Well, I was havin' a fine day 'til a certain snoop come around."

"You got any tamales to share with us, Uncle Gus?" Kelly Ann laughed.

"No," he said, his face reddening, "but if you'll quit pesterin' me, I'll give ya' an Orange Crush."

"It's a deal," she said, scampering ahead of him to the blue soda machine.

YipYap came strolling over and Kelly Ann scooped him up.

"Hi, YapYap!" she crooned, cupping the dog's face in her hand. "Can you say 'hi'?"

"Rye," croaked YipYap.

Emily couldn't believe her ears.

"Try again, YipYap," Kelly Ann coaxed. "HI" she repeated, her voiced raised to a falsetto.

"Yi" the dog whined.

"No way!" Emily said, her mouth hanging open.

"Told ya'," Gus said proudly. "Kelly Ann's one 'a the few people that can get that dog talkin'. He talks to me all the time."

"No way!" Emily kept repeating.

* * * *

Emily sat next to Miss Mattie in the center pew, as the choir's beautiful voices rose and fell to *The Little Drummer Boy.* The pulpit was decorated with green wreaths and red bows; a tall Christmas tree twinkled in the corner.

Emily closed her eyes and hummed along. *Then she saw Him...pa rum pum pum pum; the newborn King...pa rum pum pum pum...* The music soothed her soul, and she wished she could stay in this moment forever. When the song was over, they all stood as Pastor Alex read the benediction and dismissed them. Miss Mattie led the way up the aisle toward the door, greeting people, and wishing them a wonderful holiday season. Emily kept a smile glued to her face, saying, "Good morning" to one person and, "Merry Christmas" to another, nodding and smiling as parishioners complimented her church hat. Miss Mattie had loaned it to her. It was deep green and sported holly berries on its wide brim.

"You look very fetching today, my dear," the elder's wife was saying, as she shook her hand, but Emily had quit listening. She had looked up and saw Jonathan waiting for her just three pews ahead. He stood smiling at her.

"I need to find a rest room," she whispered to Miss Mattie, then turned and cut across empty pews. Miss Mattie called out to her, but she pretended not to hear, glaring at Jonathan as she hurried toward the side exit.

He looked stricken.

Good! she thought.

She bolted out the side door and made a dash for the park. She would apologize to Miss Mattie later. As she ran through the church grounds, she could hear footsteps thudding behind her.

"Emily, wait up!" Jonathan shouted.

She tried to sprint ahead, but her dress tangled around her legs. She reached down and bunched the hem together, then took off at a dead run. She could hear his footsteps thundering up behind her.

"Emily!" Jonathan said, grabbing her arm, and spinning her around.

"Let my arm go," she said breathlessly, trying to yank it away.

"Not until you tell me what's wrong," he huffed, out of breath himself.

"Nothing's wrong," she lied, her chest heaving. She was so angry, she could have knocked him in the head.

"We're not moving until you tell me what you're mad about," he said, his eyes smoldering.

She glared at him. He glared back. Then to her utter amazement, she burst into tears.

"Now look what you've done," she sobbed.

"Look what *I've* done?" he said, staring at her in disbelief. "What have I done?"

But she was crying too hard to talk—and wouldn't have told him, even if she could.

"Just tell me what's wrong," he said more gently, pulling her to his chest.

"Boys are *stupid*! You're stupid," she heaved, aware that she sounded somewhat deranged.

"We are?" he said, in a muffled voice. "Why are we stupid?"

Was Jonathan laughing?

She peeked up at him. *He was!*

Her fury mounted as she pushed him away and sputtered, "How can you like fluttering eyelashes with no brains?"

"*What?*"

"No brains! *Just little ol' Bitsy me*!" she mimicked.

"What??!!" Jonathan was laughing again. "Did you see me helping Bitsy to the medical center?"

"Why would you help Bitsy to the medical center?" she snorted.

"Because she pretended like she'd twisted her ankle," he said.

"She did *what*?"

"She saw me downtown and asked me to go to the movies with her," Jonathan said. "I told her I already had plans. Then she turned and stepped off the curb and screamed. She started limping and said she'd twisted her ankle and couldn't walk. She asked me if I would help her to the medical center."

"Really?" Emily asked in disbelief.

"Yes, really," he said. "I helped her hop all the way there." He was looking directly into Emily's eyes. "She tried to get me to carry her, but I smelled a rat. She wasn't even hurt and admitted it after the doctor called her dad—excuse me—called Big Daddy to come down." He sighed. "That whole family is weird."

"Oh..." she replied, feeling stupid.

"Is that why you're mad at me?" he said slowly. "You think I like that dopey girl?"

"You can like whoever you want," she said, trying to cover her embarrassment, "or run into flagpoles over them for all I care."

"*What?*"

"Nothing."

He reached out and tugged her hat brim down over her eyes. "You're funny!"

She swatted at his hand. "Leave my hat alone," she said, trying not to smile.

"Are we okay now?"

"Maybe," she said, adjusting her hat.

He gazed down at her, and she couldn't help staring back up at him.

"We're having a Christmas party tomorrow night," he said, his hand brushing her face. "I wanted to invite you over. Lots of food, fire in the fireplace, hot chocolate—stuff like that."

She hesitated, she had been to his house for other get togethers, but she was embarrassed to go after the scene she'd just made. "I might be busy."

She was thrilled at the utter disappointment in his eyes.

"I really don't like Bitsy," he said, still gazing down at her.

"Okay," she replied, not able to look away from him. "I'll think about it."

"All right," he said, and turned to go.

Her heart plunged. "I'm going caroling with the church tonight, are you?" she asked.

He turned around and grinned at her. "I am now," he said, giving her hat another tug.

She laughed and swatted at his hand again.

CHAPTER - 15

"Are you nervous or somethin'?" Kelly Ann asked, as she and Emily tramped through the snow the next evening, on their way to the Charles' home for their annual Christmas party.

Emily shrugged, "I'm just not that comfortable around a crowd of people that I don't know." She didn't mention that she was still a little embarrassed over getting mad at Jonathan about Bitsy.

"Well why in thunder are you goin' then?" Kelly Ann asked, scowling.

Emily glanced at her and said, "Because, if I only did the things I was comfortable doing, I'd just wind up sitting in my room for the rest of my life."

"Are you shy?" her friend asked.

"Maybe," Emily shrugged. "Whatever it is, I just think, 'Do it scared, until you're doing it brave!'"

"Hmmm," I like that," Kelly Ann said, nodding like she understood.

Emily was relieved that she didn't make a sarcastic come-back.

"I jus' hope there's people our own age ta' hang around with," Kelly Ann sighed, as they approached the house. "I'm not big on hangin' around a bunch of adults—they ask too many questions."

"Well, Jonathan will be there, and his older brother," Emily told her.

"His brother is really cute, too," Kelly Ann said, perking up. "What's his name, I keep forgettin' it."

"His name is Ed," Emily said, "and there are two younger brothers. They're little though, one's about a year old and the other around four."

"How do you know so much about their family?" Kelly Ann asked.

"Mrs. Charles has asked me to babysit a couple of times, and I've gone to other things at their house."

Kelly Ann eyed her suspiciously. "Do you like Jonathan?"

"Sure," Emily said, feigning innocence. "He's a good friend."

"You know that's not what I mean."

Emily looked at her. "I've already told you I don't want a boyfriend. Remember?"

"Oh, I remember," Kelly Ann said, grinning. "I jus' don't know if I believe it."

They rang the doorbell and stamped their boots to get the snow off. Mr. Charles, dressed in a bright red holiday sweater, swung the door open, greeting them with a huge grin.

"Well, hello ladies! Come in, come in!" he said, throwing the door open even wider, and sweeping his hand in a motion for them to enter.

"Hey, Mr. C," the girls chorused as they entered the foyer. They sat on a narrow bench and pulled their boots off, then tugged up their socks.

"Hang your jackets and scarves over there," Mr. Charles said, pointing to a coat rack which had several jackets on it already, "then come on in and join everyone."

Emily loved Mr. C's house and gazed around as she hung her jacket on a hook and stuffed her scarf in the pocket. The gorgeous wood on the staircase banisters had holly and greenery looped around it, with scattered red bows and glittery pinecones. The whole house looked like a Macy's Christmas window display, with a beautifully decorated tree twinkling in the living room, near the fireplace.

In the gathering room, family and friends were sitting in small groups talking and eating. "Attention everyone," Mr. Charles shouted. "I want to introduce some friends of ours." He extended his arms toward the girls. "Meet Emily Parks and Kelly Ann Parrish."

Everyone waved and yelled their hellos.

Jonathan and his older brother, Ed came over and Mr. Charles said, "Would you guys show the girls where all the food is, while I find your mother."

"Finally," Kelly Ann whispered, "somethin' fun with two cute boys."

Emily elbowed her, hoping nobody heard.

"The food's over here," said Ed, leading the way. Kelly Ann gave him a dazzling smile and began chatting like they were old friends.

Jonathan, who Emily noticed looked quite handsome in a deep blue shirt, offered his arm. "Glad you could make it," he grinned.

"Me too!" she replied, taking his arm.

They walked over to a buffet table and Emily's mouth began to water as she took in the platters of sliced meats, large bowls of green salad, fruit salad, two different pasta dishes, and baskets of crusty bread. Jonathan picked up two plates that were etched with silver Christmas trees, handed Emily one and began to scoop big helpings of each dish onto their plates, along with slices of turkey and roast beef.

"Sorry we don't have any cranberry sauce," he grinned.

"Me too!" she smiled back, thinking his shirt made his eyes look the exact color of blueberries.

She glanced over at the people seated in small groups and saw some of them watching her and Jonathan with that smile adults get when they think something's cute. She ignored them and looked around for Kelly Ann, spotting her with a group of young people, laughing and chatting away. Jonathan led her to a small table. As they sat down, she stared down at her plate, wondering how she could ever eat all the food Jonathan had loaded on it, but she was hungry and started right in.

"I'll get us some drinks," Jonathan said, hurrying off.

Mrs. Charles walked over just as she put a big bite of lasagna into her mouth. "We're glad you could join us, Emily," she said, sitting down in Jonathan's chair.

"Hi, Mrs. C" she said, swallowing quickly. "I love the way you've decorated your home."

"Thank you," she smiled. "My husband tells me you are taking photography lessons; how do you like it?"

"I love it," Emily said, "and I'm learning a lot."

"There's nothing that can tell a story like a good picture."

"That's exactly how I feel," Emily said. "But didn't Mr. C say that you were going to be taking photography classes, too?"

"I am after the first of the year," she replied. "Maybe we'll be in the same class together."

"That would be fun," Emily said, smiling at her.

Jonathan came back over with their drinks.

"Well, enjoy your food," Mrs. Charles said, standing up and heading over to greet some new guests in the foyer.

Emily thanked Jonathan for the drink and dug back into her food, thinking how everything tasted so wonderful.

"Wow, you must be hungry..." he said, nodding at her plate.

She looked down, surprised to see her food half eaten.

"Oh...," she said, feeling a little embarrassed. "It's really yummy!"

"For someone so small, you eat like a lumberjack!" he laughed, digging into his own food.

Unsure how to respond to that, she shrugged and returned to her plate.

"Your mom did a beautiful job of decorating your house," she told him, glancing back at the buffet table wondering if there was any dessert.

"Yeah, she's good at that stuff," he said, finishing up his plate. He noticed her staring at the buffet table. "Are you *still* hungry?

"Well, I was kind of wondering if there was any dessert..."

He laughed, and stood up. "Let's go find out."

Later, Emily tried mingling a little more with the other guests. She saw Aunt Mary and went over to her. "Merry Christmas!" she said.

"Merry Christmas, sweetie," Aunt Mary said, patting the seat next to her. "Sit down!"

"This is my first white Christmas," Emily said, as a conversation opener.

"Oh, kid," Aunt Mary gushed, "don't you just love Christmas here in Mountain Grove; it's like a picture postcard! I've lived here all my life and wouldn't want to live anywhere else in the world."

Emily agreed and Aunt Mary began telling her stories of Mountain Grove; she was just telling about General Emerson and the mysterious document he was signing when Emily felt someone standing by her. She looked up and saw Jonathan with a cup of punch in his hand.

"Thought you might be thirsty," he said, holding the plastic cup out toward her.

"Thank you," she said, reaching for the drink.

"Would you like something to drink, Aunt Mary?" he asked.

"No, sweetie, but thanks." She pointed to the empty chair next to Emily. "Do you want to sit down with us?"

He glanced at the chair. "I'd like to but Dad needs help setting up another table. Thanks anyway."

They both watched him walk away.

"That is one nice young man," Aunt Mary said, giving her a side glance.

Emily gulped down her punch.

* * * *

Emily sat on her bed cross-legged with her journal in her lap. She turned to the page titled *Emily's House* and wrote at the bottom of her list:

A house that is decorated warm & homey with bright colors and plenty of woodwork (window casings, stairs and bannisters, crown molding).

She reread it and started to close the journal, then added:

I think the spirit of the house has to be warm, too.

She didn't know if that was exactly the way to word it, but it was the closest she could come to describing the Charles' home.

* * * *

Emily emptied the Mason jar onto her bed. Five, ten, and twenty dollar bills spilled out, along with a sprinkling of one dollar bills. She separated them into piles and started counting. "Five hundred and eighty, six hundred, six hundred and twenty!" she said out loud, as she finished counting the stack of twenties. Incredible! Six hundred and twenty dollars! With her birthday gift certificate, it would be enough for everything: camera, case, chip, and tri-pod! She was so excited she could barely get the paper clip on each stack of bills. She hurriedly stuffed them into a manila envelope, deciding she would run right over to Taylor's camera shop today.

As she tore through the living room, Pearl stopped her. "Where you goin' in such a hurry?"

Emily ran over and planted a kiss on top of her wiry hair. "To buy a camera!" she all but sang. "I've finally saved enough to get just the one I've been wanting!"

"Where'd you get that kinda money?" Pearl asked suspiciously.

Emily froze, realizing the mistake she had just made.

"I've earned it doing different jobs for people around town," Emily said, deciding the truth was her only option, "but I'd appreciate it if you wouldn't say anything to Mom or Dad."

"Why not?" her grandmother scowled.

"You already know why."

Pearl looked at her a long time. "I didn't know you was interested in cam'ras."

"I'm very interested," Emily said, kneeling down by her grandmother's chair. "I've been taking photography lessons."

Pearl nodded her head and looked at her. "Well, don't worry, I won't say nothin' to nobody."

Relieved, Emily grinned. "I'll come home and take your picture later."

"Why would you ever want *my* picture?" her grandmother scowled.

Emily drew close to her. "Because you're my grandmother, and I'm starting a family album. I just want something normal in my life."

Pearl stared at her, then slowly leaned her head back on the chair and closed her eyes. "I remember wantin' the same thing when I was a girl."

She found that her grandmother had slipped her hand into hers. She squeezed it, then stood up and headed toward the door. "I'll be back soon."

"Don't be bringin' a cam'ra around me with my hair a mess," her grandmother called after her.

"I have a hat I'll let you wear," Emily laughed. "See you after while."

* * * *

Emily lifted her blue church hat out of its round box and Pearl's eyes lit up.

"Where in blazes (only she didn't say *blazes*) did you get that?" she asked.

"A friend bought it for me to wear to church with her."

"That's the prettiest hat I ever laid eyes on," Pearl said, as Emily put it into her blue veined hands.

Pearl held the hat carefully, turning it this way and that. "I always did love hats!"

"I love them, too," Emily said, taking the hat from her grandmother's hands, and setting it on her grey head.

"Oh, I'm too ugly for a hat that pretty," her grandmother protested, but left it on.

Emily fussed with the hat, setting it at just the right angle. The color of the hat intensified the color of her grandmother's eyes, and Emily was startled at how pretty she looked.

"Grandma! You look beautiful!" she laughed, then realized that she'd just called Pearl "grandma".

Pearl said nothing, just looked up at her with watery eyes.

"Hold still and let me get my camera!" Emily said, and hurried out of the room.

She had Pearl pose with her head at different angles, laughing as her grandmother got into the spirit of it, and turned her head this way and that—she even smiled once or twice.

Emily quickly snapped pictures of every pose, and then took the camera over so Pearl could see.

"See how pretty you look?" she said, bringing the pictures up on the viewing screen. They looked at picture after picture of Pearl peering into the camera, of Pearl's profile, and of Pearl sitting with the hat tilted at a jaunty angle. Emily was startled to hear a sound she had never heard before—her grandmother laughing out loud. Emily laughed, too, as they tried to pick out just the right picture for her family album.

"What are you two laughing at?" a voice snarled, startling them both.

Emily looked up to see her mother standing there glaring at them; she was still in her bath robe and slippers.

"Just some pictures," Emily said, blocking her mother's view of the camera.

"Well, keep it down," her mother snapped. "My head hurts and I don't feel like hearing any of your silly noise."

After she left, Emily tried to recapture the moment, but it was useless. Feeling foolish, Pearl took the hat off and handed it to Emily, then turned her attention back to her TV show.

Emily picked up her camera and with a dull ache, went into her room.

* * * *

"Miss Mattie!"

Miss Mattie turned toward her.

Flash! Flash! Flash! Emily shot three pictures, rapid fire.

"What on earth...?" Miss Mattie appeared dazed and unfocused. "All I can see are stars!"

"It's for my family album," Emily laughed. "I like natural shots."

"I don't think *natural* means my mouth hangin' open!"

Emily took a few more pictures around the bakery; including one of the table they always sat at. She wished someone would come in and take a picture of her and Miss Mattie sitting together. *Oh well,* she thought, *maybe later.*

"Thanks Miss Mattie, see you after while!"

"You jus' got here!"

"I'm on a picture-taking mission," she laughed, heading out the door.

* * * *

"Ike!"

Ike's head swung around and Emily snapped a picture of him hovering over his grill, spatula in mid-air.

"Got yer' cam'ra I see!" he cackled.

"I sure did, and I'm filling up my family album. Turn around and I'll get your apron, full view."

"Let me adjust my hat too..."

She fired off two more shots and went back into the dining area.

Miss Rose was putting a fork full of eggs benedict into her mouth when she saw the flash go off. Miss Violet, seated next to her, leaned forward and posed with her face tilted at an angle that caused her left earring to dangle in her glass of iced tea. Emily laughed and took her picture.

Iris Head's picture was taken as she sat looking over her real estate listings. Mr. Kingery saw her coming and sat up straight, sucked his stomach in, and posed with his *Good Eats* coffee mug in mid-air.

"Emily, whatever *are* you doing?" trilled Miss Rose, not at all happy about being captured in such an undignified pose for all the world to see.

"I'm taking pictures for my family album."

"I see," Miss Rose murmured, touched that Emily considered her family. "Do you suppose I might be in your album with another pose?"

Emily fired off four shots of Miss Rose posing demurely, but she really liked the one of her eating eggs benedict the best.

She swung her camera to the left, just in time to capture Miss Violet blotting her satin blouse where iced tea had dripped off her earrings and stained it. She used a laced handkerchief and kept her pinky extended as she daubed away. As Miss Violet bent over, the part at the top of her head revealed gray roots almost an inch long. Emily didn't take a picture of those though. She knew better.

"Tell us about this album you're putting together," Iris said, her interest sparked.

"Well," Emily began, making some minor adjustments to her camera settings, "Miss Mattie showed me her family album, with pictures taken from the time she was a little girl, and I decided I wanted a family album, too. The problem is, I don't have much family around here. Then I thought about it—and well—*you're* all my family."

"I see," Iris said, putting her hand to her chest, touched to her very core. She reached for a napkin, pretending she had something in her eye. "Would you like a group photo?" she said, her voice sounding clogged.

"No, I like pictures of you doing your everyday things," Emily told her, wondering why she sounded so funny.

Iris' nose started running and she dabbed under her eyes as streams of mascara trickled down.

"Are you okay?" Emily asked.

Iris finally gave up and just bawled into her napkin. "I didn't know you thought of me as family," she sobbed. "That's the sweetest thing I ever heard!"

Emily fired off some more shots and caught a teary-eyed Iris Head blowing her nose into a paper napkin.

"Here, let me pose," she protested, attempting to smile into the camera.

Emily laughed and took three pictures of Iris, who resembled a bleary-eyed raccoon.

* * * *

On Christmas Eve, Emily lifted the small Christmas tree from its box. Jonathan had surprised her with it yesterday, bringing it into Good Eats, where she was working the lunch shift. She remembered the look on his face when he handed it to her.

"How did you know I wanted one?" was all she could manage to say.

"I just did," he said, looking like he wanted to say more, but couldn't because customers in the café were watching.

"Thank you," she whispered, touching his face.

"You're welcome," he replied, pulling her to him for a quick hug.

The thought of his gaze warmed her as she looked around her bedroom for a place to set up the tree. She decided the dresser at the end of her bed would give her the best view.

She swept everything off the top, dusted the entire dresser with an old t-shirt, and carefully placed the two-foot tree in the center. She worked quickly, straightening the tree's wire branches, and shaping it into a miniature evergreen.

She stepped back and eyed the tree closely to make sure she had gotten the shape just right. Perfect! She was delighted with the tree's symmetry, and hurried over to plug it in. "My first Christmas tree," she said out loud, as its small twinkling lights lit the room.

She quickly changed into her pajamas, turned down her covers, and plumped up the pillows on her bed. She clicked off her desk lamp so the tree's soft glow was the only light in the room, then noticed a small switch on the tree stand and flipped it on.

Strains of *O Holy Night!* filled the room. She climbed into bed and leaned back on her pillows, staring at the tree as she listened. The small lights began to twinkle.

O holy night! The stars are brightly shining; It is the night of Our dear Savior's birth.

They sang that very song when she went caroling with the church last week. She hummed the second verse, not quite sure of the words, but remembered the third verse, and softly sang along.

A thrill of hope the weary world rejoices, For yonder breaks a new and glorious morn.

A sweet presence filled the room and Emily closed her eyes.

Fall on your knees! O, hear the angels' voices!

As the music played on, Emily sighed with a longing for something she didn't quite understand. She nestled down into her bed as drowsiness overtook her, comforted by the joy that filled the room, and the presence that filled her heart.

* * * *

The next morning, Emily peeked through her bedroom window blinds at a world blanketed with a foot of freshly fallen snow. *A white Christmas!* She was thrilled to the core.

She hunkered back into her warm blankets and began to plan her day. She knew when she walked out to the kitchen there would be a Christmas gift on the counter. There always was. She wasn't especially curious about it, and almost wished her parents would just skip that part of Christmas, along with the rest. It was silly to pretend. First, she would open her gift, and then get something to eat. She was famished since she had stayed in her room all of Christmas Eve. Her parents had their biggest fights on holidays. Next, she'd get dressed, and when she heard her parents get up, she would leave before the first shout, or first dish was thrown. She hoped they would sleep a long time, so she could stay home as long as possible. It would be embarrassing to be seen walking downtown on Christmas morning, when families should be celebrating together.

"They should sleep late," she murmured, as she threw her blankets off. "They drank enough booze last night to be in a coma 'til Easter."

* * * *

Emily stared at her Christmas gift laying on the kitchen counter. It was wrapped in green foil paper, dotted with little snowmen in red scarves. It had a wide red ribbon tied around it, and glittering pinecones pinned to the center of the red bow. Her dad had paid the store to wrap it for her. If she had tunnel vision, and saw the gift only, it seemed like a wonderful gift given by a loving father. She went back to her bedroom and returned with her camera. She took five different shots of the gift, aiming the lens carefully, so the empty booze bottles in the background didn't show. She didn't know if the pictures would make it into her family album or not; she would have to think about it. *But really, what was there to think about?* Most of her life was a pretense to the outside world, and she wanted the album to be honest. She hit the delete button five times.

* * * *

Emily heard her parents get up two hours later, and quickly threw on her clothes. She pulled on the fur-lined boots her dad had bought her for Christmas and tucked her jeans down into the tops of them. She hurriedly laced them up, then grabbed her warmest jacket, a knit hat, and wound a red scarf around her neck. She would stop briefly, thank her parents for the boots, and keep going toward the front door.

The Christmas bells at Saint Daniel's pealed as Emily walked down Elderberry Way later that day, making her heart glad. She belonged to this village and it belonged to her. Belonging. That was a pretty astounding feeling. She smiled as she thought about it, but her attention was soon diverted by the families in Emerson Park. Children were running around in bright jackets and scarves, riding new bikes and scooters, and operating their new remote-control cars, as their parents stood smiling and watching. She sighed with relief that she wasn't the only one out on Christmas day.

She heard the theater was going to be open on Christmas and walked toward Second Street, where she saw a line formed at the Grand Theatre. On the marquee, *A Christmas Story* was written in red and green letters. She was surprised to see Miss Mattie standing in line for the movie. When she spotted Emily, her face lit up, and she waved her over.

Emily ran up and hugged her. "Merry Christmas," she said, feeling extremely happy. "I thought you were going to your sister's for Christmas?"

"Me, too," Miss Mattie said, grinning as she returned the hug, "but she got called off to her daughter's who is havin' twins that decided to come early." She held Emily at arm's length. "Want to come to the movies with me? My treat!"

"I've seen this movie a million times."

"Well, Sugar, who hasn't?" she laughed. "Come on, we'll get fat together on buttered popcorn!"

Emily stepped into line, having all the warm expectations of an afternoon spent with a good friend. She couldn't have been happier. Only a few minutes ago she had dreaded a day of loneliness stretched out in front of her—and now, look at this! Good company, a funny movie, and buttered popcorn to boot!"

"Merry Christmas!" she wanted to shout.

CHAPTER - 16

Late Saturday afternoon, Emily bundled up and went looking for Kelly Ann. The Christmas holidays were over and there was a big event basketball game going on at the high school later. She wanted Kelly Ann to go with her. Ordinarily she didn't go to school events, but Kelly Ann's constant remarks about her never going anywhere had made her think that maybe she was right. She stopped in at Good Eats Café and after greeting the patrons, she asked Ike, "Do you know where I can find Kelly Ann?"

"Haven't seen her all day," he said, heading for the phone on his wall. "Let me call the house for you, I been meanin' to check in on her anyway."

He looked concerned as the phone rang and rang and no one answered. "I guess I'm gonna need ta break down and git her one of them cell phones," he sighed. "I cain't keep track of her ta save my life."

"It's okay, Ike, I'll find her," Emily said, heading for the door. "If you see her before I do, tell her I'm going to the basketball game at the high school, and to come on over."

He nodded, looking worried. She was a little concerned, too, and took off up the street for the picnic grounds. She had a hunch that she would find Kelly Ann there. Walking up Jack Pine Road, she peered through the trees to the picnic area and saw a group of kids sitting around in a huddle. *I hope Kelly Ann's not with them,* she thought.

Emily crept in further and stood in the shadow of a broad oak tree, hoping no one in the group would see her. She wanted to turn and run but was determined to see if Kelly Ann was anywhere around. Peeking out, she saw about eight kids, including Logger and Mack, sitting in a circle passing around what looked like a big fat homemade cigarette, but she knew it was pot. Each person took a puff and then handed it to the next person. Relief flooded her when she saw that Kelly Ann was not among the group, and she crept out of the trees, and headed over to the high school gymnasium by herself.

* * * *

Emily met Kelly Ann in front of the church Sunday afternoon, and they headed down the street toward Good Eats for one of Ike's good root beer floats.

"Brrrrr, it's colder 'n a possums' butt out here," Kelly Ann said, wrapping her wool scarf around the lower part of her face.

Emily nodded, pulling her jacket collar up as far as it would go. They picked up their pace as they hurried toward the café. Glen Kingery sat at the counter with his usual mug of coffee, and Emily and Kelly Ann thumped down beside him, still shivering from the cold.

"Cold enough for you gals?" laughed Glen.

"Brrrrrrr!" they said in unison.

"Weatherman said it would break by the end of the week and warm up a little," he said, as Ike set a juicy cheeseburger down in front of him.

"And we all know how accurate the weatherman is," Ike cackled.

"Oh, I almost forgot!" Kelly Ann said, turning to Emily. "I got somethin' I want to show you..."

She reached into her pocket and pulled out a pink cell phone.

"Nice!" Emily said, looking it over. "Where'd you get that?"

"From Grandpa. He thinks I need a leash, doncha, Grandpa?" she said, grinning at him.

"Not a leash, Miss Sassy," Ike said, wiping down the counter around them. "I jus' need ta be able ta get ahold of you sometimes. It's not like I kin' leave the grill in th' middle of th' day and come lookin' for ya."

"I wish you had one too, Emmy Lou," Kelly Ann said, fiddling with the keys. "We could meet up easier."

"That's not going to happen anytime soon," Emily replied, spooning ice cream into her mouth.

Ike scratched his head. "Ya' know, Em'ly," he said, "if you kin' afford about ten dollars a month, I kin' git you one on Kelly Ann's plan. Probably get a free phone, too."

"Really?"

Ike nodded.

"I'll think about it," Emily said, feeling very tempted.

"Okay, jus' let me know," he replied as he headed back to his kitchen.

Kelly Ann looked at her. "Don't you want a phone?" she asked.

"We'll talk about it later," Emily whispered.

* * * *

After the girls left, Mr. Kingery looked up at Ike, and said, "Yer gettin' generous in yer old age, Ike, buyin' a phone for yer gran'daughter an' arrangin' for Em'ly to get one."

"Not really," Ike said, pouring himself a cup of coffee. "I want it so Em'ly can git ahold of Kelly Ann anytime she wants, and vice versa. Kelly Ann's had a bunch of her so-called friends in, and they all look like they're up ta' no good. They're the bunch that hangs out in the picnic grounds smokin' and drinkin'."

"You worried about Kelly Ann?" Mr. Kingery asked, taking a sip from his mug.

Ike nodded. "I think I smelt alcohol on her th' other night."

"Kids!" Mr. Kingery grumbled, downing the rest of his coffee. "About drive ya nuts, don't they?"

* * * *

"Okay, so tell me now," Kelly Ann said, as they left Good Eats and headed up First Street. "Don't you want a phone?"

"Sure," Emily said, "but it's not that simple."

"Your parents?"

Emily nodded. "They'll never say yes. My dad likes everyone in the house to have to go through him to make phone calls."

"Well, 'scuse me for sayin' so, but that seems a tad bit controllin'," Kelly Ann said, rolling her eyes. "Would your parents even have to know?"

"They couldn't know, they'd just yell and scream," Emily sighed. "They don't know about my camera, either."

"So why doncha jus' go ahead and get the phone then?"

"It's one more thing to juggle," Emily replied wistfully. "I wish I could just tell them."

"Well, it's *their* fault you can't tell 'em nothin'!"

"I guess, but I still don't want to make bad decisions because they do."

"Been watchin' your TV doctor, huh?" Kelly Ann grinned.

"It helps me through the craziness," Emily said, smiling back at her.

* * * *

Emily was startled when she felt the vibration against her leg. She quickly dug down into her jeans pocket and retrieved the ringing cell phone.

"Hello!"

"Whoo Hooo! Lookit you!"

"Hi, Kelly Ann!"

"Am I the first call you ever got?"

Emily burst out laughing. "No one even knows I have this phone, except for you, silly!"

"Where are you?"

"On my way to Miss Mattie's."

Kelly Ann groaned. "Well, change direction an' come on over to the picnic grounds, I wantcha to meet th' guy I've been tellin' you about. He's got a friend from outta town who wants to meet you."

" *What!*" Emily cried. "Who are you talking about?"

"Never you mind, Miss Fussy," Kelly Ann said. "All I'm sayin' is this guy is really *cute*!"

Emily heard male laughter in the background.

"The picnic ground isn't my thing," Emily said, wondering if the cell phone was such a good idea after all. "Why don't we go to the movies or something?"

"'Cause I don't wanta see a movie that's nine hundred years old, that's why."

Actually, Emily didn't either. She thought a moment. "We could take the train down to Clayton; that's where the new movies are."

"Now you're talkin'!" Kelly Ann hooted. "Grab a newspaper and check to see when it starts. Call me back."

Emily heard a click at the other end.

She headed up First Street toward Good Eats. Ike always had newspapers for his customers.

"Hi, Ike!"

"Mornin' darlin', where's Kelly Ann?"

"Kelly Ann?"

"She said she was gonna be with you today."

"Oh, we're going to a movie in Clayton," Emily said, hoping he didn't ask any more questions. *Kelly Ann better not be telling her grandpa she's with me, when she's really at the picnic grounds,* Emily thought, thoroughly irritated.

"Do you have a newspaper around anywhere, Ike?" she asked, managing to keep the irritation out of her voice. "I want to see what's playing. I'm supposed to meet Kelly Ann in a few minutes."

"How're ya gettin' there?" he asked, furrowing his brow.

"We thought it'd be fun to take the train."

"Well, I'll be," he said, looking relieved. "I never thought of doin' that."

"Jus' the two of you goin'?" he asked nonchalantly, as he handed her the paper.

"Just the two of us—out on an adventure," she smiled. She looked the newspaper over and called Kelly Ann's cell phone.

"Hello..."

"There's a good movie starting in two hours," she said, telling Kelly Ann the name of it.

"I been wantin' to see that one," Kelly Ann said, sounding out of breath. "I jus' got to the train station, and it's crowded, so hurry!"

"I'm on my way."

"I'm goin' to board and save us seats," Kelly Ann said, shouting into the phone to be heard above the noise of the station. "Run! It leaves in twenty minutes."

Emily took off at a trot down First Street. Mr. Montoya was stacking fruit on a pushcart as she dashed by.

"Buenos tardes, senorita," he called to her.

"Burnos tardes," she called over her shoulder. "Can't stop, trying to catch the train..."

"Hurry, hurry," he called after her, "the 2:30 train leaves right on time."

It was five blocks to River Road, where she hooked a left and ran past Mr. Montoya's apple orchard, straight toward the train station.

There were three people ahead of her in line at the ticket window; she waited her turn, nervously checking the big clock on the wall every few seconds.

"One ticket for Clayton," she said, laying her five-dollar bill on the counter.

"It's $5.50," replied the bored ticket lady.

She quickly dug in her pocket, but a man behind her threw two quarters onto the counter. "Let's go," the man said impatiently, "or we'll all miss the train.

"Thanks," she said grabbing her ticket and bolting out the door.

Emily jumped aboard and a minute later the train began to move. She hoped the man who had given her the quarters had made it.

She went down the aisles of two cars looking for Kelly Ann, and finally spotted her at the back of the third car, in an area where the seats sat facing each other. Kelly Ann was talking to a guy sitting in the seat next to her. Emily did a double take, unable to believe what she was seeing. Kelly Ann was sitting next to Logger, gabbing away!

"Hey, Emmy Lou," Kelly Ann said, jumping to her feet when she saw her. "We were afraid you weren't gonna make it!"

"*We*?"

"Remember? I told you I had someone I wanted you to meet?"

"This is my boyfriend, Logger," Kelly Ann said, looking up at him proudly. "And this is Dylan," she said, pointing to the guy seated across from her. "Remember, I told you how cute he was!"

Emily was dumfounded. She glared at Logger and ignored Dylan, who looked about twenty, and had a face that was almost pretty—in a greasy sort of way. He gave her a creepy grin and patted the empty seat next to him.

Enraged, she turned to Kelly Ann. "I thought we were going to the movies alone," she hissed. Her heart was pounding so hard, it felt like it would hammer out of her chest.

Kelly Ann sat back down next to Logger, who gave Emily a knowing grin. The train picked up speed. "I never said 'at no one else was comin,' Kelly Ann said defensively. "Anyway, git a load off yer feet. Next stop is Clayton." She tried to sound lighthearted, but her accent had become thick as porridge. She was nervous.

Emily looked around for a seat somewhere else, but the train was packed. Not knowing what else to do, she glared at Kelly Ann and sat down next to Dylan.

"Logger says you two already know each other," Kelly Ann said, smiling up at him, as she looped her arm through his.

Logger looked at Emily with a smug grin on his face.

Seething, she ignored them both and turned and looked out the window. Her heart was thundering, and she felt like she would have a heart attack if she didn't calm down.

Kelly Ann kept trying to make small talk, but Emily refused to warm up. She could have happily throttled Kelly Ann and tossed her off the train, along with Logger and pretty boy.

The trip took about twenty-five minutes, and when they reached Clayton she stood up and said to Kelly Ann, "I'd like to talk to you a minute—in private."

Without waiting for an answer, Emily walked down the aisle out of hearing range. Kelly Ann got up and followed after her like an obedient puppy.

"Why didn't you tell me you were bringing those two?" Emily hissed, as Kelly Ann stood there blinking nervously.

"Just tryin' to have a little fun," Kelly Ann answered, her voice shaky.

"Logger is a jerk and the other guy is a creep," Emily ranted. "We need to take the next train back!"

She watched Kelly Ann's demeanor change.

"Well, I guess Logger was right," Kelly Ann said through clenched teeth. "He said you had it in for him."

"Logger is an *idiot*," Emily snapped.

"Well, sorry you think so," Kelly Ann snapped back. "He happens to be very nice to me."

Emily didn't know what to do. "Kelly Ann, we need to take the next train back," she said, punctuating each word like she was talking to a child.

"You can do what you want, but I'm goin' to the movies," Kelly Ann said, standing her ground. "Look, just come to the movies and have fun. The train back to Mountain Grove isn't goin' to leave for three hours. Are you gonna sit here all that time? Jus' come to the movies, and we'll all be back in time for the next train."

Emily didn't give a rip about the movie, but she was worried about leaving Kelly Ann alone with those two creeps. The girls were blocking the aisle and people were trying to get around them to get off the train. Emily needed to make a decision.

"I'll go, but I'm sitting next to *you*, not him!" she fumed. She would give Kelly Ann an earful when they got back home.

"Don't worry, I'll make sure we're sittin' together," Kelly Ann said, heading back toward the boys. "It's really not that bigga' deal."

"Well, it is to me," Emily said, remembering how she had told Ike they we going to the movies alone.

The movie theater was about a mile from the train station. No one talked as they walked the last few blocks. Kelly Ann had tried laughing and joking to get everyone in a good mood, but when she realized it wasn't working, she gave up. Emily bought her movie ticket and stayed glued to Kelly Ann's side as they stopped and bought candy at the concession stand. She hadn't looked at Dylan or spoken a word to him the whole trip. Inside the theater, Kelly Ann hurried down front to the middle row. "I just love sittin' way up close," she said, as she plopped down. Emily turned sideways and inched over to the seat on the other side of her. Logger sat down next to Kelly Ann; she didn't see Dylan anymore.

Good, she thought, *maybe he took the hint.*

Emily had just opened her box of Good & Plenty candy when Dylan sat down in the seat to her right. He had walked all the way around the theater to sit next to her. She glared at him and scooted closer to Kelly Ann.

"I ain't gonna bite you," he sneered.

She ignored him, settling into her seat as the movie began. She was going to clobber Kelly Ann for getting her into this. It wasn't long into the movie before she felt Dylan's arm slide around her shoulder. Infuriated, she scooted forward, grabbed the cuff of his jacket, and swung his arm back to his side of the seat.

"Keep your hands to yourself," she snapped, glaring at him.

She saw Logger put his arm around Kelly Ann, who snuggled up close to him.

Gross! she thought.

Out of the corner of her eye, she caught a flash of something and looked over just as Logger tipped up a small flask. He took a long swallow and offered it to Kelly Ann.

"What'd ya bring that stuff for?" Kelly Ann hissed, sitting up and moving away from him.

He ignored her and reached over and handed the flask to Dylan, who took an equally long swallow. The flask was passed back and forth repeatedly.

"Keep yer mitts to yerself or I'll knock you in the head," she heard Kelly Ann bark.

About then, she smelled alcohol and saw that Dylan was holding the flask under her nose, offering her a drink. She shook her head no, but Dylan kept the flask in front of her. She pushed his hand away, but he brought it right back in front of her, laughing as he did. She angrily shoved his hand out of her face, knocking the flask out of his hand into her lap. The liquid spilled all over her jeans, and the smell of alcohol filled the air.

Livid, she stood up. "I'm leaving," she said, not caring who heard.

"Aw, come on!" Dylan snarled. "Sit down!" He yanked her arm, forcing her back down into her seat.

"Don't touch her, you ape," Kelly Ann yelled, helping Emily back to her feet. "Come on, let's go."

"Sit down! "people in back of them yelled.

"'Scuse us," Kelly Ann yelled back, "but we're tryin' to get away from a couple of pigs."

The crowd laughed. "Need help?" one man yelled.

"I'll let ya know," Kelly Ann answered, grabbing Emily's arm and heading for the exit.

"Hurry, those two are gettin' drunk and crazy," Kelly Ann said, practically dragging Emily up the aisle.

"I'm not afraid," Emily said, as she slowed down, refusing to hurry. "We can call for help."

"Sure, and then they'll call my gran'pa and yer parents to come and git us. Is that what you want?"

"No," she replied, and sped up.

They ran out of the theater. "This way," said Kelly Ann, turning left.

"No, the train station is to the right!" Emily insisted.

They both looked at each other, neither one knew for sure. They went left. Up one block and down the next they ran, but nothing looked familiar. They wandered around for twenty minutes, keeping an eye out for Logger and Dylan, and found themselves in a neighborhood with new tract homes, all painted the same color. A man hosing down his driveway watched as they looked around.

"Lost?' he asked.

"Sort of," Kelly Ann told him. "Which way to the train station?"

"It's about two miles that way," he said pointing in the direction they had just come from. "Where're you going?"

"Mountain Grove," she told him.

"Well, you'd better run," he said, checking his watch. "There's only one more train up the mountain tonight, and it leaves in about twenty-five minutes."

They listened carefully as he gave them directions back to the train station, thanked him, and took off running.

"We'll never make it," Kelly Ann said, huffing and puffing after a few blocks. She slowed down, holding her side.

"We have to try," Emily said, grabbing her hand and forcing her on.

They arrived just as the train was pulling out of the station and ran frantically into the depot. "We have to be on that train, can you stop it?" Kelly Ann pleaded with the man behind the ticket counter.

"Sorry, ma'am, we have a schedule to keep," he said, shrugging his shoulders. Where're you goin'?"

"Mountain Grove."

"Well, you'll have to get there another way," he said, locking up his cash drawer. "That was the last train up the mountain tonight."

Emily felt like crying. The ticket agent began locking up the depot, and the girls went back outside and sat on a bench, trying to catch their breath. It was freezing outside, and Emily was afraid that any minute, it would start snowing.

"Who can we call?" Kelly Ann finally asked.

"Would your grandpa come and get us?"

"Well, he would, but the one little problem is you smell like a distillery," Kelly Ann said, shaking her head. "Trust me, my grandpa is *not* going to b'lieve we weren't drinkin'. He's already suspicious of me."

"Well, I can see why."

Kelly Ann opened her mouth to say something but changed her mind. "Fightin' ain't gonna help us now. Let's figure this out."

Emily wanted to yell at her not to say *ain't*—which was pretty ridiculous, given the predicament they were in.

"Okay," Kelly Ann said, trying to think it through, "so anybody in th' village will help us, the problem is choosin' the one that will *believe* us!"

She knew Kelly Ann was right.

"Miss Mattie," Emily blurted out.

"*Miss Mattie!"* Kelly Ann wailed. "I was thinkin' more of Gus!"

"Gus is a gossip; you know he'd tell his cronies."

"Well, that's true," Kelly Ann said. "But why do ya think Miss Mattie would b'lieve you? I don't think she trusts me much."

Emily didn't think so, either, but decided not to say so. "I just think she'll believe me," she said firmly, putting an end to the discussion.

Kelly Ann nodded her head and Emily called Miss Mattie's number.

"Hello," said the voice on the other end.

"Miss Mattie, it's Emily. I'm in a little trouble..."

* * * *

As the girls sat freezing on the bench outside the closed train station, Emily was filled with dread over having to give a full explanation to Miss Mattie. She didn't know how she was going do it without ratting out Kelly Ann. The blue Mazda came bouncing into the parking lot about forty-five minutes later, and Miss Mattie jumped out. "Are you girls all right?" she asked, hurrying over.

Emily hugged her. "Thanks for coming, we're fine." She saw Miss Mattie wince as she smelled the alcohol. When they were all loaded into the car, the smell of alcohol was overpowering, and Miss Mattie rolled down her window to let in some fresh air. "Someone want to tell me why I smell whiskey?" she asked, looking first at Emily in the front seat, and then at Kelly Ann in the back.

"It's my fault," Kelly Ann blurted out. As they drove back up the mountain, she told the whole story from beginning to end, without sparing herself. Emily kept glancing at Miss Mattie's stony profile as the story unfolded. She was definitely not pleased with what she was hearing.

When Kelly Ann finished telling everything, Miss Mattie said in a cold voice, "So you *tricked* Em'ly into gettin' on that train with those two boys, even tho' you knew it wasn't what she wanted?"

"Yes, ma'am," Kelly Ann replied, mournfully.

"You were dishonest; put you *and* your friend at risk goin' off with those boys."

"Yes, ma'am," she replied, barely above a whisper. "I'm really sorry..."

"Sorry isn't enough," Miss Mattie interrupted, "do you even know those two boys?"

"I've been seeing Logger for about two months."

"*Logger!"* Miss Mattie sputtered. "Does your grandpa know you were seein' that boy?"

"No, ma'am."

"Where did you meet him?"

"At the picnic grounds."

"At the picnic grounds! Now you jus' listen to me a minute, young lady..." And with that, Miss Mattie proceeded to lecture Kelly Ann until they were all the way up the mountain and back in Mountain Grove. She didn't even stop for a breath once.

"I want you to steer clear of that *place* and that *boy*, Kelly Ann. Is that clear?"

"Are you gonna tell my grandpa?"

"That's the least of your worries," Miss Mattie said, as they pulled into town. "Your grandpa can't follow you aroun' twenty-four hours a day. You got to use your own good sense!"

"Yes, ma'am." Kelly Ann was scared.

"Where do you want me to drop you, Em'ly?" Miss Mattie asked. "I want to talk to Kelly Ann a minute more."

It was dark by now, so Emily said, "Just up at the corner of Elderberry and Sycamore.

Miss Mattie gunned her Mazda up the hill.

"Goodnight, Miss Mattie," Emily said, when she got out of the car. "Thanks for helping us."

"I'm glad you called me, Sugar."

She looked in the back seat. "Bye, Kelly Ann!"

Kelly Ann just waved her hand. She looked kind of sick.

* * * *

Emily walked to the library, bundled from head to toe in a black sweatshirt over a red sweater, and she was still cold. When she went through the double doors, the heat from the library's old heater was cranked up high, blowing deliciously warm air everywhere.

"B-r-r-r-r-r-r!" Emily said, walking up to the check-out desk. She kept rubbing her mittened hands together, trying to get warm.

Mrs. Green laughed, "January and February are pretty cold in this neck of the woods!"

"I've never been this cold," Emily said, blowing into her mittens.

"Good reason to stay tucked inside here all day," Mrs. Green said, before turning to check out books for an elderly man.

As Emily went in search of adventure books, she realized she hadn't heard from Kelly Ann since Miss Mattie had rescued them two days ago. She checked her phone to see if there were any messages, but no one had called her. In a corner of the library, where no one would be disturbed, she called Kelly Ann's cell phone. It went right to her voice mail, meaning she had it turned off. Puzzled, she called her home phone.

"Hello?" Kelly Ann answered the phone.

"How come your cell phone is turned off?" Emily asked.

" *What* cell phone?" she replied irritably. "Miss Mattie ratted me out, and Grandpa took it away and grounded me for a month."

"Wow, what did he say?" Emily asked.

"He said I cain't go anywhere but school for a danged month. He said if I ever go to the picnic grounds again, he'll ground me for a year. He said if he ever hears of me seein' Logger again, he'll break his neck!"

Emily couldn't help laughing. "Well, just don't go to the picnic grounds and stay away from Logger. He's not someone you want to be with, Kelly Ann."

"How do you know?" she retorted.

She told her the story of Logger and Mack in the cafeteria.

"Well, I'm over him anyway," Kelly Ann said, after Emily had finished telling her about the cafeteria incident. "The big jerk knew I didn't like hard likker."

"He smokes pot, too."

"I don't even care," Kelly Ann said wearily. "My mama left rehab early and I'm going home. I'll stay with her the rest of the school year."

" *What?"* Emily gasped. "But why?'

"Because," Kelly Ann said, "I'm fifteen, not five! I don't need someone babysittin' me ever' minute of the day! I'm use to bein' on my own. Besides, when I was home at Christmas, I met this really cute guy and he's been textin' me. So except for missin' you, leavin' isn't all that heart breaking."

"Why didn't you tell me about the other guy?" Emily asked.

"'Cause I didn't want to hear any lectures–like th' one you're about to give me right now."

"You mean the one about you only being fifteen, and you didn't do such a great job when you picked Logger for a boyfriend?" Emily asked.

"Yep, *that* would be the one," Kelly Ann said.

Emily sighed and tried to think of what to say. "Why don't you get really picky before you date anyone else," she finally said. "Make a list of what you want in a guy, and don't go out with anyone who doesn't match the list."

"I'm going to miss you," Kelly Ann replied, ignoring everything she had said.

"I'll miss you too," Emily sighed. "When will you be back?"

"Prob'ly in the summer. Maybe Grandpa will be over bein' mad at me by then."

"Will you text me or call?" Emily asked.

"If you promise not to lecture me."

"I'll try."

They laughed, said goodbye, and hung up.

Emily didn't really feel like laughing, though, she felt extremely sad. She picked out a couple of books and took them to the check-out counter.

"You look like you've just lost your best friend!" Mrs. Green teased.

"I have, in more ways than one," she said, as she stuffed her books into her backpack and turned to leave.

Mrs. Green started to say more, but Emily was already walking toward the double doors.

CHAPTER - 17

Emily left the library deep in thought, surprised at Kelly Ann's decision to go live with her mom in Mississippi. She was also surprised that it caused her to be so sad. Walking down the library steps to First Street, flashing lights caught her attention, and she froze when she saw the street filled with all sorts of emergency vehicles. Sheriff Mobley directed traffic, while another officer controlled the crowd that had gathered in front of Miss Mattie's bakery.

What's going on? she wondered, as dread filled her.

She saw an imposing red ambulance with doors wide open, directly in front of the bakery and her heart began to hammer. Her legs grew wobbly as she flew the rest of the way down the library steps and took off at a dead run. As she ran toward the bakery, she could see medics wheeling a gurney out of the front door.

"Miss Mattie!" she heard herself screaming, as she hurtled through the crowd, nearly knocking people over.

As the crowd opened up for her, she saw Miss Mattie's still form lying on a gurney.

"Mama! Mama!" she cried, running up to her.

Miss Mattie turned and looked at her, her face wrenched with pain. "It's all right Sugar," she whispered. "It's just my leg that's hurt. I fell."

Emily grabbed her hand, sobbing.

"Listen to me, Sugar," Miss Mattie whispered. "I need you to close up the bakery an' call Blessy for me. Have her come in t'morrow." She winced with pain. "Can you do all that?"

Emily nodded her head, tears streaming down her face. "I want to come with you," she cried.

"I know you do, Sugar," Miss Mattie whispered so low that Emily could barely hear her, "but you're the only one who knows where my key is and how to handle everything. Will you do that for me?"

Mr. Charles came running up. "Mattie, what's happened?"

"It's my leg, Joe," she whispered. "I think it's broken."

"What can I do," he asked.

"Help Em'ly lock up," she whispered, then moaned.

"We need to get her to the hospital," the medic said. "She could go into shock."

They all stood back as the two medics lifted Miss Mattie into the ambulance.

Jonathan ran up as the ambulance was leaving.

"Help Emily lock up the bakery," Mr. Charles told his son. "They're taking Mattie to the hospital in Monett. I want to follow them and make sure she's all right."

"Will you call and let me know how she's doing?" Emily pleaded.

"I will," he said, "and try not to worry." He patted Emily and hurried off.

Jonathan put his arm around her shoulder and they went into the bakery to close it up.

Tears streamed down Emily's face as she emptied the pastry cases. She felt sick with worry.

"God—Miss Mattie's God—please let her be all right," she whispered, wishing with all her heart that she could have gone to the hospital with her.

"Tell me what to do," Jonathan said, coming up behind her.

"Help me fill the cases with cookies from the back," she said softly, as tears ran down her cheeks. "We need to have everything ready for tomorrow morning when Blessy comes in." She wiped tears away with her shirt sleeve. "Then we need to wash the bowls and equipment in the back."

He went over to the small sink and wet a paper towel with warm water, then came back and handed it to Emily. "Put this on your eyes and it'll help you stop crying," he said.

Emily took the paper towel and pressed it to her eyes. It felt very soothing.

"I'll fill the pastry case, and wash the bowls," he told her, after she had calmed down. "You get ahold of Blessy."

They locked up the bakery an hour later. There was still no word from Mr. Charles.

"I need to go look after the nursery," Jonathan told her. "Do you want to come with me?"

"No, I'm just going home," Emily said, feeling like she might start crying again. "You'll call me right away if you hear from your dad, right?"

"If I hear first, I'll call you," Jonathan promised, "but I think my dad will call you before he calls me."

* * * *

Emily waited the rest of the day for a call, but it wasn't until 7:30 that night that her cell phone vibrated.

"Hello," she said, cupping her hand over the phone, so her parents wouldn't hear.

"Hi, Emily," Mr. Charles said, "just wanted to give you an update. Mattie just got out of surgery and the doctor said her leg should mend just fine."

Emily let her breath out slowly, relief washing over her. "When can she come home?"

"She's going to need physical therapy," he said, "so she'll be spending a few days at Creekside Villa."

"I want to come and see her."

"I understand," he said, "but I have a feeling she won't be here at the hospital very long. Hold tight for now and I'll let you know tomorrow when you can see her."

She hated waiting but didn't have much choice since Monett was fifteen miles away. "Okay, well thanks for calling," she said, her voice breaking.

"Emily, she'll be fine," Mr. Charles reassured her.

He said goodbye and Emily turned her phone off.

* * * *

Mr. Charles was right. Three days later an ambulance transported Miss Mattie to Creekside Villa to begin physical therapy. Emily was waiting outside the building when the ambulance pulled up. She hurried over as the medics opened the back doors and lifted her out.

Miss Mattie looked surprised to see her. "Hello, Sugar," she said, smiling weakly.

Emily reached out and took her hand. "How are you feeling?"

"Tired," Miss Mattie said, and closed her eyes. The medics raised the legs on the gurney and rolled her toward the care center.

The nurses had Emily wait in the hall while they got Miss Mattie into bed. A few minutes later, Emily looked up to see Mr. Charles walking toward her.

He gave her a brief hug. "The doctor is right behind me," he said. "We're all going to talk about where to go from here."

"Is something else going on?" she asked.

"The doctor will explain everything," he told her, putting a hand on her shoulder as they walked toward Miss Mattie's room.

"I'm Dr. Blackstone," the doctor said, a few minutes later, shaking Emily's hand. They had all gathered around Miss Mattie's bed to hear what he had to say.

"I think a week of therapy should be enough to get the strength back in her leg," Dr. Blackstone said. "She'll be on crutches for a few weeks and her rehab therapist will show her how to get around on them, so she doesn't fall again." He looked down at his chart, and continued, "We've already started her on some mild heart medication..."

"Heart medication?" Emily interrupted. "For what?"

"We detected a little problem with her heart," the doctor said, looking up at her, "but with medication and the right diet, she should be fine."

"How come no one told me?" Emily asked, feeling tears spring to her eyes.

"I asked them not to say anything," Miss Mattie said. She looked at the doctor. "I didn't want Em'ly to know."

"If Emily is going to be part of your recovery team, she has to know," the doctor said.

"And I *want* to know," Emily said. "Please don't keep anything like that from me."

Miss Mattie nodded her head, looking exhausted.

"She'll need help for a few weeks when she gets home," the doctor said. He turned to Mr. Charles, "Has that been arranged?"

"My wife is making up a schedule with the village ladies who have volunteered to help out," Mr. Charles said.

"Sounds like everything is covered then," the doctor said, closing the chart. "I'll need a copy of that schedule before I release her next week."

"I'll get it to you in the next couple of days," Mr. Charles replied.

* * * *

After a week-long stay at Creekside Villa, Miss Mattie was allowed to come home. Emily insisted on taking care of her. At home, she packed clothes and toiletries in a small bag and came prepared to stay a few nights in the apartment over the bakery. To her amazement, her parents hadn't offered any resistance when she'd told them her plan.

As Miss Mattie rested on her overstuffed sofa, Emily brought her fresh water and a magazine, and insisted on plumping up her big, feather pillow.

"You're spoilin' me, Em'ly," Miss Mattie said.

"You deserve spoiling, Mama."

Miss Mattie smiled, looking tired and pale. "Sugar, are you sure you can handle the bakery after school for a while?" she asked. "It seems like too much, along with you spendin' nights with me."

"I can handle both just fine," Emily said. "How's your energy level?"

"I still feel tired, but the doctor thinks lots of rest and doin' a few exercises here at home will help." She sat up and patted the cushion for Emily to sit down beside her. "Don't you worry so much about me, Sugar. I'll be jus' fine in a few days."

"I'm glad you're better," Emily said, resting her head on Miss Mattie's shoulder. "I couldn't stand it if I lost you." She bit her lip wondering if she should have said that.

Miss Mattie chuckled, "Well I think the good Lord is gonna keep me aroun' jus' a little bit longer."

"I asked Him to, when you were in the hospital," Emily murmured.

"Well, now, Sugar, that was a fine thing to do," Miss Mattie replied, looking pleased. "And it looks like He did jus' what you asked."

Emily nodded, feeling incredibly thankful.

* * * *

"I don't know how you do this every day," Emily said to Miss Mattie, as she put up the *Closed* sign, and locked the bakery door after an extremely busy Saturday. Blessy had gotten sick, so Emily had been at the bakery since 5:00 a.m. helping Clara, then spent the rest of the day selling pastries and serving customers at the little tables. She was exhausted.

"Why honey, I jus' been blessed to do exactly what I love. That's the secret you know, to earn your livin' doin' what you love."

"I think what I love doing is photography," she said, plopping down in a chair next to her. "At least you get to sit down once in a while."

"I think that would be a fine way to earn a livin', Sugar," Miss Mattie said, with a smile that rivaled a harvest moon. "Jus' remember to keep your marks up in school so you can go on to college."

Emily stood up and took off her green apron that was dotted with purple mangos and yellow parrots and wrapped around her twice. She tossed it into the laundry bin. "Ready to go back upstairs?" she asked.

Last night Miss Mattie said she was going stir crazy sitting around the apartment all day. She was in a walking cast now, so in the afternoon Emily helped her come down the stairs and sit in the bakery for a couple of hours.

"What would I do without my girl?" Miss Mattie said, as Emily helped her to her feet. "You are an ever lastin' blessin' to me, Sugar."

"And you are an ever lastin' blessin' to me too, Miss Mattie!"

"What happened to you callin' me *Mama*?"

"I wasn't sure if you liked me calling you that," Emily said.

"There's nothin' in this world I'd like better," Miss Mattie said, hugging her close. "Your folks still okay with you spendin' so much time here?"

"They never say anything."

"Well now, don't miracles jus' keep happenin' to us?"

"Yes, ma'am, they sure do," Emily laughed, as they navigated the steep stairway.

"What do you want for dinner?" she asked, after she settled Miss Mattie on the overstuffed couch.

"Sugar, you jus' make me a quick san'wich and run on and do somethin' fun. You've been workin' hard. I'll be jus' fine with a light supper."

"There's that chicken Mrs. Charles brought over," Emily said, ignoring her request for a sandwich. "I'm going to heat it up and make you a salad, and didn't you tell me that asparagus sounded real fine to you?"

"It does sound real fine, but what sounds even finer is for you to have a little free time to yourself." Miss Mattie tilted her head and gave her a no-nonsense look. "That's what sounds fine to me, Miss Em'ly."

"Mama, if I was sick, would you fix me a sandwich and run off?"

Miss Mattie just looked at her. "You know what I'm gonna say."

"Yes, ma'am, I do, and I'm saying it too. There's no place I'd rather be than right here."

"Well then," Miss Mattie grinned, "make us both a big plate, and then run back downstairs to the bakery for our dessert."

"Now you're talkin'!" Emily said, grabbing the bakery keys and hurrying out the door. She'd get the dessert first.

* * * *

Emily sat doing her homework in the little guest room of Miss Mattie's upstairs apartment. She loved the coziness of it, with its bay window overlooking First Street. She looked around the room: there was a double bed covered with a handmade quilt, a curved armoire that held the few articles of clothing she brought with her, and a blue floral easy chair tucked back in a corner with an old-fashioned floor lamp that she loved reading by. She could hear muted traffic noise through the window and walked over to look out.

Across the street, Emerson Park was blanketed in a foot of snow. The General had a pile of snow in his lap and some stuck to the top of his head like a night cap. To the left, she saw Gilbert emerge from the church basement, bundled from head to toe. *He must've run away from his dad again,* she thought. At least he grabbed some warm clothes this time.

To the right of the park, people were hurrying up and down the library steps, which was a perfect place to nestle in when the weather was this cold. Beneath her window, people were navigating their way down the icy sidewalk; she saw Gus coming out of Good Eats. She tapped on the window and he looked up, giving her a grin that showed a full row of choppers. He waved and hurried on, his breath fogging the air like a steam engine.

* * * *

Emily was behind the cash register at the bakery Saturday morning waiting on Etta Kingery, when Mr. Charles came in.

"Hey, Mr. C!"

"How's it going?" he asked.

"Good!" she said, handing five dozen boxed donuts to Mrs. Kingery. The Village Grocer was having a grand opening of their new deli department. They had advertised free coffee and donuts for all customers coming in before noon. This was Mrs. Kingery's second trip to the bakery.

"We went through three dozen donuts the first hour we opened," Mrs. Kingery told them, "and folks are still streaming in."

Emily held the door open as Mr. Charles helped carry donuts to Mrs. Kingery's car, parked just outside at the curb.

When Mr. Charles came back in, he asked, "Who all is working here with you, Emily?"

"On weekdays, Clara and Blessy handle it, until I get out of school," she replied. "Then I take over."

"How about on Saturdays?" he asked.

"They do the baking in the morning and then it's just me," she said.

He looked concerned. "Is there anyone besides you spending nights with Mattie, or fixing her dinner?"

"No, but I don't mind," she was quick to reply. "The village ladies come while I'm in school and help. Sometimes they bring dinner."

"That's too much for you, Emily," he said. "I'll round up more help for you."

She started to protest but changed her mind. She *was* getting a little tired.

* * * *

During the nearly three weeks she had been with Miss Mattie, Emily had stopped in often at home to make sure her parents weren't getting upset about her being away, and to visit with her grandmother.

When Emily walked into the house, Pearl was in her usual spot it front of the TV. "Hi Grandma," she said, holding out a little white bag.

Her grandmother's eyes lit up like a child's. "Thank you," she squawked, eagerly taking the bag.

"It's a chocolate donut and a crème horn," Emily told her.

Her grandmother peered into the bag. "Them two are my favorite."

"I know," Emily said, reaching down and kissing the top of her wiry hair.

"You shouldn't be spendin' yer money on me," her grandmother said, looking up at her with eyes, dim and watery with age.

"Well, actually, Miss Mattie gives them to me to bring to you."

"Who's Miz Mattie?"

"The one I'm staying with. She owns the bakery."

"You ever comin' back home?" her grandmother asked.

"Sure," Emily said. "Just as soon as Miss Mattie can take care of herself again."

"That's good," she said, and gave Emily's leg a pat. "Maybe you could drop in a little more often. I miss seein' ya."

Emily was absolutely touched. "I miss you too, Grandma," she said, leaning over and giving her a bear hug.

Her dad walked into the room and glared at them.

Emily stood up. "Hi, Dad," she said. She patted her grandmother on the shoulder and started for her bedroom.

Her dad stopped her. "What'd you do, move in with that bakery woman?" he asked, looking very irritated.

Emily looked at him. "No, but she still needs my help," she replied. "I'll just be staying with her a little longer."

"Seems like she's takin' advantage of you."

She ignored the remark. "I'll be home soon."

"Where'd you say she lived?"

Emily didn't want to tell him and made a split-second decision to tell him about her cell phone instead. "She lives downtown, but if you want to reach me I have a cell phone now."

"How'd you get a cell phone?" he sneered.

"I pay a friend to be on her plan," she replied calmly.

"We don't need anyone's charity," he growled, the veins on his neck starting to pop out.

"I told you, I pay for it," she replied, standing her ground.

To her amazement, her dad didn't say any more, but just stormed into the kitchen.

She found a slip of paper and wrote her cell phone number down. She could hear her dad in the kitchen slamming drawers and swearing under his breath. She went in and handed the paper to him. "Here's my phone number if you need to reach me," she said.

At first he didn't take it and just glared at her. "Do you want it or not?" Emily asked calmly. He snatched it out of her hand.

She went to her room and grabbed a couple of warm sweaters and headed back out to the kitchen. "I'm leaving now," she told her dad, not feeling the least bit afraid. "I'll stop in tomorrow."

"That bakery woman payin' you?" her dad asked tersely.

"No," she replied.

"Good," he said. "We don't need anyone else givin' you charity."

She started to tell him it wouldn't be charity if she was working for the money.

But who cares? she thought. Why was she always trying to get her parents to see things differently? They were who they were, and they thought the way they wanted to think.

It also felt good that she wasn't the least bit afraid to tell her dad what she was doing.

"Okay, well bye," she said, then went into the living room and hugged her grandmother. "I'll try to come more often," she whispered to her.

* * * *

Mrs. Charles drove Miss Mattie to the doctor every week, and Emily always insisted on getting out of school early and going along with them so she could hear every word Dr. Blackstone said about her condition. If the truth were known, Emily only trusted herself to take care of Miss Mattie.

On this visit, the doctor gave Miss Mattie the all-clear to stay by herself. "Your progress has been wonderful, Mattie," he said.

Emily thought it was too soon for her to be on her own and said so. "I think she needs me there just a little bit longer," she told Dr. Blackstone, meaning it.

Dr. Blackstone just looked at her. "Are you sure it isn't the other way around, and you need her?"

The question irritated Emily. "No, I think she needs my help," she replied curtly. "She's still not as strong as she was before she broke her leg."

But she realized there was some truth in what Dr. Blackstone had said. She didn't want to go home.

* * * *

As Emily walked home from school, she loved the feel of the balmy air that had tiptoed up the mountain and quietly replaced the icy winds of winter. Tiny leaves had begun to unfurl from tree branches, and the air was ripe with the scent of blossoms from backyard fruit trees. Across the street, she saw Mr. Montoya setting up umbrellas to shade his wagon wheeled carts, which would soon be filled to the brim with local fruits and vegetables. He had set it up so that the sidewalk outside his produce market resembled that of an old fashioned greengrocer, complete with a hanging scale.

As she walked through the park, she spied Gilbert reading under a tree.

"Studying again, I see," she said, walking up to him. She tipped the book up so she could read the title.

"Science!" she said, sounding amazed. "Whoo hoo! Look at you!"

"Science is just 'bout my worse subject," Gilbert grumbled, "and I have ta study like a son-of-a-gun ta get a good grade. Pastor Alex has been helpin' me with it."

"Are you trying for the Honor Roll?"

"Yep," he said, trying not to grin. "School's my only way outta livin' in a trailer at the sawmill."

He closed the book and tossed it on the grass. "You heard from Kelly Ann?"

"Oh, she's texted me a few times," she said, looking up at him, "but I think she's got new friends."

"She gotta boyfriend?"

"Maybe," she said, and a thought occurred to her. "Gilbert, do you like Kelly Ann?"

His face turned red. "Yeah," he admitted, "but you better not tell anyone."

"I won't," she promised, grinning at him. "Does she know?"

"No...and that's jus' th' way I wanna leave it 'til she comes back."

"Well, she won't hear it from me," Emily promised.

"Ya'll think she's even comin' back?" he asked.

"She said she might come back in the summer."

He sighed. "I sure hope she don't gotta a boyfriend."

Emily smiled, wondering if she should help him with his English now, or wait for a better time.

CHAPTER - 18

On Saturday morning Emily's dad was pacing back and forth, from the living room to the kitchen and back again, as she hurriedly fixed a ham and cheese sandwich to take to town with her. She had to get away, her dad was on a rampage.

"I've offered 'em a discount to buy their firewood now," her dad ranted, as he paced into the living room, "but they don't get it!"

Emily quickly bagged her lunch at the kitchen counter, as her dad's anger gathered momentum. She knew she would need to stay gone all day.

"Stupid small-town hicks," he muttered, pacing back into the kitchen.

She released her breath slowly, as her anxiety level soared. The raging had been going on for the last forty minutes, and she was trying desperately to get out of the house before he headed for the booze cabinet. With the onset of warmer weather, firewood sales had trickled down to almost nothing. The wood lot was stacked to the brim with unsold wood, leaving her dad with very little to do, except drink and obsess over the whole situation.

"Dad, they'll probably start buying wood again in August or September," she blurted out, sick of hearing him go on and on.

He stopped and looked at her. "Well, since you know so much, what am I supposed to do without an income for three months?"

"You were making lots of money in the fall and winter. Did you save any of it?"

Wrong thing to say. Her dad exploded.

"Do you even *know* how much it costs to run a house?" he yelled. "You had me buyin' you enough things to make a rich man go broke! How am I s'posed to save when you got your hand out, and the grocery store has their hand out, and that jerk judge stuck me with a fine that took a month's wages!"

It's not the judge's fault you drive drunk, she wanted to say, but didn't.

He'd gotten off easy the first time he was caught drinking and driving; the sheriff had just took his keys and brought him home. The second time it happened, he was arrested, and the judge had thrown the book at him. He gave him a large fine and a lecture on how he was going to kill himself, or someone else, if he didn't change his behavior. She had heard all about it—over and over and over again. And of course, it was *their* fault, never his. His tirades were so depressing.

She went into her room and hurriedly put her hair up in a ponytail. When she checked it in the mirror, she saw that it was kind of lopsided.

"Shoot," she whispered, sticking a baseball cap over the mess. She just needed to get out of there.

"I'm sick of this place anyway," he continued, as she walked back into the kitchen to get her backpack. "Bunch of small-town jerks! Some are sayin' they're gonna burn pellets next fall instead of wood. Tree-hugging idiots!" he said, punching his open palm with his fist. "I'm lookin' for somewhere else to go."

Her stomach knotted, and she turned toward him. "You want to move?"

"What else can I do? Stay here and starve?" He glared at her and headed for the liquor cabinet.

She stood there, paralyzed with fear. *They couldn't move!*

Her mind raced as he poured himself a drink. He sat down at the kitchen table and thumbed through some papers. "I'll try and think of how you can sell your firewood, Dad," she said, not caring if it sent him into another tirade.

"Yeah, you just do that," he sneered, turning back to the papers. "In the meantime, I'm lookin' for work someplace else."

She walked up behind him and looked over his shoulder to see what he was reading. Her heart froze when she saw that he had downloaded job opportunities from the internet. She stepped in closer and saw that some of the ads had been circled in red.

"Where are you looking for jobs?" she asked.

"Anywhere I can find one," he snarled, getting up to refill his drink.

She picked up the ads and saw that the jobs were listed under different states. She felt like she couldn't breathe. Three ads under *Tennessee* had been circled, and two under *Oklahoma.* He had also circled a job offer under *Alaska.*

Alaska! Was he crazy?

* * * *

Emily left the house sick with fear. There had to be a solution! If she could just think of how to get customers for him. But how do you sell firewood in May, with a whole hot summer ahead? *If only he'd saved in the winter!* she thought, growing angry. *And all that booze they drank every day. They probably could've lived the whole summer on the money they'd wasted on that.* She was so stressed out, she found herself gulping for air.

"You solvin' the world's problems, Em'ly?" she heard someone say.

She turned and saw Gus waving at her. She'd been so deep in thought she hadn't noticed she was in front of his station.

"Well, sort of," she replied honestly, walking over to him.

"Kin I he'p you?"

"You need any firewood?"

"By jingles, I got me 'nuff firewood for two years!" he grinned. "Me 'n Ike went out when they was clearin' Possum Hill, and we both layed in 'nuff firewood to last us a *long* time. Come winter I'll be happy as a dead pig in th' sunshine!"

"Oh..."

He stared at her. "Your daddy needin' some bus'ness?"

She nodded her head.

"Hmmm," he said, scratching his head, "that's th' trouble with seas'nal business; you gotta lay up the money when it's comin' in."

She didn't want to hear it. "Well, I'm heading for the library, Gus; I'll stop by and see you later."

"Yes sir, in the winter ya gotta prepare for the summer. Prob'ly should save at least a third of yer wages."

"Okay, well tell YipYap I said hello," she said, backing away.

"Now I 'member ol' Oscar Bellamy, who used to own yer daddy's bus'ness," Gus said, warming up to the subject. "He usta save so much money he'd plum go on vacation for three months."

She couldn't breathe. "All right...I'll drop by later...need to see Mrs. Green about something..." She took off running across the street and headed for the park. For all she knew, Gus was still back there talking. As she ran, her resentment toward her dad burst into full-blown rage. He had put everything she loved into jeopardy! He just couldn't make her move!

She was shaking by the time she reached the park. She stumbled toward a weeping willow tree, ducked under its drooping branches, and slumped to the ground. She sat in the grass and hugged her knees as despair washed over her. She couldn't stand it! Why did her parents have the power to make her life so impossible? Did God hate her? She began to sob; her whole body went numb with fear at the thought of leaving Mountain Grove. She tried desperately to think of who could help her; the reality of the situation made her physically ill. Could she turn to Miss Mattie? No. She would never put that burden on her, not with her heart condition. Mrs. Green? Mr. Charles? But what could any of them do?

She curled up in a ball and began to sob quietly. "God," she whispered, "Miss Mattie's God...if you're really there, I need You to help me."

* * * *

Emily was jolted awake by children playing in the park. She looked around, confused, trying to figure out where she was, then grew calm as the willow tree branches blew gently in the breeze. She pulled out her cell phone to see what time it was, her eyes were so puffy she could barely make out the numbers.

She couldn't believe it! She had been asleep under the tree for over an hour. What now? The library wasn't an option, or any place else, with her eyes puffed up like marshmallows. She just wanted to be by herself anyway. She picked up her backpack and put her cap back on her head, pulling the bill down to cast a shadow over her eyes. Ducking out from under the canopy of the tree, she made her way behind the library, hung a sharp right and headed toward the river. She kept a watch in the distance to avoid seeing anyone, and desperately wished she had brought her sunglasses so she could hide her eyes.

Staying off the main path to the river, she walked through the bushes until the roar of the water could be heard. Only then did she walk out into the open, scooted behind a tree, and then peeked out to see if anyone was around. She spied Jonathan digging in his tackle box near the river's edge. She didn't want to see him, and quietly backed away from the tree. As she did, the heel of her flip-flop caught on a tree root and she tumbled over, nearly doing a backward somersault. She popped up, flew back into the bushes, and took off running. She had only run a few feet when she felt something sharp. Looking down, she saw that one of her flip-flops was missing, and she was running barefoot over rocks. She had no choice, but to go back for her shoe. She got down on her hands and knees and crawled back over to where she had fallen. She peeked out from behind a bush, scanning the ground for her flip-flop, but it was nowhere to be found. She glanced up and saw something moving in the breeze. It was her flip-flop dangling from a Manzanita branch. She crept toward it, snapping a twig that cracked like a cannon. She quickly reached up and yanked the shoe down and scrambled back into the bushes.

As she hurried away, her elbow began to sting. Stopping to look at it, she saw it was bleeding profusely from a deep cut, and the sting felt like she was being peppered by a swarm of bees. She took the corner of her shirt and wiped it off the best she could, picking out bits of leaves and dirt. *So much for first aid,* she thought, holding her shirt against the wound as she hurried on through the brush. She found another trail downstream that led to the river. She peeked out warily, and not seeing anyone, walked out onto the sandy beach area.

"How come you're trying to hide from me?" said a voice, from behind her.

She shrieked as she spun around. Jonathan was sitting on a rock watching her.

Frightened and furious, she asked, "Why'd you follow me?"

"Why did you hide behind a tree, and run back into the bushes so I wouldn't see you?"

"You *saw* me?"

"Of course I saw you," he laughed, "you're wearing bright red!"

"Oh..."

"What's wrong with your eyes?" he asked.

"Nothing," she said, heading back into the bushes.

"Emily," he said, following her, "it's not safe to walk through brush, you should stick to the main trail."

"I don't care," she said, and hurried on, hoping he would just go away.

"What's wrong?" he asked, holding her arm.

She tried to pull away, but he held tight.

"Just tell me what's wrong," he said gently.

The tears started again; uncontrollable tears. She sank down on a fallen log and hid her face in her hands. He sat down next to her and put his arm around her, not saying a word. He gently rubbed her back as she sobbed. Then she started hiccoughing and couldn't stop. They both laughed as it echoed through the woods.

"I need a tissue," she whispered, her head turned away so he couldn't see her face.

He got her a paper towel from his tackle box.

"Don't look at me," she said, as she reached for it. "My eyes look like a monster."

"You don't look like a monster," he said, handing her the paper towel. "You're pretty."

Her heart leaped. *Jonathan thought she was pretty?*

"Can I borrow your sunglasses?" she asked, keeping her face turned away.

He pulled them off and handed them to her. She kept her head down as she slipped them on. They were too big and she had to keep pushing them back on her nose.

He grinned—until he noticed her elbow. "Emily, you're bleeding!" he said, pulling her elbow up so he could have a better look. "You must've cut it when you did that somersault."

She was mortified. "You saw me fall, too!"

"Of course I saw you," he said, as he checked her wound, "you sounded like an elephant crashing through the brush." He went over to his tackle box and pulled out a small first aid kit.

She glared at him. "You could've at least *pretended* like you didn't see."

"I'm not a very good pretender," he said, opening the kit.

She started to say something, but realized she was glad he didn't pretend.

"Let me see your elbow," he said, pulling a small wet cloth out of a foil packet.

She raised her arm and he began patting the wound; it felt like the swarm of bees had returned.

"Ouch," she said, jerking her arm away.

"Be still," he said, holding her elbow firmly, "it's an antiseptic. You've got all kinds of junk in that cut."

He dabbed at the area getting out bits of bark and dirt. She flinched but didn't move her arm again.

"That's a really bad cut, but I don't think you need stitches," he said, peering closely. He found a large band-aid and carefully covered the wound.

"Keep an eye out for infection," he said, returning the supplies to his first aid kit. "I tried to get all the junk out, but with all the animal poop in the woods... well, you know."

"Gross!" she said and stood up to go. "No I didn't know, but thank you. I'll see you later."

"I really wish you'd tell me what's wrong."

She hesitated, realizing she actually wanted to tell him.

He waited.

She sat back down. "My dad's talking about moving."

His eyes narrowed. "Why would he do that?"

"Because no one is buying his wood and because he thinks Mountain Grove is the cause of all his problems."

"What?" he snorted. "How could he possibly blame a town for his problems?"

"Because that's the weird way he sees things. It doesn't do any good trying to figure it out. I've tried."

"Okay," Jonathan said, "so what happened to all the money he made this winter when wood was selling?"

She found herself telling him everything, even about her dad being stopped for drunk driving again, and the heavy fine.

"Whew!" he said when she had finished. "And you're sure he hasn't saved *any* money?"

"Jonathan, they drink *all* of the time. It costs a fortune for three people to drink as much as they do. I've calculated it, and it's way more than we pay for rent."

She wondered if she was saying too much but decided she didn't really care. It felt very good to have someone to talk to, and she was tired of protecting her parents.

"Well then, we have to come up with a solution," he said. "Not about their drinking, that's their beast to battle, but maybe we could come up with a solution for selling the firewood."

He didn't say anything for a few moments, just sat deep in thought. "What do you think about making up flyers to try and drum up business for him?" he finally asked.

"You mean hand them to people?"

"No, I mean use a staple gun and put them on telephone poles—but yes, we could hand them to people too, or at least leave a flyer on their doorstep. Maybe we could take the train to Clayton and leave flyers all over the neighborhoods."

"Why couldn't we leave them at houses in Mountain Grove?"

"We will. But let's go down the hill into Clayton, too." He looked at her. "I think it might be good for you to get away from everything here for a while."

His concern touched her deeply.

"We could go to the library and make up a flyer," she said, growing excited. "Maybe run off a thousand or so. Do you think a thousand flyers is too many?"

"A thousand would sure tell us if people are going to respond," he said, growing excited with her. "Did you say your dad would give them a good deal if they bought wood now?"

"That's what he said this morning."

"Call him and ask the best deal he would give on a cord of wood, and then we'll get started on the flyers."

She looked at him. "I can't."

"Why can't you?"

"Because he'll be drunk by now and get mad if I bring it up."

He shook his head. "Emily, just try. If he gets mad, he gets mad! You can always hang up."

She hesitated, but he was right. She *could* just hang up.

* * * *

The phone rang and rang before her dad answered.

"Dad, it's me, Emily. If someone wants to buy wood from you, how much for a cord?"

"What's their name?" he asked.

"I don't know their name. I'm going to put up flyers for you."

"I don't need no one's charity," he snorted.

"It's not charity. It's me helping you."

"Three hundred?" he growled into the phone.

Emily listened for a few seconds, then quickly pressed the *off* button on her phone.

"What's wrong?" Jonathan asked.

"He started swearing about the sheriff again," she said, looking up at him.

Jonathan laughed first, then they both laughed, and took off for town.

"Are my eyes still puffy?" she asked, lowering the sunglasses.

"Let me see," he said, peering closely. She could feel his warm breath on her cheeks. "They're better, but still pretty puffy."

She left the sunglasses off, hoping the breeze would help the swelling.

Jonathan made plans as they walked. "So, he's agreed to sell a cord of firewood for three hundred dollars then, right?"

"That's what he said," she shrugged. "But he may change his mind ten minutes from now."

"If he does, he does," Jonathan said, as they crossed First Street and headed toward the library. "We'll go by what he says now. If he's already looking for work in other towns, we have to do something quick."

Emily liked it that he used the word *we*.

CHAPTER – 19

Emily and Jonathan hurried through the library doors, waved hello to Mrs. Green, and headed for the computer tables.

Jonathan got right to work on the computer as Emily looked over his shoulder. First he typed, *"Special Deal on Firewood,"* then pressed the Caps Lock key and in bold letters wrote, ***BUY NOW AND SAVE!!!*** He went out on the internet and found a drawing of logs burning in a fireplace for visual effect.

He did a little more typing then asked, "What do you think?"

Emily studied it for a second. "Add *Free Delivery,"* she murmured.

"Does he deliver for free?"

"He does now," she laughed.

He added her dad's phone number and put a border around the whole thing. He leaned back in his chair as Emily gave it a final inspection.

"Put my cell number on it, too, in case he doesn't answer his phone," she said.

Jonathan typed a little more. "Anything else?" he asked.

She looked it over. "Seems fine to me."

"We'll go use my dad's copy machine," he said, as the flyer printed out.

She hesitated. "I don't want your dad to know everything I told you."

"Nobody's going to hear it from me," he said, rising from his chair.

They waved good-bye to Mrs. Green, and headed out the double doors.

They walked in the back gate of Bloomin' Happy and Jonathan flashed a copy of the flyer to his dad. "Okay if we use your copier and a couple of reams of paper?"

Mr. Charles gave the flyer a quick glance, looked at Emily and said, "No problem." He left to go help a customer and Emily was relieved he didn't ask a lot questions.

They waited for the first fifty copies to print out, grabbed them off the tray, and took off for town with Mr. Charles' staple gun.

"We'll be back later for the rest of the copies," Jonathan called out to his dad.

Mr. Charles waved, as they hurried out the gate.

"We'll put these first flyers up on telephone poles," Jonathan said, stopping at the first pole they came to. Emily held the stack of flyers as he stapled the first one at eye level. "After we get these put up, we'll go back and get the other copies and put flyers on doorsteps around Mountain Grove," he said, stepping back to look at the flyer. "Then tomorrow morning, we'll catch the seven o'clock to Clayton and stay there until the rest of the flyers are passed out." He smiled down at her. "Sound like a plan?"

She nodded happily. "Thanks for helping me."

"No problem. Can't lose my fishing buddy, can I?" he said, tugging the bill of her cap down over her eyes.

* * * *

Emily awoke at five-thirty the next morning, quickly dressed and headed for the kitchen. She had decided to make Jonathan a nice lunch for helping her. She knew boys ate a lot, so she packed two extra sandwiches, put in some drinks, then found some fruit and sliced up some cheese. She looked around the kitchen for something else to bring, wishing she had bought a pastry for him. She glanced at the clock. If she hurried, she would just have time to run by the bakery. She knew he loved apple fritters.

"Morning, Miss Mattie!" she sang out, as she burst through the bakery door.

"Well, good mornin', Sugar! What in the world are you doin' out this early?" Miss Mattie grinned.

"Jonathan and I are going into Clayton to pass out flyers for my dad's wood business. His business is down with summer coming on."

"I see," Miss Mattie said, looking concerned. "Didn't he save any money durin' the winter?"

Emily shook her head.

Miss Mattie leaned in closer and peered at her. "Your eyes are kinda puffy. You been cryin'?" Miss Mattie noticed everything.

"I was yesterday," Emily admitted. "But everything is going to be okay now."

"Why were you cryin', Sugar?"

"My dad wants to move someplace else to work."

"Oh Sugar...no!" she cried.

"It's okay, Miss Mattie," Emily assured her. "Jonathan and I are going to drum up plenty of business for him."

"Well, now," Miss Mattie said, her smile growing as big as the harvest moon, "passin' out flyers is a fine idea."

Emily glanced up at the wall clock. "I need to hurry, we leave at seven!"

Miss Mattie quickly put two apple fritters in a bag and refused to take any money. "My treat for you and that fine friend of yours," she smiled, handing her the bag. "I'll be home from church after one o'clock, so give me a call; I want to hear all about your trip.

Emily reached over and planted a kiss on her soft brown cheek. "You're the best!" she said hurrying out the door. Outside, she hooked a right and took off for the train station.

She got there at 6:45, but didn't see Jonathan. She hurried over to buy her ticket and saw him buying them both one.

"I can buy my own," she said, reaching into her pocket.

"I've got it," he said.

The trained pulled out right at seven. He put both their backpacks on the shelf overhead and sat down next to her.

"I ran off a map of neighborhoods in Clayton," he said, unfolding a paper. "We'll start here." He pointed to a neighborhood north of the train station. "Then we'll head in this direction." He glanced down at the bag in her lap. "What smells so good?"

"I got you something this morning at Miss Mattie's," she said, opening the bag. "Apple fritters. They're still warm."

"Wow! Thanks!" he said, sounding extremely happy. "I forgot to eat this morning."

They had both forgotten to eat breakfast and dug into the bag like eager children. At first they were going to split one and save the other for lunch, but they were too hungry and wolfed both of them down.

"Did I ever tell you that you eat like a lumberjack?" he laughed, as she finished off her fritter.

"I was hungry," she said, licking the icing off her fingers.

They settled back in their seats. Emily's full stomach and the clickity-clack of the train made her sleepy. She closed her eyes for a minute.

When she woke up, the train was slowing down and she realized she had her head on Jonathan's shoulder. She sat up quickly, checking to make sure she hadn't drooled on his shirt.

"I slept a long time," she said, looking out the window, as Clayton came into view.

"You sure did," he said, "and you snore when you sleep."

"I do?"

"Just a little. Like Gus' dog."

She knew that YipYap snored like a sawmill. "No I don't!" she laughed, whacking his arm. She hoped she didn't anyway.

When the train came to a stop, Jonathan grabbed their backpacks and they both hopped off. The train station brought back memories of the last awful time she was here with Kelly Ann and those two creepy boys. There was the bench they had sat on waiting for Miss Mattie to come and rescue them.

Jonathan helped her put her backpack on, then looked over the map. "Okay, let's head this way," he said, pointing north.

They had about 800 flyers left; they had handed out nearly 200 flyers in Mountain Grove the day before. When they reached the first neighborhood, they decided that each should take a side of the street. They walked up to every doorway and left a flyer on the doorstep. It was hot and tiring work, but they delivered about 300 flyers before lunch time.

Around noon they walked by a park. "Let's eat here," Emily said, spotting a water fountain. They hurried over and took long drinks.

A sprawling oak tree stood in the middle of the park and they headed for its shade. Emily unzipped her backpack and took out a small tablecloth and spread it out, then motioned for Jonathan to sit down. "I packed a picnic for us," she said.

His face lit up. "Good, I'm starved," he said, looking at her with that funny look he got sometimes. His intense blueberry-colored eyes made her nervous, as she fumbled in her backpack and pulled out a sandwich.

"Thanks!" he said as he eagerly bit into it. "Any iced tea in that magic pack of yours?"

"How'd you know," she said, bringing out two bottles of peach Snapple.

"I didn't know, I was only kidding!" he laughed, as he twisted off the cap and downed half the bottle.

He looked at her. "Your eyes are still a little puffy," he said, peering closely. "They're probably sensitive to the light, you should wear my sunglasses." He started to take them off.

"I brought mine," she replied, digging into the backpack. "Do my eyes still look like marshmallows?"

"Only the miniatures," he smiled.

She laughed and got a sandwich out for herself.

Jonathan leaned back against the tree chewing happily on his sandwich. "How'd you keep this so cold?"

"Blue Ice," she said, as she pulled out sliced cheese and fruit, and set it in front of him.

He looked up at her and she noticed that his eyes twinkled like his dad's. "Man, you're gonna spoil me!"

"You deserve to be spoiled," she said, loving the intense color of his eyes. "Thanks for helping me."

* * * *

They worked into the late afternoon going from neighborhood to neighborhood. It was hot and exhausting. They still had about 150 flyers left when Jonathan checked the time.

"Oh my gosh," he said, "the last train leaves in twenty minutes!"

They stuffed the flyers into his pack and took off running. After about five blocks she slowed down. "I can't run anymore," she gasped.

"You have to," he said, grabbing her hand and pulling her along.

After three more blocks, he stopped and took her backpack, lightening her load. "Come on, pokey," he laughed, pulling her by the hand again.

She hurried along, wondering if she should tell him this was her second time to run for the last train to Mountain Grove. They were both gasping for breath as they hopped aboard the train and collapsed into their seats. The train started up with a lurch and they put their heads back on the seat trying to catch their breath.

"Thanks again," she said, smiling up at him.

"No problem," he smiled back, reaching over and brushing a strand of stray hair from her face.

She turned and watched out the window as houses and businesses flew by. She soon felt a gentle rise as they started climbing the mountain. As pine trees whizzed by, she heard a soft snuffling sound. Jonathan was sleeping with his mouth slightly open. She hoped he'd snore even louder so she could tell him that he sounded like the train whistle. She waited, but his snore just stayed at a low snuffling sound.

I'll tell him he sounds like a train whistle anyway, she laughed, scooting closer in case he needed a place to lean his head.

* * * *

Emily headed for the bakery before school the next morning; she had forgotten to call Miss Mattie last night to tell her about the trip to Clayton. As she walked along, she kept hoping that her cell phone would ring.

"How'd it go yesterday, Sugar?" Miss Mattie asked first thing, when she walked through the door.

"Great! Sorry I forgot to call. We handed out almost all the flyers, and Jonathan is putting some at Bloomin' Happy for Mr. C to give to customers. I brought these in to see if you would mind handing them out."

"My pleasure," Miss Mattie said, stacking them right by her register. "Do you have time for one of my world-class donuts?"

"I'll come in after school," she said, heading for the door. "I want to give some flyers to Mr. Montoya and see if Mr. Kingery will let me put one up on the bulletin board at his grocery store."

Just before she got to the door, her phone started ringing.

"Hallelujah!" shouted Miss Mattie.

"Hello!" Emily said, so excited she nearly dropped the phone.

Y'all got any pine wood? a gravelly voice asked.

"No, we have oak. It's all dried and none of it's green."

Naw, I'm lookin' for pine. There was a click at the other end.

Miss Mattie looked at her expectantly.

"He wanted pine," she sighed.

"Jus' wait for the next call, Sugar. It'll be comin'."

But it didn't come. Emily silenced her phone at school but checked it every half hour for a message. She grew heartsick as the morning and afternoon wore on, and not another call came in. There was another thought nagging at the back of her mind. Her dad was drinking from morning till night and she didn't know how he'd handle a customer, even if one did call. She decided to go straight home after school and check out the situation there. The house was silent as she walked in. She tiptoed down the hall to her parents' room and listened at the door; they were both snoring. She knew that they had been up drinking all night, but it was weird that Pearl was still sleeping.

She went into the kitchen to check the bulletin board and saw that her dad had tacked up one of the newspaper ads from yesterday. This time the job listed under *Tennessee* had a star by it. Frightened, she picked up his cell phone from the kitchen counter and scrolled to the incoming calls. There were three calls from area codes she didn't recognize; the only local call was when she had phoned him two days ago. No one had called her dad about firewood. She sighed and glanced up at the clock. It was almost three o'clock and Pearl was in bed. That was weird. She went down the hall to Pearl's room and listened at the door. She didn't hear any snoring, so she knocked, then quietly opened the door. Pearl was sitting on the edge of her bed with one house slipper on her foot and the other one in her hand. She didn't turn her head when Emily walked in—just sat staring straight ahead.

"Pearl, are you okay?" she asked, walking over and laying a hand on her shoulder.

Pearl's face looked lopsided, and when she tried to say something, it sounded garbled like she was from another planet.

"Pearl, what's wrong," Emily cried, kneeling down beside her. Pearl just sat there like she was in a trance.

Her phone rang, making her jump.

"Hello?"

"I got Mr. Galloway here, Sugar," Miss Mattie's voice rang out cheerfully, "and he wants to buy some 'o your daddy's wood!"

"Miss Mattie, something's wrong with my grandma."

"What it is, Sugar?"

"I don't know. Part of her face is droopy and when she talks it's all weird sounding."

"Dear Lord," Miss Mattie gasped. "Sugar, what's your address, I'm sendin' for an ambulance."

She gave it to her and Miss Mattie told her she'd call back in a few minutes.

Emily ran to her parents' bedroom and banged loudly on the door.

Her dad mumbled something from the other side.

"Dad, something's wrong with Pearl!" she yelled at the door.

There was no response and she banged again.

She ran back to her grandmother's room where Pearl sat looking muddled and confused. She sat down and took Pearl's cold hands into hers. "Help is coming, don't be afraid," she said. In the distance she could hear a siren.

She ran outside and waved her arms as the ambulance turned onto Sycamore Lane. It pulled up in front of her house, two medics jumped out, and they all ran into the house. She flew down the hall and pointed to Pearl's room.

"What's your grandmother's name?' one medic asked, as he began to examine her.

"Pearl," Emily whispered.

"Looks like she's had a stroke," the other medic said, after a quick examination. He ran for the gurney.

"You live here alone with her?" the other asked.

"No, my parents are here, but I can't wake them up."

The medic looked alarmed.

"They're drunk, not sick," she replied miserably, and went over to her grandmother and put her arm around her.

When the medic returned with the gurney, they asked her to step out of the room while they took her grandmother's vitals. As she waited in the hall, she could hear them talking.

"There's something more going on than a stroke," one medic said.

"She's as stable as we're going to get her," the other said. "Let's get her to the hospital before she arrests."

They quickly rolled the gurney out into the hallway, and Emily heard a clamor from her parents' room. Her dad stumbled out into the hallway just as they were wheeling Pearl past his door.

"What the ______?" He uttered an obscenity.

"Pearl's had a stroke, Dad," she said, her voice choking up.

"Oh God," he snapped, "like I don't have enough problems."

A flash of utter hatred shot through her. "Just go back to bed," she said evenly. "I'll take care of her."

He shook his head and went back into his room.

"What's wrong?" she heard her mother ask crossly.

"Pearl's sick," he grumbled. "Emily's takin' care of it."

She heard the bed creak as he crawled back into it. She was trembling as she followed the gurney through the house. She saw her backpack and grabbed it, determined to ride along in the ambulance.

"I want to come with my grandmother," she said, and without waiting for an answer, climbed into the back of the ambulance with Pearl.

"I don't know if we can carry minors," one of the medics said.

She looked imploringly at the other.

"Sure we can," he said, pointing to a small chair for her to sit in. "Buckle up tight!"

Her cell phone started ringing as the ambulance took off and she silenced it, watching as the medic hooked her grandmother up to monitors.

"Step on it," the medic shouted to the driver, "her heart's doing the hokey-pokey back here."

The siren went on, the ambulance picked up speed, and they were soon careening around corners. The medic braced himself to keep his balance, as the ambulance swayed back and forth.

"Stay with us, Pearl," he kept shouting.

Emily watched in horror as the medic worked desperately, grabbing syringes one by one, yanking the cap off with his teeth, and plunging them into her grandmother's arm, then dropping them to the floor. Paralyzed with fear, she watched the empty containers roll back and forth across the floor as the medic began CPR on her grandmother.

* * * *

The ambulance hurtled through the mountain pass to Monett. Emily sat rigid on the hard plastic seat as the paramedic worked to save her grandmother. She looked once and saw her grandmother move her hand and knew she was still alive.

"Please, God," she whispered.

When they pulled up to the hospital, the ambulance doors flew open, and the paramedics jumped out. One of them told Emily to wait in the waiting room as they rushed the gurney through the emergency room doors. Her phone buzzed in her pocket as she entered the waiting room, and she quickly took it out, hoping it was Miss Mattie.

"Hello!"

"*Do y'all deliver half cords to Clarksville?*" asked a gruff voice on the other end. *"I only have 'nuf money for a half cord."*

She didn't know what the man was talking about at first; yesterday seemed a thousand years away.

"No, only full cords," she said, and then heard her phone power down. She looked at the dead cell phone trying to figure out what had happened and realized she had forgotten to charge it.

She sat down on a brown leather couch in the waiting room. It was cold and uncomfortable. She sat for over an hour, wondering what was happening to her grandmother. She thought about calling Miss Mattie back digging through her backpack for the charging cord.

Before she could find it, a nurse came out and asked, "Is the family for Pearl Miller here?"

She hurried over. "I'm her granddaughter."

"Are your parents here?"

She shook her head and the nurse's eyes swept the waiting room, like she didn't believe her.

"Has someone notified your parents about your grandmother?" the nurse asked.

"Well, they were notified when the medics came and took her away in an ambulance," Emily said.

The nurse's eyes bugged out slightly. "And what did they say?" she asked.

"They didn't say anything, they went back to bed."

The nurse stared at Emily in disbelief. "Oh...well," she stammered, "come on back and see your grandmother. But we really do need to get ahold of your parents."

Good luck, she thought, as she followed the nurse down the hall.

"My name is Nurse Malcolm," she said, pointing to the name badge that hung around her neck. "Your grandmother is critically ill," she explained in a low voice. "The doctor will come in and talk to you as soon as he can." She swiped a card at the double doors that read ICU and both doors swished open. The room was circular with twelve patient's rooms circling the nurse's station. A nurse sat at the desk watching monitors; there was one for each patient. Nurse Malcolm led her to Room 3. Her grandmother lay still and gray on the bed, with wires attached to her chest and tubes coming out of everywhere. The room was as quiet as a tomb, except for the machines beeping and hissing. She knew at a glance that her grandmother was very sick. She had a tube down her throat and taped to her face—and every time the machine swished, her chest would rise. It frightened her, and she just stood in the doorway staring, unable to make herself go in. She heard the double doors swing open and saw Miss Mattie rush in looking this way and that. When she spotted Emily she hurried over.

"Sugar, how's your grandmother?" she asked breathlessly, glancing toward the bed. She walked slowly over to Pearl's side. "Dear God," she whispered.

Emily stayed in the doorway too frightened to move. "Is she dead?"

"No Sugar, but she's very sick." Miss Mattie held her hand out, and said, "Come on over —it's okay."

Emily walked over and grabbed Miss Mattie's hand with both of hers and looked down at her grandmother all sunken in the bed. "She looks so old!" she whispered. The rise and fall of her chest was eerie and Emily looked away.

A tall, stern-looking doctor walked in.

"I'm Dr. Bradley," he said.

Miss Mattie looked at him evenly and said, "I'm Mattie Cooke, and this is Emily, the patient's granddaughter."

"I see," he replied, not bothering to mention that only family members were allowed in ICU.

"Mrs. Miller is very sick," he said, getting right to the point. "She had a stroke and on the way to the hospital, she had a heart attack. She's having trouble breathing so we've put her on a machine that's breathing for her."

The room began to swim around Emily, and she swayed toward Miss Mattie.

Miss Mattie helped her ease down into the chair. "It's all right Sugar, it's all right."

"Is she going to die?" Emily could barely utter the words.

"We don't know," the doctor replied frankly. "We're doing everything we can to take care of her, but only time will tell."

* * * *

The evening shadows stretched long over the room as Emily and Miss Mattie sat, talking softly. Occasionally Miss Mattie would hum a quiet hymn or stand up and check on Pearl.

Around 7:00 p.m. Miss Mattie asked, "Are your parents coming up?"

"I don't think so," she said, too ashamed to make eye contact.

Miss Mattie started to say something but didn't. "Well, Sugar," she finally said, "you need to come with me, and let's get you some nourishment. It's prob'ly been a long time since you ate.

"I don't want to leave her," Emily replied, shaking her head.

"I know leavin' is the last thing you want to do," Miss Mattie said, rising from her chair, "but she's in fine hands, and I'll bring you right back in the mornin'."

Emily hesitated, not knowing what to do. Other than her backpack, she hadn't brought a thing with her–including money. She couldn't ask Miss Mattie to drive her home to pick up some things and bring her back. It would be too hard on her.

"You need to listen to your mama," Miss Mattie said, holding out her hand. "This could go on for a long, *long* time. You need to pace yourself. You come along with me now and we'll get you some supper."

She felt so torn. She knew that if she didn't leave, Miss Mattie wouldn't leave either. She couldn't put her health at risk. In the end she took Miss Mattie's hand and they both went over to Pearl.

Miss Mattie said, "Lets' pray for your grandmother, Sugar."

Emily bowed her head, praying with all of her heart, as Miss Mattie said the words.

"Lord God, we leave Em'ly's grandmother in Your hands. Watch over her, heal her, and give her back to Em'ly. Amen"

"Amen," Emily whispered, then leaned over and kissed her grandmother good-bye. She looked so fragile, as though she could just slip away after the next breath.

"Watch over her, God," Emily whispered, as they left the room.

They stopped at Harper's Café in Monett for a bite to eat before their trip home. After they placed their orders, Miss Mattie asked, "Any more calls for firewood?'

Startled, she remembered her phone needed charging. She saw an electrical plug near their booth and plugged it in. She waited until the phone charged enough to make a call, and then called her voice mail. As she pressed buttons to receive her messages, she silently begged there to be calls for firewood, but the only message was from Jonathan, asking how the firewood sales were going.

She returned to her seat. "No calls for firewood," she sighed.

"Don't forget Mr. Galloway, the man who came into my bakery. He wants a cord," Miss Mattie smiled.

That was some good news she had forgotten about. Maybe her dad had received calls by now, too.

It was dark when Miss Mattie dropped her off at home. Her dad's truck was gone, and when she let herself in, the house was quiet. She walked into the kitchen, saw two empty cardboard boxes and her blood ran cold. There were two more boxes in the living room, and all the pictures had been taken off the wall. Her stomach did a somersault. *They couldn't be moving, not when Pearl was so sick.* She heard the front door open and her dad came in carrying three more boxes.

"What are you doing?" she asked.

"I got the job in Tennessee," he said, swaying slightly. He had been driving drunk again.

"We can't move. What about Pearl?"

"She can come, too."

"Dad, listen to me," she said, her voice breaking, "Pearl's had a stroke *and* a heart attack."

"Well then," he said, staring at her bleary eyed, "we'll send for her when she gets better." He set the boxes on the floor. "I gotta take this job anyway. I haven't made a rent payment here in three months."

"You're behind on the rent?" she asked, in disbelief.

"Yep," he said, glaring at her.

"Did anyone call you for firewood?"

"Three people," he said, pulling moving blankets out of one of the boxes. "That'll get me jus' about what I need to move us."

She wheeled around and went looking for her mother; she found her in the small office at the computer.

"Pearl's had a stroke and a heart attack; she's on a breathing machine," she blurted out.

Her mother turned in the swivel chair and stared blankly at her.

"Don't you want to go to the hospital and see her?" Emily finally asked.

"Is she asking for me?"

"She's not conscious."

"Well then, it's not going to matter to her whether I'm there or not."

"She might die," Emily said, not believing what she was hearing.

"Don't start it, Emily," her mother snapped. "We barely spoke to each other when she was well. What would we talk about now, even if she did wake up?"

Emily just stared at her.

"Anyway," her mother grimaced, "you know hospitals creep me out."

"It's not about *you,*" she said, incredulously.

Her mother turned back to the computer.

"So you'd move without her?" Emily asked, refusing to be ignored.

Her mother turned and glared at her. "We're being evicted from this place on Wednesday," she said evenly. "Where do you suggest we live while you're playing nursemaid?"

Wednesday? She backed away from her mother. She wouldn't say another word about moving. All she knew was that she was not going with them.

CHAPTER – 20

The next morning Miss Mattie was out in front of Emily's house at seven o'clock, sipping coffee and listening to Pastor Goodnight out of Alabama, on her car radio.

"Good mornin', Sugar," she said, as Emily slid into the passenger's seat.

"Good morning," Emily replied, putting on her seat belt. "I forgot about your bakery—who's watching it?"

"Clara's helpin' me," Miss Mattie said, putting the car into drive and making a U-turn. "My bakin' is all done, and she can run the cash register 'til I get back." She turned left on Elderberry Lane and headed for Highway 110 to Monett.

As she barreled the car up to seventy, she turned the radio down. "So did your daddy get any calls about firewood?"

"Three."

Miss Mattie glanced at her. "You don't sound very excited about it."

"My dad's moving anyway, he already found a job in Tennessee," she said dully.

"What!" Miss Mattie yelped, nearly driving off the road. The car in back of her honked and the driver shouted something as he passed her.

"What about your grandmother?"

"My dad said they'd send for her when she got better."

"Dear Lord," Miss Mattie said. "When are you leavin'?"

"*They're* leaving pretty soon," she said, putting her head back on the seat. "I'm coming up with another plan. I'm not leaving my grandmother."

"What! "Miss Mattie yelped again, careening out onto the soft shoulder. "Your parents

wouldn't leave you." She steered the car back onto the road and looked at her. "Would they?"

"I don't know," she said, wishing Miss Mattie would just keep her eyes on the road. "I just want to concentrate on getting my grandma better right now."

"Well, what will you do?" Miss Mattie asked.

"I'm not sure," she murmured. She actually had a pretty good idea of what she was going to do, but she didn't want to burden Miss Mattie with it.

Miss Mattie started to say something, but Emily's cell phone rang. She looked at the small screen and saw it was Jonathan.

"So how many orders have you received?" he asked, his voice fairly crackling with excitement.

"Three."

"I knew it!" he laughed. "You'll probably get even more calls today."

"Jonathan, my parents are still moving anyway."

"What!"

She didn't want to say too much in front of Miss Mattie. "My grandmother is really sick. I'm in the car with Miss Mattie—she's driving me to the hospital."

"Emily, they can't..." was all she heard before her phone died.

She looked at the bars. She had forgotten to plug it in last night when she got home, and the little charge she'd given it at the café hadn't lasted. She would have to remember to plug it in at the hospital.

Miss Mattie resumed their conversation. "So why can't your parents jus' wait until your gran'mother is better?"

She knew she'd told Miss Mattie too much already. "We'll see what they do," she replied, forcing her voice to sound somewhat cheerful. "Things will work out."

* * * *

Her grandmother looked about the same when they arrived back at the ICU, but Nurse Malcolm said her blood pressure had soared during the night, and they had trouble getting it down.

Miss Mattie pulled up a chair to sit down and catch her breath. Emily thought her face looked tired and drawn. *Why did I even let her drive me this morning?* she scolded herself. Miss Mattie couldn't run a bakery and help her. It was too much.

"Mama," Emily said, setting her backpack in a corner, "I know you need to get back to the bakery. As you said last night, this could go on for quite a while." She looked at her evenly. "I'll be fine by myself."

Miss Mattie opened her mouth to protest, but then said, "Are you sure, Sugar?"

"Positive, and I'm going to spend the night if her blood pressure goes up again. Maybe she'd do better if I were here."

Miss Mattie hesitated.

"Now you need to listen to me, Mama," Emily said, putting her arms around her. "I'm fine and I want you to take care of yourself. I can handle *this*, but I couldn't handle it if you weren't in that bakery for me every time I walked through the door."

Miss Mattie looked at her. "Well, in that case," she finally said, reaching for her purse, "you'll have to let me give you some money to buy yourself a good supper. They have a nice cafeteria in the basement," she pulled out some fives and tens, "and we passed a Foster Freeze about two blocks down the road. You have to promise me you'll eat and take care of yourself."

"It's okay, I have money," Emily protested. "And I'll take the bus home, so don't worry about that."

"No way, young lady," she replied, meaning it. "If you don't spend the night, I'm comin' back for you and that's that!" She held the money out. "Now your mama wants to buy your supper for you," she smiled.

Emily took the money, and threw her arms around Miss Mattie, hugging her good-bye. On her way out, Miss Mattie walked over and said good-bye to the nurse and gave her a phone number to reach her, with strict instructions to call anytime.

"I'll call you if things get worse," the nurse promised, and with a final wave Miss Mattie walked out the double doors.

Emily went over and sat by her grandmother. It seemed lonely and eerie in the quiet room and she almost regretted sending Miss Mattie away. She pulled up the high-back chair, which she discovered became a rocking chair when the side latch was released. She rocked back and forth and tried to settle in; she still had to study for her finals at school. Her mind wandered as she studied, so she tried to plan her day. She had two sandwiches in her backpack. She would go to the cafeteria for a drink later. If her grandmother's blood pressure stayed down, she would go back to Mountain Grove tonight. Wednesday was eviction day for her parents, and she had to make plans. She turned back to her history book and reread the same paragraph three times before she finally tossed it aside. She couldn't sit here trying to absorb a book when her world was crumbling at her feet. She only had two days.

The enormity of what she was doing was overwhelming. She pulled out a piece of paper to list what she would need just to exist. She figured the basic things she needed were food, soap, shampoo and toothpaste. She had plenty of clothes, and she could go to the laundromat on Second Street to wash them. She put laundry soap on her list. She thought she could keep herself supplied with the things she needed by working for Miss Mattie, Ike, and Mr. Charles. She figured out what she made a week working Wednesdays at the bakery, and a day or two a week at Bloomin' Happy, and Good Eats. It wasn't a lot of money, but if she was careful, she would make it okay.

Her greatest need right now—and the one that concerned her the most—was a place to stay. Mr. and Mrs. Apple were still in Florida. They had called the bakery, and left word with Miss Mattie that they would be back in the summer. But she wouldn't impose on them anyway, with Mr. Apple's bad health. It was the same reason she didn't want to worry Miss Mattie. *Older people make you feel safe, but they're kind of a fragile bunch,* she decided. She'd get her grandmother well and figure out where to live later. In a pinch, she could sleep at the hospital. One day at a time, and one problem at a time, was the only way she could handle it and keep breathing.

Emily grew restless and her stomach began to rumble. She looked at the time. One o'clock, no wonder she was hungry. She stood up and stretched, deciding it felt better to be tucked away with Pearl in this quiet place, than the craziness of her house. Nurse Malcolm had explained how to read Pearl's blood pressure on the monitor. She kept an eye on it all morning, thankful it was staying down.

She grabbed her backpack, deciding she would go to the cafeteria for a drink, and then go outside and eat her lunch in the fresh air. She took the elevator down to the first floor and went in search of the cafeteria. As Emily walked into the lobby, she was more than a little surprised to see Jonathan burst through the front doors. She hurried over to him.

"Jonathan, what are you doing here? Why aren't you in school?"

He looked distraught and somewhat angry. "Emily, I've called every hospital in the county trying to find you," he said.

"You did?" she asked, puzzled. "You look weird, what's wrong?"

"*What's wrong*?" he asked, in disbelief. "You tell me you're moving and on your way to the hospital, and the phone goes dead. I've been trying to call you back all day!"

"Oh, I forgot to plug my phone in. I didn't know you'd be worried."

"Didn't know I'd be worried?" he blustered. "Why do you think I helped you with the flyers and walked around Clayton all day? I don't want you to move!"

"You don't?"

"Emily, are you *crazy*! I..."

"You, *what*?"

He just shook his head. "I just don't want you to move, that's all."

She didn't understand the feeling of joy that swept over her. "I'm sorry I worried you," she said, touching his arm.

He sighed. "Is your grandmother doing okay?"

"She's stable," she replied, looking around the lobby for a spot where they could talk privately. "I'd take you to her room if I could, but only family members are allowed."

They sat down on a small couch behind some potted plants. She didn't know if she should tell him she wasn't moving with her parents. He would try and help her, and she needed to handle it herself.

"When are you moving?" he asked, looking tired.

"When I went home last night, they had already brought moving boxes in, and all the pictures were down."

"Is there any way to change their mind?"

"No, I tried," she said, looking at him evenly. "The biggest thing is, they haven't been paying the rent—they *have* to move. I didn't know that, or I wouldn't have bothered with the flyers."

He nodded his head and looked so depressed that she felt sorry for him.

"I'm not going with them," she blurted out.

He stared at her. "How can you *not* go with your parents?"

"I don't have that part worked out yet," she said. "I just know I'm not leaving my grandma."

"Emily..." he started to say, but just shook his head. "How can you stay?"

She suddenly felt lighthearted and very sure of herself. "I'll get it to work out, you'll see."

"But *how*?"

"Well, I'm not really sure," she smiled, "but I'm a pretty self-sufficient person, you know."

"Yes, I've noticed that," he said, grinning slightly himself.

She had an idea. "I'll go check on my grandmother," she said, jumping up. "When I come back, let's go to the Foster Freeze down the street. I'll buy you an ice cream for all your trouble."

He stood up and looked at her, then touched her cheek. "Did I ever tell you that you're *crazy*?"

"I think so," she grinned, "and I couldn't agree with you more." She whirled around and ran for the elevator before he could say anything more. How could she be feeling so lighthearted in the midst of this awful situation, she wondered.

* * * *

"How'd you get here anyway?" Emily asked Jonathan, as they ate their soft cones.

"The bus," Jonathan said. "I called every hospital I could think of, but no one would give me any information. I had to wait for Miss Mattie to get back and she told me where you were."

She lapped up the ice cream streaming down over her cone. "What time does the last bus leave back for Mountain Grove?"

"At seven. Want to ride with me?"

"I was thinking I'd spend the night with Pearl, but, so far, her blood pressure has stayed down." She bit into her cone. "I'll keep an eye on her, and if the medicine keeps it down the rest of the day, I'll go with you."

"What's your next step?" he asked, popping the last bite of cone into his mouth.

"I have to find a place to stay," she said, then let the bombshell fall. "My parents are being evicted on Wednesday."

"*Wednesday!*"

She nodded. "That's why I want to go back tonight. I have to do something quick."

"Tell me what you're thinking of doing."

"Well, it's kind of sketchy, and I don't want anyone else to know..." She leaned in and told him her plans.

* * * *

There was no change in Pearl the rest of the day and Emily wondered if she would ever open her eyes again. Her blood pressure had stayed under control, so Emily decided to take the bus back with Jonathan, who was in the waiting room studying for finals. She called Miss Mattie as they walked toward the bus stop to let her know the plans.

When she got home that evening there were even more boxes packed and stacked in the kitchen. In her bedroom, she saw a note from her dad scrawled on a piece of cardboard: *Emily—pack your room.* She didn't know exactly how she would tell him she wasn't going, but she needed to do it quickly. Her dad had left some empty boxes on her floor, and she began to pack only those things she wanted to keep with her. The furniture would go with them, all she would take were her clothes and things she had bought with her own money. An incredible sadness settled over her as she emptied out drawers and closet. This was the end of living with her family—such as it was. She pushed all thoughts about the future out of her mind. It was way too scary.

It was well after midnight before she had her things packed. She pushed the boxes she wasn't keeping out into the kitchen, and went back to her room, tumbling into bed, exhausted.

* * * *

She overslept the next morning, and when she walked out into the kitchen her dad was taping up boxes.

"You all packed?" he asked.

She nodded and went for it. "I'm thinking I'd like to stay here for a while. It would be easier and cheaper for you and mom, and I could look after Pearl until she's better. Plus, I could finish out my school year." She held her breath, waiting for his answer.

"Where would you stay?" he asked stiffly.

"With friends."

"I don't know..." he said, rubbing the back of his neck.

"Just think about it. I'm late for school and have to run."

So far, so good, she thought, as she went to get her backpack. *If he was going to get mad and tell me no, he would've done it by now.* She felt a little more light-hearted as she took off for school thinking this whole thing might be easier than she thought. She hurried up the road that led to the school, planning out her day. She would need to go to the office first and explain why she hadn't been there yesterday. Her cell phone rang, interrupting her thoughts. "Hello?"

Emily, it's Nurse Malcolm. Your grandmother had another heart attack.

"My grandma...?" She was stunned.

She's in pretty bad shape, Emily. You might want to come back to the hospital as soon as you can. We've left a message with your parents.

She didn't reply, just whirled around and took off running full speed for the bus stop.

* * * *

At the hospital she rang the ICU buzzer for them to let her in and flew through the doors when they swung open. The curtains had been pulled over the glass window in her grandmother's room and she couldn't see inside. She started to go in the door, but Dr. Bradley was there and asked her to wait outside.

She backed up to the nurse's station. "Is she dead?" she whispered to the nurse.

"No, but she came very close," the nurse told her honestly.

Emily sat down and put her head in her hands. "Did you call Miss Mattie?" she asked.

"I was just getting ready to," the nurse said. "Is there any way to reach your parents?"

She shook her head. "No, and they won't come anyway. I'll call Miss Mattie, you don't need to."

"Are you sure?" she said, "I promised I would."

"I'll call her now," Emily said, knowing that if the nurse called, Miss Mattie would hurry to the hospital. Emily didn't want that. She couldn't lose both of them. She called Miss Mattie and downplayed the horror of what was going on, promising to keep her updated. She got off the phone as quickly as she could and went back into ICU where Dr. Bradley was just coming out of her grandmother's room.

"She's stable for now," he said, "the next few hours will tell her outcome."

She nodded her head miserably. "Can I see her?"

He walked with her back into the room.

She looked at the monitor and saw that her grandmother's blood pressure was soaring. Her skin was translucent, and she looked like a small, wrinkled doll. Emily reached out and held her icy hand. The hours flew by with no change. Emily was afraid to leave, and stayed glued to the bedside, watching her grandmother's chest rise and fall...rise and fall...rise and fall. If her grandmother looked like she stopped breathing, Emily stopped breathing, too.

The nurse finally came in, "Take a little break, sweetie. Run down and get something to eat and walk in the fresh air for a while."

She hesitated.

"We'll call you, just like we did before, if there's any change," the nurse promised.

She went down the elevator and called Miss Mattie to update her.

"You want me to come down, Sugar?" Miss Mattie asked her.

"No, there's nothing you can do and I'm okay. I just wanted you to know that I'm spending the night here."

"You have money for your supper?"

"Yes, Mama, I surely do."

Miss Mattie chuckled, "All right Sugar, phone me in the mornin' or if you need me in the night, the phone is right by my bed."

"Would you call the school and tell Mr. Godfrey where I am?"

Miss Mattie promised she would, and they hung up.

She had six more days of school, with finals at the beginning of next week. She needed to study. She hurried down to the cafeteria and bought a sandwich and drink. She started to eat it there, but grew worried, and took it back up to her grandmother's room. She tilted the high back chair to a comfortable angle, propped up her history book and studied as she ate.

The afternoon and evening wore on with no change in her grandmother's vitals. About nine o'clock the nurse brought a blanket and pillow and showed her how to let the back of her chair down to make a narrow bed. All through the night, Emily got up and checked on her grandmother, holding her hand and telling her that she was there with her. Sometime around four in the morning Pearl's blood pressure dropped.

Emily awoke to the clatter of the food cart being rolled from room to room. The nurse brought in a breakfast tray. "Eat up," she smiled. "It's your grandmother's tray and I don't think she'll be eating today."

"How do you think my grandma is doing?"

"Well, it's good that her blood pressure dropped, but she's got a long way back. Eat your breakfast and then think about going home for a while. We'll call you if there's any change."

Emily didn't want to leave at all, but there were things she needed to do that wouldn't wait–such as convincing her parents to let her stay, and getting her boxes stored somewhere. After that, she would just stay at the hospital until she figured things out. She put on her backpack and walked out to the nurse's desk. "I'll be back later. Is my number still posted, so you can call me if anything happens?"

"Got it right here, sweetie," the nurse smiled.

"Please, call me for anything," Emily said, wondering how she was going to bear the next few hours away.

"I promise," the nurse said. "Try and get some rest."

It would be a long, long time before she got a chance to rest, she thought, as she walked out the double doors to the bus stop.

****

She got off the bus in Mountain Grove and trudged up Elderberry Lane, bone weary. The first thing that needed to be done was to see what her dad had to say about her staying. His truck was not in the yard and the blinds were all closed, which was weird. She took out her key and unlocked the door. The house echoed, as the front door opened and banged against the door stop. The first thing she noticed was that the boxes were all gone.

"Dad? Mom?" she called, not quite believing her eyes. Her heart froze as she walked from empty room to empty room, calling their name. Chills ran up and down her spine as she realized that everything was gone, including her parents.

CHAPTER – 21

Emily stood in the empty house, panic stricken. Had she lost track of the days? She quickly calculated: Sunday, Monday, Tuesday. Today was Tuesday, and her parents didn't have to be out until Wednesday. Where were they? She ran out to the wood lot to see if her dad's truck was there.

It was empty.

She dug her phone out of her pocket and turned it on. Her hands trembled as she brought up *missed calls* on the screen. Surely, they had tried to get ahold of her.

No calls.

She went back into the house and opened the door to her bedroom. There were all the boxes she had packed to keep. Her dad had pushed them over to a corner of the room; an envelope was propped up on one of the boxes, with her name written on it. She tore open the envelope. Inside were three twenty-dollar bills and a note:

Emily--

We decided it was ok for you to stay. We'll call with our address when we get one. We're leaving tonight. Don't know when sheriff will show up.

Dad

She stared at the note, hardly able to breathe. They had sneaked out in the middle of the night, without even trying to contact her. Her disbelief turned into horror, and she slid down to the floor leaning up against the packing boxes. *It couldn't be!* Surely her parents wouldn't just drive off and leave her—not without making sure she was safe and had a place to stay.

What should she do?

All she could think of was that she desperately needed a shower. The rest of it was so overwhelming, she couldn't think about it. But there were no towels. She looked at the boxes, remembering that she had wrapped her lamp in a beach towel when she packed it. She just had to remember which box.

As she lathered up her hair in the hot shower, she pushed down her panic, and tried to come up with an idea. Her first thought was Miss Mattie, but she quickly x'd that off her list of options. She was afraid that Miss Mattie's health was still too fragile to involve her in a mess like this. That left two options: spend the night here or go ask Pastor Alex if she could stay in the church basement.

She didn't want the sheriff to find her here, so that left only one option.

* * * *

When she knocked on the parsonage door, Pastor Alex opened it dressed in jeans and a t-shirt.

"Emily!" he smiled, throwing the door open. "Come in!" He gave her a quick hug and led her into the living room.

"What's up with Emily today? Needing the church basement to house another homeless friend?" he teased.

She just stared at him.

He quit smiling. "You really *do* need the basement to house a friend?"

She nodded her head yes.

"Who?"

"Me."

"*You?*"

About then, his wife walked in; she went over and hugged Emily. "What did I just hear about Emily needing the church basement again?" Penelope smiled.

"Emily needs the basement for herself this time," the pastor said slowly to his wife.

"*Oh,*" she murmured, quickly sitting down on the couch. "Come, sit down, and tell us all about it, Emily," she said, patting the seat next to her.

Emily took a seat, wondering how to tell them; she had forgotten to think it through on the way over. She decided to go with the condensed version. "My grandmother had a stroke and a heart attack," she said, looking up at the pastor's wife. "My parents left for Tennessee, where my dad has a new job, and I need a place to stay for a few days, until I can make other arrangements."

"Your parents just left you here?" Penelope asked, her eyes bugging slightly.

Emily nodded. "I told them I didn't want to go with them."

"*So they just left you?*" Pastor Alex asked, punctuating every word.

Emily almost laughed at the sight of the two adults with jaws dropped, and eyes bugged out like Frisbees.

"I just need a place to stay for a few days, until I can get something figured out long term," she said, plunging in with both feet. "Plus, I still have to study for my finals, which we take on Friday. After that I'll take care of everything."

"Wow!" Pastor Alex said, looking at his wife, then back at Emily. "Do you have any idea what you'll do after that?"

"I'll probably have to go into foster care," she said, sounding much more confident than she felt.

"Do you have a place to stay tonight?" the pastor inquired.

"No, they took my bed."

For some reason, they all burst out laughing.

"Emily, Emily," he chuckled, "you are something else."

The laughter broke the tension, and Emily began to relax a little.

"Where are all your belongings?" he asked.

"Still at the house, but I need to get them out because the sheriff is coming today." She figured she may as well tell it all. "My parents haven't been paying the rent."

"I see," he said, rubbing the back of his neck. "Do you have a lot of things?"

"About eight boxes."

"Okay then, let's take this a step at a time," he said, deep in thought. "Use the basement tonight and we'll figure the rest out tomorrow."

She hesitated. "Could we figure the rest out on Friday, after school? I need to study for my finals and I'm going to be spending most of my time at the hospital."

He nodded, "Friday it is then. How about food? Are you hungry?"

"No, they gave me a breakfast tray at the hospital before I came here."

"Well, the next thing on the agenda is to get the boxes out of your house," Pastor Alex said, rubbing the back of his neck again. "I bet Joe Charles would bring them over in his truck. Would you like me to call him?"

She shook her head. "I'm going back over to the house and I'll call on the way over." She would talk to Jonathan and have him ask his dad.

* * * *

"They just left without telling you!" Jonathan sputtered, when she explained why she was calling.

This was getting to be exhausting. "Yes," she replied slowly, "but I still have a plan. I just didn't plan on this."

He was silent for a moment. "My dad is gone with the truck for about twenty minutes, but we'll be right over when he gets back." He paused. "Emily, are you *sure* they didn't just go shopping or something?"

"I'm sure," she replied evenly. "See you in a while."

She hurried to get the boxes out of her house, dragging them out the door, and pushing them onto the lawn. Her parents had left the house a mess and she didn't want anyone seeing it.

She was waiting on the lawn when Mr. Charles' truck came roaring up. He and Jonathan jumped out and hurried over.

"Emily..." Mr. Charles said, but suddenly found himself at a loss for words. He looked at her boxes. "Do you have any idea where your parents are?" he finally asked.

"I don't know," she shrugged tiredly, "somewhere in Tennessee. My dad's supposed to let me know when they get settled."

He shook his head in disbelief. "Did they leave you money to live on?"

"A little, plus I have my own money from working."

Jonathan started loading her boxes into the back of the truck. He wasn't saying anything, and she could tell that he was angry.

"Wouldn't you rather stay with Mattie, than in the church basement?" Mr. Charles asked.

"No," she replied emphatically, "and I rather she didn't know about this until I get things figured out. I don't want to worry her; she hasn't been out of the hospital all that long."

It seemed surreal as she watched them load up her boxes. She started to get into the truck, then she remembered her garden. Grief shot through her, and she tried to keep her lips from trembling.

Jonathan noticed immediately. "What's wrong?" he asked.

"My garden..." she whispered.

"Go see it," Mr. Charles offered. "We'll wait here."

"No," she whispered, not wanting to take up any more of their time. "I'll walk back up after we unload the boxes. I need to leave a note for Mr. and Mrs. Apple."

It only took a few minutes to carry her few belongings into the church basement. After they had set the last box down, both Jonathan and Mr. Charles lingered, trying to think of what more they could do for her. It got awkward.

"Thanks for bringing my stuff over," she said. "I'm going to walk up and leave a note for Mr. and Mrs. Apple and have one last look at my garden." She choked up again on that one.

"I'll go with you," Jonathan said.

"It's okay," she assured him. "I just want to sit in my red chair a few minutes. Thanks so much—both of you."

Mr. Charles hugged her. "Emily, are you *sure* you wouldn't rather just stay with Mattie?"

"No, she's done enough," she replied firmly.

She hugged them both and took off walking toward Sycamore Lane, knowing they wouldn't leave unless she left first.

On the way, she checked her cell phone to make sure it was on. She kept hoping it would ring, and it would be her parents making sure she was okay.

"That little fairy tale is probably not going to happen," she murmured to herself, as she unlatched the gate to her backyard.

She walked to the archway of her garden and stood a moment, taking it all in. It was the prettiest time of year, when every bloom fairly exploded with color. The sun's slant on the greenery added a depth that only enhanced the riot of colors. It all but took her breath away. There was her red chair that she'd worked so many hours on—sanding it and picking out just the right shade of red to spray paint it. It was a part of her sanctuary, her sanity. She went to it and sat down, wishing with all her heart that she could keep it. She stared down at her pansies, as a slight, warm breeze blew them back and forth. It seemed like they were waving good-bye to her.

She leaned her head back and closed her eyes against the sun's glare. An incredible sadness settled over her. This wasn't going to be as easy as she'd thought. Hot tears flowed down her cheeks and ran back toward her ears.

Her mind insisted that she think about what was happening: *Your mom and dad left you, and they don't care what happens to you.* The tears came faster, as her mind recited the words over and over and over again. She put her chin down so the tears didn't run into her ears anymore.

* * * *

After slipping a note under the Apple's front door, Emily went back to the church basement and got a few things to take to the hospital with her. Her cell phone rang and she yanked it out of her pocket, hoping against hope that it was her parents. She peered at the screen and saw that it was Miss Mattie. She didn't know what she was going to tell her yet, so she didn't answer. Then noticing the time, she hurriedly stuffed her books into her backpack, deciding to talk to Gilbert before she went to the hospital.

She stopped by the parsonage. "I may not be back tonight if my grandmother isn't doing any better," she told Penelope.

"Why don't you call us either way, so we know," the pastor's wife said.

"Okay, I will," she said, turning to go. She turned back. "And thanks for everything."

"Wait just one minute," Penelope said, raising her finger. She hurried off down the hall and returned a few seconds later.

"Here," she said, handing Emily some folded twenty-dollar bills, "for food, or anything else you need."

"I have money," she began, but Penelope interrupted her.

"Please take it," she said softly. "I want you to."

She hesitated.

"Please..."

Emily took it and threw her arms around the pastor's wife. "Thanks," she whispered, holding her tight.

* * * *

Emily went in search of Gilbert. She could always find him in the library, or in the park, studying. This time she found him in the park, reading under the shade of a sycamore tree.

"Hi, Gilbert," she said, thumping down beside him.

"Whas' up?" he asked.

"Gilbert, I need to ask you about foster care. How do you get into it?"

He looked at her like she'd lost her mind. "You mean you wanna go into foster care?"

"No, I don't *want* to," she explained, "but my dad got a job in Tennessee, and he and my mom left. I don't want to leave Mountain Grove or my grandma, and I don't know what else to do."

"They left without you?" he asked, incredulously.

Was there an echo in this mountain, she wondered, having heard the question asked repeatedly today.

She nodded and said, “Yes, Gilbert, they left without me. I told them I didn’t want to go with them, if that makes any difference.”

“Jeez, Em’ly, what kinda parents you got,” he said, shaking his head.

She just stared at him.

“I know, I know, I’m a great one to talk, right?”

“I just need some advice from you, Gilbert,” she sighed, “not a critique of my parents.”

“Not a *what* of yer parents?”

“Gilbert!”

“Okay, okay, my advice is that you should go live in th’ church basement or down at th’ river!”

“I *am* living in the church basement for the next few days,” she said.

“Well, why do ya need foster care then?”

“Because Gilbert, I need a place for two or three *years*, not two or three days.” She looked at him. “You know...until I’m eighteen.”

“It’s done through th’ county,” he replied, sounding irritated. “Th’ office is in Clayton.”

“That’s all you know?”

“That’s all,” he shrugged. “They come an’ git me, I don’t go to their office and volunteer, ya know.”

“Well, thanks,” she said, and started to get up.

“Ya’ll prob’ly won’t be thankin’ me onc’t you go live there.”

She sat back down. “What’s so awful about foster care, Gilbert?”

“The home ain’t awful,” he said. “What’s awful is havin’ people tell ya what ta do. Go to school, do yer danged homework, take a shower, go to bed. I’m usta takin’ care of myself, not livin’ by a bunch of rules.”

“Is it like a regular home life?” she asked.

“I ‘spose,” he mumbled. “They giv’ ya foster parents—and they was nice—but like I said, I druther be on my own, out in th’ woods with my dogs and all. I don’t like bein’ in a house with a buncha people breathin’ down my neck.”

“Well, it’s good that they were nice to you.”

"Yeah, they was nice, and 'at ol' social worker came 'round all the time, and if they wasn't nice, I coulda' told her. She asked me all th' time how it was goin'."

"Well, I'm just checking out my options right now," she said, wondering if talking to Gilbert had been such a good idea.

"I say, take the option of livin' at the river," he said, meaning it.

She burst out laughing. "I think that would get pretty cold in the winter!"

"Well, worry 'bout that in th' winter," he said. He peered closely at her. "You got any bruises on you?"

"No, why?"

"I was thinkin' it would be quicker to get in if someone was hittin' ya."

"Is getting beat up the only way you can get into foster care?"

"No, there's other things. If yer parents' ain't givin' you no food, sexual 'buse, or if they're puttin' you in some kinda danger."

"But they *will* take you if you're under eighteen and your parents have left you, right?"

"Sure, it's called 'bandonment," he said, pleased to be such a wealth of information. "Ain't you ever heard of that?"

"Abandonment?"

He nodded.

"Sure, I've heard of it," she said, getting to her feet. "I'll find out where their office is and go talk to them about it. Thanks for your help, Gilbert."

"You heard from Kelly Ann?" he asked, offhandedly.

"Last I heard, she was coming for a visit in June or July. You still missing her?"

"Yeah," he sighed, "all the dern time."

* * * *

As Emily hurried up the hospital steps, she couldn't quit thinking about her parents. She felt like she was in a dream; a nightmare that was really happening to her. She pushed the thoughts to the back of her mind and ran to the elevator, wishing she hadn't stayed away from her grandmother so long. When she got to ICU, it seemed like forever before they answered the buzzer to let her in. She tiptoed into her grandmother's room and peeked over the bed railing, surprised to see two eyes looking back at her.

"Grandma!"

Her grandmother gave a little wave and closed her eyes. She didn't wake back up for quite a while, but her color and blood pressure were better. Emily sat with her all afternoon, and even though it was hard to do, she decided to go back to Mountain Grove so she could go to school in the morning. She'd missed too much already, and she needed to get ready for her finals.

She wrote a note saying she'd be right back after school tomorrow, and put it on the bedside table. Nurse Malcolm promised to read it to her when she woke up again. "There's a good chance she won't be in ICU after tonight," Nurse Malcom said. "They usually put people out on the main floor once they can breathe on their own."

* * * *

It was almost dark when Emily got back to Mountain Grove and she went directly to the parsonage to tell them she was back. When Penelope opened the door, a wonderful aroma floated out.

"Emily, we were just sitting down to dinner," she said, swinging the door wide open. "Come and join us!"

"Thanks, but I need to study for my finals," she said. "I just wanted to let you know I was back."

"Well, you still need to eat," the pastor's wife said, all but pulling her into the house.

Penelope served up bowls of thick soup, with chunks of beef swimming in seasoned vegetables. They said grace and tucked into their bowls.

"Yummy!" Emily said, after the first spoonful.

"Thank you," Penelope smiled, and passed a basket of warm bread.

"How's your grandmother doing?" Pastor Alex asked.

"She opened her eyes and sort of waved at me!" Emily replied, spreading butter liberally on her bread.

"Wonderful! Did she talk?"

"No, but she can't talk–she has a breathing tube down her throat."

"Have you heard anything from your parents?" Penelope asked.

She shook her head. It was embarrassing, and she wished people would stop asking her.

"To let you know my plans," she said, changing the subject, "I'll take my finals on Monday. Then on Tuesday, I'll go to Clayton. Gilbert told me that's where the foster care offices are."

"Oh, yes," Penelope said, "that's where we went when we got our foster care license."

"You have a foster care license?" Emily asked.

"Yes, we used to do foster care, and we still have a license," she smiled. "That's why we can let you and Gilbert stay here until you know what you're going to do long term; we've been in contact with Tori at Social Services." She offered Emily more bread, then continued, "We don't do active foster care anymore; it turned out to be too much when Alex became a full-time pastor, and our home now isn't big enough." Penelope looked at her. "How will you go look into foster care on Tuesday? Don't you have school?"

"Yes," Emily replied, "but nothing is going on. Just class parties and signing yearbooks. You know, that kind of stuff."

"Well, you don't want to miss that, do you?" she asked.

"Actually I do," Emily replied, looking at her evenly. "By then, everyone will know my parents have left, and it would just be awkward and embarrassing. It doesn't sound like any fun."

"I see," the pastor's wife replied. "How are you doing right now?"

"Well," she replied hesitantly, "I thought all I wanted was to be able to stay in Mountain Grove–and I'm glad I did. But I didn't expect this other feeling."

"What other feeling?" Penelope asked.

Emily looked up at her. "I feel abandoned."

No one said anything for a moment.

"Is there anything we can do for you, Emily?" Penelope asked, laying a soft hand on hers.

"Well, if you have more soup, I forgot to eat today."

They all laughed and steered clear of any serious talk for the rest of the meal, much to Emily's great relief.

* * * *

Emily thanked Pastor Alex and Penelope for dinner and left early for the basement to study. She sat on the bed, and as she pulled books out of her backpack, there was a light knock at the door. When she opened it, Jonathan stood there smiling.

"Jonathan!" she said, feeling a rush of happiness.

"I have something for you," he grinned, stepping aside.

Emily peered past him and gasped. Sitting just outside the door was her red chair.

Emily put her hand over her mouth, unable to say a word, as Jonathan carried the chair in and set it in a corner.

He hugged her and said, "There's one more thing." He went back outside and returned holding a glazed pot of blue pansies. "These are from my dad," he grinned, "for your *next* garden."

Tears sprang to her eyes. He set the pot of flowers near her red chair. She kept her hand over her mouth, unable to speak.

"It's okay, don't say anything," he said, looking down at her. He touched her cheek. "My dad's waiting in the truck. I'll see you tomorrow." He hugged her for a long time and left.

She went over and sat down in her red chair, rocking back and forth as the tears flowed. She caressed the pansies as they smiled up at her.

* * * *

After school Emily got on the bus and headed for Monett to see her grandmother. On the way, she phoned Miss Mattie, knowing it was a busy time of day at the bakery and she wouldn't have time to ask a lot of questions.

"Cooke's Bakery..."

"Hi, Miss Mattie!"

"Sugar, where *are* you?"

"On my way to see my grandma." She could hear lots of noise in the background.

"How's she doin'? I called the hospital an' they said she was better."

She heard Miss Mattie counting out change to someone.

"She is much better," Emily said. "Well, I know you're busy so I'll let you go. I'm studying for my finals so I'll probably have my phone off, but you can leave me a message."

"Okay, Sugar, your folks still talkin' 'bout movin'?"

"Yes, but I'll talk to you about it later. Bye!" She quickly clicked her phone off.

She started to press the *off* button on the phone, but hesitated. Without giving it another thought, she called her dad's cell number. It rang once...twice...a recording came on...

"The number you have reached has been disconnected..."

It couldn't be! She must've dialed wrong. She hurriedly redialed the number, but it was true–her dad's phone had been disconnected. *He must not have paid that bill either,* she thought dully. She could barely breathe as the pain in her heart grew. Her parents really didn't care what happened to her.

When Emily walked into her grandmother's room the next day, she couldn't have been more surprised. The breathing tube had been removed and her grandmother was sleeping peacefully. She tiptoed back out to the nurse's station.

"When did they take the breathing tube out?" she asked Nurse Malcolm.

"This morning," she smiled.

"I can't believe my grandmother looks so good, when she looked so awful yesterday."

"It's wonderful, isn't it," the nurse agreed. "When you come in tomorrow, she'll probably be out of ICU."

Emily went back to her grandmother's room and pulled out her schoolbooks, putting all her other problems aside. If her grandmother was going to be okay, she could deal with the rest.

* * * *

Her cell phone rang at about eight-thirty that evening.

"Hello!"

"Are you ready to leave yet?" asked a male voice.

"Jonathan! Where are you?"

"I'm down in the lobby studying, and there's only one more bus back to Mountain Grove tonight. It leaves at nine."

"I thought the last one left at ten," she said, alarmed. "I'll be right down."

She gave instructions for Nurse Malcolm to call her if there were any changes with her grandmother, grabbed her backpack, and flew out the door to meet Jonathan.

"You didn't have to come all this way to ride the bus with me," she panted, as they sprinted down the street toward the bus stop.

"It's dark and not safe," he said, "of course I did."

"Well, thanks," she huffed, trying to keep up with him. She really didn't like riding buses at night, and the thought of going into the church basement alone creeped her out.

They made it to the bus stop with a few minutes to spare. Two men, with caps pulled down over their eyes, walked up and waited with them, giving side glances at Emily. She moved closer to Jonathan and he put his arm around her.

"See, I told you it wasn't safe," he whispered to her.

"Where's the stupid bus," she whispered back.

Once they were on the bus, there weren't any seats together, so Jonathan had her sit on a seat in the aisle, while he stood next to her hanging onto the pole. The two strangers sat near them. Emily turned the overhead light on and studied all the way back to Mountain Grove. Jonathan put in ear plugs and listened to a Spanish lesson for finals, keeping an eye on the two men, who still had their hats pulled down over their eyes. When the bus pulled up to the stop in Mountain Grove, the two strangers stayed on the bus, much to Emily's relief. The bus stop was about half a mile from the church and they hoofed it on over. Jonathan waited outside while she checked the bathroom and under the bed. She didn't like going into an empty room.

"All clear," she smiled, sticking her head out the door. "Thanks again, Jonathan."

"No problem," he grinned, reaching through the door to hug her goodbye. "I'll let the Britton's know you're back.

Her heart fluttered as he hugged her. She didn't understand the feeling that made her want to stay wrapped in his arms forever.

"Thanks for everything," she said, as he let her go. He smiled, touched her cheek, and left.

She sat down in her red chair and quickly pulled out the cell phone, hoping for a message from her parents. There was only one message from Miss Mattie, telling her to drop by the bakery sometime. She sighed and went in and took a shower.

As she left the school grounds the next day, she could've jumped up and clicked her heels together, she was so happy that finals were over with. It seemed like she might have done well on them, too.

The relief of her finals gave her courage. *Now to Monett to see Pearl,* she thought, *and on Tuesday, to Clayton to apply for foster care.* The rest would be a piece of cake.

CHAPTER – 22

When Emily arrived at the hospital the next day, she checked at the front desk to see if her grandmother had been moved. The receptionist looked it up on the computer and told her that her grandmother was out of ICU and now in Room 303.

"Thanks," Emily said, and as she turned toward the elevator, she noticed the hospital's gift shop. Not knowing if there was anything she could afford to buy, she went in anyway and immediately spotted a glass case displaying a variety of chocolate candy. Her grandmother loved chocolate, so she dug into her backpack for money to buy some. She went up the elevator to the third floor holding a polka-dot bag of chocolates, tied with a silver ribbon. When she found Room 303, the door was closed and she knocked gently. There was no answer, so she went in and saw her grandmother propped up on two pillows, napping.

"Grandma," she whispered.

Her grandmother's eyes flew open, when she saw it was Emily, she smiled.

Emily froze.

Her grandmother only smiled with one side of her mouth. The whole left side of her face drooped, and when she tried to speak, only a garbled sound came out. She appeared confused and closed her eyes again.

"Don't go back to sleep just yet," Emily said, forcing herself to sound cheerful.

Her grandmother just shook her head sadly, and Emily realized that her grandmother hadn't been sleeping, but was just depressed over what had happened to her.

"You just need a little more time," Emily whispered, squeezing her hand. "It will probably clear up with time."

Her grandmother shook her head, and kept her eyes closed.

Emily sighed, and went out to the nurse's desk. "When will I be able to talk to Mrs. Miller's doctor?" she asked the nurse.

The nurse checked her records. "Dr. Blackstone is taking over her case, since she'll probably go into a nursing facility in Mountain Grove, where his practice is."

This was the first time Emily had thought about where her grandmother would go after the hospital. But what the nurse said made sense; she would need physical therapy. She was also glad her grandmother would have the same doctor who had cared for Miss Mattie. She liked him.

"Dr. Blackstone has already made his morning rounds," the nurse continued, scrolling through the pages, "so he'll probably stop in this evening. He usually makes evening rounds around seven-ish."

Emily decided that she wouldn't leave the hospital until the doctor came in.

* * * *

Dr. Blackstone came in at seven on the dot. "Hello, Emily," he said.

"You knew this was my grandmother?" she asked.

"Yes," he said, "Mattie told me."

Emily wondered what else she had told him.

Dr. Blackstone checked Pearl over, having her do different things to see if there was any improvement. He checked her heart. "Hmmm," he said, patting her leg.

Emily followed him out into the hall and got right to the point. "Is her paralysis going to get any better?"

Dr. Blackstone looked at her, as though he was debating on how much he should say.

"I want to know everything," she said, evenly.

He nodded. "I doubt that she will improve much," the doctor said, looking directly at her. "We're going to try physical therapy, of course. But I don't think you'll see a lot of improvement. Our biggest focus will be to help her regain her speech."

"Will she be able to walk?"

"I don't think so."

"How about eating?"

"Her swallowing reflex shut down for a while, but that's coming back."

"So how do I take care of her?" Emily asked simply.

The doctor looked puzzled. "Where are your parents?"

Apparently, Miss Mattie hadn't told him everything. "They're in Tennessee," she said.

"I see," he said, running his hand over the back of his neck. "So, you're it."

"I'm it."

"I'll get her into Creekside Villa in a few days," he said, taking a piece of paper out of his coat pocket, and jotting down some notes. "To answer your question, Emily," he said, tucking the paper back into his pocket. "The way you can take care of her is to visit her, talk to her, touch her."

"What else can I do?"

"Nothing," he replied frankly. "Right now her left side is totally paralyzed and she needs round the clock care."

"When will she be transferred?"

"Not for another week." He looked at her. "Emily, I'm going to be running more tests on your grandmother's heart and liver. I'm concerned about some of the test results we have already run."

"What's wrong?" Emily felt her heart drop.

"I don't know for sure yet, but I suspect damage from all her years of drinking," he said quietly. "Did she drink beer or hard liquor?"

"Hard liquor," she replied, realizing that Miss Mattie had filled Dr. Blackstone in on her family situation.

He sighed. "Well, I'll let you know what the tests show."

She held out her hand. "Thanks for telling me everything," she said, shaking his hand solemnly.

He smiled, shaking her hand with a firm grip. "Let me know if you need any more questions answered," he said, then turned and went into the next patient's room.

* * * *

"Well, it looks like you'll be going to Creekside Villa in Mountain Grove for physical therapy next week," Emily said to her grandmother, trying to sound upbeat. "They'll help you regain your speech first, the doctor said."

Her grandmother reached up and touched the left side of her face, her eyes questioning.

Emily had to tell her the truth. "We don't know about the paralysis yet, but physical therapy can work wonders."

The respiratory therapist came in to give her grandmother a breathing treatment. "We want to make sure your grandmother doesn't get pneumonia," the therapist explained, as Emily looked at her, questioning.

While the treatment was going on, Emily dashed down to the cafeteria. On the way, she decided to peek into the lobby to make sure Jonathan wasn't there again.

She saw him from a distance, slouched down in a chair reading. He looked up as she walked toward him. "Hey, I was just going to call you," Jonathan said.

"You're crazy!" she laughed. "How long have you been here?"

"About an hour. We'll have to leave pretty soon, it's almost eight thirty."

"I'll run back up and say good-bye to my grandmother," she said, suddenly feeling lighthearted. "She's not in ICU anymore!"

Jonathan smiled and gave her a thumbs-up.

* * * *

"Hey Miss Mattie," Emily sang out, as she hurried through the bakery door.

"Good mornin', Sugar," Miss Mattie smiled, handing a customer a box of maple donuts. She came around the counter to give Emily a hug, looking positively electrifying in a cobalt blue apron with yellow stars, smiling moons, and jagged yellow thunderbolts darting this way and that.

"I'm on my way to the hospital," Emily said, loving the smell of cinnamon, as she hugged Miss Mattie. "My grandmother's out of ICU."

"Now isn't that jus' fine, Sugar!" Miss Mattie said, with a smile as bright as a new moon.

"There's a sad part too," Emily said, feeling her spirits plummet. "She's paralyzed on her left side, and the doctor doesn't know if it'll get any better."

"Oh, I'm so sorry," Miss Mattie replied, giving her an extra squeeze. "Will they try phys'cal therapy?"

She told her about Dr. Blackstone's plans for her grandmother at Creekside Villa.

"What about your folks, Sugar? They still talkin' 'bout leavin'?" Miss Mattie asked.

"Yes," she said, avoiding eye contact. "I need to run, Miss Mattie. I have to catch the bus to see my grandmother. I just wanted to drop by for a minute."

"What are you goin' to do if they leave?" Miss Mattie asked, eyeing her suspiciously.

She gulped again, trying desperately to think of a truthful answer. She couldn't make eye contact with Miss Mattie.

"They already left, didn't they?" Miss Mattie asked.

"Yes, ma'am."

"An' where are you stayin'?"

"In the church basement."

Miss Mattie's eyes got big as dinner plates. "Now why would you stay in a *basement,* when I have a perfectly good bedroom right over our heads?"

"I'm just staying there until I can make permanent arrangements," Emily gulped.

"What kinda' perm'nant arrangements?"

Emily sighed. "I'm looking for a foster home."

Miss Mattie's mouth literally fell open. "You're lookin' for *what*?"

"A foster home..." and she poured out the whole story.

"My goodness gracious," Miss Mattie murmured, when Emily had finished. "Why didn't you come to me with all this?"

"Miss Mattie..." she began, groping for words. "You've already helped me enough, and there's nothing you can do about all this."

"You might've given me a chance."

"I don't want to trouble you with all my problems," she replied, looking at her evenly. "You have to take good care of yourself."

"Oh Sugar, I'm fine..."

"You're *almost* fine," she interrupted her, "but you're not all-the-way fine."

"Well, I already know a perm'nant place you can live," Miss Mattie said, ignoring her last remark.

Emily looked puzzled. "Where?" she asked.

"With me, of course!"

Emily swallowed hard. "Thank you so much, Miss Mattie, but no. We're talking *months, years*, not just a few days."

"Now, now Sugar..."

"No," she said, interrupting her again, "it's too much."

"But, Sugar..."

"We aren't going to talk about it, Mama," she said, picking up her backpack. "All I want is for you to take good care of yourself. I can handle all of this, but I couldn't stand it if something happened to you." She quickly hugged Miss Mattie and hurried out the bakery door before the tears started.

Emily's heart felt crushed as she hurried toward the bus stop, tears flowing down her cheeks. She couldn't think of anything she'd love more than living over the bakery with Miss Mattie. But with her heart condition, Emily wasn't about to put that burden on her and risk her health. "I can't lose you, too, Mama," she whispered, as she crossed the street to the bus stop. As the bus roared away from the curb, Emily settled into her seat and sent Jonathan a text message, telling him she would be back in town before dark and not to come for her. Then she took out a train schedule to plan her trip to Clayton on Tuesday morning.

As the bus carried her toward Monett, she put her head back on the seat and closed her eyes, feeling the dark clouds of depression gathering. She had tried to be brave, but she would absolutely love to live with Miss Mattie, instead of moving in with people she didn't even know.

* * *

On her way to the train depot Tuesday morning, she decided to stop in at the bakery and see Miss Mattie. The truth about her parents was out now, and she missed Miss Mattie more than she could bear. She didn't want to avoid her anymore.

Miss Mattie looked up at the clock as she walked into the bakery. "Aren't you goin' to be late for school, Sugar?"

"I took my finals yesterday and I'm not going to school today, I'm taking the train into Clayton," she said, as she set her backpack down and peered into the pastry case. "I'll take a jelly donut, please."

When she looked up, Miss Mattie was just staring at her. "Whatever in this world would make you miss school and go into Clayton?" she asked.

"I already told you about it," Emily said. "It's for foster care."

"But, Sugar..." she started to protest.

"Please don't say anything," Emily interrupted. "I've been avoiding you, but I need you in my life, and I need to be able to talk about this without worrying you. Please don't say anymore." She looked steadily at Miss Mattie, "I have to do this."

Miss Mattie stared back at her. "All right Sugar, I understand," she finally said. "Thanks for lettin' me know." She got a jelly-filled donut out of the pastry case and put it on a doily-lined china plate, then turned with a smile, and said, "Now let's have us a good visit, and you tell me all about your gran'mother."

Emily hugged her. "Thanks, Mama," she whispered.

* * * *

Emily got off the train in Clayton and looked at the directions she'd downloaded from the internet. She had about a two mile walk ahead of her to the county offices, she decided. At least it was a beautiful day, and she certainly wasn't in any hurry. When she got there, she climbed the steps to the county building, pulled open the massive glass door, and was met by a security guard at the entrance.

"Which way to the foster care offices?" she asked the guard. He didn't say a word, just pointed to the stairway.

The office was at the top of the stairs. She went in and was greeted by the receptionist.

"May I help you?" the woman asked, peering over pink reading glasses.

"Yes, I was wondering how to check into foster care?"

"How to *what*?" she asked, removing her glasses.

"Check into foster care," Emily repeated slowly.

"Is your home unsafe?" the woman asked, appearing to be quite alarmed.

"Well, I don't have one anymore," Emily replied, matter-of-factly.

"Let me get Mrs. Mertz for you..."

Mrs. Mertz wasn't quite sure of what to do, either; it seemed that Emily had come to the wrong office. This office was for licensing people to have a foster care home.

Mrs. Mertz took her arm, and said, "Let me show you where to find Child Protective Services. I think that's the office you need." She had quite a grip and didn't release Emily's arm until she was safely in the hands of the CPS people.

"Good luck!" Mrs. Mertz smiled, toodling her fingers as she left.

Emily was escorted into the inner sanctums of the CPS office. She found herself sitting across the desk from a pretty redhead.

The woman smiled warmly. "I'm Miss Tori," she said, and reached across the desk to shake Emily's hand.

"I'm Emily," she replied, loving the woman's smile.

"What brings you here today, Emily?"

She decided to get right to the point. "I've been abandoned and I'd like to check into foster care."

Miss Tori reached for a pen and paper. "Why do you think you've been abandoned?" she asked evenly.

"Because my parents left for Tennessee and didn't take me," she replied, liking it very much that Miss Tori stayed calm, and her eyes didn't bug out like the other adults she'd told.

"Do you know where they are?" Miss Tori asked.

"No, they said they'd send me an address when they get one," she said. "But even if they do, I don't want to move. My grandmother is sick and I'm not going to leave her, plus my parents drink and scream at each other all the time and it makes my stomach hurt."

"Do they hurt you when they're drinking?" Miss Tori asked, calmly.

"No."

"Do they threaten you?"

"No. They just swear and throw things."

"At you?"

"No."

"Do they touch you inappropriately?"

"No."

"Is there food in your house to eat?"

"There was, but there's not a house anymore."

Miss Tori scribbled down some notes. "So, what you're telling me, Emily, is that your parents have left the state, and you don't know where they are, and you need temporary foster care."

Emily nodded. "Yes, that's exactly it." She was liking Miss Tori better all the time.

"You have also said that your parents are alcoholics," she continued, "and you don't want to live with them anymore, even if they do send for you?"

"That's part of it," Emily said. "The other part is they're leaving my grandma behind. She's just had a stroke and a heart attack and I want to stay with her."

"Can she take care of you?" Miss Tori asked.

"No, I want to take care of *her*."

Miss Tori took more notes, and then asked, "Where are you staying now?"

"In Mountain Grove. At the same church basement that Gilbert did. Do you remember Gilbert?"

"Oh yes, I remember him," the social worker chuckled. "He's a free spirit and doesn't like foster care much.

"I noticed," Emily laughed along with her.

Miss Tori smiled and said, "Pastor Alex has been in contact with our agency about your temporary arrangement. I'm glad you're still there."

Emily nodded.

Miss Tori twiddled her pen and thought for a moment. She finally said, "Emily, we'll try and locate your parents, and see what they have to say. Abandonment does qualify you for foster care, although foster care usually happens when parents can't care for their kids, or it isn't safe for the kids–like Gilbert. They are being abused or neglected in some way.

"Only my nerves are abused," Emily said, with a shrug.

"I understand," Miss Tori smiled, "and right now, I bet you're feeling abandoned.

Emily nodded, not trusting herself to speak as tears welled up.

"Do you think your parents would agree to any kind of counseling for their alcoholism, or be willing to get help with their parenting skills, once we do locate them? We have a lot of programs for that kind of help."

Emily shook her head. "No, they'd never agree to that."

"Do you have a cell phone number for your parents, or do you know of any relatives they might be staying with?"

"I've already tried my dad's cell phone and it's been disconnected. He didn't have much money, and probably didn't pay the bill."

"How about friends or relatives?" Miss Tori asked.

Emily almost laughed. "My parents don't have any friends, and if there's family out there somewhere, I sure don't know about it."

"Well, let's take this one step at a time," Miss Tori said, pulling out a folder and putting Emily's information in it. "Since

Pastor Alex has a foster care license, you can stay there until we locate a more permanent foster family for you. Right now, we don't have any foster parents in Mountain Grove, but I'll do some calling and be in touch with you. I'll also be trying to locate your parents."

Emily hoped with all her heart that she didn't find them but didn't say so.

Miss Tori stood to her feet. "I'm glad you came in, Emily," she said, smiling like she really meant it. "From what I've heard, you have a lot of support in Mountain Grove. That's really good. Here's my card. I want you to call me if you think of any questions or have any other concerns."

* * * *

As Emily stepped down off the train in Mountain Grove, she was exhausted and light-headed with hunger. She hadn't risked stopping in Clayton for something to eat since her track record for missing—or nearly missing—trains was a bit unnerving. It was late afternoon, and the only thing she had eaten all day was the jelly donut. She toyed with the idea of going home to the church basement for a bowl of soup but didn't really want to be alone. Her second option was to order something inexpensive off Ike's menu. That thought made her happy and she headed for Good Eats Café.

"Hi Ike!" she called back to the kitchen, as the screen door at Good Eats slammed behind her.

"Why hello, darlin'," Ike grinned, hurrying out of his kitchen, spatula in hand. "Long time no see."

"I know, I've missed you," she grinned back, thumping down on a red stool at the counter. "My grandma got sick and I've been going to the hospital in Monett every day."

"So I hear," he said, handing her a menu. "I also heard 'bout you stayin' in th' basement over at th' church."

Word spread fast.

"I didn't want to leave my grandma when my dad got a job in Tennessee," was the only explanation she offered, before changing the subject. "I'm starving! My mouth's been watering for one of your good cheeseburgers."

"Okay, one cheeseburger comin' up," he grinned, giving his spatula a twirl. "With summer vacation comin' on, mebbe you'd be interested in workin' for me a little more often."

"Sure, just let me know which days," she said, feeling suddenly energized.

One problem solved; now all she needed was a permanent place to stay.

She looked around the café as she waited for her burger. The only other customer was a man hunkered over a cup of coffee in the back booth.

Ike came back a few minutes later and set a cheeseburger in front of her. She gulped when she saw the mound of fries that accompanied the burger. She had meant to say "no fries," since it cost more.

"Kelly Ann will be comin' for a visit soon," Ike said, wiping his already clean counter with a white dish towel. "You two stayed in touch?"

She was shaky from hunger and tried to remember if she'd eaten dinner last night. "We text," she said, between bites, "but we haven't been talking much lately."

He shook his head. "Her mama said there's been a boy comin' 'round." He glanced at her half-eaten burger. "Let me get you somethin' to wash that down."

"Water is fine..." she started to say, but Ike was already scooping ice cream into a tall soda glass.

"I got me a new brand of ice cream and I need th' o'pinion of a root beer float expert," he grinned, pulling the handle on the soda dispenser.

This was going to take a big bite out of one of her twenty-dollar bills, she thought. She needed to be more careful.

"Yummy," she said, tasting the float Ike had set down in front of her. She spooned creamy bites of ice cream into her mouth. "Ummm! Your new ice cream *does* taste better. More vanilla-y."

"New dairy salesman come 'round and pestered me 'til I give in and tried it," he said, filling her glass with more root beer. "Bought some milk and butter from him, too." He added another scoop of ice cream to her glass.

The man in the booth got up and put money in the juke box. An old Elvis Presley tune came on, and Ike hummed along, as he eyed her plate. "Seems like you got a hollow leg today," he said, nodding toward her plate.

She looked down, surprised to see her burger was gone. She laughed, pouring catsup on the fries. "I was really hungry."

"You want another burger?"

"No thanks," she said, digging into the fries.

When every fry had been eaten, she took her spoon and reached deep into her soda glass for the last bite of ice cream. In the background Elvis crooned, *Love Me Tender*.

"Well," she said, wiping her mouth with a napkin, "I need to get going and go visit my grandma."

She took a final swig from her straw and laid her twenty-dollar bill on the counter. "Thanks Ike," she smiled, sliding the money toward him. "That was really good."

He pushed it back to her. "Yer money's no good in here t'day, young lady."

" *What?* No way, Ike," she said, sliding the twenty toward him again.

"Listen, Em'ly," he said, pushing the money back across the counter, "we're fam'ly here and it's my guess you didn't eat much t'day and maybe even yesterday. Right?"

She tried to remember when her last meal was.

"I can't really remember," she replied honestly.

"Well, it's my guess you ain't put a fork to yer mouth in a coupla days," he said, peering at her intently, "and you need to give me a chance fer my "Pass It Along Club."

"What's a "Pass It Along Club?" she asked.

"Well, darlin'," he said, his brow furrowed, trying to think how to say it just right, "what it means is, there's been a few times in my life when I was a little short on cash, an' someone he'ped me out."

"Really?" she asked.

"It's th' truth," he said, raising his hand. "I been in some real fixes, an' times got tough. Kinda like the tough time yer goin' through," he said, looking at her evenly. "So, I accepted he'p from some good people along th' way, with th' idea that when times got better fer me, I'd pass it along to the next fella'."

He picked up the twenty and handed it to her. "When times get better for you, you can do the same thing and *pass it along*. Sorta keep my club goin', he said, with a wink.

She went around the counter to hug him. "Thanks, Ike," she said, "and I promise I'll pass it along someday."

"And I know ya will," he said, awkwardly patting her back. "Now you jus' run on, an' go take good care of that gran'ma of yers."

CHAPTER – 23

It was official. She had talked with Dr. Blackstone, and her grandmother would be taken by ambulance to Creekside Villa sometime Thursday afternoon, three days from now.

"You'll travel in high style by ambulance to Mountain Grove," she told her grandmother later, trying to cheer her up. "I'll be able to walk over and see you every day."

Her grandmother only nodded and looked away. Her paralysis hadn't improved, and even though they'd started her speech therapy, she was flat-out depressed, and no amount of Emily's chirpy chatter seemed to make any difference. She'd told her grandmother about her parents' leaving town, but all Pearl did was shrug. Emily sat quietly with her for another forty minutes watching TV, then realized she couldn't afford to stay a minute longer. There was only one more bus leaving for Mountain Grove. Pastor Alex had talked to her about her last two days at school and she had wound up promising him she would go. She wished she hadn't. She really wanted to spend the night here at the hospital with her grandmother.

She leaned down and kissed her good-bye. "I'll be on the first bus after school tomorrow," she whispered.

As Emily left the room, she turned for a final wave good-bye, but her grandmother had turned her face to the wall. She lingered a second trying to think of what she could do or say, but she had to go. She flew down the hall toward the elevator, wondering if the stairs would be faster. The elevator doors were open and she hurried inside. When the elevator reached the first floor she bolted out, flew through the front doors, and out into the street, surprised that it was already so dark. She had exactly twelve minutes to run to the bus stop.

Okay, this is creepy, she thought, as she hurtled down the empty streets. She hung a right at the next corner, and as she approached the bus stop, she saw two men huddled by the bench. She slowed down, then stopped. They looked like the same two creepy guys she had seen when she was with Jonathan last week; she wouldn't go a step further until she saw the bus coming.

The men noticed her and one ducked his head, whispering to the other. Alarmed, she looked around for a place to run. There were only closed businesses in the immediate area, and no one in sight.

Two blocks in the opposite direction she could see the light of a Burger King.

One man got a creepy grin on his face and nudged the other man. Emily's heart began to race, and she slowly backed up in the direction of Burger King, not taking her eyes off the two men. As they took a step toward her, terror washed over her and she turned to run.

Just as she took off, she heard the sweet sound of the bus's roar. It sailed past her and pulled up to the bus stop. The doors swung open. The two men stared at her and she froze. A passenger came out and stood on the steps of the bus, but she kept her eyes glued to the men.

What should she do, the bus was going to pull away soon?

"Emily, come on," the passenger shouted.

She looked up. *Jonathan!*

She hurtled toward him, speechless with terror. Her feet felt weighted, as though she were running in slow motion. She kept her eyes on Jonathan, who held the door open until she was safely aboard. She huddled in a seat next to the window, trembling. Her stomach hurt and she felt like she was going to throw up. She kept glancing toward the door, but the two men didn't get on.

Jonathan sat down next to her. "I thought you weren't going to ride the bus alone after dark," he said angrily.

"I know, I know," she mumbled miserably, leaning her head against the cool window. She squeezed her stomach trying to stop the pain.

"What's wrong?" he asked.

Her stomach rolled. She grabbed her backpack and fumbled with a plastic bag stashed inside.

"Are you sick?" he asked.

She nodded, as she struggled to get the plastic bag open.

Jonathan took it from her and held it open. Her stomach rolled again, and she heaved into the bag, mortified as wave after wave of nausea hit her, and she vomited all of her lunch.

Jonathan found some tissue in the backpack with one hand, while holding the vomit bag in the other. Emily hurriedly wiped her mouth and reached for the plastic bag, threw the dirty tissue in, zipped it, and put it under her seat. She wanted to crawl under the seat with the bag, she was so embarrassed–or better yet, crawl under the bus.

"Are you okay?" he asked.

"No," she whispered, and leaned her forehead against the cool window, keeping her eyes closed. She was utterly mortified.

They were halfway to Mountain Grove before she spoke again. "How did you know I was still in Monett?" she asked, still keeping her eyes closed.

"Ike told me you'd left late, and I knew you'd stay late."

She peeked out from under her lashes and stared at his profile; his jaw was white and clenched. He was still angry.

"I promise I'll leave before dark when I come home tomorrow," she said. "I only go to Monett two more times. After that my grandma goes to Creekside Villa."

"Emily, didn't you see those two creeps looking at you?" he asked, angrily. "They weren't there to catch the bus."

She shuddered.

"Wait for me after school," he said, heatedly. "I'm coming with you."

She didn't argue, and they finished the bus ride in silence.

When the bus pulled up to the curb in Mountain Grove, they got off and began walking down First Street toward the church. As the bus roared by, Emily stared after it.

"Guess what?" she said.

"What?" he replied, irritably.

"I left the throw-up bag under the seat."

As they watched the bus's taillights disappear into the night, Jonathan started laughing. Emily tried to appear indignant, but couldn't, and she also began to laugh. They walked on, laughing, as passersby turned and stared at them.

"I'm sorry I upset you," Emily said, after they had walked a couple of blocks. "I couldn't stand to leave my grandma, so I waited until the last minute to go. I would've spent the night, but I need to be in school tomorrow.

"School isn't worth your life," he said, some of the anger returning to his voice. "You should've changed your plans when you saw it was dark."

She sighed. He was always so logical. She didn't bother telling him that she had promised Pastor Alex she would finish the last two days of school. He would just say that didn't matter either.

"What are you thinking about?" he asked, as they walked along.

"If I should tell you that I promised Pastor Alex I'd finish the last two days of school," she said, looking up at him, "and that's why I left, even though it was dark."

"That doesn't matter," he replied, right on cue. "You could've called him and explained."

She looked up at him and chuckled, liking his clinched jaw, and even liking his seriousness.

"What's so funny?" he asked, looking down at her.

She looped her arm through his. "Thanks for coming for me," she said.

"You're welcome," he murmured. She noticed his jaw had softened, and she was pretty sure his eyes lit up when she took his arm.

When they reached the church basement, Jonathan waited outside while she checked under the bed and in the bathroom.

"No robbers or ghosts sharing a room with me tonight," she smiled, as she walked back outside.

He grinned reaching over to hug her good-bye.

"Don't hug me," she said, pulling away. "I'm stinky from throwing up."

"You're also crazy," he murmured, hugging her anyway.

* * * *

Only two more days of school, Emily thought, as she walked into the school cafeteria for lunch. Bitsy saw her and got up from the table she was sharing with three other cheerleaders.

"Oh Em'ly," Bitsy cooed loudly, as she walked toward her, "I heard all 'bout your awful tragedy."

"What tragedy?" she asked, wondering how much Bitsy knew.

"You know, your fam'ly 'n all. Ya'll must be worried half sick, havin' your mama and daddy run off and leave you that way."

Emily stood there speechless, as everything around them became quiet.

"They didn't just *run off*," she said, mortified, because that's exactly what they had done.

"Why don't you jus' shut yer pie hole," Emily heard someone say behind her. She turned, and there was Gilbert with his food tray, glowering at Bitsy.

Bisty's eyes grew round with alarm. "Well, if you aren't just about the nastiest person I ever met," she snarled.

"If ya wanna see nasty, go look in th' mirror," he said, his face red with anger.

Bitsy's faced flamed, and she stamped her foot. "Well, you jus' wait 'til I tell Big Daddy 'bout this," she howled. "Yer gonna be sorry you ever poked your nose where it didn't belong."

"Well now, that just 'bout terrifies me to pieces," he mocked. "You and yer daddy are both a coupla weird-o's."

Bitsy opened her mouth to say something, then closed it. Opened it, closed it. She finally made some sort of high-pitched scream and stomped back over to her friends. They gathered around her whispering and pointing at Emily, who didn't know what to do. Should she buy her lunch or leave?

"C'mon Em'ly," Gilbert said, heading toward the lunch line. "Never mind that lil' barr'cuda."

Emily was ravenous, so she followed Gilbert. Besides, cafeteria food was too cheap to pass up. Gilbert stood in line with her while she got her food. She loaded up her tray, realizing the confrontation with Bitsy certainly hadn't affected her appetite a bit. They found a table near a window on the other side of the cafeteria and sat down.

"Thanks, Gilbert," she said, biting into her grilled cheese sandwich.

"Wasn't nothin'," he shrugged. "Someone needs to knock her out."

Emily chuckled, and dug into the applesauce, which had been liberally doused with cinnamon. "Ugh," she shuddered, and turned to her vegetables.

"Ya'll gettin' enough ta eat there in the basement?" Gilbert asked, downing his own applesauce in four bites.

"I have plenty of soup," she said, tasting her chocolate pudding. "Pastor Alex told me to help myself to the pantry."

"I might bring ya some food, too," he said, glancing down at her plate. "Ya'll gonna eat that applesauce?"

She shook her head and pushed her tray toward him, wondering how he could possibly bring her food, but decided not to ask. Then, out of the blue, she found herself asking, "Gilbert, are you going to college?"

He stopped eating, spoon frozen in midair. "How in blazes (only he didn't say *blazes*) would I do that," he growled. "Ya gotta have brains and money ta go there."

"You have good brains, Gilbert. You read all the time," she said, polishing off her grilled cheese. "I think you'd do great in college."

"Well thanks for reassurin' me on th' brains aspect, now there's that lil' problem of money. I ain't got none."

"Getting money isn't that hard," she replied, opening up a small juice bottle. "They'll either loan you the money, or give it to you, if your grades are good enough—you know, a scholarship. And you can always work while you're in college."

"Well, my grades was in th' toilet last year."

"Yes, but you've brought them up this year," she said. "They only look at your high school grades when you apply for college, so just keep up the good work." She smiled at him. "You can do it, I know you can."

"Are you goin' ta college?" he asked.

"Sure, why wouldn't I?"

"Same reason I wouldn't."

"Well, if you won't let your situation stop you, then neither will I."

"I'll think about it," he said, "but I sure ain't gotta clear picture how I'd do all that."

"You'll have to work on your English, too."

"What's wrong with m' English?" he asked.

"Well, for one thing, try not to say *ain't*. It's definitely not a college word."

"Okay, I sure don't *got* a clear picture of how I'd do all that."

This is going to be a tough row to hoe, she thought, quoting Gus. But she knew Gilbert was smart, and he had already broken her reading record at the library.

* * * *

After school, she hurried down the street toward the bakery. It seemed a hundred years since Miss Mattie had called the ambulance for her grandmother, but it had actually only been about ten days ago. In a little over a week and a half, her life had turned upside down and sideways. The day was beautiful, not too hot, just a lovely mountain day with a warm breeze blowing through the pines. She walked through the bakery door with a smile so big, it lifted her ears. She expected to see a big smile coming back at her, but only Clara stood behind the counter.

"Afternoon, Em'ly," she said.

"Hi, Clara, where's Miss Mattie?"

"Oh, she went off. Had some bus'ness to take care of."

"Oh," Emily said, more than a little disappointed. Miss Mattie was always in the bakery after school. A thought occurred to her. "She's not sick, is she?"

"I dunno," Clara said, shrugging her shoulders. "She didn't tell me nothin' 'bout where she was goin'."

"Was she all dressed up?"

"Yessum'. She pretty much dressed to the nines, and lookin' real sharp."

Puzzled, she bought an apple fritter and headed back out the door. She didn't want to stay and eat it if Miss Mattie wasn't there to keep her company. Before going back to the church basement, she checked the sanctuary to see if Miss Mattie had gone to one of the ladies' prayer meetings she sometimes attended, but there were no ladies gathered today. She checked the Sunday school rooms. All empty. It had to be a doctor's appointment she decided, as fear found a place in the back of her mind.

In her room later, she glanced at the half-eaten apple fritter sitting on the bedside table and decided she should have something more substantial to eat. She went into the church pantry, which was the size of a small room, and rummaged through some of the cans. There was a can of cream of celery soup, and one of potato with ham, which she mixed together in a saucepan and set on the hotplate. She sat cross legged on the bed eating the soup out of a plastic bowl. It had been two days since she'd seen Miss Tori about foster care, and she hadn't yet heard a word from her. She set her bowl down and checked her phone for messages, but there hadn't been any calls.

She dialed her dad's cell phone number on a whim, thinking maybe it was reconnected. All she got for her trouble was the same recording she had heard the last time. *What kind of people just drive off and leave their daughter?* she wondered. It was like something out of a Grade B movie. No, make that a Grade Z movie.

* * * *

She was up early Thursday morning, so exhilarated to be free for the whole summer that she nearly danced with joy. Three months relief from Miss Graham; three months relief from whispers behind her back; three months relief from probing questions. Hallelujah! She was free!

She plumped the pillows up on her bed and snuggled in for a good read, the pleasantness of the room making her want to stay in all day. When her stomach began to rumble, she hopped into the shower and got ready to go to the bakery. Her mouth was watering for one of Miss Mattie's good maple bars and she wanted to tell her all about her trip to Clayton. An hour later she stood flabbergasted, once again staring at Clara behind the register. *Had Miss Mattie deserted her?* She ached with disappointment.

"She gone again," Clara said, dipping into what appeared to be a snuff pouch.

"When will she be back?"

"She didn't tell me nothin'," Clara replied, sticking a pinch of tobacco into her cheek. "I jus' know I'll be here 'til closin'."

She tucked the small pouch back into her apron pocket as a customer walked in. Miss Mattie had asked her not to use snuff when she was behind the counter–but Miss Mattie wasn't here.

Emily went back to the church basement, with the maple bar in a bag, unable to dismiss the fear that loomed in her mind. She tried reading again but couldn't concentrate. She decided that she couldn't stand being in this room another second and jammed her feet into her shoes and turned off the lights. As she hurried out the door, she nearly tripped over a brown paper bag filled to the brim with groceries. Astonished, she picked up the bag and saw, *from Gilbert,* scrawled on the side. She carried the grocery bag into her room and rummaged through its contents. There were cans of tuna fish, bread, cheese, ham, mayonnaise and mustard. When she saw the lettuce and tomato, her mouth began to water.

She went into the pantry where she had seen a tiny refrigerator and dragged it out into the bedroom area. *Now if it just works,* she thought, as she plugged it in. A little light came on and she heard the hum of its motor. "Yes!" she said, dancing a little jig. She made two sandwiches and quickly ate one, then went back into the pantry and found a plastic bag. She wrapped up the second sandwich for later. As she put it in her backpack, she remembered the plastic bag of vomit on the bus ride the other night and felt embarrassed all over again. "Don't think about it," she said out loud, praying that the sight of her throwing up into a baggie would be forever erased from Jonathan's mind.

As she cut across the park and headed toward Creekside Villa, she saw Gilbert studying under a tree.

"Thanks for the food, Gilbert," she said, walking up to him.

"Yer welcome," he grinned. "I forgot to tell ya', I been workin' over at the Village Grocer. Pastor Alex he'ped me get a part-time job over there."

"Nice!" she said, smiling.

"I get a discount on m' groceries, too."

"Double nice," she said. "Well, I'm on my way to visit my grandma, I just wanted to thank you. I really appreciate it."

"Aw, wasn't nuthin'," he said ducking his head and returning to his book.

She reached down and hugged him.

* * * *

Emily went up to the nurse's desk at Creekside Villa and asked if her grandmother had arrived. The nurse checked her records. "She'll be here around two o'clock," she smiled. "We have her room all ready—number 208."

"That's next door to Mrs. Tupper," Emily said, and took off down the hall.

"I'll be in Mrs. Tupper's room if you'll let me know when my grandma gets here," she called over her shoulder. She couldn't wait to tell Mrs. Tupper who her new neighbor was going to be.

When she walked into the room Mrs. Tupper's face lit up and she held out her hand. "Why Emily, how very good to see you," she said, barely able to speak above a whisper.

Emily took her hand. "I haven't been able to come and see you for a while because my grandmother had a stroke," she explained, liking the warm, papery feel of Mrs. Tupper's skin.

"I'm so sorry to hear that," she whispered.

"She's coming here for therapy today," Emily said, "and guess what?"

"I can't guess," she warbled.

"She's going to be right next door to you!"

"Well, is that so?" Mrs. Tupper whispered, looking pleased. "I'm sure we'll be great friends."

Friends? Emily hadn't thought of that. Would her grandma even be friendly with people?

"She may be a little shy at first," was all Emily could think of to say. "The stroke took away her speech, but they think it will come back with therapy. I think she's depressed too," she added.

"The poor dear, I'm so sorry," Mrs. Tupper warbled. "Tell her I'll be praying for her."

Emily didn't know how praying would go over with her grandmother, either. She realized that she had only seen her grandmother interact with a television set–never with people, or God. They visited for a while, then she heard wheels swishing down the hallway and a nurse popped her head into the room and said, "Emily, your grandmother is here!"

She hugged Mrs. Tupper and hurried next door to her grandmother's room.

As she walked in, the nurse held her finger to her lips. "Your grandmother is exhausted from the trip," she whispered, "sit with her, but let her rest and not talk just yet."

Emily nodded and quietly sat down. Pearl's eyes were closed, so she took a book out of her backpack. The nurse must not have looked at her grandmother's records yet, she thought, or she would know that her grandmother couldn't talk, even if she was rested.

* * * *

Emily awoke early Friday wondering how to spend the morning. Her grandmother had physical therapy until eleven, then needed to rest, so she couldn't see her until the afternoon. She decided she would go to the bakery and see Miss Mattie. It was odd, but she missed Miss Mattie more than she did her parents.

Her thoughts were interrupted by her cell phone ringing and she grabbed it up.

"Hello!" she said, thinking it was her dad.

"Emily, it's Miss Tori."

Miss Tori! She had almost put foster care out of her mind.

"Emily, I wanted to touch bases with you. We don't have a foster family that's available in Mountain Grove just yet, so we'd like to place you temporarily with a family in Monett, or we have a family in Clayton. You could meet them both and be involved in deciding which one you'd like to live with. What do you think about that?"

She didn't have to think about it. "No," she said, emphatically. "My grandmother is here and this is where I want to live."

There was a short pause on the other end of the line, and then Miss Tori said, "I will contact Pastor Alex and see if you can stay a few more days, but Emily, we'll have to place you soon."

"Have you contacted my parents?" she asked, holding her breath.

"No. Are you sure they didn't give you *any* clue as to what town in Tennessee they were moving to?"

"No, they didn't tell me," she said. *And even if they did, I wouldn't go live with them,* she thought.

"I'll get back to you soon," Miss Tori said, "but consider Monett and Clayton, just temporarily."

She didn't respond. She knew she would never move away from Mountain Grove, even temporarily. This was her family. If they tried to make her live in another town she *would* go live at the river. Well maybe not the river, but she would figure something out. The phone call chased away whatever peace she had felt and left her feeling wary. She couldn't wait to go see Miss Mattie. But then again, Miss Mattie always knew when she was worried, and she would not be able to tell her why. Borderline depressed, she knew she should just stay away from the bakery, but she needed to talk to someone. She pulled out her long-neglected journal.

Dear Journal,

I'm living in a church basement now. A few days ago, I had a home, but now I don't. One by one, the villagers are finding out that my parents left me. I didn't want to go to Tennessee with them—but it's so embarrassing the way they just left me. They didn't check to make sure I had a place to stay, or enough money. They just got into the pick-up and left in the middle of the night—and they haven't called once to see how I'm doing.

Maybe the embarrassment should be theirs and not mine. Pastor Alex and Penelope said I am brave—so did Ike and Mr. C. I think they're proud of me.

Another thing I keep remembering is what Pastor Alex told me is in the Bible: Even if your mother and father forsake you, I will lift you up (that's God talking). It means God's got my back.

Miss Tori freaked me out when she talked about a foster home away from Mountain Grove. I'm in over my head on this one. I'm thinking about giving the God thing a try. E.

* * * *

On her way to the care home, she decided that she would at least walk by and make sure Miss Mattie was in the bakery, and not off somewhere. She crossed the street and sauntered by, quickly peeking through the bakery's glass door. Sure enough, there was Miss Mattie waiting on a customer. She sighed and kept going. She liked it when life was simple and hoped it would be that way once she found a foster home. As she sauntered down the hall of the care home, she heard laughter coming out of her grandmother's room. When she walked in, there sat Mrs. Tupper in her wheelchair laughing with her grandma. She couldn't have been more shocked if they had been doing handstands together.

They both looked up at her with laughter in their eyes.

"Hope I'm not interrupting anything," she smiled.

"Not at all, come right on in," whispered Mrs. Tupper in her shaky voice. "I had the nurse wheel me down so I could get acquainted with your grandmother. She's a delight!"

A delight? Emily went over and hugged her grandma, noticing that she was wearing a pretty pink bed jacket, and her hair was nicely brushed.

"You look so pretty," Emily told her, "where'd you get the snazzy little robe?"

"Oh, I gave it to her," beamed Mrs. Tupper. "I had an extra one, and thought she'd like it. She does look pretty in pink, doesn't she?"

"Yes, she does!" Emily said, then hugged Mrs. Tupper. "Thank you," she whispered.

She wanted to let them continue their gab session, and looked for an excuse to leave. "Does anyone want some juice or a soft drink?"

Her grandmother nodded her head and held up one finger to show she wanted the first thing offered. Mrs. Tupper said she would have a Sprite. Emily took off, hoping they would go back to talking, although the conversation had to be pretty one-sided. She stayed away about twenty minutes, strolling down to the refrigerator in the hall and talking to a few of the residents.

"I was a War Bride, you know," Mrs. Tupper was telling her grandmother when she returned. "My Oliver served in Germany."

Emily handed her the Sprite.

Mrs. Tupper thanked her, and Emily watched in amazement as she downed about two-thirds of it. "My, I was thirsty," she whispered.

She helped her grandmother, putting the drink into her right hand.

Mrs. Tupper reached over and patted her grandmother's leg. "After a few therapy sessions, Pearl will be able to tell me all about her life."

They both saw the shadow cross her grandmother's face, and her smile slowly disappear.

Uh oh, she shouldn't have said that, Emily thought.

Mrs. Tupper caught the expression and said, "Well, I must be getting back to my own room now—and Pearl, if you don't want to talk about your life, its fine with me. We can just be "right now" friends."

Her grandmother nodded her head and blinked a thank you.

CHAPTER – 24

Saturday morning began beautifully, promising to be a warm day. After breakfast, Emily walked across the street to visit Gus at the gas station. She had become curious as to how fast the news was spreading about her parents' leaving her, and what was being said about it. She had been avoiding people because she was embarrassed by her predicament, but a subtle shift had happened, and now she was only curious. *A great way to feel,* she decided, as she walked briskly across the gas island.

"Anybody in here have an Orange Crush?" she called out, as she walked into Gus' office. Gus was leaning back in his wooden desk chair, napping with a ball cap over his face. His feet were propped up on a stack of oil cans, and his dog slept at his feet.

Gus awoke with a start and squinted at her through sleep laden eyes. "Well, looky who's here, YipYap," he said, with a grin, "it's Miss Em'ly!"

"Morning, Gus," she said cheerfully.

He and his dog got slowly to their feet. "Ow!" said Gus, twisting his shoulders this way and that. "Gotta derned crick in my shoulder." He rubbed the tender area, then spun his right arm around in circles like a propeller.

Emily heard a pop.

"There we go, good as new," he exclaimed, with a smile that showed an even row of choppers.

He gave her a quick hug. "How's Miss Em'ly t'day?

"It is well with my soul," she said, laughing as she hugged him back.

"It's wha'?" he asked, peering down at her.

"Nothing," she laughed. "It was a song I heard the church choir practicing last night."

"Oh, that's right. I heard you was camped out over in th' church basement now. How's it goin'?"

"It's going good. I'm lined up for foster care," she said, deciding to tell it all.

"Well, I'll be danged," Gus said, rubbing his chin. "Hmmmm." It appeared that even Gus could be at a loss for words, and she hoped those weren't tears in his eyes.

"You have any Orange Crush?" she asked, changing the subject.

"Ya know I do, little lady. How 'bout some Ritz crackers thrown in."

"Yum," she said, heading for the box that held the cracker supply. Crackers with peanut butter, Orange Crush, and a sprinkling of village gossip were all that was needed to get the conversation to a happier level.

"So tell me all 'bout this foster care yer goin' into," Gus said, returning to the subject, as they sat munching.

She told him everything Miss Tori had said, sparing no details—even the part about temporary foster care being available in Monett and Clayton.

"Well, I guess that's not too far away," he said.

"I'm *never* going to live any place but here," she said, giving YipYap's chin a thorough scratching. "You're all my family, and I'm *not* leaving."

This time, she was sure she saw tears in his eyes, and was relieved that a customer pulled up. Gus went out to wait on them. She found YipYap's wire brush and gave him a head-to-toe brushing. He nuzzled her and she would have sworn he gave her a big smile.

* * * *

"Emily dear," Mrs. Apple said, when the door swung open, "we were wondering when you'd come by to see us."

"Come on in, Emily," Mr. Apple yelled from the living room.

She walked in and hugged them both hard. "How was Florida?"

They both started talking at once, each giving every detail of their trip, from a weather report to how firm the mattress was on their bed, and then a timer went off in the kitchen.

"Stay for lunch, Emily," Mrs. Apple said, hurrying to her stove. "I've just made a pot of chicken noodle soup, and you can tell us where you've moved to, and everything you've been doing."

Emily realized they had heard nothing about her parents' leaving her. "Well, hold onto your hats," she said, as she walked into the kitchen, "have I ever got a story to tell you!"

* * * *

Mr. and Mrs. Apple sat there with their soup spoons frozen in mid-air, and a look of utter disbelief on their faces.

"Your parents just *left* you?" Mrs. Apple kept repeating.

"Well, I told them I didn't want to go," Emily said.

"And they just *left* you?"

"For heaven's sake, Helena—YES, they just left her," Mr. Apple blustered. "Now quit hammering the girl, and let's help her figure out what to do."

"Well, I already have a plan," she said, reaching for a homemade yeast roll, and slathering it with butter.

They sat with their spoons still poised in mid-air waiting.

"I've signed up for foster care," she said biting into her roll. It was delicious and she was starving.

"You *what*?" they both said in unison.

She wished she could eat and explain it all later—but it didn't look like that was going to happen. They still hadn't touched their soup.

"Eat your soup before it gets cold, and I'll tell you everything," she said, taking a couple of quick bites from her own bowl. It was *so* good!

"...and she said that right now they only have a foster care family available in Monett and one in Clayton," she told them, managing to get in a few more spoonfuls of soup. "So, I told her no, that I just want to live in Mountain Grove. She's supposed to call me back in a couple of days."

Their soup spoons were frozen in mid-air again. Finally, Mr. Apple said, "You are a *most* extraordinary young woman, Emily!"

"Oh, well thanks!" she replied, popping another bite of roll into her mouth.

"Emily, you can stay with us..." Mrs. Apple started to say.

Emily shook her head, interrupting her. "If it was just for a few days, I would. But this is *years* we're talking about. I'm only fifteen."

"Well..." Mrs. Apple began, glancing at her husband.

"No," Emily said adamantly, "this will all work out fine. You two travel a lot, and I want you to be able to keep doing that. I'll come and see you when you're home—I just won't be next door." She smiled. "But thanks for your offer."

"Please let us help," said Mrs. Apple, "there must be *something* we can do for you."

"Well," she said, "is there enough soup for me to have seconds?"

* * * *

When she hugged Mr. Apple good-bye, it seemed like he didn't want to let her go.

"Emily, promise you'll come by often, and tell us right away when you know where you'll be living," Mrs. Apple said, openly weeping.

"Don't cry," Emily said, hugging her tight. "I promise."

Mr. Apple tapped her on the shoulder, and when she turned around, he stuffed some twenty-dollar bills into her hand.

"You don't have to do that," she said, blinking back tears of her own,

"We want to do *something,* Emily," he said, squeezing her hand, "please don't refuse us."

Later, she sat on her bed with the twenties spread out in front of her. *A hundred and twenty dollars!* She couldn't believe Mr. Apple had given her so much. She felt like tossing the bills in the air and letting them rain back down on her, like she had seen in the movies.

* * * *

Her cell phone was ringing when she emerged from the shower the next morning.

"We've found a foster care family for you in Mountain Grove, Emily," Miss Tori's voice rang out, sounding very pleased.

Emily felt like the wind had been knocked out of her, and she couldn't breathe for a moment.

"Emily, are you there?"

"I'm here," she replied slowly. She had never really come to grips with the fact that she would actually be required to move into a complete stranger's house, where she wouldn't know a soul.

"I know it's a lot to grasp, but we want you to meet the family first," Miss Tori was saying. "Would Wednesday work for you?"

"Where would we meet?"

"Well, it seems a little silly for you and the foster family to come all the way to my office in Clayton," Miss Tori replied, pausing as she thought, "so let me see what public buildings are available to meet at in Mountain Grove. After the initial visit, if you're comfortable with the family, we'll set up a second visit where you can stay at their house. Perhaps spend a night or two with them."

"Okay," she said, feeling her stomach roll.

Miss Tori said she would call back later in the day, with a place and time to meet on Wednesday.

Emily sat staring at the floor with the phone in her hand. *This is too scary*, she thought. *What if I don't like them? Or they don't like me?* She felt like she was suffocating.

She decided to head for the river, got dressed, and threw some things into her backpack. She started to cross through the park but stopped in her tracks when she realized that what she really wanted was someone to talk to. The second realization that hit her was that *someone* was Jonathan. She turned and hurried toward Bloomin' Happy Nursery, hoping with all her heart that he was working today. As she flew down the sidewalk, she spotted Jonathan loading shrubs into a customer's pick-up, and relief flooded over her.

His face lit up when he saw her. "Hey!" he said, as she walked up to him.

"Hey, yourself," she smiled back. "I was on my way to the river, do you want to come?"

"I can't," he said. "My dad's gone, and I'm the only one here."

"Miss Tori found a foster care family for me in Mountain Grove," she blurted out.

"No kidding!" he said. "Are you excited?"

She was as surprised as Jonathan when she burst into tears. They were standing in the middle of the parking lot, and she knew all the customers at Good Eats could see her out the café's side window. She turned her back to the street and faced Jonathan. "Do you have any tissues inside the nursery?" she asked, as she wiped away tears with the back of her hand. She could feel her nose starting to run.

"We'll find something," he said, putting an arm around her and shielding her from view, as they walked across the parking lot and through the nursery gate.

He led her to a chair tucked behind lattice work on the patio. "Did you change your mind about foster care?" he asked, handing her a sheet from a paper towel roll.

"I don't know," she sniffed. "I feel like I'm suffocating all of a sudden." She hid her face behind the paper towel, trying to control her sobs.

He pulled up a chair beside her and put his arm around her as she wept; she leaned her head against his chest.

"Are you worried if you'll like the family?" he asked.

She nodded, keeping the paper towel over her face.

"Are you worried if they'll like you?"

She nodded again.

"Don't hide your face," he chuckled, "I've already seen you with marshmallow eyes, remember?"

She hiccupped behind the paper towel but didn't take it down.

He tried again. "Are you afraid you'll be trapped?"

She nodded.

"Do you want things to just stay the way they are?"

Once more, her head bobbed up and down.

"Well, that's the way I feel about *any* new situation."

"You do?" she asked, peeking over the paper towel.

"Sure, everyone does. But in most situations, you just have to get through it, then you can go back home. But if you go into foster care, you *will* be home."

"That's what's really bothering me," she said, her voice sounding like a clogged drainpipe. "I don't want to be stuck. Do you think Pastor Alex would let me back in the basement if I hate the foster care home?"

"Sure he would, but I bet you'll like it," he smiled, brushing a strand of hair out of her face. "Why don't you just take it a step at a time? When you meet the family, you'll know if you're going to be comfortable around them. If you're not, tell the social worker. No one's going to make you go somewhere you don't want to be."

"Are you sure?" she asked.

"Are you somewhere you don't want to be right now?" he asked.

"No."

"Well then, don't feel powerless—because you're not."

She felt like she could breathe again. "Thanks," she said, smiling at him.

"You're welcome," he replied, smiling back. "Just take it a step at a time."

She spent the morning at Bloomin' Happy helping Jonathan tidy the grounds and stock shelves. A lot of customers came in and they didn't get a chance to talk much again, but throughout the morning Jonathan would look over and smile at her, making her feel like everything was going to be fine. About one o'clock her cell phone rang. Jonathan was showing gardenias to a customer, but she saw him glance over at her.

She answered, and it was Miss Tori. "Emily, how does two o'clock on Wednesday afternoon sound for the first meeting?"

"Okay," she replied. "Where?"

"At the library. I talked to a Mrs. Green and she said we could use her office."

"Okay," Emily said again, feeling like she couldn't breathe.

"You sound worried, Emily," Miss Tori said. "Don't be. You're really going to like this family."

"I hope so," she whispered.

Miss Tori laughed. "See you Wednesday!"

Jonathan walked over after the customer paid for her flowers. "Well?"

"I got my execution date and place."

"Emily..." he said, laughing.

She laughed too. "Okay, okay, I'll take it a step at a time."

* * * *

As much as she tried, Emily couldn't get *Wednesday at two o'clock* out of her mind. *Who was this foster family? Did they have other children? Would she have her own room?* At one point, she went so far as to pick up her cell phone and call Miss Tori. She wanted to ply her with every question that was clamoring around in her mind. But Miss Tori wasn't in, and she didn't leave a message.

She spent half of Tuesday writing down all the questions she had for the family during their first meeting, and the other half figuring out what to wear. She dropped in on Pastor Alex and Penelope to let them know what was going on. She didn't want them to think she was trying to live in the church basement forever—even though she wished she were.

* * * *

She awoke at five Wednesday morning and couldn't go back to sleep. It was still dark, so she snapped on the light and plumped her pillows up to read. She looked at the clock and started the countdown: *nine hours until she went to the library to meet the foster family.* Around seven, she awoke again with her reading book resting on her chest. She threw the covers back and went to the window to see what kind of day it was. *Beautiful, with a slight breeze,* she observed, looking out on the park.

Seven hours to go.

She took a shower, then made a breakfast of granola and bananas. She pulled out the money Mr. Apple had given her and took out a twenty-dollar bill. Her *just in case* money. Just in case of *what,* she wasn't sure, but she didn't want anything at this meeting to take her by surprise.

Six hours to go.

She paced for twenty minutes and tried to think of what she could do for the next few hours, but nothing came to mind. She was too nervous to make small talk with people. She left the basement, walked around to the front of the church and mounted the steps, going quietly in through the double doors. She entered the sanctuary and sat down on the pew in the front row and felt like she could breathe again. She closed her eyes and just rested in the peace and quiet. After forty-five minutes, she got up to leave, glancing at the large clock on the back wall of the church.

Two hours to go.

At one o'clock, she took another shower and began to dress. She started to put on a skirt and blouse, but in the end, just wore capris and a pullover. She brushed her hair and decided to wear it long, and the sides pulled back with a brown comb.

At 1:55, she left the basement and walked across the park toward the library. She didn't remember going up the steps, only watching in slow motion as her hand reached out and grabbed the handle of the double doors. She pulled it open.

* * * *

She held her breath as she walked into the library, looking left and right for Mrs. Green, who wasn't in sight. She was surprised to see Gus and Ike grinning at her by the check-out desk.

What in the world were they doing in the library? she thought. She waved and they both gave her a thumb's up.

Mr. Charles was standing near the fiction section; he also gave her a thumb's up.

What's going on? she wondered.

Miss Rose and Miss Violet were over by the card catalog with Mitzi, who was outfitted in a party dress. They smiled and waved hankies at her.

Was this a dream? she wondered, as she walked toward the office. Then she saw Jonathan leaning against a reading table.

"What's going on?" she whispered, as he came over and offered his arm.

"Need an escort?" he smiled.

She held onto his arm, more puzzled than ever, as she saw other villagers scattered throughout the library. There was Pastor Alex and Penelope, Iris Head, and Mr. Montoya all giving her the thumbs up. Montana stood to the side with his camera and blinded her with the camera flash as she walked by. Stars danced in front of her eyes, as he gave her a thumbs up, also.

What was going on? Everyone grinned at her like she had won the lottery.

When they reached the office, Jonathan knocked, and Miss Tori opened the door.

"Hello, Emily," she smiled, "ready to meet your new family?"

She didn't trust herself to speak, and just nodded.

Miss Tori threw open the door and Emily walked in. The only person she saw was Miss Mattie sitting near the desk.

Emily was confused. "Didn't the foster family show up?" she asked, turning to Miss Tori.

"Yes," the social worker grinned, her hand sweeping in Miss Mattie's direction.

Emily didn't understand for a second. "*Miss Mattie?*" she whispered. "Miss Mattie isn't a foster parent."

"I am now, Sugar," she smiled, holding a piece of paper out toward her.

Emily went over and read it, then looked up at Miss Mattie.

"What does it say, Sugar?"

"It says that the State of Virginia has licensed you to be a foster parent."

"Mmm hmmm," Miss Mattie grinned. "*Now* will you come live with me?"

Emily was flabbergasted. "You did all this for me?"

Miss Mattie stood up. "I b'lieve I heard you say a few times that I was your mama, didn't I?"

She nodded.

Miss Mattie tilted her head. "Well, don't you think a daughter oughta be livin' with her mama?"

Emily flew into her arms. "I don't want you to get sick," she said. "Dr. Blackstone said your heart..." She couldn't finish the sentence.

"Oh now, Sugar, I'm not gonna get sick," Miss Mattie crooned, holding her tight. "There's nothin' in this world that I want more than to have you livin' with me."

Emily heard a thundering round of applause, and turning around, she saw villagers laughing and clapping for her.

"You all *knew*?" she asked incredulously.

"We all heard about two hours ago," Mr. Charles said, trying to control the grin that had spread across his face.

Miss Rose couldn't resist, and burst out singing, "For She's a Jolly Good Fellow." The villagers joined her and sang three rousing choruses, with no one having a clue about how to sing the feminine version.

* * * *

Emily looked around her new bedroom, scarcely believing what had just taken place. Before she left the library, Miss Tori had asked, "Do you still need to think about it, Emily, or do you approve of your new family?"

"I approve," was all she could manage to croak, before her throat constricted. She threw her arms around Miss Tori and hugged her.

She had gone back to the church basement at four o'clock, packed her things, and put the room in order. At five o'clock Mr. Charles and Jonathan had come and loaded everything up in Mr. C's Dodge Ram and carted it over to the bakery.

"I can't believe it," she murmured, as she looked around. Miss Mattie had redecorated the bedroom, changing it from a guest room, into her room. "A *daughter's* room," Emily whispered.

There was a new oak dresser with a round mirror, and a matching chest of drawers next to a beautiful armoire. The floor was covered with a brightly colored modern rug; a nightstand stood right by her bed, with an old-fashioned lamp of pink and green for her to read by. Mr. C had even set her red chair and bowl of pansies near the window. It was all so homey and so perfect. It took her breath away.

She sat on her double bed, kind of bouncing to get the feel of it, and thought about the mental stress she had put herself through these last few days. She flopped back on the bed and stared up at the ceiling with unbridled relief. Her relief was *double,* because not only had she been worried about foster care, but also about Miss Mattie. All those days Miss Mattie had been gone from the bakery had been spent—not in secret visits to the doctor—but in Clayton doing paperwork, to become her foster mother. She stood up and walked to the large window overlooking First Street. Looking across the street, there was Gilbert reading under a tree in the park. She wanted to knock on the window and yell, "Look where I'm living!" But knew she would attract the attention of everyone walking down First Street, and Gilbert wouldn't hear her anyway.

Later that night, as she lay in her darkened room thinking of all the smiling faces that had surrounded her today, and all that Miss Mattie had done to make this possible, she was overwhelmed with feelings of incredible gratitude.

"Thank you," she whispered into the darkness, before falling into a deep sleep.

* * * *

Early the next morning, she heard her cell phone ringing and struggled to wake up. She answered in a voice heavy with sleep. "Hello..."

"Em'ly?" a male voice barked.

"*Dad?*" she whispered, her heart rate going through the roof.

"I only gotta minute," he said, "but we're in Tennessee now and we rented us a little one bedroom."

A one bedroom? she thought but didn't say anything.

"We'll send for you later," he continued, "after everything gets settled and Pearl gets better an' all that."

"Okay," she replied weakly.

"I gotta new phone number too."

"I saw it on my phone," she said, barely speaking above a whisper. "I'll write it down."

"Okay, if you call, do it after seven, so I don't use up my minutes."

"I'll remember that," she said, wanting nothing more than to hang up before he told her where they were living. She had promised Miss Tori she'd let her know if she found out.

He said goodbye and the line went dead.

"A *one* bedroom?" she said out loud. He had no intention of sending for her, and she felt stung to the core.

"A one bedroom," she repeated, and threw back her covers. She heard Miss Mattie rattling pots in the kitchen and padded out to see her.

Miss Mattie took one look at her and said, "What's wrong, Sugar?"

"My dad just called me."

"And?"

"They only rented a one bedroom."

Miss Mattie's face lit up. "Hallelujah! You're safe."

"Safe?"

"They won't send for you," she said, beaming.

"I'm *safe*," she said softly, as the realization washed over her.

"Thank You, Lord," Miss Mattie hooted. "They only rented a one bedroom,"

Emily laughed, and they both began dancing a little jig.

"This is our freedom dance," Miss Mattie sang, waving her hands, as they danced all around the living room hooting and cheering.

"I'm free," Emily laughed, waving her arms.

In the bakery, Clara scowled up at the ceiling, wondering what all the thumping was about.

CHAPTER - 25

"I heard from Dad this morning," Emily told her grandma, later that day when she went to visit her.

Her grandmother's eyes appeared interested, so she continued, "They found a house." She didn't know if she should tell her grandmother that it was only a one bedroom.

Her grandmother's eyes clouded, and Emily suddenly realized that her grandma didn't want to go live with her parents either.

"It's okay," she said, reaching for her grandmother's hand. "I like it here better, too, and I can tell that Dad won't force us to go there."

Her grandmother's eyes looked relieved.

"They only rented a one-bedroom," Emily whispered, smiling at her grandmother.

Relief spread over Pearl's face.

"Guess where I'm living?" Emily grinned, changing the subject. "Right downtown over the bakery!"

Her grandmother's eyes lit up.

"I'll bring you a donut from now on when I come to visit."

Her grandmother actually smiled—with half her mouth anyway.

Later, while Pearl napped, Emily went next door to see Mrs. Tupper and invited her to visit her grandma later.

"I heard you have a new home over the bakery!" Mrs. Tupper warbled.

"I sure do," Emily smiled, thinking that the news about her living arrangement had traveled at supersonic speed this time.

"The night nurse told me," Mrs. Tupper added proudly.

Emily laughed, happy that this time it was good news that had sped through the little village.

****

Emily bounced into Good Eats early Saturday morning ready to work.

"Good mornin,' neighbor!" Ike smiled. "How d' you like livin' next door?"

"I love it!" she laughed. "I'm living in a fairy tale."

"Well now, that's 'bout the best news I heard in a long time," he grinned, showing new teeth that resembled Gus' choppers. "How do ya like m' new dental work?" he said, baring his teeth for her.

"Looks like you and Gus go to the same dentist," Emily said, peering intently at his mouth.

"Yep, two peas in a pod," he laughed, handing her an apron.

"Have you heard from Kelly Ann?" she asked, putting the apron bib over her head.

"I sure have," Ike said. "She'll be here next week."

Part of Emily was excited, and part of her didn't know how to feel. Kelly Ann rarely called or texted anymore. "Did you tell her I live downtown now?" she asked.

"Yes, ma'am, I surely did," he grinned, "an' she was happy as peach pie for ya."

At two o'clock, when the last of the lunch crowd left, Ike said, "I think I can handle it now Em'ly, if you want some time to visit yer gran'ma."

"Thanks, I do want to," she said, untying her apron and throwing it in the bin.

"Millie's goin' to see her gran'baby on Wednesday if you want to help with the lunch crowd then."

"I'll be here!"

"I'm real happy for ya,' Em'ly," he said, grinning at her. "You and Mattie will be real good for each other."

"I hope so," she replied evenly. "I don't know how I can ever repay what she's done."

"Jus' remember our talk, darlin'," he said. "What you do is "pass it along" to the next person when the time comes. You'll get yer chance. You jus' remember what old Ike said."

"I'll remember," she said. "I'll write it in my journal and never forget."

He gave her a thumbs up. "That's the ticket," he said, heading back to his kitchen.

* * * *

When Emily walked into Creekside Villa to see her grandmother, the nurse at the front desk called her over. "Emily, Dr. Blackstone was looking for you a few minutes ago."

Her heart fluttered. "Is something wrong?" she asked, afraid of the answer.

"He wants to go over your grandmother's test results."

She hurried to her grandmother's room. As she rounded the corner, she nearly collided with Dr. Blackstone.

"The nurse said you were looking for me," she said, her heart thumping.

"I need to talk to your parents," the doctor replied firmly.

"My parents are still in Tennessee, but you can talk to me."

Dr. Blackstone wasn't put off that easily. "I need to talk to them about your grandmother's prognosis and treatment. Would you have them call me at this number," he said, handing her his card.

"I'll take it, but they won't call you," she said, staring down at the card. She looked up at him. "Could I talk to you for a minute in private?"

"Sure," he said, looking puzzled. He led her to a door that read, "Medical Staff Only".

It was a break room and two nurses sat talking in a far corner. Dr. Blackstone led her to the other side of the room, where they sat down at a small chrome table. Emily tried to think of how to tell him about her parents without making them seem like monsters. The doctor sat looking at her, waiting. She realized there wasn't any easy way to tell it, so she just blurted out the whole story. Dr. Blackstone didn't react or interrupt, he just sat quietly and listened.

"So now I'm living with Miss Mattie over the bakery," she concluded. "I just got a phone number for my parents, but please don't ask for it. I don't think they'll care what you want to say to them, but I do. So, would you just tell me?"

She watched his face soften.

"So, you're in foster care now?"

She nodded.

"You like it there?"

"I love Miss Mattie."

He didn't say anything, just stared out the window for a second.

"What are you going to do when you're eighteen and won't be in foster care anymore?" he asked.

She thought that was an odd thing to talk about, but said, "Go to college. Miss Mattie says I have to keep my grades up, so I do."

"Good," he said, looking at her evenly. "I was in foster care when I was your age."

"*You* were in foster care?" She couldn't have been more surprised if he had told her he'd done backflips over the moon.

He nodded. "I felt like a toss-away item when I first went into the foster care system. Do you ever feel that way?"

"Well," she said, mulling it over, "when I think, *how could my parents just leave me,* I feel tossed away. So, I try and focus on how the villagers treat me. I see their teeth smiling at me and that makes me feel better."

Dr. Blackstone burst out laughing. "Well, I never had a village full of people smiling at me, so I had a lot of stuff to work through. It sounds like you're a little ahead of the game."

It was the first time Emily had seen the doctor laugh, he usually seemed so grumpy. "I listen to the TV doctor, too, and that helps," she told him.

"Good, I listen to him too," he said, leaning back in his chair. "Are you close to your grandmother?"

"When I was younger I wasn't. I was just scared of her, and wouldn't go near her until she passed out," Emily said, matter of factly. "Then a few months ago, Mrs. Green told me I should try hugging my family and it might work. It only worked on my grandma, and we started talking. She told me we looked alike, and I let her wear my Sunday hat that Miss Mattie bought me. I have pictures of us laughing together." Her voice caught and she had to gulp back tears. She was terrified of what Dr. Blackstone was going to tell her. "Please just tell me about her test results," she said, her voice quivering.

He looked at her. "The years of your grandmother's drinking have taken their toll," he began slowly. "The test results show she has extensive liver damage, and there was damage done to her heart when she had the heart attack."

"And her stroke?" she asked, just wanting to hear it all, and get it over with.

"Her paralysis is permanent," he began, "a little of her speech has returned and that's what we'll focus on." He looked at Emily a moment, then said, "She probably doesn't have very long to live."

Emily felt like the wind had been knocked out of her. "Does she know?" she finally managed to ask.

He nodded. "People have a right to know if their life is ending, so they can make the necessary arrangements, mend relationships, whatever they would need the time for."

"What did she say when you told her?" she asked, her voice trembling.

"She's concerned about you," he said, running his fingers through his dark hair. "I'd advise you to give her all the details of where you're living and let her know you're happy. Let her write out everything she needs to talk to you about. Visit her often and laugh with her." He looked at her evenly. "Emily, you can't protect her from death, so don't try. Just be with her."

She nodded, unable to keep back the tears.

Dr. Blackstone handed her some napkins from the dispenser and said, "Let me see that card I gave you."

She pulled it out of her pocket and slid it across the table.

He scrawled a phone number on the back. "Here's my cell phone number, so you can reach me anytime," he said, handing the card back to her. "Let me know if I can help you with anything." He checked his watch. "I have an appointment with another patient's family, so I need to go," he stood up, hesitated, and then said, "My life eventually went very well, Emily, and I believe yours will too." He patted her shoulder and walked out.

She sat for another twenty minutes bringing her emotions under control, fanning her eyes so they wouldn't be red when she saw her grandmother. When she walked into her grandmother's room, two nurses were rolling her bed toward the back wall.

"What's going on?" Emily asked.

"She's going to have a roommate," the nurse said. "We've had a sudden influx of people, and when that happens, we double residents up."

Emily kissed her grandmother's forehead and smiled at her. "How're you doing, Grandma?"

Her grandmother shrugged.

"I brought a white board, so you can write down whatever you want to say," Emily told her, pulling it out of her backpack. "I thought that would be easier than the pen and paper we've been using." She started to put it on the bedside table, but her grandmother signaled she wanted to write. Emily held the board while her grandmother squiggled across it with a felt tip pen.

When she was through Emily looked down at what she had written:

I have money in bank. Want you to have it.

With all of her being, Emily wanted to throw the white board across the room and yell that she didn't care about the stupid money, but her grandmother's eyes looked desperate, and she remembered what Dr. Blackstone had told her.

"Okay," she said. "Which bank?" She felt like her heart would break.

Her grandmother wrote down the name of the bank and added, *for your college.* Emily nodded, and bit her lower lip. She started to take the white board away, but her grandmother shook her head and wrote, *give me paper & pen.*

Emily got them out of her backpack, propped the pad of paper up and handed her the ball point pen.

With a shaky hand Pearl wrote the date and one sentence: *I want my money to go to my granddaughter, Emily Parks.* Pearl tapped on the bed rail with the pen to get the nurse's attention and waved for her to come over.

The nurse peered down at the paper. "You want me to witness the signing, right?" she asked.

Pearl nodded and signed the paper, then tapped on the pad for the nurse to sign, also.

"Grandma..." Emily started to say, feeling like her heart would break.

But the nurse calmly wrote, *Witnessed by* and signed her name. Her grandmother ripped the page off the pad, and handed it to Emily, with a pleading look in her eyes.

"I'll take good care of the paper, I promise," Emily said.

Her grandmother nodded and lay back on her pillow, exhausted.

The nurse took her hand. "Mrs. Miller, I'm going to have your wishes typed up, and a notary come in later this week."

Her grandmother nodded.

"What do you mean?" Emily asked, just wanting to get the ordeal over with.

"The paper you have will relieve your grandmother's mind for now," the nurse explained, "but having it notarized will make it easier for you to get the money out of the bank—later."

"I'm not worried about it," Emily said.

"Yes, but your grandmother *is,*" the nurse replied, looking at her evenly.

After the nurse left, Emily tried to make things more cheerful. "Have you seen Mrs. Tupper today?" she asked.

Her grandmother shook her head, and wrote on the white board, *not for 2 days. she is too weak.*

Emily suddenly had an idea. "I'll be right back," she said.

She hurried out to the nurse's desk. "Have you assigned a roommate to my grandma yet?"

* * * *

Forty-five minutes later Mrs. Tupper was wheeled into the room with Pearl. "Here's your new roommate, Grandma," Emily said, watching her eyes light up.

"I've missed you, Pearl," Mrs. Tupper warbled, waving a veined hand. "Would you roll my TV set in too, Emily? I have the cutest movie I want Pearl to see."

Emily rolled the set in and went down to the cafeteria to pop some popcorn. She hurried back with their snack and drinks and pulled up a chair between the two beds. They spent the next hour and a half laughing their heads off over Mrs. Tupper's movie. *This is the best I can do for you, Grandma,* she thought, as she looked over and watched her grandmother laughing.

After the movie, Dr. Blackstone poked his head into the room. "There you are, Mrs. Tupper, I didn't realize they'd moved you to this room.

"Oh yes," Mrs. Tupper warbled. "I moved in with Pearl; we're great friends."

He came in and nodded to each of them, then said, "Excuse us for a minute." He pulled the privacy curtain around Mrs. Tupper while he examined her.

When he was through, he pushed the curtain back and said good-bye.

"I just love him," Mrs. Tupper whispered. "Poor thing lost his wife about a year ago. He went from bouncing down the halls, to a mere shadow of the man he used to be."

So that's why he looks grumpy, Emily thought, *he's just sad.*

* * * *

Dear Journal,

It's been a month now since my life changed. I need to write down the date everything became different–July 20th–that's when I came to live with Miss Mattie.

My life is normal now. I smell dinner cooking at night and Mama fixes me breakfast in the morning. If I'm not up yet, she leaves it in the oven warmer before she goes downstairs to the bakery. She lets me come and go pretty much as I please, and calls me on my cell phone to see how I'm doing.

It's peaceful now. I don't wake up in the middle of the night listening to people fighting, I haven't seen an empty booze bottle in a month, and there are no locked doors shutting me out. Home is a nice word now, and not one that gives me a stomachache. E.

* * * *

"Sorry I'm late, Grandma," Emily said, sailing into her room the next day, with a vase overflowing with daffodils, roses, and daisies.

Mrs. Tupper smiled from her bed, and Emily stopped to let her take a whiff of the flowers.

"Lovely," Mrs. Tupper whispered, burying her face in the bouquet.

"They're from Bloomin' Happy Nursery," she said, placing the flowers where both her grandmother and Mrs. Tupper could see them. "Mr. Charles sent them."

Her grandmother nodded, looking like she didn't feel very well. Emily noticed that her nose was kind of bluish.

"Having a bad day?" she asked, taking her hand.

"Write," her grandmother mouthed, wiggling her fingers to show that she wanted a pen.

Emily opened a small drawer and brought out the white board. It seemed to take a lot of effort to write today, and when her grandmother was through, she pushed the white board toward Emily.

Have you heard from yr daddy & mama?

"Dad called me once," she replied.

Are you going to live with them?

She looked at her grandmother's face wondering where this was going. "No. I want to live here and they only rented a one bedroom, so they probably aren't really expecting us to come."

Did you tell them about me?

"I haven't told them a lot," she replied evenly. "Would you like me to tell them?"

Alarm filled her grandmother's eyes; she shook her head and mouthed, "No."

Need to tell you something, she scribbled.

"Okay," she said, but her grandmother was pointing toward Mrs. Tupper.

"You don't want her to know?" Emily whispered.

Her grandmother shook her head and Emily peered around the privacy curtain; Mrs. Tupper was napping.

"She's asleep," Emily said, "go ahead and tell me." She pushed the white board toward her and Pearl quickly printed a few words and pushed it back.

Emily glanced down and read it, then read it again. Her heart began to hammer; she couldn't believe what it said.

You have a sister.

"I have a sister?" she gasped, barely able to get the words out.

Her grandmother nodded.

"*How?*" she stammered. "*Where?*"

She was born 4 yrs before you. Yr mama couldn't keep her so my cousin in Georgia took her.

"I have a sister in Georgia?" she asked, in utter disbelief. "Are you in contact with her?"

Pearl shook her head and wrote: *We were but yr daddy found out & had a fit. He watched the mail from then on & we didn't have phone to call on.*

"Is he my sister's father, too?"

Her grandmother shook her head and mouthed, *No.* She wrote: *They sent picture & yr daddy saw it. Said he never wanted you to know. He wouldn't let yr mama or me talk about it.*

She remembered the picture she had found. "Was it a picture of her in a blue party dress?" she asked, and her grandmother nodded.

All this time she'd thought the picture of the red-haired baby was her. She had even put it in her family album. Puzzle pieces fluttered into place and she knew why her mother had been so upset when she showed her the picture. It also explained why her dad had their mail sent to a post office box. He'd even taken the mailbox down from the outside wall to make sure the postman couldn't deliver mail to the house.

"How many years since you've heard from your cousin?" Emily asked, feeling like she couldn't breathe quite right.

Her grandmother thought a minute, then wrote: *about 8 yrs. Your sister's name is Eva.*

"Eva," Emily said softly. *I have a sister named Eva.* She felt like a wrecking ball had swung out of nowhere and bashed her in the head.

She tried to calculate. "If she's four years older than me," she murmured, "she must be eighteen or nineteen by now." She looked at Pearl. "What town did they lived in?"

Moved a lot. Last town was Lewiston, Ga.

This was unreal.

Her grandmother's eyes were getting droopy like she was about to fall asleep. Emily pushed the white board back toward her. "Grandma, *please*, write down every scrap of information that you can remember about your cousin and Eva. Full names, birthdates, everything—even if it doesn't sound important." She had seen TV shows about people searching for family members and knew the tiniest bit of information could be important. Her grandmother looked up at her and shrugged like there wasn't any more to tell. They heard Mrs. Tupper stirring from her nap.

"Are you still here, Emily?" she warbled, from the other side of the curtain.

Emily went over to her bed. "Do you need something?"

"Yes, please. Some water with ice. I hate to ring the nurse for it."

She didn't know what to do; her grandmother might fall asleep.

"I'll be right back," she said, grabbing Mrs. Tupper's small pitcher and hurrying out the door.

She flew to the ice machine in the small kitchen and filled the pitcher, and then glanced around to see if they had set out any snacks. If Mrs. Tupper was eating, she wouldn't distract her grandmother. She found some pretzels and sailed back down the hall to their room.

When she walked in, Mrs. Tupper was gabbing away. Someone had pulled the curtain back all the way. Emily set the water and pretzels down, trying to think of how to close the curtain again. She handed Mrs. Tupper a glass of ice water and hurried over to see if her grandmother had written anything.

Cousin's name, Joyce Miller, was scrawled across the board.

"Do you know her birthday, Grandma?" she whispered.

She shook her head and yawned.

"How old is she?"

She pointed to herself.

"Your age?"

She nodded.

Emily realized she didn't even know how old her grandmother was. "How old are *you*?"

81, her grandmother wrote in a shaky hand.

"When is your birthday?"

March 2.

How sad was this—year after year had gone by, and nobody had paid attention to that day. She realized that she didn't even know her parents' birthdays.

"Is there anything else you can remember?" she asked.

But Pearl had lost interest, exhausted, she turned away from her.

Emily alternated between wanting to shake Pearl, or just go home—and never come back. She didn't do either one but sat staring at her grandmother's back.

Why hadn't it occurred to Emily that she didn't know her parents' birthdays? Was she selfish, too? Was it inherited? Her grandmother rolled over and Emily noticed her blue fingernails again. She looked away. The doctor had told her it was from lack of oxygen, but she didn't want to think about it anymore. She glanced at the clock, desperately wanting to run out the door. Emily looked down at the white board Pearl had set aside, and knew instinctively that Pearl was all through, and couldn't—or maybe wouldn't—give her any more information about her sister.

My mother left two daughters behind. The thought came out of nowhere, making her stomach wrench. It was almost impossible to believe!

Pearl's eyes were closed, and Emily watched as her blue veined eyelids twitched every now and then. *Would you be here with me if I was the one in the hospital?* Emily asked her silently. But she thought she knew the answer.

"I'll leave and let you have your nap, Grandma," she said, after a few minutes had passed. "I need to get back home and help with dinner."

Her grandmother nodded her head slightly but didn't open her eyes.

"Bye, Mrs. Tupper," she said, on the way out.

"Goodbye, dear, see you tomorrow."

Maybe, Emily thought.

When she got outside, she began to run. She ran all the way to the bakery and flew up the stairs to Miss Mattie.

"Sugar, what's *wrong*?" Miss Mattie asked, as she burst through the living room door.

"I have a sister," she blurted out.

"You have a *sister*?" Miss Mattie asked, in disbelief. "Where?"

"In Georgia. Pearl told me but I can't get much information out of her." She went to the sofa and sank down. "What if I'm like them, Miss Mattie?"

"What if you're like *who*?" she asked, her voice filled with concern.

"How could I live with them all my life, and not be like them," Emily whispered. "I'm trying to be different, but what if I didn't make it?"

Miss Mattie sat down next to her and drew her close. "Sugar, you made it jus' fine," she crooned. "You're th' sweetest girl this side of th' Mississippi."

"But I'm not sweet!" Emily cried. "When I was sitting with Pearl today, I wanted to run away and not see her dying anymore, and I'm so angry that she might not try and remember any more about my sister." She bit her lip, blinking away tears. "I'm not going back."

"Oh Sugar, you'll go back," Miss Mattie said, holding her close, and resting her chin on her head, "and that's th' absolute proof you're different than your fam'ly. You run wherever you're needed without a thought for yourself, and there's not a selfish bone in you."

"Yes, there is."

"Well, I suppose we all act a tiny bit selfish sometimes," Miss Mattie murmured. "But you aren't a selfish person...I know that! She smiled at her. "Here's a little secret I learned. People who worry 'bout bein' selfish, usually aren't."

Emily wondered if it were true.

Miss Mattie held her at arm's length. "Now tell me this news about havin' a sister."

* * * *

Emily spent all Saturday morning on the computer at the library typing in *Eva Miller,* which she believed to be her sister's name. But it seemed like there were hundreds of people with that name living in Georgia.

Mrs. Green came over to her and said, "It looks like something serious is going on!"

"What do you mean?" Emily asked, feeling bleary eyed after staring so long at the computer screen.

"You've been glaring at that computer, and biting your lip for hours," Mrs. Green said.

Emily sighed and rubbed her eyes. "I found out from my grandmother that I have a sister," she replied, wearily.

For once, Mrs. Green was at a loss for words. "Oh my," she kept repeating, as Emily told her everything Pearl had said.

"Well, how does it all make you feel?" Mrs. Green finally asked. "I can't even imagine finding out that kind of news. Are you excited?"

Emily thought about it. "No," she replied evenly, "I'm angry and frustrated. My family is selfish and self-centered. I feel like I never want to see any of them again."

"Wow," Mrs. Green said. "Pretty strong stuff, huh?"

She nodded.

Mrs. Green pulled up a chair next to Emily's. "Do you know what I'd do right now if I were you?" she asked, peering at her over her reading glasses.

"What?" Emily sighed.

"Check out a nice adventure book and go home and rest. Quit thinking about it for a while. It'll start sorting itself out."

Emily looked at her doubtfully. "You really think so?" she asked, leaning back in her chair, exhausted from the whole mess.

"I really do. And if you'll write down what information you have, I'll put Mr. Green to work finding more information about your sister. He's a whiz at this computer stuff."

Emily decided to take Mrs. Green's advice, and like an obedient child wrote out all the information she had about her sister and handed it to the librarian. Then she found a book, checked it out, and went home. She lay in her quiet room over the bakery and read the rest of the afternoon, refusing to think any more about her family.

CHAPTER – 26

Emily sat holding her grandmother's hand, thinking that she slept a lot these days. When she was awake, Emily asked her questions about her life, her mother's life, and what she knew of her sister's life. Puzzle pieces floated into place. Not all of them, but she had a little better picture.

Pearl went from being reluctant to share anything, to filling up her white board with everything that came to her mind. When it first happened, Emily could barely keep up with all the information flowing from her grandmother's felt tip pen. She soon gave up trying and pulled out her cell phone and took pictures of whatever Pearl had written on the white board. The next time she came to visit, she brought a yellow-lined tablet for her grandmother to write on so that she would have a permanent record.

Emily had the nurse take pictures of her and her grandmother together and put them in frames all over Pearl's room. She blew up the picture of her grandmother in the blue church hat, and Pearl laughed when she saw it.

"See how pretty you are, Grandma," she told her again.

Now, when she sat anywhere near her, her grandmother would reach out a hand for Emily to hold. So here she sat, holding Pearl's hand while she napped, thinking how strange that things change so quickly.

Her grandmother's skin looked a little bluer today, her fingernails too. "I love you, Grandma," she said out loud. Pearl's eyes fluttered open and she smiled.

"Love you, too," she mouthed and closed her eyes again.

* * * *

Emily sat with Miss Mattie on the church pew holding her hand. There were no tears as Pastor Alex said the eulogy for her grandmother, and spoke of her last weeks with Emily, and the relationship they had developed. Emily wasn't really listening. She was trying desperately to remember all the things that were going right in her life. She found that gratitude calmed her heart when it wanted to go careening over a cliff. She tried her best to listen to Pastor Alex as he talked about what Jesus had to say about death, but his voice faded to the background as she started ticking off on her fingers the things she was grateful for:

Thumb to little finger, she had made her grandma laugh out loud in her church hat.

Thumb to ring finger, she was living with Miss Mattie over the bakery.

Thumb to middle finger, Ike had offered her a summer job.

Thumb to index finger, thumb to index finger. She couldn't think of anything else. Sadness swept back over her and she decided to remember later.

"In my Father's house are many mansions," Pastor Alex was saying, as he quoted Jesus, "if it were not so, I would have told you..."

She had called her dad at work the morning Pearl died. He sounded awkward and tried saying a couple of meaningless things. She couldn't remember what they were anymore.

"Are you doin' all right?" he finally asked, and she wanted nothing more than to just hang up the phone. It was weird how after so short a time, her dad seemed like a distant person she had once known.

"I'm okay," she told him, and he said something about telling her mom, then they'd hung up. There was no talk of her coming to live with them.

She thought about what Pastor Alex had just said about God building mansions in Heaven for the people He loves. What did her own father offer? Nothing. *No room at the inn.* She felt Miss Mattie tapping her leg and realized she had chuckled out loud over her miserable joke. Pastor Alex was leading everyone in the Lord's Prayer. *Thy kingdom come, Thy will be done,* she mouthed the words. The church was filled with her new family; every pew was full. She looked over at Gus, who had closed his service station for an hour to come for the services. Across the aisle she saw Ike and wondered how he'd managed to leave the café and come here. She added these two people to her grateful list and even decided to be grateful to her dad for choosing this place to bring her to. Maybe someday she would be able to let go of the rest.

She looked down at her red dress. She knew you were supposed to wear something dark to a funeral, but she didn't want to. Pearl liked bright colors, and Miss Mattie said it would be fine. Her heart swelled with gratitude when she thought of Miss Mattie. She leaned her head on Miss Mattie's shoulder, and her new mama patted her leg. Someone from the choir began singing *How Great Thou Art* and the people stood to their feet. After the service they were supposed to go into the fellowship hall for lunch. She would be so glad when this was over; all she wanted was to go to her home over the bakery.

Everyone was filing out now, patting and hugging her. Emily thanked them all for coming. Miss Mattie whispered, "Remember to invite them to the fellowship hall for lunch."

Emily said all the right words with one part of her brain, but the other part kept thinking random thoughts. The Charles family sat across the table from her in the fellowship hall. She never did remember what she had on her plate that day; she just kept trying to stay focused, making polite replies every now and then. Twice Miss Mattie nudged her because her mind had drifted off. Jonathan was asking her something, but she didn't know what he was saying. She looked at him across the table, he was a blur. She used the corner of her napkin to dab at her eyes. There seemed to be continuous tears, like a stream flowing over a small precipice. Even when she woke at night her cheeks were wet.

She watched as Jonathan picked up his plate and walked around the table to sit next to her. He leaned over and whispered, "I'm going fishing later today. Want to come?"

"Yes," she whispered back. *Yes, yes, yes, she wanted to come. Why didn't they run out the door right this minute, in fact.*

He went back to eating.

She leaned over, her head brushing his shoulder. "What time?" she whispered.

He answered, but her thoughts had already sailed away, and when she picked up her fork she realized she hadn't a clue what he'd told her.

"I'm sorry," she whispered, "I forgot to listen. What time did you say?" To her amazement she didn't listen the second time, either.

She looked at him not knowing what to do.

When he saw the look on her face, he put down his fork. "Listen to me, Emily," he said, taking her hand.

"I can't concentrate," she said, her tears flowing unchecked over the precipice. She could feel the whole table watching them.

"It's okay," he said, his thumb stroking the top of her hand. "I'm going to come by the bakery at two o'clock."

She nodded and looked away.

"Don't look away, or you'll forget again," he said, squeezing her hand. "Look at me."

She turned and watched his lips. He repeated, "I'll be by at two."

She nodded and looked over at the Charles family, wondering what they must be thinking, but they were getting to their feet and clearing the table. Emily looked down at her plate; she hadn't eaten much, but she didn't care, she just wanted to run away to the river.

People came up to her and murmured one thing or another. She couldn't focus and forgot what they said as soon as they said it. Miss Mattie was leading her by the arm now and at last they were going home. She glanced back over her shoulder as they left and saw that the church congregation had stayed behind to clean everything up; she didn't even know some of these people, but they'd pitched right in to help.

Pay attention to what these people are doing, a voice inside her said. She pulled her mind out of its fog and hurried over to them. "Thank you," she said, walking up to each one and hugging them.

Miss Mattie smiled from the doorway and waited for her.

* * * *

She sat on the big rock as Jonathan waded out into the river. She would fish later. For now, she just wanted to watch the water and listen to its roar. Jonathan kept glancing over at her. She knew he was concerned about her, but his worry weighed her down. She laid back on the rock, feeling its warmth under her plaid shirt and jeans; she clasped her hands under her head, and stared up at the sky. Maybe Jonathan would think she was taking a nap if she just lay still. She closed her eyes.

She felt a shadow over her and drops of water hit her arm.

"Wake up, sleepy head," Jonathan said, standing over her. She shaded her eyes and looked up. The sun was low in the sky and Jonathan had taken off his waders and put his fishing pole somewhere.

"Want to fish?" he asked.

"No, I just want to sit here," she said, rubbing her eyes as she sat up.

"You okay?"

"Not really—but I will be."

He nodded, and she was glad he didn't insist that she be okay right now.

"My parents' are bar-b-cuing tonight," he said. "They wanted me to invite you over."

Part of her wanted to go, and part of her didn't.

"Okay," she finally said.

"I need to get back and help them; you ready to leave yet?"

She nodded and held out her hand so he could pull her up. He helped her up, but he didn't let go of her hand.

"I'm sorry you have to go through all of this," he said, looking into her eyes. "If I could take it off of your shoulders, and put it on my own, I would." He pulled her close to him.

She rested her head on his chest. "I know," she whispered, and wondered, once again, at the flutter of her heart.

He let her go and slid down the rock, then reached to help her down. They both hopped from rock to rock until they were back on shore. He picked up his waders and she reached down and picked up his fishing pole, carrying it for him. He put his free arm around her as they walked back to town. Her heart fluttered again and she realized she loved the safety of his arms.

* * * *

Emily was working the register at the bakery as a steady stream of customers filed in Saturday morning. Miss Mattie was making an extra batch of donuts since they had run out of them at 10:00 that morning.

Jonathan walked in, looked at the line of customers then went over and stood near her as she bagged up donuts and other pastries for the customers.

"Wow," he grinned. "I've never seen it this busy."

"I don't know what's going on," she shrugged, grinning back at him.

"I'll come back this afternoon," he said, heading for the door. "I have something I want to show you."

"What?"

"I'll be back later," he grinned, not telling her.

She was busy for the next two hours but kept trying to guess what Jonathan might want to show her. She loved surprises.

Her phone buzzed in her pocket and she pulled it out. A text message from Jonathan read:

nursery 2 busy 2 leave. come ovr when yr thru wrking. "Rats!" she thought. She wanted to know now.

At 3:00 p.m. she all but ran out the bakery door and headed straight for Bloomin' Happy. She walked through the gate and looked around for Jonathan.

"He's in the market getting something to eat," Mr. C said behind her.

She turned and smiled at him. "Busy day?"

"Yes, it is," he said. "Jonathan said you were having the same customer load at the bakery."

"It was crazy–and I still don't know why so many people came in."

"Maybe it has something to do with the end of summer," he shrugged. "Did Jonathan tell you the news?"

"What news?" she asked, just as Jonathan came out of the Village Grocer with a pint of orange juice and a deli sandwich.

"I didn't get the chance to tell her," Jonathan said, "she was too busy at the bakery."

"Well, I'll let you two talk," Mr. C said. "I'm going to make a quick delivery to some folks on White Pine Road. Looks like business has slowed down enough for me to leave."

"Okay, so what's the news?" she asked, as Mr. C headed out the gate.

"Not going to let me eat first, huh?" he smiled.

"No way. I'm too nosey," she laughed.

Jonathan set his food down on a small table and pulled papers from his back pocket. "Remember, I told you that I applied last year to go to school abroad?" he said, handing her a brochure with a picture of England.

All Emily saw were the words, *Student Foreign Exchange Program* and her heart sank. She looked over the brochure. "So, have they accepted you for next year?" she said, forcing her voice to sound cheerful.

"No, not next year–this year," he said, studying her face. "In September."

"Oh, *this* year," was all she could manage to say, as her heart crumbled.

"I'll only be gone from September to December," he hurried on to say, "then I'll be back for a month at Christmas. Then back to

England from February to the end of May." The excitement was gone from his voice.

"You took me by surprise," she said, with a forced laugh, praying she wouldn't cry.

"I applied before any of this happened to you," he said apologetically. "It seemed exciting at the time."

"It is exciting, Jonathan. You get to go on an adventure."

"I don't want to leave you," he said, pulling her close to him.

Then don't! she wanted to say, feeling safe, and warm, and wonderful in his arms.

She pulled back from him. "It's only for a while and it'll be a great experience," she said, with a forced smile. She was determined to choose all the right words.

"But I don't want to leave you," he repeated. "Especially not now."

"I'll be okay—and you can send me a post card of Big Ben and the Queen," she said, forcing her voice to sound lighthearted.

"I could reapply for next year," he said, brushing a strand of hair back from her face, "after your life calms down a little bit."

"No, you should go this year," she said, meaning it, "you might not get another chance." Her heart had shifted, and she really wanted what was best for him.

A customer walked through the gate. Jonathan looked from her to the customer and back again. "Don't' leave, I'll be right back," he said. "You can have half my sandwich if you're hungry."

She sat down in the canvas chair and looked at his ham and cheese sandwich and dill pickle. She hadn't realized how hungry she was. When he returned she was just finishing up the half he'd offered.

"Well, I see my news didn't spoil your appetite!" he laughed, handing her the other half of the sandwich. "I'll go get another one."

She started to refuse, but she *was* hungry. "Needs more mayonnaise," she said, taking a bite of the pickle.

"I'll bring you some," he grinned, as he swung open the door to the store.

"So, you really don't mind that I'm going, huh?" Jonathan said when he returned, handing her a packet of mayonnaise.

She ripped open the packet with her teeth and gave the other half of the sandwich a thorough dousing. "Well, I'll really miss you. But I'll also be happy for you that you get to go."

"Which way will you feel the most?" he teased.

"I'm not telling," she smiled, biting off a huge mouthful of sandwich.

She chewed for a minute. "Do you know anything about the family you'll be living with?" she asked, hoping they didn't have any daughters.

"Not a lot," he said, "they're older and don't have any kids." He smiled at her. "Were you wondering if they had any daughters?"

She wadded up her sandwich wrapper and threw it at him.

* * * *

On Saturday, Emily was browsing the fiction section of the library trying to decide if she wanted to tackle a book of over eight hundred pages. The sheer weight of the book in her hand was daunting. As she tried to make up her mind, her cell phone signaled a text message.

She pressed a button on her phone and was surprised to see the message was from Kelly Ann. It read: *where r u?*

@ library, where r u? she texted back.

Her phone sounded a few minutes later, and the incoming text read: *turn around.*

Emily spun around, and there stood Kelly Ann grinning at her.

"Kelly Ann!" she cried, surprised at the joy she felt at seeing her. They hugged, dancing around in a circle, laughing and talking at the same time.

"Shhhhh," a stern looking man hissed from his easy chair in the corner, while others in the library glanced up from their reading material.

"Let me check this book out and we'll go somewhere else and talk," Emily whispered.

Mrs. Green had her head down doing paperwork when they approached the check-out desk. Emily cleared her throat with an exaggerated, *Ahem.*

Mrs. Green looked up. "Kelly Ann!" she yelped, with a grin that made the tops of her ears rise. She hurried around the desk and gave her a warm hug. "What a surprise to see you," she grinned. "How long are you here for," she asked, holding her at arm's length.

"Just a few days," Kelly Ann replied.

"Well, welcome back!" the librarian said, giving her an extra squeeze before going back to the line of people checking out books. "We'll talk more later," she smiled, handing Emily her book. "It's so good to see you."

When they exited the library, Emily laughed and said, "Your accent is as thick as soup again."

"Vegetable or chowder?"

"Oh, chowder, all the way," Emily said, and they both laughed.

"Come on, let's go ta Grandpa's," Kelly Ann said, turning in the direction of Good Eats Café. "He's springin' for lunch t'day."

As they walked the tree-lined street, Kelly Ann asked question after question, wanting to be brought up-to-date on the villagers. Emily recited all the news she could think of, wondering if she should be including herself in the update, since she and her family were probably the number one news item in the village. She decided to let Kelly Ann bring the subject up.

"I saw Carlotta at Gus's station twice last week," Emily said, as they neared the café. "I bet those two get married someday."

"Naw, not Uncle Gus," Kelly Ann cackled, as they pulled open the screen door of the café.

"Not Uncle Gus *what*?" Gus asked, from his stool at the counter.

"We're havin' girl talk, Uncle Gus," Kelly Ann laughed, hurrying over to hug him.

"Girl talk 'bout me?" he asked, hugging her back.

"Em'ly thinks you're gonna marry Carlotta," she grinned.

"Oh law, forgit I asked," Gus said, throwing a ten-dollar bill on the counter. "I'm gettin' back ta' my station before you two give me indigestion."

"Let me in on the secret," Millie said, as she picked up his plate and the money.

"The secret is, these two girls are snoops and I'm leavin'," he said, jamming his ball cap on his head. "And if yer nice and don't ask questions, you can keep th' change."

"Deal!" Millie said, stuffing the change into her pocket.

He glanced at the girls. "You two kin stop by later for an Orange Crush if ya leave yer snoopy questions at the door."

"Party pooper," Kelly Ann said, reaching over and giving him another hug. "It's good to see you, Uncle Gus."

"You, too," he said, patting her back. "Glad yer' back in our neck of th' woods." He waved as he left, the screen door slapping closed behind him.

"What can I git you girls?" Millie asked.

"We want cheeseburgers all the way, with fries and root beer floats," Kelly Ann said, "and give the bill to Gran'pa."

"Story of m' life," Ike smiled, as he came out of his kitchen. "Sure good to see you two girls sittin' together at my counter again."

"It feels great to be sittin' here with you and Em'ly, Grandpa," Kelly Ann replied, as Emily nodded her head in agreement.

Emily decided later that it must not have felt that great for Kelly Ann to be with her, because after they finished their burgers, they said goodbye with promises to get together that evening. But Emily didn't see Kelly Ann again. She found out later that Kelly Ann had spent the rest of her visit with old friends at the picnic grounds.

* * * *

"I'm leaving the third week in August," Jonathan said to Emily, as they sat together in the park. He had seen her reading under a Sycamore tree and come over to talk.

"That's not very long from now," she replied, her heart dropping.

He fiddled with a small twig lying on the grass. "What're you going to be doing while I'm gone?" he asked.

"Oh, take a trip to Paris," she quipped. "Maybe visit the White House."

"Busy girl," he replied, grinning.

"What I'll actually be doing," she said, looking up at him, "is helping Miss Mattie with the bakery and going to school."

"I'm going to miss you," he said, his eyes locking onto hers.

"Be sure to email or text me every day, okay?" she said, wondering if he could hear her heart hammering.

"I will," he said, looking like he wanted to say more. He took her hand instead.

* * * *

When it came time for Jonathan to leave for England, Emily went to the airport with him and his family. Just before he boarded the plane, Jonathan went down the line of his family and hugged his dad and mom and brothers. His mother cried, making the situation all the more heart wrenching. When he got to Emily, he hugged her. "I'll send you a picture of the Queen," he whispered.

"Don't forget Big Ben," she whispered back.

After a long hug, he started to leave, then hugged her again. Emily hoped nobody saw the tears in her eyes as he headed toward the escalator. Halfway up, he turned for one last wave at everyone, but he kept his eyes on her.

Emily's heart felt as heavy as a stone as she walked back to the car with his family.

* * * *

Emily didn't sleep very well the night before school started. The dread of whispers behind her back, and nods in her direction, made her lie awake staring at the ceiling. She knew there was nothing she could do, except get it over with. To her great surprise, the first day of school was pretty uneventful. The story of her parents' leaving town without her was old news by now, she guessed, feeling immensely relieved. Even Bitsy was pleasant to her.

"How's that cute Jonathan gettin' along across the Pond?" Bitsy had asked, when she saw Emily in the cafeteria.

"Across the *what*?" Emily asked, feigning ignorance.

"Ya'll know, 'cross the ocean," Bitsy chirped.

"Oh, good," Emily said. "He likes England."

"Well, tell him my feelin's are hurt," Bitsy pouted, pushing out her lower lip. "I gave him my email address jus' b'fore he left, an' he hasn't written me one time yet."

"Oh, really," Emily said, suddenly feeling very lighthearted.

"Ya'll don't happen to have his phone number, do ya?" Bitsy said.

Emily gave her a big smile. "Just ask him to send it when he emails you," she said, twiddling her fingers good-bye, as she hurried off.

CHAPTER - 27

"I heard from Kelly Ann and she wants ta come out sometime in October or November an' live with me again," Ike told Emily, as she sat at his counter sipping a root beer float.

"In the middle of the semester?" Emily asked, holding the straw up so it dripped ice cream into her mouth.

"Yeah, it's kinda weird," Ike replied. "Musta decided all of a sudden. She didn't mention it when she was here." He shrugged. "Seems like somethin's goin' on."

"Like what?" she asked.

"Beats me," Ike shrugged. "But when you reach my age, you jus' get feelins about stuff."

* * * *

Emily was in her room studying when her cell phone chirped, signaling a message. She pressed the button and the download sign came on. She laughed out loud as half of Jonathan's face appeared on the screen, with Queen Elizabeth in the background. The phone chirped again and another picture of the Queen appeared. In this one she was waving to the crowd, with a purse dangling from her arm.

Emily looked at the first picture again, wishing it showed all of Jonathan's face. A picture of the Queen was fun, but she really wanted to see him.

Congrats on queen sighting, she texted to him.

I'd rather b taking pictures of u, he texted back.

Her heart skipped a beat as she pressed the phone to her face. She missed him so much.

* * * *

Emily walked along the tree-lined street, on her way to visit Mrs. Tupper, loving the blush of red, yellow, and orange that tinged the leaves on the trees overhead. It was hard to believe that fall was almost here. Within a couple of weeks, the trees would be ablaze with color, and the roads filled with tourists snapping pictures of the fall colors. She sniffed the air, hoping for the first whiff of smoke from the villagers' wood burning stoves.

Across the street at St. Daniel's, she heard the nuns practicing for the Wednesday night song mass. She had been to it twice now and enjoyed the music immensely–especially the Blues Sisters.

* * * *

Emily sat on the edge of Mrs. Tupper's bed, laughing with her, and bringing her up to date on everything that had gone on since her last visit.

Mrs. Tupper had heard most of it already from the night nurse.

"You probably know more than I do," Emily laughed. "Tell me your news."

Mrs. Tupper smiled and in a warbled voice filled Emily in on details of village life that Emily had never even heard of.

"The night nurse needs to write a gossip column," Emily laughed.

"Perhaps she should," smiled Mrs. Tupper. "Now, tell me what you hear from that young man of yours." She lay propped up on pillows looking like a young girl eager for a story.

Emily sighed, wishing Mrs. Tupper wouldn't call him *her* young man. "He'll be home sometime in December for Christmas, but he isn't *my young man,* Mrs. Tupper. We're only friends."

"Oh, pish-posh," Mrs. Tupper warbled, with a wave of her hand. "I saw that gleam in his eye for you. I'm ninety-four, dear, I *know* what that gleam means."

"Oh..." Emily murmured, not knowing what else to say.

"Has he sent you any pictures recently?" Mrs. Tupper asked, her eyes starting to droop. Excitement exhausted her.

"Yes, but I already showed you the ones of him in front of famous places."

"Well," Mrs. Tupper quavered eagerly, "may I see your new ones?"

"Sure," Emily replied, scanning the pictures on her phone for one to show her. She realized she didn't want to show her *any.* They were too personal.

Maybe she could show her the one of Jonathan standing in front of the sidewalk florist, holding out a bouquet of flowers, as though he were giving them to her. *No, not that one,* she thought, and hurriedly scrolled to the next picture.

She laughed out loud at the picture taken inside a candy shop, with Jonathan holding out a chocolate turtle, her favorite candy. He had texted that he ate it in her honor.

"You seem very selective about what you want me to see," Mrs. Tupper warbled, a mischievous grin on her face.

Emily gave up and held the phone out so Mrs. Tupper could see as she scrolled through the pictures.

"Just as I thought," Mrs. Tupper whispered, "he cares very much for you." And with that, she closed her eyes and slept, peaceful as a child.

* * * *

"You heard any more from Kelly Ann," Gilbert asked Emily, as he bagged her groceries at the Village Grocer.

"Ike told me she's coming in October or November," she replied, tucking some carrots down into the bag.

"Oh really?" Gilbert said, his face lighting up. "But why in the middle of the school year?"

"I don't know," she shrugged. "Ike doesn't know either."

"You want me to carry this bag for ya?" Gilbert offered.

"All the way to the bakery?"

"Sure," Gilbert shrugged. "It's what I git paid for."

"I'd like it very much, then," she smiled, handing him the grocery bag.

Gilbert waved to Mr. Kingery. "I'm makin' a delivery, be back in a few minutes."

Mr. Kingery nodded and went back to talking to a customer.

"So how's ol' Jonathan doin'?" he asked as they walked up First Street.

"He's having fun and likes England a lot," she said.

"He ever find that ol' Ben guy?"

Emily laughed. "Yes, he found him and sent a picture. Want to see it?"

Gilbert nodded and they stopped at the corner so she could bring the picture up on her phone.

She found the picture and handed it to him. "There's Big Ben!" she said, trying to keep a straight face.

"Where?" Gilbert asked.

"Big Ben is a clock," she laughed.

He glanced up at her and shook his head. "You two are crazy," he said, as they continued down the sidewalk.

She laughed. "Do you want to see other pictures he sent?"

"Sure, why not," he replied.

They stopped again and she showed him a picture Jonathan had taken of himself in front of Westminster Abbey, one in front of an English Starbucks, and one in front of his high school.

"He takes pictures of himself in front of stuff?" Gilbert asked, wrinkling his brow.

"Mmm hmm," she replied. "I asked him to. I wanted to see pictures of him, not just places."

"What's this one?" he asked, scrolling to a picture of Jonathan sitting at a small table by himself, with two drinks on the table.

"You weren't supposed to look at that one," she laughed, grabbing the phone out of his hand.

"What's he doin'," Gilbert laughed, "waitin' for a date?"

"No," she replied airily, "he's wishing I were there having lunch with him."

Gilbert just stared at her, and they both burst out laughing.

"You two really ARE crazy," he cackled.

"I couldn't agree with you more," she tried to say, but couldn't because she was laughing so hard.

Later in her room that night, Emily heard her phone chirp and when she picked it up she saw that it was another picture from Jonathan. This one was a close-up of his face with Westminster Abby in the background. She glanced at the palace, and then stared for a long time at Jonathan's face. His lips looked soft, and she wondered how it would feel to kiss them.

* * * *

On a Sunday morning in late October, Emily sat in the church pew next to Miss Mattie in her most recent church hat, purchased from the *Catalog of Fine Hats*, bought just before Jonathan left for England. It had cost her way too much money, but she had never seen a hat more beautiful. It was fawn colored with a small brim, and a russet-colored ostrich feather that swooped back on one side. Miss Mattie said it looked beautiful with her red hair. She thought back to when she wore it to church the first time and remembered that Jonathan's eyes lit up like Fourth of July sparklers when he saw her. He had been sitting in the pew just a little ahead of her to the left, and he'd turned every so often to steal a glance of her. The memory of it still warmed her. She definitely loved this hat.

As Emily, and the rest of the congregation finished singing, "It Is Well With My Soul", Emily glanced up from her hymnal, then glanced again, not quite believing her eyes as she watched Kelly Ann walking up the church aisle. She looked over at Miss Mattie whose jaw had dropped, also. Emily hadn't heard from Kelly Ann since early summer.

Kelly Ann didn't notice Emily, and sat down next to Miss Rose, who gathered up her purse and Bible to make room for her. Kelly Ann–the person who'd always made fun of church–now sat quietly listening to the sermon. Emily kept stealing glances at her. Kelly Ann sang when she was supposed to sing, and looked at Miss Rose's Bible with her, when scripture reading was going on. She didn't do one sassy thing all during the service. *Incredible!* Emily thought. This was a miracle on the same level as the parting of the Red Sea, healing the deaf, and maybe even the feeding of the five thousand.

After the service, Emily stayed in her pew waiting for Kelly Ann to notice her. When she did, she smiled and calmly made her way over to Emily, stopping to greet people.

Kelly Ann gave Emily a hug, and then reached over and hugged Miss Mattie. "Good mornin'," she said warmly.

"Good mornin', Kelly Ann," Miss Mattie said, with a smile as bright as a moonbeam. "Welcome home."

"Thank you, ma'am."

Emily was so shocked by her quiet demeanor that, other than saying hello, she couldn't think of one thing to say.

"Will you be staying in Mountain Grove for a while now?" Miss Mattie asked.

"Yes'm for a little while," Kelly Ann replied. "My mama was havin' too many struggles with not drinkin', so she decided to go to this one place and get it taken care of once and fer all. But she had to commit to stay there for somethin' like nine months to a year, so I guess ya'll will be stuck with me for a while."

"Well now, aren't you jus' so proud that your mama had the courage to do that," Miss Mattie said. "We'll be sure to remember her in our prayers."

"I 'preciate that," Kelly Ann replied, without a hint of sarcasm.

If you aren't doin' anything this afternoon," Miss Mattie said, "we'd be happy if you'd join us for Sunday dinner. I'm roastin' a plump chicken."

Kelly Ann looked surprised at the invitation, but said, "Well sure, I'd like that. Can I bring somethin'?"

"No," Miss Mattie smiled, "jus' bring yourself and a good appetite. Come over 'bout four." She glanced up at the front of the church. "You girls excuse me for a minute; I need to talk to the choir director before he gets away."

As Miss Mattie hurried off, Emily fumbled for something to say. "Do you want to go do something?" was all she could come up with.

"Like what?" Kelly Ann asked, stifling a yawn.

"I don't know, walk down by the river or see a movie."

"Hmmm, let's walk. I've been tryin' to do more of that."

"Are you trying to lose weight?" Emily asked.

"Naw, walkin's jus' good for you."

"Oh!" Emily replied, not recalling that Kelly Ann had ever been into health. "Well, let's meet in front of the library at eleven."

Kelly Ann nodded, gave her a brief hug and left, stopping to shake hands with various townspeople on the way down the aisle.

Emily just stared after her in disbelief.

* * * *

As Emily and Kelly Ann walked down Second Street toward Jack Pine Road, Emily asked about her mother.

"She had a coupla slip-ups and it scared 'er," Kelly Ann said. "She decided she doesn't want to live that way anymore. Seems like she's really changed. Anyway, this place has a success rate that's through the roof, and she asked me if I cared if she went, since I would need to stay with Gran'pa an' all."

"Do you mind?"

"Naw, not really. It doesn't much matter where I live now."

"What do you mean?"

"Nothin'," she replied, and changed the subject. "How's it goin' livin' with Miss Mattie?"

"I love it," Emily said, and told her everything about her parents' moving.

Kelly Ann listened quietly, then said, "And you lost your grandma, too?"

Emily nodded. "Everyone's gone, so all of you are my family now."

"Wow, and I thought I had it rough," Kelly Ann said, shaking her head. "At least I have Grandpa."

"And I have Miss Mattie," Emily grinned. "She's my mama now."

"And a darned cute mama, she is," Kelly Ann laughed, giving her a quick hug.

They sat for over an hour on the big rock at the river, talking their hearts out. Emily tried to find out more about Kelly Ann's boyfriend, but she changed the subject every time Emily brought it up.

Exasperated, Emily finally blurted out, "Why don't you want to talk about him?"

"Cause he's a dirt bag," Kelly Ann said, tossing a twig out into the river.

"So, you aren't with him anymore?"

"Nope," she replied, but her bottom lip was trembling.

"Are you okay?"

"I will be," Kelly Ann said, biting her lip.

"What do you mean?"

"Just some things goin' on," she said, tossing another twig into the water, "but I'm not ready to talk about it yet."

"Okay, well I'm here when you are."

Kelly Ann nodded her head.

"I forgot to tell you the biggest news..." Emily said.

"There's *more?"* said Kelly Ann.

"I have a sister," Emily blurted out.

"You have a *what*?"

"A couple of weeks before she died, my grandmother told me I have a sister somewhere."

"Oh my gosh! Are you lookin' for her?"

"I started to, but then Mrs. Green took the information and gave it to Mr. Green. She said he's good at that stuff. He's been giving me updates, but nothing solid yet."

"Oh my gosh! Are you just so excited or what?"

"It doesn't seem real," Emily replied, tossing pebbles into the river.

"Oh my gosh," Kelly Ann kept repeating.

"I think I will find her eventually, but actually..." Emily hesitated, not knowing if she should say it or not.

"Actually *what*?" Kelly Ann asked, turning and looking at her.

"When you were living here before, I thought of you as my sister."

"You did?" Kelly Ann gasped.

Emily nodded. "But then you didn't stay in contact with me. I thought you liked your other friends more than me, so I didn't know what to think anymore. I missed you, though."

"I'm sorry," Kelly Ann said, looking at her. "I was so stupid."

"It's okay."

"No it's not."

"Well, I'm just glad you're back," Emily said. "And I still cared about you even if you were being stupid."

"Thanks," Kelly Ann laughed. "Yer a great sister."

Emily grinned. "Want to walk a little more?"

"Okay, then I'm goin' home for awhile. I'm sleepy."

"Too many late movies?"

Kelly Ann just shrugged and hopped down from the rock.

"You aren't sick are you," Emily asked, as they walked back to town.

"No, I'll be fine. It was nice of Miss Mattie to invite me over," she said, changing the subject again.

They parted ways with Emily reminding her that dinner would be at four.

"Don't worry, I won't forgit," Kelly Ann said, and with a final wave, headed across the park to cut between the houses.

Emily spotted Gilbert sitting under a tree reading and lingered to watch his reaction when he saw Kelly Ann.

Even from across the street, Emily could see Gilbert's smile go from ear to ear. He stood up and threw his arms around Kelly Ann, who looked surprised and took a step back. They talked for a few seconds, then Gilbert reached out and touched her arm before Kelly Ann continued on home.

* * * *

"Sugar, I'm goin' down to Clayton this afternoon to do a little shoppin'," Miss Mattie said as they ate breakfast Monday morning. "Would you like to come with me? Blessy is watchin' the bakery."

Emily thought for a moment and said, "Sure, I'd like to come. Could we make a stop on the way, though?"

"Stop where?" asked Miss Mattie, spreading strawberry jam on her biscuit. "There's no town between here and Clayton."

"You'll see," Emily said, making a mental note to bring her camera.

"That was a real nice visit with Kelly Ann last night," Miss Mattie said, as she drove her Mazda down the mountain to Clayton.

"She sure has changed," Emily said.

"Yes, ma'am, she sure has," Miss Mattie agreed.

"Wonder what caused it?"

"Well, Sugar, sometimes people jus' grow up."

"Turn here!" Emily suddenly shouted.

"What on earth," Miss Mattie yelped, pulling off the road.

"The town sign," Emily said, pointing to the clearing where it stood. "I want to take a picture of it."

"Oh, well now I see," Miss Mattie grinned, driving slowly over the bumpy dirt road. She pulled up in front of the sign in a cloud of dust, and they both got out. Emily read it out loud:

Welcome to Mountain Grove!

We Aren't Just a Town, We're a Family.

"You want me to take your picture standin' in front of it, Sugar?" Miss Mattie asked.

"No thanks," she replied. "I just want a picture of the sign."

"What're you gonna do with it?"

"Hang it on my bedroom wall," she replied, choosing different angles and firing off several shots. "Miles Taylor at the camera shop said he'd enlarge it for me."

"I see," her mama replied, looking pleased.

* * * *

On Tuesday, Emily and Kelly Ann sat at the counter at Good Eats. Millie set two root beer floats down in front of them, and smiled at Kelly Ann. "Glad yer back, honey, and I hope you stay a long time," she said, and patted her shoulder as she went to wait on another customer.

"Thanks, Millie," Kelly Ann called after her. "I hope I do, too," she whispered.

Emily gave her a side glance, but Kelly Ann was already slurping root beer through her straw. Ike came out and set platters of cheeseburgers and fries down in front of them. "Eat up ladies," he beamed and hurried back to the kitchen. Customers poured into the café as the noon hour approached. They welcomed Kelly Ann with warm greetings, gentle teasing, and big hugs.

Emily had gobbled down half her burger when she noticed Kelly Ann was only nibbling at hers. She watched as Kelly Ann ate half a fry, then tossed the other half back down on her plate.

"Aren't you hungry?" she asked.

"Th' grease upsets my stomach a lil'," Kelly Ann said, gently rubbing her belly. "I think I'm jus' tired today. Maybe I'll take this with me and go home for a nap."

"*A nap?"* Emily said, nearly choking on her food. "Have you started taking one every day?"

"I've jus' been a little tired lately," Kelly Ann replied, sliding down off the stool. She walked around the counter and got a "to go" box and put her cheeseburger and fries into it, then sat back down while Emily finished eating, keeping the box on her lap.

When Ike came out and glanced at their plates. "How were the burgers, ladies?" he asked.

"Yummy!" Emily replied.

Kelly Ann echoed the same thing, keeping her "to go" box out of sight.

* * * *

Miss Mattie had a big grin on her face as she stirred shredded cheese into their scrambled eggs.

"What're you thinking about?" Emily asked.

"I'm thinkin' my daughter is havin' a birthday next Saturday and I'm wonderin' what to plan for her."

Emily was more than pleased that she had remembered, but said, "Let's just do something small and simple. Kelly Ann is taking me to the movies Saturday night."

Her mama turned and looked at her. "I thought you enjoyed your big birthday party last year."

"I did, but this year I just want something small."

"You sure?"

Emily nodded.

As her birthday approached Emily wondered if she would hear from her parents. She didn't think about them that much, but special events like birthdays sent her mind rocketing to the past. It'd been a while since she'd called them, only once since her grandmother died. There hadn't been much to say, and after a few awkward sentences, they'd hung up. Emily had called because she wanted to make sure they were still a few hundred miles away. Her parents were unpredictable, and it made her nervous wondering if they would suddenly change their mind and come and get her.

She woke up on her birthday full of anticipation. Her mama wouldn't tell her what she had planned, but Emily had heard her speaking in low tones on the phone in her bedroom a number of times.

When she walked out into the living room she saw a huge Mylar balloon with *Happy Birthday* written on it tied to the chair at the kitchen table. There was a note on the table that read:

Happy Birthday Sugar! Your breakfast is in the warming oven. Be dressed in something pretty by 11:30. Blessy says to come downstairs so she can give you a birthday hug.

Mama

* * * *

"Where are we going?" Emily asked as she and her mama hurried down the street dressed to the nines, complete with church hats.

"Oh, you'll see," her mama grinned.

Emily laughed, and picked up her step.

They turned right on Elderberry Way and walked toward the church. "I'm having something at the church?" Emily asked.

"No, Sugar, not the church, the parsonage."

Penelope opened the door, dressed for high tea, with a full brim hat, long gloves and a boa. "Come right on in," she grinned. They followed her into the dining room where a circular table had been decorated with a lovely damask cloth, candles, and fine china. A beautifully decorated cake with her name on it sat in the middle of the table. Seated at the table were Mrs. Green and Mrs. Apple, both garbed in boas, long gloves, and wide hats–and both with huge grins on their faces.

"Happy Birthday!" they both chorused, rising from their seats and hurrying over to hug Emily.

Penelope handed Emily and Miss Mattie a set of gloves and boas. They giggled like schoolgirls as they put on their attire for high tea and took their seats at the table.

* * * *

Dear Journal,

Today is my sixteenth birthday and I had the best birthday party with the women who have helped me most in my life. I wonder how Mama knew. It was so fun. We were all dressed for tea and each of the ladies said something nice about me and their hopes for me. Penelope said the best prayer for me before we ate, and I hope it comes true.

But as I think about it, what I've needed most in my life has already come true. What other girl has such great women in her life. I told them all so, and Mama cried.

E.

* * * *

As fall turned into winter, Emily grew excited as village shops began to deck themselves out in Christmas finery. She had a spectacular view from her room over the bakery of the church, and its Nativity scene. Even the library, on the other side of the park, put lights shaped like candles in every window, and wreaths with red bows on its huge doors.

She turned from the window when she heard the knock at the door. She had invited Kelly Ann over to help her bake cookies for the residents at Creekside Villa. Kelly Ann had been keeping to herself a lot lately, and it had been Miss Mattie's suggestion that they invite her.

"Who wants to sample a warm sugar cookie," asked Miss Mattie, later in the day, as she pulled them out of the oven.

"Yummy," said Emily, biting into one. She handed one to Kelly Ann.

"It's good," Kelly Ann murmured, taking a few nibbles.

"You feelin' okay, Kelly Ann?" Miss Mattie asked, eyeing her with concern. She reached up and felt Kelly Ann's forehead.

"I'm all right," Kelly Ann replied, looking listless and pale.

Miss Mattie started to say something, but suddenly Kelly Ann bolted from the kitchen and ran to the bathroom, where they could hear her vomiting.

"She must have the flu," Emily said, getting out of her chair to go help her.

"Just give her a minute," Miss Mattie said, holding her arm. "I don't think it's the flu."

Kelly Ann returned to the room a few minutes later looking sheepish. "I'm so sorry," she said, putting her face in her hands.

"Are you okay?" Emily asked.

She shook her head no.

Miss Mattie scooted over and put her arm around Kelly Ann. "Honey, do you have somethin' you need to tell us?"

Kelly Ann lowered her head, and Emily watched as tears coursed down her cheeks and plopped on her blouse.

"What's wrong, Kelly Ann?" Emily asked softly, scooting her chair over next to her.

Kelly Ann gulped, and it was a second before she answered. "I'm pregnant," she whispered.

Emily felt like someone had hit her in the head with a sledgehammer. She looked up at Miss Mattie, who didn't appear to be at all surprised.

"How far along are you, honey?" Miss Mattie asked gently.

"A little over four months, I think," she sobbed.

Emily looked at Miss Mattie in disbelief.

"There, there, don't cry," Miss Mattie crooned.

Emily couldn't think of one thing to say, and just sat there staring at the two of them. *Pregnant? Kelly Ann pregnant?* Her mind refused to believe it.

Miss Mattie patted and shushed as Kelly Ann wept with grief. Emily wanted to run from the room.

"Does your granddaddy know?" Miss Mattie asked.

"No, no one knows," she cried softly.

"How about the baby's daddy?"

"He knows, but he just got mad and left when I told him," she said, and began to sob. "I don't want him around anyway. He's a dirt bag."

Emily sat in a daze as they talked on. Finally, Kelly Ann said she needed to go home and lie down. She got up to leave.

"I think you'll feel better if you jus' tell your granddaddy and get it over with," Miss Mattie said, helping her put her jacket on. She reached out and hugged the young girl, holding her close.

"You're right, I'll tell him," Kelly Ann said, hugging her back.

She turned to Emily. "Everything will work out," Emily said in a stilted voice, but she didn't really believe it.

"Are you mad at me?" Kelly Ann asked, her eyes pleading with her not to be.

"No," Emily lied.

She walked Kelly Ann down the steps. "I'll call you tomorrow," Emily said coolly, not sure if she really would.

Kelly Ann started to say something, but just nodded and turned to go.

When she got back upstairs Miss Mattie was sitting on the couch with her head back and eyes closed. Emily went over and sat by her. "I just can't believe it," she said, angrily.

"Well, it's true, Sugar," Miss Mattie replied, opening her eyes and looking at her. "She's gonna need lots of support."

"Plus, she picked a terrible father for the baby," Emily said, growing even angrier.

Miss Mattie surprised her by chuckling. "Sugar, when a girl starts makin' bad decisions for herself, she isn't too likely to be lookin' out for a baby that's not even conceived yet."

"Well, I'm mad at her."

"Tell me what you're mad about," Miss Mattie said.

"I'm mad that she ruined her life, mad that the baby has a crummy dad, mad that she was *stupid!*" Emily sputtered.

"Anything else?" Miss Mattie asked, looking at her evenly.

"Probably," she said, feeling herself soften, "but I'll get over it."

"That's good, because this isn't about you," Miss Mattie reminded her. "It's about Kelly Ann and the little one she's carryin'."

"Her whole life has changed."

"Yes, it has and that's what she's cryin' about," Miss Mattie replied. "She's grievin' over her mistake and doesn't need any anger from us. She's already plenty mad at herself."

"I guess," Emily sighed.

"This is an opportunity to help someone in need," Miss Mattie continued, "and it doesn't matter how we feel about it. We do plenty wrong and God keeps helpin' us."

Emily sighed again. "I'll go see her tomorrow and do better."

"Maybe you should give her a quick call tonight," Miss Mattie suggested. "I bet you'll both sleep better if you do."

Emily nodded, went into her room, and dialed Kelly Ann's number.

When Kelly Ann answered, she said, "I just wanted you to know that I'm here all the way for you."

"Thanks," Kelly Ann whispered. "Are you still mad?"

"No," Emily said. "I just had a thousand different emotions going through me at once. I wanted you to know that I'd like to be involved, and help you plan if you want me to."

"Thanks, Emmy Lou," she said, sounding relieved.

"You're welcome," Emily said, meaning it.

"Did I ever tell you that you're a great sister?" Kelly Ann asked.

"And I'll be an even better aunt when your baby comes," she answered.

"Thank you," Kelly Ann said, with a sigh. "That means everything to me."

* * * *

Two days later, Emily was upstairs in her room reading when her phone chirped. She picked it up and saw that it was a message from Jonathan. When she pressed the download button, his face appeared in front of a familiar statue. She did a double take. It was the General!

She hurried to her window and looked down at the park where Jonathan stood bundled up from the cold, grinning and waving at her. She nearly burst with happiness as she flew out the door and down the steps, her feet barely touching. She sprinted across First Street where Jonathan stood grinning at her, hesitated a second, then flew into his arms. He stared down at her and she gazed up at him. His face came toward hers and she stood on her tiptoes. She was right. His lips were very soft.

* * * *

"Hurry or we're gonna be late for the party," Mama called to her from the kitchen. They were going to the Charles' home for their yearly Christmas party.

"Just another five minutes," Emily yelled, as she positioned the nail. She gave it three blows with a hammer, and then tested it to make sure it would hold. She lifted the large picture, hung it on the nail, then stood back to see how it looked.

Perfect! she thought, as she stared at the enlarged picture she'd taken of the town sign just outside of Mountain Grove. She read the words out loud:

Welcome to Mountain Grove!

We Aren't Just a Town, We're a Family.

"Em'ly!" her mama called again from the kitchen.

"Coming," she said, tossing the hammer on her bed.

They both bundled up and went out the door into the crisp night air. Emily hummed as she thought of seeing Jonathan again, and wondered what the New Year would bring. They hurried down the snowy sidewalk past shops shimmering with Christmas lights, and draped in green and red, with a wreath on every door. The bells rang at St. Daniel's and they quickened their step.

About the Author

Sharon Armstrong resides in Northern California with her husband, Chuck, and a large extended family.

Her love of children and teen-agers is the primary reason for writing *Emily's House.* She served on a hotline, counseling young woman for over ten years.

Much of their story is Emily's story.

SharonArmstrongAuthor@gmail.com
Facebook: SharonArmstrongAuthor
Instagram: sharonarmstrongauthor
Webpage: SharonArmstrongAuthor.com

Emily's story continues in book two. Sign up for updates so you will be notified when it is released.

Made in United States
Orlando, FL
16 April 2022

16906168R00187